John Lacy

The Dramatic Works of John Lacy

Comedian with Prefatory Memoir and Notes

John Lacy

The Dramatic Works of John Lacy
Comedian with Prefatory Memoir and Notes

ISBN/EAN: 9783744777476

Printed in Europe, USA, Canada, Australia, Japan

Cover: Foto ©Andreas Hilbeck / pixelio.de

More available books at **www.hansebooks.com**

THE DRAMATIC

WORKS OF JOHN LACY,

COMEDIAN,

WITH PREFATORY MEMOIR AND NOTES.

MDCCCLXXV.

EDINBURGH: WILLIAM PATERSON.
LONDON: H. SOTHERAN & CO.

TO

JAMES ROBINSON PLANCHÉ, Esquire,

ETC. ETC. ETC.,

WHOSE ELEGANCE OF STYLE IN

DRAMATIC COMPOSITION,

MORE ESPECIALLY IN

HUMOROUS POETIC ILLUSTRATIONS OF

HEATHEN AND FAIRY MYTHOLOGY,

HAS FORMED ONE OF

THE MARKED FEATURES OF THE ENGLISH STAGE

FOR UPWARDS OF THE LAST HALF CENTURY,

THIS VOLUME IS DEDICATED,

WITH THE MOST SINCERE REGARDS OF

THE EDITORS.

CONTENTS.

PREFATORY MEMOIR.

JOHN LACY, comedian, the author and adapter of the dramatic pieces in this volume, was born in the vicinity of Doncaster. According to Aubrey, he "came to London, to ye playhouse, 1631," and apprenticed himself to John Ogilby, who at that time exercised the vocation of a dancing-master. This latter meritorious individual, born at Edinburgh in 1600, was the means, at the age of thirteen, along with his mother's combined industry, of releasing his father, a gentleman who had dissipated a good estate, from the King's Bench Prison, and assisting him to pay his debts. He then became apprentice to one Mr. Draper, who kept a dancing-school in Gray's Inn Lane, "and in a short time arrived to so great excellency in that art, that he found means to purchase his time of his master, and sett up for himselfe." In addition to his teaching, Ogilby figured occasionally in court masques, until an accident unfitted him for such public displays. "When the Duke of Buckingham's great masque was represented at court, he was chosen, among the rest, to performe some extraordinary part in it; and vaulting and cutting capers being then in fashion, he, endeavouring to doe something extraordinary, by misfortune of a false step when he came to the ground did spraine a veine on the inside of his leg, of which

he was lame ever after, which gave an occasion to
say, 'that he was an excellent dancing-master, and
never a good leg.'"*

Shortly before the Rebellion, John Ogilby went
over to Ireland, to teach in the family of the Earl
of Strafford, the Lord-Lieutenant, who appointed
him Master of the Ceremonies for that kingdom,
and assisted him to build a little theatre in St.
Warbrugh Street in Dublin; but, the Rebellion
breaking out, his theatre was ruined and he lost
everything. He returned to England in 1648,
and printed a translation of Virgil made by himself. At the age of sixty he betook himself to
the study of Greek, and translated Homer's Iliad,
which Pope mentions that he read when a child
" with a pleasure that left the most lasting impression on his mind." In anticipation of the
Restoration, he printed "the fairest impression
and the most correct of English Bibles that ever
was yet done, in royall and imperiall paper.". He
also printed and published *His Majesty's Entertain-
ments at his Coronation*, in folio, with cuts, 1662. In
the same year he returned to Ireland. and, in virtue
of his patent as Master of the Revels, built a new
theatre at Dublin at a cost of two thousand pounds,
"having disputed his right with Sir William
D'Avenant, who had obtained a grant." While
at Dublin he wrote a play, called *The Merchant of
Dublin*, which was never printed. He published
a translation of Homer's *Odyssey* in 1665, and, in
his retirement at Kingston-upon-Thames, during
the plague, wrote among other works a second
volume of his *Paraphrase of Æsop*, which he called

---

* Aubrey's *Lives of Eminent Men*. London, 1813. 8vo.
Vol. ii.

his *Æsopiques.* Having lost all he had, except five pounds, by the great Fire, he made proposals to print an English atlas, and was encouraged by the King and the nobility to make an actual survey of the roads of England and Wales, by which the posts were regulated. He was appointed his majesty's cosmographer, and died 4th September 1676.

Under such a master as this, and retaining the friendship of such a man during his subsequent career, it cannot be doubted that Lacy was largely benefited.

A writer, supposed to be Motteux, in the *Continuation of Langbaine's Lives of the Dramatic Poets,* in treating of Lacy, says he was "originally a dancing-master;" but further than his having apprenticed himself to Ogilby to learn the art, apparently in connection with his theatrical pursuits, there is no record of his ever having been a teacher. The same writer observes, of his personal appearance, that he was "of a rare shape of body and good complexion," which other authorities confirm.

During the Civil War, he, like the majority of his brother actors, betook himself to the "passage of arms," and procured a commission as lieutenant and quartermaster under Colonel Lord Gerard, afterwards the Earl of Macclesfield. He returned to the stage at the Restoration, and became a universal favourite, more especially in eccentric comedy. Pepys was a great admirer of his, and numerous are the entries in his diary respecting him. Noticing his appearance, 21st May 1662, in the play of *The French Dancing-Mistress,* he says, "The play pleased us very well, but Lacy's part, the dancing-mistress, the best in the world." On

the 22d May, he again says, "We by coach to
the theatre, and saw *Love in a Maze*. The play
hath little in it, but Lacy's part of a country fellow,
which he did to admiration."

On the 10th June, in the year following, he
again went, with some friends, to see *Love in a
Maze*. "The play is pretty good, but the life of
the play is Lacy's part, the clown, which is most
admirable; but for the rest, which are counted
old and excellent actors, in my life I never heard
both men and women so ill pronounce their
parts."

"12th June 1663.—To the Royal Theatre, and
there saw *The Committee*, a merry but indifferent
play; only Lacy's part, an Irish footman, is beyond imagination."

Four years afterwards he again sees the same
piece, with a different impression as to its merits :—

"13th August 1667.—Sir W. Pen and I to the
King's House, and there saw *The Committee*, which
I went to with some prejudice, not liking it before,
but I do now find it a very good play, and a great
deal of good invention in it ; but Lacy's part is so
well performed that it would set off anything."

As Lacy figures prominently in the following
graphic account of the production of Howard's
Change of Crowns and its consequences, we give
it in Pepys' own words :—

"15th April 1667.—To the King's House by
chance—where a new play ; so full as I never saw
it ; I forced to stand all the while close to the
very door, till I took cold, and many people went
away for want of room. The King, and Queene,
and Duke of York and Duchesse there, and all
the Court, and Sir W. Coventry. The play
called *The Change of Crownes*, a play of Ned

Howard's *—the best that I ever saw at that house, being a great play, and serious; only Lacy did act the country gentleman come up to Court, who do abuse the Court with all the imaginable wit and plainness about selling of places, and doing everything for money. The play took very well."

16th April 1667, Pepys, going with his wife to see again *The Change of Crowns*, was surprised to find that the play had been changed. "However in, and there Knipp came into the pit. Knipp tells me the King was so angry at the liberty taken by Lacy's part to abuse him to his face, that he commanded they should act no more, till Moone went and got leave for them to act again, but not this play. The King mighty angry; and it was bitter indeed, but very fine and witty. . . . Pretty to hear them talk of yesterday's play, and I durst not own to my wife that I had seen it."

"20th April.—Met Mr. Rolt, who tells me the reason of no play to-day at the King's House. That Lacy had been committed to the porter's lodge for his acting his part in the late new play, and, being thence released to come to the King's House, he there met with Ned Howard, the poet of the play, who congratulated his release; upon which Lacy cursed him, as that it was the fault of his nonsensical play that was the cause of his ill-usage. Mr. Howard did give him some reply; to which Lacy answered him that he was more a fool than a poet; upon which Howard did give him a blow on the face with his glove; on which Lacy, having a cane in his hand, did give him a

---

* Younger son of the first Earl of Berkshire, and brother to Sir Robert Howard.

blow over the pate. Here Rolt and others that discoursed of it in the pit did wonder that Howard did not run him through, he being too mean a fellow to fight with. But Howard did not do anything but complain to the King of it; so the whole house is silenced, and the gentry seem to rejoice much at it, the house being become too insolent."

On 1st May 1667, and 28th April 1668, Pepys commends Lacy's admirable acting of the clown in *Love in a Maze;* and on 13th July 1667 he has this entry : "Yesterday Sir Thomas Crewe told me that Lacy lies a-dying; nor will receive any ghostly advice from a bishop, an old acquaintance of his, that went to see him."

Lacy, however, recovered from this serious illness, and survived it for several years; but he did not appear upon the stage so frequently as he had previously done. He is thus again noticed by Pepys :—

"19th January 1668-69.—At noon eat a mouthful, and so with my wife to Madam Turner's and find her gone, but The. staid for us; and so to the King's House to see *Horace.* This the third day of its acting—a silly tragedy; but Lacy hath made a farce of several dances—between each act one; but his words are but silly, and invention not extraordinary as to the dances; only some Dutchmen come out of the mouth and tail of a Hamburgh sow. Thence, not much pleased with the play, set them at home in the Strand."

"The famous Mr. Lacy," Mr. Wilkes observes in his *View of the Stage,* 1759, 8vo, "was an excellent low comedian, and so pleasing to King Charles."

Rymer, in his *Dissertation on Tragedy,* speaks of him thus :—"The eyes of the audience are prepossessed and charmed by his action before aught of the poet can approach their ears."

Langbaine says of him :—" He was a comedian whose abilities were sufficiently known to all that frequented the Theatre Royal, where for many years he performed all parts that he undertook to a miracle, insomuch that I am apt to believe that as *this* age never had, so the *next* never will have, his *equal*, at least not his *superiour*. He was so well approved by Charles II., that he caused his picture to be drawn in three several figures in the same table, viz. that of Teague in *The Committee*, Scruple in *The Cheats*, and Galliard in *Variety;* which piece is still in being in Windsor Castle."

Galliard is a character in the Duke of New-castle's *Variety ;* Teague, a low Irishman, is in Mr. Robert Howard's *Committee*, a comedy which has since been reduced to a farce, under the title of *Honest Thieves;* and Scruple, a canting, mercenary Nonconformist, in Wilson's *Cheats*, whose style of hypocrisy and casuistry was doubtless very enter-taining in that day, when the original, now long become quite obsolete, was to be met with in every street.

Aubrey thus notes :—" His ma^tie. (Ch. II.) has severall pictures of this famous comedian at Wind-sore and Hampton Court, in the postures of severall parts that he acted, *e.g.* Teag, L^d. Vaux, the Puritan."

A copy of the painting in compartments at Windsor Castle was amongst Mr. Harris' theatri-cal portraits which were sold by the hammer of George Robins in 1819. It fetched eleven guineas. The romancing auctioneer, probably imagining that the three characters were all assumed in one piece, described Lacy as " the Matthews of his day."

Langbaine further says:—"I remember in Shirley's *Changes*, the deceased Mr. Lacy acted Johnny Thump, Sir Gervase Simple's man, with general applause ;" and, speaking of Falstaff, "this part used to be played by Mr. Lacy, and never failed of applause." Downes chronicles his successes in these three lines :—

"For his just acting all gave him due praise,
His part in *The Cheats*, Jony Thump, Teg,* and Bayes —
In these four excelling ; the Court gave him the bays."

Geneste gives this list of the chief characters he played :—

In Vere Street, about 1662, Scruple, in *The Cheats.*†

Theatre Royal, 1663.—Teague, in *The Committee.*†

1664.—Captain Otter, in *The Silent Woman.* Ananias, in *The Alchemist.*

1665.— Sir Politick Would-be, in *Volpone.* Monsieur Raggou, in *The Old Troop.*†

1666.—Sir Roger, in *The Scornful Lady.*

1667.—Sauny the Scot.† Country gentleman, in *The Change of Crowns.*† Johnny Thump, in *Changes.*

1669.—Drench, in *The Dumb Lady.*†

1671.—Bayes.†

1672.—Alderman Gripe, in *Love in a Wood.*†

1673.—Intrigo, in *Love in the Dark.*†

"He probably," says Geneste, "acted French-love in the English *Monsieur ;* Pinguister in *All Mistaken ;* Tartuffe ; French valet, in *The Mock Duellist ;* the English Lawyer ; Bobadill."

Langbaine continues :—"Nor did his talent wholly lie in acting ; he knew both how to judge

---

* Teague in Howard's works is spelt "Teg."
† Originally.

and write plays. And if his comedies are somewhat allied to French farce, it is out of choice rather than want of ability to write true comedy. We have three plays extant under his name :—

"*The Dumb Lady, or The Farrier made Physician.* A comedy. 1672.

"*The Old Troop, or Monsieur Ragou.* A comedy. 1672.

"*Sir Hercules Buffoon, or The Poetical Squire.* A comedy. 1682."

Besides these three plays, a fourth is attributed to him, *Sauny the Scot,* which, although produced in 1667, was not printed until 1698, but with Lacy's name on the title-page.

Pepys thus mentions the reception of *The Old Troop :*—" 31st July 1668.—To the King's House to see the first day of Lacy's *Monsieur Ragou,* now new acted. The King and Court all there, and mighty merry. A farce."

In the *Poems on State Affairs,* it is insinuated by Sir George Etherege that Lacy participated with Hart in the favours of Nell Gwyn. Be that as it may, he is known to have been her first instructor in the art of acting, the lessons she received from Hart being subsequent.

Lacy lived to an advanced age. His death occurred on Saturday, 17th September 1681, and he was buried " in the further churchyard of St. Martyn's-in-the-Fields on the Monday following."

JAMES MAIDMENT.
W. H. LOGAN.

EDINBURGH, 1st *January* 1875.

THE DUMB LADY.

The Dumb Lady ; or The Farrier made Physician.   As it was acted at the Theatre Royal.   By John Lacy, Gent. London : Printed for Thomas Dring, at the White Lyon, next Chancery Lane end in Fleet Street.   1672.

This play is founded on Molière's comedy *Le Médecin malgré lui*. "If," says Langbaine, "the reader will take the pains to compare them together, he will easily see that our author has much improv'd the French play." Geneste has this entry: "*Dumb Lady; or the Farrier made a Physician.* This farce, in five acts, was put together by Lacy. The main plot is taken from Molière's *Mock Doctor;* the catastrophe is borrowed from Molière's *Love's the best Doctor.*" The *Dumb Lady* was not printed till 1672, but it was probably acted about this time, as Softhead, in the first act, says, "I'll die a virgin martyr." Massinger's *Virgin Martyr* had been revived in 1668. Lacy concludes his Epistle to the Reader with hoping that his play will prove as beneficial to the printer as it had *formerly* been to himself. There are no performers' names to the Dramatis Personæ, but Lacy no doubt acted "Drench, the Farrier."

The plot of the *Médecin malgré lui*, simple in itself, has, through the instrumentality of those who wish to throw a doubt upon the originality of Molière, been ascribed to foreign sources. One has it, that "this excellent poet has taken the plot of that humorous piece from a history related by a certain German writer, Adam Olearius;" while another says: "It has been recently proved that *Hop o' my Thumb* is but another rendering of an Indian fable; and that *Cinderella* too, and many other popular stories, come from the Egyptian Rhodopia. The story of Molière's *Médecin malgré lui* has been found by M. Cosquin in a Sanscrit collection, 'La Couka Saptali.'"

The former thus proceeds: "This Olearius published, in 1647, his *Scientific Journey to Moscow and Persia;* which history, being translated into French as early as the year 1656 by the celebrated Wickefort, might have been read by Molière before the *Médecin malgré lui* was, for the first time, brought upon the stage in 1666."

"The history in question," he continues, "is briefly as follows :—The Grand Duke Boris Gudenow, who reigned during the years 1597 and 1605, was, according to the relation of Olearius, very much afflicted with the gout. At a certain period, when he suffered very severe pains, he caused it publicly to be proclaimed at Moscow, that he would reward with extraordinary favour and great riches the man, whoever he might be, that would relieve him from those pains. It seems that no one voluntarily appeared to earn the favour of the Grand Duke ; and, indeed, no wonder, for a doctor had his whole existence at stake in those times in Russia if his cure failed upon some high or noble patient ; and Gudenow was in the habit of making the surgeon, as if he considered the latter as absolute master of nature, responsible for the result of his art.

"The wife of a certain bojaar, or councillor of the cabinet, who received very harsh treatment from her husband, took the advantage of this public edict of the Grand Duke to revenge herself, in a cunning manner, on her cruel husband. She therefore had the Duke informed that her husband possessed an infallible remedy for the gout, but that he was not sufficiently humane to impart it.

"The bojaar was immediately sent for to court, and strictly examined. The latter declared, by all that was holy, that he was unacquainted with any such remedy, and had not the slightest knowledge of medicine. But oaths would not avail him ; Gudenow had him severely whipped and confined. When, shortly after, he was again examined, he repeated the same declarations, adding that this trick was probably played upon him by his wife ; the Duke had him whipt a second time, but more severely, and threatened him with death if he did not speedily relieve him from pain. Seized with terror, the bojaar was now entirely at a loss what to be at. He promised to do his best, but requested a few days in order to have the necessary drugs gathered. Having, with great difficulty, had his request granted, he sent to Ozirbalt, two days' journey from Moscow, in order to get thence all sorts of drugs which were to be had there. He sent for a cartload of them, mixed them all together, and prepared therewith a bath for the Duke, in the hope of his blind cure proving successful. Gudenow, after having used the bath, really found some relief, and the bojaar had his life spared him. Nevertheless, because he had known such an art, denied his knowledge of it, and refused his assistance to the Grand Duke, the latter had him again thoroughly whipt, and after being entirely recovered, he gave him a new dress, two hundred rubles, and eighteen slaves, by way of a present. In addition to this, he seriously admonished the doctor never to be revenged on his wife. It is said that the bojaar, after this occurrence, lived many years in peace and happiness with his spouse."

The second account, as found by M. Cosquin in "La Couka Saptali," is as follows :—"In the town of Pantchapoura lived a king called Satroumardana. His daughter, named Madanarekha, had an abscess in her throat. The doctors applied all kinds of plasters, but without effect, so at last they agreed that there was no remedy for the disease. Then the King proclaimed in every country that he who cured the Princess should be richly rewarded. The wife of a Brahmin who lived in a village, having heard the proclamation, said to the messenger, 'My husband is the most skilful magician and charmer in the world. Take him with you ; he will cure the Princess.' And she said to her husband, ' Pretend to be a magician and a charmer, and go boldly into the town to cure the Princess. You won't waste your time.' The Brahmin went to the palace and to the Princess, sprinkled her with water, blew at her, and imitated the charmers, muttering the while between his teeth. Suddenly he cried out at the top of his voice, and uttered a farrago of the most absurd words he could think of. On hearing all these strange utterances, the Princess was taken with such a fit of laughter, that the abscess broke and she was cured. The King, transported with joy, overloaded the Brahmin with presents."

There is another adaptation of *Le Medecin malgre lui*, in the shape of a ballad farce by Henry Fielding, called *The Mock Doctor, or the Dumb Lady Cured*, and acted at Drury Lane in 1732. Geneste, remarking upon the English translation of Molière's plays (1739), reminds us respecting *Le Medecin malgre lui*, that Mrs. Centlivre used a great part of it in her *Love's Contrivance*, 1703.

The "high-born and most hopeful prince," to whom this drama is inscribed, was the eldest of the three natural sons of Charles II. by Barbara Villiers, wife of Roger Palmer, Earl of Castlemain, better known as Duchess of Cleveland, a dignity conferred by her royal keeper in testimony of the high opinion he entertained of her " personal" virtues,*— at least, so runs the preamble of the patent of creation.

At the date of the play the hopeful prince enjoyed the title of Earl of Southampton, "as," says Collins, the Peerage writer, "heir of his mother, the Duchess of Cleveland," that being her second title. Upon the first of April 1673 he was installed a Knight of the Garter, and upon the 10th of September 1675 was created Duke of Southampton, Earl of Chichester, and Baron of Newberry, with remainder to the

* *Collins' Peerage*, vol. i. p. 56   London, 1741. 8vo.

heirs male of his body, whom failing to his younger brother George, Duke of Northumberland. Upon the death of his mother, at her house of Chiswick, in the county of Middlesex, on 9th October 1709, the title of Cleveland, under the limitations in the patent, devolved on her eldest son Charles.

His Grace married, when eighteen, Mary, heiress of Sir Henry Wood, the elder brother of Thomas, Bishop of Litchfield and Coventry. The Duchess died in 1680, and was buried in Westminster Abbey. By her he had no issue. This lady seems to have brought him a very handsome fortune, as in Michaelmas term 1685 he had a decree in Chancery against the Bishop for £30,000, "as part of his lady's fortune."

In 1694 the Duke took to wife Anne, daughter of Sir William Pulteny of Misterton, in the county of Leicester, by whom he had three sons and three daughters. He died 9th September 1730, and was succeeded by his eldest son William, who dying without issue in 1774, the titles of Cleveland and Southampton became extinct, and remained so for more than half a century, when the Dukedom of Cleveland was revived in the person of the Earl of Darlington, the heir of line of Lady Grace Fitzroy, the second daughter of Duke Charles, who married Henry Vane, son of Lord Barnard. Her eldest sister Barbara died unmarried, and her youngest sister, Lady Anne, who married John Paddley, Esq., departed this life at Waterford, Herts, the 23d of January 1769.

TO THE HIGH - BORN AND MOST HOPEFUL
PRINCE CHARLES, LORD LIMRICK, AND
EARL OF SOUTHAMPTON.

GREAT SIR,—When I began to write this dedication my hand shook, a fear possessed me, and I
trembled; my pen fell from me, and my whole
frame grew disordered, as if blasted with some
sudden upstart comet. Such awe and reverence
waits on dignity, that I now find it fit for me to
wish I had been refused the honour of my dedication, rather than undertake a task so much too
great for me. How shall I excuse this bold and
saucy fault? How shall my mean, unworthy pen
render you your attributes? Now I find presumption is a sin indeed. I have given myself a wound
beyond the cure of common men : heal me, then,
great sir; for where princes touch, the cure is infallible. And now, since you so graciously have
received my Farrier, who dares say he is no Physician? When you vouchsafe to call him Doctor,
he has commenced, and from your mouth he has
taken his degree; for what you say is, and ought
to be. Such a power is due to you from the
greatness of your blood. I and my abject muse
had perished but for you ; and in such distress
whither should we flee for shelter but to him that
has power to spread his wings and cover us? And
you have done it generously. Yet am I not to
wonder at this virtue in you, since your high birth

can do no less for you than to make you good ; and you are so. And may that goodness and humility which so early appears in you increase to a full perfection ! May your virtues prove as beautiful as your person ! May they still endeavour to out-vie each other, yet neither obtain, but still walk hand in hand till your virtues in you be reverenced by all mankind, and your lovely person honoured by all women ; and so may you continue to a long and happy life. But I need not wish this, nor the world doubt it, for already you're possessed of all those virtues that men hereafter may reasonably expect from you ; for, being supported with ma-jesty of one side, and with so admired and beauti-ful a mother on the other, besides her great and honourable birth, on such sure foundations you cannot fail our hopes ; and that you never may, shall be for ever the prayers of your most faithful and most obedient servant,

JOHN LACY.

THE EPISTLE TO THE READER.

GENTLE reader (for so most epistles begin), being conscious of my own weakness (for so they go on), I let thee know my own modesty had kept me from the press, but for the importunity of friends (and so they make an end).

By this, you see, poetry consists more of fancy than truth. So do the poets too, or else why should they seem ashamed to come into the press, when I know their bowels languish within them till they are there, vain-glory being the chief ingredient that makes up the spirit of poetry, and the grand inducement that puts us all in print? There is a kind of charm in poetry—'tis like tobacco and chemistry; for if you once take the one and undertake the other, you are fixed to the freehold never to be parted. So fares it with the dabblers in the dew of Parnassus: no revilings, no shameful reproaches can discourage us; still we write on, still we are fixed to the freehold. I have observed how much more precious to a poet the issue of his brain is than that of his loins, for I have known them bury children without grief or trouble; but the issue of their brain is so dear and tender to them, that if you go about to persuade them but to cut a play or poem shorter, they are so concerned, that every line you cut is valued at a joint, and every speech a limb lopped off. Without doubt, there is a kind of madness in poetry, or else how can a man be so vainly possessed as to think his

own works exceed all other men's? That there
are such men is but too true, for I myself have
thought so of my own poetry; and when I, that am
so mean an under-shrub, do prove so vainly mad,
the tall cedars, sure, must needs be shaken with
outrageous fits; and in those fits they write rap-
tures, and fly to the skies, and get among the
gods, and make such work that you would swear
they're all breaking up school and coming down
amongst us. For my part, I wonder they have
not come all this while; I'm sure they have been
sufficiently provoked. I thank my incapacity I am
not so far gone in poetry as to arrive at those fits.
Yet I have this to say, that I have had my ends
upon poetry, and not poetry upon me; for if
poetry had gained its ends on me, it had made me
mad, but that I having my ends on it appears in
my getting money by it, which was shown plenti-
fully on my poet's days; but that I thank my
friends for, and not the desert of my plays. And I
wish, reader, that you may prove as kind to the
printer as you were to me when you were a hearer;
and that my farrier may prove as good a servant
to him as formerly to me, who am, reader, your
humble servant,

JOHN LACY.

PROLOGUE.

HERE I am, and not asham'd who know it,
I humbly come your *forma paup'ris* poet:
Not Hector-like, that one half-year has writ,
And fights th' other half to defend that wit.
Nor have I brought you here a second play,
Like him that pretends preaching twice a day;
And when you gravely come i' th' afternoon,
He puts you off with repetition,
Saying, you may remember in the morn
I told you thus, and so, and where, and when;
So spins out his hour with the same again.
Though such things pass on those that sermons
    hear,
It will not do with play-judgers, I fear.
I would you had their grace, and they your wit;
Sermons would then be hard as plays to hit,
And easy scenes would pass upon you, when
Grace above wit abounds in gentlemen.
How would the poets all rejoice to see
This age appear i' th' old simplicity—
To have your wives and you come ten times o'er,
To see the pudding eaten in Jane Shore;
To cry up the bold Beauchamps of the stage?
There was a blessed understanding age.
I would you were such but for one three days,
Till the poor poet gather up his bays;
Or else my less than fifth-rate wit, I find,
Will force me beg you'll not be just, but kind.
Yet use me as you please, my comfort is,
Philosophy can no farther go than this :—
If by your vengeance I must needs be worried,
I'm not the first small poet has miscarried.

THE ACTORS' NAMES.

GERNETTE, . . . *An old rich gentleman.*

OLINDA, ... *His daughter, pretending dumbness, and after that mad-
ness.*

Squire SOFTHEAD, . *Her suitor.*

LEANDER, ... *Her lover, but not permitted.*

DRENCH, ... *A farrier, beaten to a Doctor.*

ISABEL, ... *His wife.*

JARVIS, ... *Servant to* Gernette.

NURSE, ... *His wife, and housekeeper to*
Gernette.

Mrs. NIBBY, . . . *Cousin to* Gernette.

Mr. OTHENTICK, . *A parson, and brother to*
Leander.

Three DOCTORS *of physic.*

WOMEN-SERVANTS *attending on* Olinda.

Two FOOTBOYS.

Two WHIPPERS *of Bedlam.*

PATIENTS.

NEIGHBOURS.

THE DUMB LADY.

ACT I.—SCENE I.

Enter JARVIS *and* SERVANT.

Ser. The like was never heard of—to have a sweet young lady, as she was going to be married, to fall dumb!

Jar. If my wife had done so too, I think it had been ne'er the worse for the commonwealth; but it would make any woman dumb to be designed for such a fop as Squire Softhead.

Ser. He is a fop of a new stamp. I would not marry a milkmaid to him.

Jar. I would he had my wife, or any that would make him a cuckold! He has turned away twenty servants because they do not call him Squire oft enough. I shall be sick every time I hear the word Squire, he has made it so ridiculously loathsome.

Ser. He has been called so from his cradle in the country, where the title of Squire had always great worship, till the fool crept in amongst them, of which he is chief.

Jar. Yes, faith, for if there were an army of fops,—as truly I think they might be raised here, —Squire Softhead must be General. He has one faculty: he will maintain a quarrel within three words of striking, and then he will eat cold custard.

Ser. Hang him! But dost thou think my young mistress is dumb indeed?

Jar. You saw the doctors could not cure her. But if she do counterfeit, do not blame her, for 'twere pity upon pity that the Squire—a pox squire him!—should have her. Here they all come!

> *Enter* GERNETTE; *his* DAUGHTER, *led by* SERVANTS *as dumb;* SQUIRE SOFTHEAD, *her suitor;* NIBBY, *and* JARVIS.

Ger. To have my child struck dumb upon her intended wedding day, and to have the doctors give her over, too! O my unhappy stars!

Soft. Are the stars such unhappy things? Are they the cause of her dumbness? By the heart of a horse, if I thought so I'd complain of 'em.

Nib. Complain of the stars! Who would you complain to, good Squire Softhead?

Soft. I'd complain to the sun and moon; I warrant you they'd not uphold them in their rascally twinkling tricks.

Nib. Alas, poor Squire, the sun is always in haste; he ne'er stays to hear complaints.

Soft. Why, then, I'll watch them when they fall; and if the proudest star of them all light within my ground, by the heart of a horse, I'll have an action of trespass against them; and if the law once take hold of 'em, I'll warrant 'em for twinkling again in haste.

Nib. You were best get a star-trap to catch 'em in.

Soft. I warrant you a law-trap will do as well.

Nib. Do you think your daughter had not better be dumb and dead than marry such a ridiculous brute as this?

Ger. Oh, but his estate lies so sweetly round mine, that when she understands the blessing she'll doat on him as I do.

Nib. Marry, the devil doat on him! Why, sir, he never comes into her chamber but he is all of a foaming sweat, throws off his periwig—and no one knows whether he or that smells rankest; then he runs to the looking-glass, rubs his head with the dressing cloth, puts on his periwig, then combs out the powder upon his mistress, so makes a scurvy leg, and leaves her. There's a lover, with a pox to him! But, Squire, why do you profane the stars so?

Soft. Profane! There's a company of vagabond wand'ring stars that do nothing but run up and down the sky to tell fortunes, just like our gipsies i' th' highway; I know 'em well enough. Heart of a horse, to lose a wife for want of three words! If she had said but "to have and to hold," we had had no further use of her tongue as I know of.

Nib. Why so, Squire?

Soft. Do not call me Squire, mistress. Bare Squire, without Softhead, sounds scurvily, and 'tis scurvily done to call me so, and as scurvily I take it; and, by the heart of a horse, if you were not a woman, I'd wound you scurvily.

Jar. Truly, methinks, there's such a sympathy betwixt Squire and Softhead that 'tis a thousand pities to part them.

Nib. I beseech you, Squire, which is the ancientest family, the Softheads or the Haufheads?*

Soft. The Softheads are the ancientest family in Europe, for Adam's youngest son got a knock in his cradle, and the Softheads ever since derive themselves in a direct line from him.

---

* Hauf-rockton. Quite silly.— *Yorsh.*

Ger. How does my child ? Thou hast thy health, I hope ?

Olin. A-a-a-a-a !

Soft. Heart of a horse, I believe she counterfeits dumbness; but I have a trick to make her speak again, if you'll give me leave.

Ger. With all my heart, sir; what is it ?

Soft. Why, I'll go call her jade and whore, and that will provoke her to call me rogue and rascal, you know.

Ger. Though it be upon such rude terms, I would be glad to hear her speak, sir.

Soft. Come on ! Why do not you speak the words of matrimony, you jade, that you might be my wife, you little whore ? Look you, sir, she has given me an answer.

[*She takes him a cuff o' th' ear.*

Ger. Ay, but 'tis but with her hand, sir.

Soft. However, 'tis an answer, sir; and she may marry me with her hand as well as with her tongue, for it seems to me to be the stronger confirmation.

Ger. Squire, if you love my child, endeavour to find all possible helps. Where's my servants ? Run and ride all ways imaginable; leave no ground unsearched, nor means unthought of, to recover her.

Nib. And, good Squire Softhead, find out a wise man to cure her. Do you know one when you see him ?

Soft. By my troth, to my knowledge, I never saw a wise man in my life.

Jar. Do you send a fool to find out a wise man ?

Nib. If he cannot find a wise man, a wise man will find out him quickly.

Ger. Come, lead my child to her chamber, and

ride all ways and all countries to find out wise and able men. [*Exeunt all but* JARVIS *and* SOFTHEAD.

Soft. Jarvis, how shall we do to know a wise man when we see him? What marks and signs have they?

Jar. Why, their dress and their speech they have from the stool of formality; and they have likely a bald head with a satin cap on't, a narrow band with a broad hat; a cane growing in their hands, with the silver head always bobbing at their lips; and they that are thus habited are taken for wise men.

Soft. Why, then, I may be a wise man if a silver cane will make me so; but, prithee, what do these wise men do?

Jar. By'r lady, that will puzzle a wise man to tell you, for I never heard of anything that was wisely done in my life; therefore I think wise men do nothing.

Soft. Then I will be wise, whatsoever it cost me, for I love to do nothing above all things i'th' world. But come, let us go the right way to find a wise man now.

Jar. I'll warrant you go right, for we'll go directly east.

Soft. Why, you fool, the wise men came out o' th' east, and dost thou think to find them there when they left the place?

Jar. Ay, but, sir, they returned back into their own country again.

Soft. Did they? Why, then, the wise men of the east are not so wise as the wise men of France; for if they get into another country, the devil cannot drive them home again. [*Exeunt.*

Enter DRENCH, *a farrier, and* ISABEL, *his wife.*

Dr. I say, dame Isabel, I'll have it my way!

B

Isa. Have it my way! Why, who are you, sir? Art thou any more than my husband, fellow? How camest thou thus audacious, then, to say, I'll have it my way? Say that again, and by the faith I have in my confidant, my gallant shall make thee an example.

Dr. Aha! have you your confidant and your gallant, wife?

Isa. Yes, that I have. You know when the great ones have done with a fashion, it comes amongst we mean madams into the country at last; and I have as much privilege due to me as any freeborn people in the world has, and we women will maintain the liberties of the subject with our lives and fortunes.

Dr. By'r lady, wife, you rant like a freeborn subject indeed! But, pray you, what do you with the word "freeborn subject"?

Isa. I have it to show that I am one of the freeborn, and may have my gallant, with all the perquisites belonging thereunto.

Dr. Why, thou stragglest as far out of the bonds of matrimony as if thou'dst a good jointure to justify thee in't. There is a thing called *duty*, wife; the parson, you may remember, said so when he married us.

Isa. I no more remember what the parson said when he married us than what he has said ever since when he preached.

Dr. The jade's mad beyond recovery; a pox of the liberty of the she subject! Wife, there are five children by the fireside; pray you, how many of 'em's mine, wife? I think 'tis high time to ask that question.

Isa. I must not be so much concerned with thee as to call thee husband; therefore, Mr. Drench, the first child was yours.

Dr. And whose are the rest ?

Isa. The rest are mine, fellow; let that suffice thee!

Dr. And but one of them mine, wife ?

Isa. No but one yours, and for this following reason. After my first child, you neglected your family duty, Mr. Drench; and when you grew negligent of me I grew careful of myself, and from that care came the rest of my children, Mr. Drench.

Dr. And those four children, it seems, are freeborn subjects ? I find a wife a little modish is worse than a wife a little oldish. Wife, I'll downright poison your freeborn children.

Isa. O thou ungallantified beast! wouldst thou destroy thy own flesh and blood ?

Dr. Not mine, but I will yours, wife.

Isa. Why, are not man and wife one flesh ? and then are not your children mine, and mine yours, Mr. Drench ?

Dr. Faith, I doubt this argument is the general security that mankind has to warrant their offsprings legitimate.

Isa. Sirrah, talk of poisoning my children, and I'll have thee so gallantified !

Dr. Gallantified! Prithee what's that, wife ?

Isa. To be gallantified is to be soundly cudgell'd, sirrah. There is another point of she doctrine for you.

Dr. Pray you, let me ask you a question, madam. Nay, be not ashamed to be called madam, for as mean people as yourself has the impudence to own it. Therefore, madam, are you true to your gallant ?

Isa. Ay, by my life am I! I else deserve to lose my privileges, and be a bondwoman, ay, and condemned to my own husband.

Dr. That part of me that's gentleman forgives thee freely for that; but the rough part, which is farrier, must be revenged; and though your gallant carry your cudgel of love, I carry your cudgel of chastisement. I plead my privileges, wife, and must beat you; take this, and that, and that, and this! [*Beats her.*

Isa. Help! murder, murder! Will you kill me, you villain?

Dr. Kill you? Alas! this is but compliment, wife, and 'tis a new fashion come into the country, wife; so I have it to show you that I'm one o' th' freeborn, wife. [*Beats her again.*

Isa. Murder, murder! help, murder!

Enter a NEIGHBOUR.

Neigh. What's here? Fie, fie, neighbour Drench! Hold, for shame! What, beating your wife?

Isa. Ay, marry is he, sir; what's that to you suppose I long for a beating? I have been getting him in a good humour this two months to do it, and now you must disturb us.

Neigh. Nay, if you long for a beating, I'm sorry I disturbed you. I have done.

Isa. You wicked fellow, do you know what you've done? You have taken him off of the sweetest humour. I see by his looks I shall not get another blow off him to save my life.

Dr. The jade is mad beyond all cure.

Neigh. Ay, for none but a madwoman would long for a beating; but farewell, neighbours. I have done.

Dr. You're an impertinent fellow to begin. Men that part rencounters are often killed or hurt, and therefore you ought, neighbour, to be soundly cudgelled. [*Beats him.*

Neigh. Nay, good neighbour, hold, hold!

Isa. You see he has taken off his anger from me, and now you must have all the sweet blows, you rascal!

Dr. So he shall, for if I had known thou hadst longed for a beating, thou shouldst not have had a blow to 've saved thy life ; but you shall have it.

[*Beats him again.*

Neigh. Hold, hold, hold! If ere I part man and wife, if ere I put my hand betwixt the bark and the tree again, may my fingers bear fruit and the boys rob my orchard! A woman to long for a beating? What a blessing 'twere if all our wives would long so! [*Exit* NEIGHBOUR.

Dr. Now I know you long for a beating, wife, lest you should miscarry I'll beat you wonderfully.

Isa. Hold, hold! my longing is over indeed.

Dr. Is it? Why, then, I'll to the wood and drench a sick horse ; and by that time I return I hope you may come to your longing again, and then I shall plead the liberty of the subject, and claw your freeborn sides again. [*Exit* DRENCH.

Isa. To be beaten thus! If I be not revenged, say I'm a woman without gall or invention. Let me think a little. They say when a woman means mischief, if she but look upon her apron-strings the devil will help her presently. I'll try him. Who is here?

Enter JARVIS *and* SOFTHEAD *to her.*

Soft. We may search long enough; the devil a wise man that I can find or hear of.

Jar. Ay, but, sir, you must know there be several sorts of wise men ; and our business is to find out a wise physician.

Isa. Either the proverb's false or the devil's
very dull, for he has helped me to no invention
yet.   [*Aside.*

Soft. But all the professed doctors which we take
to be wise physicians have given her over, you see.

Jar. Ay, but there may be skilful and wise men
in physic that do not profess it.

Soft. You say very true, for I was cured once
o' th' bellyache by an old woman and a warm
trencher, when all the doctors i' th' town had given
me over.

Isa. God-a-mercy, devil; I have it, i' faith ! These
gentlemen have given me a hint for a revenge
upon my barbarous husband.   Gentlemen, I overheard your discourse, and I find you are in great
distress for a wise physician.

Soft. What then ? does such a country creature
as thou know anything that's wise ?

Isa. I know not what your worship means by
wise.

Soft. I dare swear thou dost not, for I, that am
a squire, scarce know myself.

Isa. But, sir, I can help you to the most excellent physician upon earth ; but then he's a man of
the most strangest humours.

Soft. 'Slid, no matter for his humours, so he be
wise ! Where is he ?

Isa. Why, in that very copse, blooding and
drenching of a sick horse.

Soft. Why, that's a wise farrier, not a wise physician, woman !

Isa. But he is a famous physician of Padua, and
has retired himself on purpose to avoid patients.

Soft. Then he is a fool, and no physician ; for
the wise doctors never leave a patient whilst he
has either breath in 's body or money in 's purse.

Isa. Ay, but, sir, this is not a man that values money.

Soft. Then, I say, he is not a wise man. Come away, Jarvis, this cannot be he we look for.

Isa. Why, you must know, sir, he exceeds the world for physic; but then his humour is to deny his profession, and acknowledge nothing but ignorance. Then, sir, he looks so like a farrier, that you would swear he were one indeed; then he is such a clown.

Jar. The greater the scholar, still the more clown; and the further he is gone in learning, the more ignorant still in other things.

Soft. Ay, but is he far gone in physic? Can he make a dumb woman speak?

Isa. A dumb woman speak! I'll undertake he shall provoke a dumb devil to speak.

Soft. That's the wise man I want; pray you, where is he?

Isa. Why, sir, he is easily spoke with, but you'll find it wonderful difficult to get him to a patient. Neither gold, compliment, nor other fair usage could ever yet work upon him; and yet there is a way to gain him.

Soft. Heart of a horse, pox to him! what way can that be?

Isa. A way that you'll think strange, but very true. He could never yet be brought to a patient without being rudely used and soundly cudgelled to it.

Soft. Nay, by the heart of a horse, he shall want for no beating!

Isa. Ay, marry, sir, that will do it, and nothing else i' th' world; yet he will carry his seeming simplicity so cunningly, that I hold a wager you come away persuaded that he is no physician.

Jar. I hold a wager he shall own it; I'll make him commence doctor else with a good cudgel, I warrant you. But is he such a rare physician?

Isa. Truly, sir, but two days since he brought a madwoman to her wits again that was suspected never to have any; nay, he has taken men's legs and arms off, and set 'em on sound again.

Jar. That's beyond Surgeon's Hall; sure he can conjure.

Soft. I'll be hanged if this fellow be not a spy of the virtuosos, and is come hither disguised to betray secrets in nature.

Jar. But does he take no other fees but beating, mistress?

Isa. Of a certain, nothing else, sir.

Jar. I would some doctors I know could be brought to that: I would want no physic, nor he should want no fees, i' faith!

Isa. Gentlemen, you'll find him in the wood with a leather apron, and a hammer by his side, as if he were a real smith; and he studies as much to be a farrier now as formerly a physician. And as his drink was altogether wine before, now, farrier-like, he studies all sorts of ale, and drinks them soundly, too. So farewell, gentlemen; you'll find all things true as I have said, and my rascal, I hope, will be cudgelled from a farrier to a doctor.

[*Exit* ISABEL.

Jar. Why, this is such an humorous physician as yet I have not heard of.

Soft. 'Slid, we should have asked the woman one thing: it may be he delights to be beaten with one sort of cudgel more than another.

Jar. We'll be so civil as to ask him that, if he puts us to it. But come, let us into the wood and find him out!

Soft. Hark! I hear the trees hurl * in the wood. 'Slid, here's a man coming towards us; I hope 'twill prove the doctor.

Jar. By mass! he has a leather apron on, and a hammer by his side.

Soft. 'Tis he! What if we cudgel him before we speak to him?

Jar. Not for the world, sir; that would be rude indeed.

Enter DRENCH.

Save you, sir.

Dr. Save me, sir? Spare your compliment till I'm dying, and then I'll thank you for 't.

Soft. By the heart of a horse, I like him for that; for what should a man be saved for till he is dead, you know?

Jar. Sir, in short, we come, having business with you, to pay you all the respect and reverence that's due to your worship.

Dr. Respect, reverence, and worship! You're very merry, gentlemen. Pray you, sir, what part of me is it that you find worshipful?

Jar. Oh, sir, it is your virtues that we admire.

Dr. Virtue! I never heard the word in my life; no, nor the use on 't.

Soft. Thou speak'st like an honest man, for, by my troth, I see no sign of virtue about thee.

Jar. 'Slid, you'll spoil all to be so blunt with him. Sir, we understand you are a great doctor.

Dr. I understand myself to be a great horse-doctor, sir.

Soft. But pray you, sir, be a man-doctor for my sake. By this cudgel, it will be the better for you, if you knew all!

Jar. Sir, in short, we know you to be a famous

* Rattle.

doctor of Padua, and we wish you would leave these abject thoughts of being a farrier, and follow your own worthy profession of physic.

Dr. Now you provoke me, sir. Do you think a farrier inferior to a physician? He is the son of a mare that thinks a horse has not as many diseases as a man.

Soft. And he is the son of a whore that thinks a squire has not as many diseases as a horse. And, friend, take heed how you make comparisons, for you'll have all the squires i' th' country about your ears upon this score.

Dr. Country squires I shall deal well enough with, and I shall justify a horse has more diseases than a squire, and take the honour of knighthood to help you.

Soft. You lie! and for the honour of squirehood I'll die a virgin martyr!   [*Offers to draw.*

Jar. Hold, hold, sir! the latter end of a squire's argument is still quarrelling.

Soft. Without quarrelling, then, I'll prove that squire and squiress have more diseases than a horse.

Dr. Ay, with the diseases of their own, that nature never meant them, I grant you.

Soft. And first, I prove a squiress, that is, a woman, may be dumb.

Dr. And I answer, a horse cannot speak—set that against that. And yet I'll undertake to make a horse speak before you shall make a woman dumb, sir.

Jar. Good squire, let us mind our business. In short, sir, will you own your profession? Are you a doctor or no?

Dr. A pox of a doctor! I am a downright farrier. I can give you a drench, or cut you for the staggers when you're drunk; I have no more learning than a horse. Pray open my head, and see if you can find a physician there.

Jar. Since no means but the extremity will make you own your profession, we will cudgel you with as much compliment as we can, sir.

Soft. A cudgel is but a coarse compliment, I confess.

Dr. Hey, good boys, i' faith! What a devil mean you, gentlemen?

Jar. Squire, do you strike the first blow.

Soft. No; do you, Jarvis, for the first blow will bear an action, you know; and thou'rt a poor fellow, he can recover nothing of thee.

Dr. What a devil's the matter?

Jar. Fall on, fall on! Will you confess you're a doctor?   [*Beats him.*

Dr. Hold, hold, hold! I will be a physician!

Jar. Will you own you are one, sir?
[*Beats him again.*

Dr. I am one, I am one! Hold, I am a very good physician; I feel I am.

Enter ISABEL.

Isa. Yes, gentlemen, he is a rare physician; and would confess it, too, but that he would not lose the pleasure of a cudgel, for once a week he longs for a beating. Now you and I are even, sir.
[*Exit* ISABEL.

Dr. A pox upon you, is this your design? I'll be revenged, you jade, to the purpose. If I should say she is my wife, and that I'm a very blacksmith, they'd not believe me; 'twere but the way to be cudgelled again.

Jar. Nay, come, sir. What! are you falling into a relapse again?

Dr. No, no; hold ! As the woman says, I am a doctor.

Jar. Ay, and so famous, that you can take off broken limbs and set them on sound again.

Dr. Well, I will own all this rather than have my bones broken. And, now I remember, you fetched me once before out of this great wood, in Plato's great year, as my master called it.

Soft. Pray you, sir, how long is that since?

Dr. Why, next strawberry time, it will be complete six-and-thirty thousand years.

Jar. Ho, boy !

Dr. Ay, and I remember I poisoned somebody at your request.

Jar. No, sir, I do not remember that.

Dr. But I do, sir; by the same token you gave me a hundred pieces for a bribe, tied up in a laced handkerchief.

Jar. I remember now as well as can be.

Soft. But I do not remember I hired him to poison anybody, nor do I remember I'm six-and-thirty thousand years old. A pox of your Plato's great year, and his little year too!

Jar. Pray, sir, remember your mistress will ne'er be cured else.

Soft. Nay, rather than so, I will remember anything.

Jar. Look you there, sir; you see we both remember; therefore, I pray you, go with us to cure a distressed lady.

Dr. My business in physic is killing, not curing, I assure you; for as there is your man-tailor and your woman-tailor, so there is your killing doctor and your curing doctor—distinct professions, I assure you.

Jar. But, sir, you must own curing as well as

killing, or else we shall court you with a cudgel again.

Soft. As we did in Plato's great year, you know, Jarvis.

Dr. I do not remember that ye beat me then.

Soft. But I remember it; by the same token you gave me my laced handkerchief back when you had put the gold in your pocket.

Dr. Now I do remember. Hold, hold!

[*Offers to beat him.*

I do own curing, and, since there is no remedy, I confess I am a doctor; but if all men should take their degrees as I have done, we should have but small commencements. I once served a mountebank, and have some of his canting terms, and for aught I know, may prove as good a physician as if I'd served an apprenticeship at Padua. Well, gentlemen, what disease is it I must cure?

Soft. You must help a lady that is dumb, and has lost her speech.

Dr. How! dumb, and lost her speech too! That's a great work. If she had only lost her speech, I could have cured her, or if she had been but dumb; but to be dumb and speechless too, her case is very desperate. Would I'd my wife and all the neighbourhood at that lock!

Jar. But we must entreat your utmost skill, for 'tis a sad thing for a woman to be speechless.

Dr. Ay, and dumb; but 'tis a sadder thing for a man to be a fool, for certainly he is a changeling that has a dumb wife and would have her speak again. Are you in love with a woman's sting?

Jar. Why do you call it a sting, sir?

Dr. Because, sir, a woman has no tongue; they're tongues in men's mouths, but they're called stings in women.

Jar. But, sir, this lady never spoke an angry word—not so much as to a servant!

Dr. But she will do if I cure her, for I've an unlucky hand that way; yet for her sweet disposition's sake I'll preserve her. And now I'll answer to the name of doctor with as much confidence as a quack dressed up in all his ignorance.

Soft. Will ignorance make men confident? 'Slid, would I'd a little ignorance too!

Jar. Ay, if you had but a little, 'twere very well, sir.

Dr. Let me see how to behave myself like a doctor, now. I will first take your mistress by the pulse, and look up gravely at the ceiling all the while; then ask what she took last, and when she'd a stool,—and there's half a doctor's work. Then I'll prescribe something that will neither do hurt nor good, so leave her to luck; and there's the other half of the doctor. Then, to amuse the people, I'll give her the powder of a dried dock-leaf with apothecaries' hard name to it; and if that will not mend her, I'll give her a drench, for women have sturdy stomachs, and why not as strong of constitution as horses?

Soft. Heart of a horse, thou'rt a delicate mad doctor! Sirrah, wilt thou give her a drench?

Dr. Why, a drench is a potion, and a potion is a drench; only the distinction is, when you put it into a horn, then 'tis a drench for a horse; and when you put it into a vial-glass, 'tis a potion for a man. Nay, I'll discover all their cheats.

Come, my Squire Softhead, never fear thy wench,
She shall be cured by learned Dr. Drench.

ACT II.—SCENE I.

Enter GERNETTE, SOFTHEAD, JARVIS, *and* NURSE.

Ger. And is he so famous a physician, say you?

Jar. Why, sir, Esculapius, as you call him, is a mere mountebank to him.

Soft. Ay, and that fellow Galen Hippocrates, as you call him, not worthy to be his apothecary. He can conjure, for he'll cure a wooden leg, make it flesh and blood, and set you up sound again!

Jar. Nay, if he like your pulse, he'll give you a lease of your life for term of years.

Nur. I would he would give me three lives in mine, and begin them all at fifteen again.

Jar. Is not one life sufficient to make a man a cuckold, but you'd have three to do it in?

Nur. Yes, because I'd make thee a monster, that my child and I may live upon showing thee.

Ger. You talk of wonders; I long to see him.

Jar. He is i' th' next room, sir; but 'tis the maddest doctor, and of the strangest humours.

Soft. So he is, for, by the heart of a horse, we were fain to bribe him with a cudgel before he would own being a doctor.

Nur. A downright sir reverence of a doctor! I say, get her a worthy husband, and say I told you so.

Ger. You're a foolish woman, and talk of that you understand not.

Nur. Understand not? Sure I should know what a woman wants as well as you. I say again, a pox of your doctor! get her a good husband! A plaster of true love clapped to her will do her more good than senna or rhubarb.

Ger. Did I not provide her a good husband?
Was she not to marry the Squire here?

Nur. A precious morsel of him! How came
you to be a Squire, with a pox, with your soft head,
and your little head, and your no head at all?

Soft. Bear witness, she says I have no head at
all!

Nur. Thou mayest take it and throw it to the
dogs for any brains there's in 't.

Soft. I will not call you whore, gentlewoman,
but, by the heart of a horse, your husband's a
cuckold; and he is not only an English cuckold,
but also an Italian cuckold—that is to say, he is a
cuckold both before and behind.

Nur. Sirrah, cudgel him, or lie in the truckle-
bed all thy life!

Jar. I'll rather cudgel thee, for I believe every
word he says.

Nur. For shame! Proffer her a husband of her
own choosing. Let her have Leander!

Ger. She shall never be his Hero.

Nur. If she perish in the Hellespont, at your
peril!

Ger. Hellespont?—how came you by that fine
word?

Nur. Honestly enough.

Jar. As honestly as you came by your child, I
think.

Nur. I have seen Mr. Hellespont in a puppet-
show, and Hero, and Leander too.

Ger. Talk no more of Leander, I know him not;
but whoe'er he be, he is not to be compared with
the Squire here for wealth.

Nur. Is your Squire boobe, loobe, poope, to
stand with Leander for parts and person?

Ger. Do you know his parts?

Nur. No, but I have heard of him and his parts.

Soft. Grant me patience, for I have much ado to forbear calling you whore, forsooth !

Nur. Do, if thou dar'st ! Is wealth to be named the same day with love ? I scorn that comparison, though I'm o' th' wrong side o' th' teens, i' faith.

Ger. Hast thou any sense of the fopperies of love left ?

Nur. Dost thou call sweet love foppery ? Though thou 'rt my master, thou 'rt a beast. Go, go to bed and die ; what dost thou in this world ? Let the doctors give him physic ; nobody else has need on 't !

Jar. You 're very bold with your master, wife.

Nur. He has been as bold with me ; let that suffice you, husband. I have so fresh in my memory the sweet effects of love, that I wonder mankind should be such beasts as to forget it.

Ger. Go, give your child suck, for that's your talent, and meddle no more.

Jar. That's another sign 'tis none of my child, for why should he be so careful to have the child suck if it were not his own ?

Soft. Look you, friend, your wife has abus'd me, and 'tis not civil to call her whore to her own face ; but I tell thee to thy face she is a whore rampant, and in heraldry thou 'rt a cuckold passant.

Jar. Ay, sir, and my wants make me a cuckold couchant, or I'd ne'er endure it.

Soft. Oh, here come's our delicate, humoursome doctor, i' faith !

Enter DOCTOR.

Ger. Squire, go bid them make my daughter ready to receive the Doctor.

Soft. I do not care to go, for she has her wild

C

Irish chambermaid, that always calls me Squire Pogemihone, and then laughs at me.

Ger. Pray you, go, sir. You're very welcome, sir; I have very much desired to see you.

[*Exit* SOFTHEAD.

Doct. Hippocrates says, I pray you be covered.

Ger. Pray you, in what chapter of Hippocrates does he bid you be covered?

Doct. In the first chapter of keeping your head warm.

Ger. A pleasant gentleman, and I love his humour. But, sir, concerning my daughter, who is very sick, sir——

Doct. I am very glad on 't, sir; and I would you and your whole family were sick, lame, or blind, that I might have the honour to cure you.

Ger. Why, this is the strangest doctor. He had need of good parts to bear out his humours.

Doct. And now, sir, I pray you, what's your daughter's name?

Ger. Olinda, sir, at your service.

Doct. Olinda! a pretty name to be cured.

Ger. Sir, I'll see if my daughter be ready to come forth to you. [*Exit* GERNETTE.

Doct. Your servant, sir; and what woman is that, I pray you?

Jar. The nurse of the house, sir.

Doct. By'r lady, a pretty piece of household stuff, and a fine ornament for a couch. I do salute you, nurse, and I would I were that happy suckling that shall draw down the milk of your favour and affection, nurse.

Jar. Her pulse beats not thereabouts, sir! Hands off, for she's my wife, sir!

Doct. I cry you mercy, sir. I congratulate you for having so handsome a wife, and your wife for having so worthy a husband. Your breasts, sweet nurse——

Jar. Pray you, hold, sir! Half this courtesy would serve.

Doct. Worthy sir, I cannot declare enough how much I'm your servant! Delicate breasts, nurse.

[*His hands upon her breasts still.*

Nur. At your service.

Jar. Oh, devil take you, sir; let my wife's breasts alone!

Doct. Sweet sir, I must see her breasts; it is the doctor's duty to look to the nurse's milk.

Jar. You shall not look to her milk; I'll look to your water for that, sir!

Doct. You will not hinder me from following my profession. Alas! I must not only feel her breasts, but I must know whether she be with child or no.

Jar. Sir, my wife is not with child.

Doct. But she must be with child. What say'st thou, Nurse?

Nur. If your worship think it be for my health, sir.

Doct. Thou wilt die in a week, else.

Nur. Do you hear that?

Jar. A pox of your mountebanking, sir! My wife is sound and well, and shall have no doctor.

Doct. Sir, I know you're a man of sense, and I beseech you hear reason. A sweet nurse!

Nur. Oh, dear Doctor!

Jar. A pox of your sense and reason! Give me my wife, sir!

Doct. But, sir, I'm from home, and want a woman. I hope you'll be civil to a stranger; if you come my way, I'll be as kind to you, sir.

Jar. The devil take your kindness! Give me my wife.

Doct. Give me a reason for't; for look you, sir, your wife is either with child, or else she has a tympany. Nurse, show me your legs, they may be swelled and dropsical; a sweet woman may be cast away here for want of a little looking to.

Jar. Let my wife's legs alone, or I'll downright thrust you out o' th' room!

Doct. Sir, I find you're choleric; but I'll give you a purge shall make you so patient, that if you saw me lie with your wife you should not have so much gall left as would make an angry line in your face.

Nur. Now, good husband, take physic.

Doct. God-a-mercy, Nurse!

Nur. In troth, sir, he is always so fretful, and so cholericly jealous!

Jar. I'll make you an example!

Doct. Such another word, and I'll put thee in a fever, and keep thee in't a year. I tell thee, fellow, thy wife is not well, and I will give her a gentle gentile glister. Prithee be sick, Nurse.

Nur. Yes, sir, I am sick; and if you please you shall give me a gentle gentile, as you call it.

Jar. You are no more sick than I am, housewife!

Nur. Sure the doctor knows better than you or I whether I be sick or no; and I find I am sick, and I do so long for a gentle gentile what d'ye call it?

Jar. My master is coming, or I'd give you such a gentle gentile!

Enter old GERNETTE, *his* DAUGHTER *led in by* SERVANTS, *and* SQUIRE SOFTHEAD.

Ger. Sir, I have brought my daughter; and I

beseech your best care of her, for the world's gone with me if she die.

Doct. Hold, sir! People do not die so easily without the help of a physician.

Ger. A notable droll, and puts me in great comfort.

Doct. Is this she? A very pretty patient, and one a man may venture on in sickness or in health. Come on, sir, let me feel your pulse!

Ger. I am not sick, sir.

Doct. But your daughter is, therefore give me your pulse. Why, by your pulse, I find your daughter is dumb!

Nur. Oh dear! how he hits on 't!

Jar. Hits on 't? You'd be hit on 't too, would you? He may thank his knowing on 't before.

Ger. But, sir, 'tis strange that you should know my daughter's disease by my pulse.

Doct. Sympathy does it. I find you have no faith here in the sympathetical powder, therefore cannot know our sympathetical way of practice. When any man or woman is sick in Greenland, they always send the next of kin to the doctor; and by that pulse the disease is known and the patient cured.

Soft. Pray, Doctor, feel whether I be dumb or no.

Nur. Let me feel your pulse, husband. Oh, I am sick, and the Doctor must physic me, or I die!

Jar. The devil has found a new way to make a cuckold.

Ger. But what may be the cause, think you, of her dumbness?

Doct. Why, sir, according to the sense of Aristotle——

Ger. Aristotle was a philosopher, sir.

Doct. Ay, and a physician too ; I know what I say.   Heart ! I had like to have been gravell'd ! I say again, according to the sense of Hippocrates.

Ger. Ay, marry, sir, he was a physician indeed.

Doct. Ay, and a philosopher too ; therefore no matter which of their opinions I take.

Jar. By my troth, I think so too.

Doct. And therefore, as I said at first, according to the sense of Aristotle, women are dumb because they cannot speak.

Nur. A sweet doctor ! I always thought so, indeed.

Jar. Have you tasted of his sweetness, you quean ?

Nur. Not yet, but I hope I shall do, you rogue !

Ger. But, sir, are there many reasons for dumbness in a woman ?

Doct. Several, sir. A woman may be dumb when she has no mind to speak ; and she may speak when nobody has a mind to hear her. This is natural philosophy, now.

Ger. Why, you speak as if it were sullenness in their sex, and not a defect in nature, nor other accident.

Doct. I do so. In some romance, perhaps, you may have read of a woman's being dumb; but sure no man seriously ever heard of a woman that could not speak.

Nur. He is i' th' right, i' faith ; this is the doctor of doctors, i' faith.

Jar. Again the Doctor ? I would he were hung about thy neck !

Nur. By my troth, so would I, to determine thy jealousy !

Ger. But pray you, sir, why should you think a woman cannot be dumb ?

Doct. Why, sir, your men that have endeavoured
to find out the perpetual motion have come near
it, I confess, with their clocks and pendulums;
but Aristotle says, Fix a dial-plate to a woman's
mouth, and if the perpetual motion be not there,
let them never hope to find it; and if it be there,
'tis infallible a woman cannot be dumb.

Enter a FOOTBOY.

Boy. Squire, forsooth, here is a letter.

Soft. A good boy! Squire and forsooth does
well together; they're very suitable. But hold!
this letter is not big enough to have business in 't,
nor little enough to be a challenge. Heart of a
horse, a downright challenge!—[*Reads the letter*]—
and if he be as stout as Hercules, I'll fright him
out on 's fighting, or he shall fright me!

Ger. But touching the cause of my child's disease, sir.   [*Exit* SOFTHEAD.

Doct. Why, you must know, her dumbness may
proceed from the string-holt.

Ger. The string-holt! Why, that's a disease one
of my horses has now in the stable.

Doct. I grant you, sir; but we of Padua call a
lameness in the tongue the string-holt, from that
very string which you call the greedy worm.—A
pox on me, I shall betray myself a farrier!—[*Aside.*]
—And this dumbness proceeds from a contraction
or shrinking of that nerve or string, which shrinking proceeds from stomachous fumigations, which
proceed from certain exhalations or influence of
the stars, called in Arabic—do you understand
Arabic?

Ger. Not a word—not I, sir.

Doct. A gentleman, and not speak Arabic! Why,
where have you been bred?

Ger. I neither speak Arabic, Latin, nor any language but my mother tongue.

Doct. What blessed luck is this for me ! How shall I do to explain it to you, then ? For optimum purgamentum, cantaridem, venetreclum — do ye conceive me, sir ?—vinum cum drammum, scirramoucha scrupulum ; and this is just your daughter's case, sir.

Nur. Hoboy, Doctor! he claws it away with Latin, i' faith !

Jar. Still commending the Doctor ? You'd have him claw you away with Latin too, would you not, you jade ?

Nur. Ay, faith, or with Greek either, you knave !

Ger. Sure he's a learned man, if one could understand him. Pray you, if you please, state her case in English.

Doct. Why, this is worse than all the rest. Why, you must know, sir, that the vapours passing from the right side, where lies the heart, unto the left, where lies the liver, the lungs, which in Latin we call Armion, having communication with the brain, which in Greek we call Nazmathon, by intermedium of the Vena cava, which in Hebrew we call Rabshack, and in Arabic Helgoshob——

Nur. Thou beast ! when wilt thou know Rabshack and Helgoshob ? O most divine Doctor!

Jar. Divine ! Is it come to divinity now ? Why, then, you hope to be saved by him ?

Nur. I'll venture with him into Rabshack and Helgoshob, whate'er befalls me.

Ger. Ragshag ? Sir, I understand these tongues less than Latin.

Doct. I'm sorry for 't, sir ; did you but know the sweet sound of Hebrew and Arabic, you would never speak your mother tongue again.

Ger. Sir, I like your discourse well, only where you say the heart lies on the right side and the liver on the left, which is contrary to all anatomists I ever heard of.

Doct. How shall I answer this? Pox on him, he makes me sweat!—Why, sir, it is true that in time of health the heart lies on the left side, and in most diseases too; but in dumbness, the heart by some strong passion being turned and whirled to the right side, till by art it be returned and whirled back to the left, neither man nor woman can possibly speak; and that is the positive cause of all dumbness.

Nur. O dear Doctor, I cry still!

Jar. Is it come to dear Doctor, now? Is he your dear, you whore?

Nur. He is not yet, but he shall be, you cuckold!

Jar. Cuckold! Remember this.

Nur. I do remember thou art one, and I will remember to continue thee so.

Ger. Sir, I am well satisfied. Now, if you please, let us proceed to the cure of my daughter.

Doct. Oh, there's the point! Why, there be several ways to cure, and twice as many ways to kill; for we learned physicians with too much study have likely a worm in our heads, and when that worm wriggles the mind alters, so that we change our fashions as much in physic as the court and gentry do their clothes. But come, get my patient to her bed, and when she's warm give her a lusty dose of sops and wine.

Ger. How! sops and wine! Sure that will make her drunk, sir.

Doct. The better, sir; for when people are drunk, they are apt to speak their minds. I work by natural causes. You see by the virtue of

cakes and wine how women tattle at a gossiping.
No man ever knew a dumb woman at a christen-
ing or a gossiping but she talked before she went
away.

Nur. The Doctor's i' th' right, I'll be sworn; I
know it by experience. O brave Doctor!

Jar. Brave Doctor! I' faith, proclaim your love
with him.

Nur. By my troth, so I will, with the first
opportunity.

Doct. So lead her to bed, and let Nurse drink
with her to countenance her.

Nur. I will indeed, Mr. Doctor; I will be sure
to obey your commands.

Doct. And when you have drunk smartly, bring
me word how it works, Nurse.

Jar. You shall be hanged first, Doctor.

Doct. And be sure, Nurse, come alone still; for
you know she may have something to say to me
that is not fit for her husband to hear.

Jar. A pox on you! must my master pimp for
you too?

Ger. Pray you take your fee, sir.

Doct. By no means; no cure no money with me,
sir. But pray you be careful of my patient, and be
sure to send Nurse still to me.

Jar. I must be a cuckold, and cannot avoid it.

Ger. Sir, I shall send to you, but perhaps not
Nurse.

Jar. So my master is jealous of her as well as I!
Now 'tis plain he got my child. How many points
o' th' compass am I a cuckold?

Doct. I hope I shall make that rogue mad for
beating me.

Nur. Your servant, Mr. Doctor.

Doct. Your servant, Nurse.   [*Exeunt.*

Enter LEANDER *and his* FOOTBOY.

Lea. Boy, did Squire Softhead receive my note so cheerfully ?

1 *Boy.* Yes, sir; and withal he told me he wondered that he heard not sooner from you, being, you know, he was to marry your mistress.

Lea. Is he so brave ? I shall the better digest my ruin if I find honour in him; yet he with all his merits can never deserve her. 'Tis strange if he should fight, for they say he is a very ass. Oh, here he comes !

Enter SOFTHEAD *and his* BOY.

Soft. Sirrah, yonder he is; will you be sure to do as I bid you ?

2 *Boy.* Yes, I warrant your worship.

Soft. Just when you see my vest off, that's your time.

2 *Boy.* I'll be sure to do it, sir.

Lea. Save you, sir.

Soft. Damn you, sir, why ? Why the pox save me, sir?

Lea. Because your poor servant hath an occasion to kill you and send you to heaven. But why damn me, sir ?

Soft. Because your poor servant hath an occasion to kill you and send you to hell, sir.

Lea. This is uncharitable language from a dying man, as you are, sir.

Soft. I scorn dying; I've an estate will keep me alive in spite of a duel, sir. I scorn but to be very charitable. Where wilt thou be buried, fellow?

Lea. Let me be killed first, I pray you.

Soft. Nay, by the heart of a horse, doubt not that, sir ! And if you'll have a tombstone over you,

write your inscription, and my stonecutter shall do
it. Nay, I scorn but to be charitable, sir.

Lea. Good rich Squire, make your will, for die
you must.

Soft. What a pox should I kill thee for, that has
nothing to leave me for my pains ?

Lea. Now you are not civil, sir.

Soft. I scorn but to be as civil as any man !

Lea. You shall find me so too, for I'll see you
buried in the flaxen your grandam spun herself,
and left your worship for a winding-sheet.

Soft. And I'll be as civil to you, sir, for I'll see
you buried in flannel. And, sir, to show myself
civil, if you have a mind not to fight at this weapon, I'll stay till you choose another ; nay, if you
have a mind not to fight at all, for civility's sake
I'll have no mind to fight at all neither—I scorn
to be behindhand in civility !

Lea. Now, no more words, sir, but strip and
take your fortune.

Soft. Pull off, boy ! And, sir, I must have you
know that I long as much to go out of this world
honourably as you to stay in it honourably.

2 *Boy.* This is my cue, I take it.

    [SOFTHEAD'S BOY *runs away with his master's
        sword.*

Soft. And to show you I kill you, sir, merely
upon honour, and not upon malice, I lovingly embrace you, sir.

Lea. Embrace an ass ! Leave your fencer's
tricks, and take you to your sword, sir !

Soft. Then a pox on you, sir ! and give me my
trusty sword, boy ! How ! the rogue is run away,
and with my sword, too ! Why, sirrah rascal, come
back, you treacherous rogue ! Come, this must be
your plot, sir, to hire my boy to run away with my

sword, sir. Why, rogue, traitor to my honour, come back!

Lea. This shall not serve your turn, Squire; my boy shall run and overtake him, I'll warrant you.

Soft. I scorn to be beholding to you or your boy, sir. I'll run and overtake him myself, sir; and I charge you upon honour to stay till I come back, sir. [*He runs off as fast as he can.*

Lea. This is the newest coward I have known! He has cozen'd me, for, as I live, I thought he would have fought, for he bore it up to the very point of danger. Sirrah, there's a vest for you, and run after him and cudgel him till he be all over black and blue!

1 *Boy.* You could not have put me upon a better employment, sir. [*Exit* BOY.

Enter DOCTOR.

Doct. By your favour, sir, I was looking out at my window, and as I thought I saw a duel towards, so I came.

Lea. To prevent it?

Doct. No, by my troth, sir; my business is not to prevent wounds, but to cure 'em. Where is the other that fought you? Nounze, you have made quick despatch; have you killed him and buried him already?

Lea. No; he is gone very safe, and no wound about him but that of his honour.

Doct. Was it not Squire Softhead, sir?

Lea. It was so, sir; and how he has behaved himself you shall know anon. But, sir, I guess you are the doctor that undertakes the Dumb Lady?

Doct. I am so, sir.

Lea. You're happily come, sir, for I have earnest business with you.

Doct. Why, ay, the dulness of your eye shows you have—let's see, let's see—a very dangerous and highflying pulse.

Lea. I am not sick, sir.

Doct. You are loth to confess. Come, I see you have a clap, sir.

Lea. By my honour, not I, sir.

Doct. Do not let it go too far; modesty has spoiled one-half of the town gallants, and too much confidence the other half, so that there's no hopes of any of you.

Lea. If you please, sir, I shall acquaint you with my business. My name, sir, is Leander; perhaps you may have heard of me.

Doct. I have heard of a naval knight called Sir Hero Leander; are you the man, I pray you?

Lea. You are merry, sir, but my affair is serious. You have a dumb lady your patient to whom I am a servant, and she, sir, has an equal love for me. Now, being by her father barred of all means of coming together——

Doct. You would have me do it, and so pimp for you?

Lea. Not pimp, sir; but I would fain oblige you to befriend us.

Doct. Befriend us? a modest phrase for pimping. I begin to find that physic is but one part of a doctor's trade; and I shall gain the character of Chaucer's seamstress, for says he,

" She keeps a shop for countenance,
    But bawdeth for her sustenance."

So I shall physic give for countenance,
    But pimping's my chief maintenance.

Lea. Sir, I know you may bring me to the speech of her. I mean no pimping, sir.

Doct. Whatever you mean, the thing is the

same, sir; for how can I help you to the speech of
her but I must bring you together? And if I bring
you together, what's that but pimping, sir?

Lea. But I mean in the way of honesty, sir.

Doct. Honesty? Indeed I have heard 'twill make
men rich and brave, but I never heard of honesty
in the case before. Sir, the profession will not
bear it. And would you make a pimp of a physician? O most horrible indignity!

Lea. Pray you, sir, be pacified, and let this show
you that I can be grateful.   [*Gives him a purse.*

Doct. Is there a fee belonging to that part of a
doctor too? I begin now to think that pimping is
no such scandalous thing as malicious men report
it. Sir, you have given me such strong reasons to
think so well on 't, that I believe none rail at it
but such as would be glad of the employment
themselves. And, sir, as you call it, I will help
you to the speech of her, or befriend you, or pimp
for you.

Lea. Your servant, sir. I must now reveal a
secret to you. You must know, sir, the lady
feigns this dumbness for love of me, and to avoid
marriage with this Squire Softhead.

Doct. I knew there was some trick in 't. 'Twere
impossible else, either by nature, art, or misfortune,
a woman should be dumb; for take a woman's
tongue, and pluck it up by the roots, I'm sure in an
hour another would grow i' th' room on 't. But
come, sir; you shall shift you, and pass for my
apothecary.

Lea. That I think an excellent way, and nothing
better.

Doct. We cannot miss to cure her now. I shall
get credit as I am her physician, and money as I
am your bringer together, or your pimping friend.

Thus shall I be your advocate and protector.
[*Ring.*
And venerably called both bawd and doctor.

ACT III.—SCENE I.

Enter DOCTOR, *and* LEANDER *like an apothecary.*

Lea. This habit will pass me for an apothecary;
I only want some of their canting phrases.

Doct. Why, faith, you are as well qualified for
an apothecary as I am for a physician. You have
trusted me with your heart, and now I'll trust you
with my simplicity. I am no doctor, but was
forced to own being one—why and how I'll tell you
hereafter; but having served a mountebank, that
and my great share in impudence has made me
famous.

Lea. Is it possible impudence should have such
virtuous effects ?

Doct. Yes; yet some men rail at impudence, and
speak it vicious, when the jest is, they that rail
most at it make most use on 't. 'Tis doubtless the
greatest blessing in the world, and most men do
their business by it.

Lea. But if you be so ignorant, sure impudence
should not bear you out, especially in this learned
profession.

Doct. Oh, sir, it is the securest cloak for ignorance of all arts ! Other professions are liable to
miscarriages and questionable; but the physician
may kill from the fool to the senator, from the
beggar to the blood-royal, and ne'er be called in
question ; the dead was never so uncivil yet as to

come out o'th' other world to complain of the physician.

Lea. 'Tis a sign they're civilly used where they are. But do you not study at all?

Doct. It needs not, for the great study of physic is come to nothing now but letting blood; and it falls out well for me, that am a downright farrier.

Lea. How! is your real profession a farrier?

Doct. Yes, faith; and with the same fleams I let horse's blood I use my patients to; and the horse's drench is the potion I give to men; and I cure more than I kill, so that I am the only doctor that has found out horse and man to be of one constitution.

Lea. But how comes letting of blood so much in fashion?

Doct. Oh, sir, 'tis à la mode Paris. If your corn does but ache against rain, what says the doctor? Let him blood. Nay, if you be troubled in conscience, they'll let you blood for that too.

Lea. They let not blood for the small-pox, I hope?

Doct. But they do; and 'tis the opinion of Padua that 'tis as sure a way to kill as an old woman and saffron is to cure.

Lea. How came you by that velvet coat?

Enter a SEAMAN'S WIFE, *a* COUNTRYMAN *with an urinal, and an* APPRENTICE *with an urinal, with other* PATIENTS.

Doct. Oh, here come patients! Mark my confidence.—[*They press to the Doctor.*]—Good people, one at once; let the woman be served first. Now, woman, what want you?

Wife. That that nobody can help me to, the worse luck, sir. I am a seaman's wife, sir, that

D

has been married this dozen years, and I have never a child; and please you, and I would fain have a child, sir.

Doct. And wouldst thou have me get it?

Wife. I would fain have your worship give me something that will, sir.

Doct. By my troth, I have nothing about me at this time can do it. Why, look thou send thy husband to sea; that often makes the wife fruitful.

Wife. Alack, sir, I have tried all ways, both by sea and land, and nothing will help me!

Doct. I do prescribe thee a lusty wine-porter, and he shall be thy gallant.

Wife. And it please your worship, I have tried your gallant, and your top-gallant, and your top-and-top-gallant, and all will do no good, sir.

Doct. By my troth, go try the mainyard too, and if that fail thee, thou'rt a barren woman of a certain; but come i' th' evening to me! after a glass of wine I may have something to help thee.

[*Exit* WOMAN.

Coun. And it please your worship, I am a poor man.

Doct. I have never a medicine for that disease. Prithee begone, fellow.

Coun. My wife, and it please you, lies dangerously sick.

Doct. If thou be'st poor, trouble thyself no further; she'll die of a certain. But art thou so poor thou canst not come to the point?

Coun. I would entreat your worship to visit her; and here's an old angel for you.

Doct. This is but one of the points; there's two-and-thirty in the compass, fellow. However, I'll come see her. She rules the roast when she has her health, does she not?

Coun. Ay, but too much, to my sorrow, sir.

Doct. Thou hast a stable, hast thou not ?

Coun. Yes, and it please you.

Doct. Then take me your wife, and tie her up to the rack-staves ; and be sure you give her no hay, for I mean to blood her and drench her.

Coun. Why, sir, that's as I serve my horse when he is sick !

Doct. But I know thou'rt a henpecked fellow, and such women as do command in chief I physic them as I do horses, and all little enough, too ; but first take her and ride her off on her legs.

Coun. That's more than I, and your worship to help me, can do, sir. But I hope your worship will come. [*Exit* COUNTRYMAN.

Doct. Yes, yes. What are you, sir ?

Prent. A prentice, sir, that has brought my mistress' water, sir.

Doct. Has your mistress ne'er a maid, but she must send her water by her prentice ? A foolish custom ; I cannot break 'em on 't. Let me see ; but are you sure this is your mistress' water ?

Prent. Yes, and it please your worship.

Doct. How sure are you ? Did you see her make it ?

Prent. I did not see her make it, but, and it please you, I heard her make it.

Doct. Why, I find by thy mistress' water, friend, that thou art almost out of thy time.

Prent. Yes, truly, within three months, and it please you.

Doct. I knew it. Why, here is twenty visible things in this water ! Your master is out of town about a purchase, is he not ?

Prent. Yes, and it please your worship.

Doct. And you are removed out o' th' garret to

lie in the next room to your mistress, to keep spirits from her, are you not?

Prent. By my troth, and so I am, and it please your worship.

Doct. The water shows it plainly. Hold! ha! I find your mistress is apt to dream much, and is frighted, and walks in her sleep, and comes to your chamber to be awakened, does she not?

Prent. By my truly, she has been so troubled with these frights since my master's absence that I have never had a good night's rest since he went; for she'll come in her sleep and throw herself upon my bed, and then I lie as still as can be, and then she rises like a madwoman, and throws all the clothes off, and makes such work with me that I'm ashamed your worship should know it. Then tell her on't the next day, and she runs away and laughs at me.

Doct. I know her disease. Commend me to thy mistress, and tell her, because I'll make a perfect cure on't, I'll come and lie in the next room to her myself, and thou shalt go into the garret again.

Prent. And it please your worship, my mistress perhaps may not like that so well, sir.

Doct. She will like it, I know; 'tis variety must recover her. Go tell her I'll not fail her.

[*Exit* PRENTICE.

Lea. Here comes Squire Softhead, that ran away with a trick to save his honour.

Doct. I see your boy has cudgelled him to some purpose.

Enter SOFTHEAD.

Soft. Save you, Doctor! a word in private. Can you keep a secret?

Doct. 'Tis the first point of my profession, secrecy.

Soft. Despatch that fellow out o' th' way quickly, then.

Doct. He is my apothecary, and as much to be trusted as I am. But how came your face so?

Soft. Honourably of my side! You must know I have fought a duel with a damned coward, a rascal called Leander.

Lea. Now must I be abused, and dare not take notice on 't!—But, sir, is it possible Leander should be such a coward?

Soft. Do you know him, sir?

Lea. Very well, sir.

Soft. Is he your friend, sir? If he be, I am sorry I said so of him, sir; but if he be not your friend, he is a coward, and I'll justify it, and a rascal, and I'll maintain it. Yet, sir, if you have the least relation to him, I shall be very ready to eat my words rather than disoblige you.

Lea. Sir, he is neither relation nor friend of mine, neither care I a farthing for him, sir.

Soft. Then he's the son of a whore, and I'll tell you how he served me. Just when we were stripped, and ready to go to it, the base rascal hired my boy, it seems, to run away with my sword.

Doct. That was base indeed.

Lea. I cannot believe so unworthy a thing of him.

Soft. Rather than offend any man, I'll say I hired my boy myself to run away with my sword. I can be no civiller, sir.

Lea. Rather than so, I will believe Leander did it, sir.

Soft. Sir, I thank you heartily, and I will justify all that Mandevil or Coriat writ for your sake, so you believe it yourself, sir.

Doct. But how was the duel, if the boy ran away with your sword?

Soft. Why, I ran after him, got my sword, and came honourably to him again, and I drove him honourably round the field; and all that while his boy got behind me dishonourably and cudgelled me damnably, that I am ashamed it should be known.

Lea. Nay, sir, it shall ne'er be known for us; but if the boy cudgelled you behind, how came you thus black and blue before?

Soft. Why, he beat my head and shoulders so devilishly that it came quite through to th' other side, that my face is all over Coventry blue. Therefore, good Doctor, report I am your patient and desperately wounded, and there's twenty pound; and I'll have a red scarf with a great fringe about my arm—methinks that looks valiantly; and here is a sword has been up to the hilt in blood; and if you hear Leander be killed, not a word who did it, on your lives!

Lea. Sir, to tell you true, we came just now from dressing of Leander's wounds; and to be plain with you, if you did it, your life is in danger, for he cannot live above two dressings more.

Doct. Therefore, if you would escape hanging, flee your country.

Soft. Heart of a horse, I did neither wound him nor kill him!

Lea. No! did you not confess just now you did? Besides, your sword is all bloody up to the hilt, which will hang you if there were no other witness in the world.

Soft. Heart of a horse, I shall be hanged with a trick of my own!

Doct. I'll get money out of him.—Sir, we can

do no less than send for a constable and apprehend you.

Soft. O dear Doctor, thou wilt not be such a rascal, I hope!

Doct. I'll be revenged of you for beating of me into a doctor, when I had a mind to conceal my parts; therefore get me a constable.

Soft. I am disgraced and dishonoured if you do; and that's all you can do to take away the reputation of a poor Squire, for I did not kill Leander.

Lea. Why, how came your sword so bloody?

Soft. If you must needs know, 'twas with killing of a sheep, sir.

Doct. A sheep? Why, are you not ashamed, as you are a Squire, to own that?

Soft. There's no shame in it, sir, for 'twas a ram sheep, sir, and he assaulted me; and in my own defence I killed him honourably and fairly.

Doct. This excuse will not serve, for Leander is dying, and we must apprehend you.

Soft. Since you are such a rascal, I'll give you a hundred pound to conceal all that I have said.

Doct. Tell us the whole truth of your duel, and give me two hundred pound, as you did for the last man you killed in Plato's great year.

Soft. A pox of your Plato, and your two hundred pound! But, since there's no remedy, you shall have it, sir.

Lea. And withal, tell us the truth of your duel, and we'll swear to be true to you.

Soft. Why, then, by the heart of a horse, we fought not one stroke, but my boy ran away with my sword, as I contrived it, and I seemed to run after him to fetch it again, and so ran quite out o' th' field. And this is the truth, by the heart of

a horse! Then Leander's boy ran after me, and
cudgelled me, as you see, Coventry-wise.

Doct. Well, sir, go into my chamber and send
for your money, and I'll release you and keep your
counsel faithfully.

Soft. To give a physician two hundred pounds,
and not so much as one clap cured for it! O dishonour to true Squirehood for evermore!

[*Exit* SOFTHEAD.

Enter ISABEL.

Doct. 'Slid, Pothecary! here is my wife! I'm
resolved I will not own the quean; for, first, she'll
obstruct our design, next, I owe her a revenge.
Hark you! we must have some device to be rid of
her.   [*Whispers.*

Lea. I understand you very well.

Isa. Save your worship!

Lea. Would you speak with anybody here,
woman?

Isa. Pray tell his doctorship's worship that
here's his wife.

Lea. Alas, poor woman, his worship has ne'er a
wife!

Isa. Who told you so? Were you by when his
worship was unmarried again? I must and will
make bold to speak to him. Good Doctor Dog-
bolt, how long have you been worshipful?

Doct. Feel her pulse, feel her pulse, Pothecary!

Isa. I'll take you over the face if you feel anything about me, you beastly fellow!

Lea. Prithee, begone, woman, for I assure thee
Doctor Drench has ne'er a wife.

Isa. But there is a horse-doctor Drench, a
farrier, that has a wife.

Doct. Ay, the farrier Drench may have a wife,

but I assure thee Doctor Drench has none ; therefore begone, woman !

Isa. Are you too proud to own your wife, you
ungrateful rascal ? Who made you a doctor but
my invention and a good cudgel ? I'll spoil your
trade of physic, sirrah !

Doct. Now is your time, Pothecary, to be rid of
her.

Lea. 'Tis enough ! But, Doctor, do you hear
the strange news that's abroad ?

Isa. O lack ! what news is it, I beseech you,
good sir ?

Lea. I do not speak to thee, woman.

Doct. Well, what is it ?

Lea. It seems there is an edict made, and it
goes very hard with poor women, I confess.

Isa. Now, good sir, as ever you came of a woman,
tell me quickly what it is !

Lea. I will not tell my tale to the woman.

Doct. Then tell me, I pray you.

Lea. Why, sir, there is a new edict made, that
no woman, upon pain of death, under such a degree
or quality, shall presume to have a gallant, or any
man but her own husband.

Isa. And all this upon pain of death ? 'Slife !
who would not be a rebel at this rate ?

Lea. You say very true ; and upon this hard
usage there are twenty thousand women in arms,
and have made a formal remonstrance, wherein
they declare for the privilege of the she-subject,
and will live and die for the freeborn women of
England.

Isa. Ten thousand blessings upon them !
Where are they, I beseech you, sir ?

Lea. They're drawn up upon Hounslow Heath,
and are now marching to besiege Windsor Castle.

Isa. Though I sell all I have, and undo my children, I'll have a regiment, whatsoever it cost me!

[*Exit* ISABEL.

Doct. I saw the cage stand open by the stocks. Throw this purse into 't, and say I sent it; and when she is in, lock the door and bid the boys hoot at her and call her bawd, and then I am revenged for her beating she procured me.

[*Exeunt.*

Enter NURSE.

Nur. I find the Doctor has a mind to gallant me. He has such a winning way with him; he swears 'tis a thousand pities such a rascal as my husband should e'er enjoy me, and such like fine terms, that 'tis hard, I swear, to withstand him. But yet one's honesty—Why, I confess, honesty's a fine thing to read of in a romance, but I do not find the practice of it so followed as to make it a fashion; therefore, if Doctor's love hold, I shall—I shall—I cannot help it, husband, I shall.

Enter DOCTOR.

Doct. Nurse, how happy am I to meet with thee alone! Ah, rogue, methinks I could e'en run through thee now!

Nur. Ay, so ye all say; but I am sure I could never see it yet.

Doct. Now, good Nurse, grant me my suit.

Nur. Truly, Doctor, so I would, if it were not for my honesty.

Doct. Thou fool, there is no such thing as honesty! The word honesty is a mere bugbear that jealous husbands invented to keep women in awe with, as raw-head and bloody-bones frights children; that's all, i' faith.

Nur. But is it possible that should be true, Doctor?

Doct. Nurse, it is so true that I'll show thee a reverend book, called St. Aratine's, where you shall be convinced there's no such thing as honesty.

Nur. Say you so? Nay, then, dear Doctor, give me physic. Here comes my husband. What woman's that with him?

Enter JARVIS *and* ISABEL.

Doct. 'Tis a patient of mine that has twenty diseases besides a Neapolitan pox.

Nur. What disease is that, Doctor?

Doct. 'Tis a new-fashion'd disease came fresh with the last packet.

Nur. Have we not old-fashion'd diseases enough of our own, but we must send for new ones over?

Jar. What a villain is this Doctor! First, not to own his wife; next, with a trick to trepan you into the cage; then make the boys throw dirt at you and call you bawd. But why do you weep?

Isa. To think that ever I should live to be called bawd. If he had called me whore, 'twould ne'er have vexed me; but to be called bawd is to be thought an old woman unworthy of copulation.

Jar. Troth, malicious people may call you bawd, but, I protest, I think you far worthy to be called whore; therefore, pray you, wipe your eyes.

Isa. I thank you for your good opinion, howsoever.

Jar. If it please you, madam, I'll make my opinion good.

Nur. Here is a rogue! to be jealous of his wife, and yet play the whoremaster himself!

Isa. Look you, there's Doctor Devil for you! that will not own his wife.

Jar. And my wife with him ! Take no notice of
them. I believe he has made me a cuckold of all
colours—of the red, and the green, the yellow, and
the blue bed. A pox on him ! Faith, be revenged,
and make his caps too little for him.

Isa. By my gallant, so I would, if it were not
for my honour.

Jar. Honour ? I'll not come near your honour ;
that's an airy thing that lies i' th' crown of your
head. My request lies lower, quite another way.

Isa. Look, look ! how familiar Doctor Dog is
yonder. Oh for revenge !

Jar. A pox on him ! I'm not able to endure this.
Go you in there.—Are you in your closet, sir ? If
you be, come out and see a fine sight quickly, sir.
Oh, look ! look ! this cursed Doctor ! [*Exit* ISABEL.

Nur. We had need be careful of our credits,
Doctor, for the world is grown so base, that if they
should but see a man and a woman in bed together
they would swear they were naught straight.

Doct. Fear nothing, Nurse.   [*Kisses her.*

Jar. Look, look, look ! I am no cuckold to
speak on.

Enter GERNETTE.

Ger. Is it so ? What a false quean is this to use
me thus !

Jar. Use you thus, sir ? 'Tis use me thus, with
your favour. 'Slid, why are you concerned ? 'Tis I
am the cuckold, sir.

Nur. 'Slid, Doctor, my master sees us kissing ; I
am utterly undone.

Doct. Feign yourself in a sound, and I'll seem to
rub you to fetch you to life again. Alack ! help,
help ! Who's within there ? Help ! Oh, are you

there, sir? Good sir, run for a glass of cold water;
I have much ado to keep life in her.

Ger. Ay, with all my heart! and glad 'tis no
worse. [*Exit* GERNETTE.

Jar. Why the devil must he fetch water? Why
could he not have sent me? I find I shall be the
staple cuckold for all the kingdom.

Nur. What a rascal art thou to fetch my
master!

Jar. Oh, you counterfeit quean! you are not in a
sound, then?

Nur. No, you jealous rogue! but I'll counterfeit
again as soon as my master comes, and he shall
believe it, too.

Doct. Here he comes; fall into your sound again,
quick!

Enter GERNETTE.

Ger. Here, here! Alack, poor Nurse, she does
use to have fits.

Jar. Ay, a pox on her, more than e'er her
mother had. Sir, give her no water; she counterfeits; she spoke as sensibly since you went as ever
she did. Deny it, Doctor, if you can.

Doct. What an uncharitable villain art thou to
forge such a wicked lie! This rogue is made sure.
[*Gives her water.*

Ger. Come, you wicked knave, and help to
lead her to her bed; you'll never leave your
jealousy. [SERVANTS *and* JARVIS *lead her off.*

Jar. Oh, oh, oh! she'll pull my ear off, sir!

Doct. That's a sign of a strong fit, sir; but lay
her upon her bed and she'll recover. 'Slid, sir, I
never was so surprised in my life! I was consult-
ing with Nurse about your daughter's health, and

all o' th' sudden she fell into my arms in a sound. But now for your daughter, sir.

Ger. Despatch, and bring my daughter hither with all care.

Doct. And, good sirs, bid my apothecary come in.

Ger. What apothecary is it, sir? Cannot you cure her without an apothecary?

Doct. No, sir; you speak as if you were jealous.

Ger. Not jealous, sir, but I love to know who comes in my house.

Doct. Neither apothecary nor doctor shall trouble you; so fare you well, and cure your daughter yourself, sir.

Ger. Nay, sweet Doctor, leave me not in this distress!

Doct. Be not jealous, then.

Ger. Be not angry, then. Hey ho, Doctor, my heart misgives me that my child will be stolen.

Enter APOTHECARY.

Doct. I'll warrant you whilst I am in your house.—He smokes us, I doubt.

Ger. I thank you, sir. Is this your apothecary?

Doct. Yes, sir.

Ger. What the reason may be, I know not, but my heart rises at him though I never saw him before.

Doct. You make your life miserable with foolish phantasms. Pray, sir, bid him welcome.

Ger. Why, you're welcome, sir; but, to tell you truly, I like you not.

Apot. If you please, I'll be gone, sir.—Do you think he has no hint of our design?

Doct. No, no!—Nay, sir, if he go, I'll go with him.

Ger. Nay, I beseech you both, stay! for I doubt

my child is dying. Oh, here she comes! Good sir, look upon her.

Enter OLINDA *in a couch; two* WOMEN.

Doct. Apothecary, feel her pulse!

Ger. Is not that your office, sir?

Doct. Yet again? Why, he is the most learned man in Europe, and, to my shame, I find I cannot cure her without him. Go, go, feel her pulse!

Apot. I fear my over joy will discover me.

Doct. Meantime, I'll tell you, sir, 'tis a great question amongst we learned of Padua whether men or women be hardest to cure. Some are of one opinion, some another; meantime there be potent arguments on either side.

Ger. He is very long feeling her pulse, methinks.

Doct. Pray you, mind you me, sir. First, we hold that women being naturally more cold than men, and cold being an enemy to life, it follows their cure must needs be more difficult and dangerous.

Ger. How many pulses has he to feel that he is thus long about it?

Doct. You do not mark me, sir. I do not love to be slighted when I'm in argument.

Ger. I do mark you, sir.

Doct. Then, I say, 'tis generally held at Padua, that women, when they take physic, ought to have their potions much more stronger than men, because physic cannot work so well upon cold and phlegmatic bodies as upon hot and dry. You do not hear me, sir.

Ger. They're very close together, methinks!

Doct. A sign he minds his business; and this was the opinion of the great Cham of Tartar's chief physician, that was fellow-student with me at Padua.

Ger. A pox of your great Cham! I must know why he dwells thus long upon her pulse. Have you conveyed no letters to her, sir?

Doct. What an uncivil question's that! Come, Pothecary! Let your daughter die, and you perish, the world shall never make me visit her again.

Ger. Dear Doctor, do not leave me in this extremity. Mr. Pothecary, will you be my over-throw too?

Apot. I'll do no man service that affronts me thus.

Ger. Good gentlemen, bear with an old man's passion! Good Mr. Apothecary, go to my child again!

Apot. No, not I, sir; I shall but convey letters.

Ger. Nay, then, you're cruel. I beseech your pardons, gentlemen.

Doct. Well, sir, we see it is your weakness, and we pass it over; go to your daughter whilst we consult a little.—We must press to have her to your house to cure her.

Apot. Good! And if he refuses that, I'll persuade her to counterfeit madness; I have a design in 't.

Doct. And that she may appear the more mad, let her tear all her clothes off, for a madwoman naked has such antic temptations.

Apot. I should be loth any man should see her naked but myself, Doctor.

Ger. Well, gentlemen, what have you concluded of?

Doct. Sir, he must feel if he can discover of what side her heart lies.—I'll keep him in discourse the meanwhile.

Ger. Must he feel her heart, Doctor? Still it runs in my mind this apothecary will do me a mis-chief. Nay, be not angry!

Doct. Nay, I forgive you; I see an old man's

twice a child. Pray you walk into the next room ;
I must talk in private with you.

Ger. I should sound if I should leave my child
with the Apothecary.

Doct. Let's talk here, then ; for look you, sir.

[*They walk, and seem to talk earnestly.*

Olin. I'll observe all your directions ; for if he
will not let me go to your house, he shall find me
mad enough, doubt not.

Apot. You see how jealous he is, therefore we
have no other hopes of enjoyment left but by this
means.

Olin. I'll do my part ; fear not.

Ger. Sure he feels something more than her
heart all this while.

Doct. If there be occasion, we must stick at
nothing.

Apot. Why, sir, according to your opinion, I
have found her heart on her right side.

Ger. Most wonderful ! Pray you, what may be
the reason, gentlemen ?

Apot. Love is certainly the cause on 't ; and for
her cure this is no place of convenience, therefore
she must be removed to my house.

Ger. To thy house, thou wicked fellow ! I told
thee at my first sight of thee I did not like thee.

Apot. But there is all things ready that cannot
be removed hither, sir,—my tubs, my baths, and
my sweating-house.

Ger. I like it not. It is a plot to steal my child ;
I doubt so. Nay, be not angry, gentlemen, I do
but doubt so.

Doct. You would make a man forswear doing
you any service.

Ger. I crave your pardons once more. Is there
no art left to make her speak ?

E

Doct. Yes, I could make her speak presently; but I doubt it will be but wildly, sir, for love has shaken her brain exceedingly.

Ger. Let me have the comfort to hear her speak of any fashion, good Mr. Doctor.

Apot. You shall, sir. Pray you, madam, chew that in your mouth. Sir, you shall see the effects of it straight. Before you speak, put out your tongue, and wag it two or three times.

[*He embraces her.*

Olin. Let me alone! I'll do anything to purchase thee, my dear Leander!

Ger. Why does he embrace her so? I do not like it, sir.

Doct. 'Tis something in order to her cure. I think you're mad, sir; you'll spoil all. He is but shaking her heart right.

Ger. I'm sure he shakes mine every time he touches her.

Olin. A—a—a—a.

[*She rises up and stares, and wags her tongue.*

Ger. Oh, bless my child!

Doct. Be comforted, sir, for now it works.

Olin. A—a—a—a.

Ger. Is this your working? The devil work! my child is undone!

Doct. Nay, now her tongue wags, she'll not be long ere she speaks; fear not.

Olin. Who are all you, sirs?

Ger. She speaks! she speaks! Make me thankful to you for it, worthy Mr. Doctor and Apothecary!

Olin. What art thou? whence camest thou? and whither wouldst thou?

Ger. Oh me, I fear my child's distracted!

Doct. I told you, sir, her sense was a little shaken.

Olin. Pray you, is not that the devil in black, sir?

Doct. No, I'm but a doctor yet, madam; I shall not take my degree of devil these seven years.

Apot. Yet, if you please, madam, he shall commence devil presently.

Olin. Then, good Doctor Devil,—for you shall lose none of your titles here, sir,—help me to tear that beard off that old, wrinkled, weather-beaten, tanned old face.

Ger. I am thy father, child!

Olin. I hope thou art not. I'd rather be a bastard than have thy ill-nature in me.

Ger. I am thy old father, child.

Olin. I hate anything that's old!

Ger. Wilt thou break thy old father's heart?

Olin. Nay, that's more precious to me than my father, which is my dear looking-glass. I would break that if it were old, for sure the devil invented old people on purpose to cross young lovers; they could ne'er have been so cruel else to poor Leander!

Ger. My child is undone; she weeps for Leander.

Olin. Yes, and will weep again and again for Leander. Leander, Leander, Leander! Why, you do not love Leander; for which sin, good Doctor Devil, take him into your territories, and let him fall desperately in love with a young she-devil, and let that she-devil have a cross father that will not let them come together, and then he'll feel the torment his poor child endures.

Ger. Doctor, this has too much sense and satire in 't to be madness.

Doct. Oh, sir, 'tis madness to a high degree, and dangerous madness too!

Olin. You look like Leander, sir, you are so young and handsome! Sure you are Leander!

Apot. Yes, madam, I am so.

Ger. No, no, no, Pothecary! Do not say so, I charge you. What does he mean by holding up his finger so impudently? [*He beckons.*

Doct. He makes signs to let you know he must say as she says to please her, for in Padua we deal with mad folks like those that catch dottrils: when they stretch out a wing, we must stretch out an arm; if they stretch out a leg, you must do so too; else if we should cross her, she may fall into a raging fit and tear us all to pieces.

Ger. O most accursed madness!

Olin. Why would you absent yourself so long, Leander? Why lay you not your rosy cheek to mine, and throw your arms with sweet embraces about your lover? I doubt you're false, Leander!

Apot. Madam, may the earth open as I kneel, and make me an example of falsehood, if any unconstant thought be in me!

Ger. Why, villain Pothecary, talk no more so to her. Why the devil does he kneel? He speaks as feelingly as if he were concerned.

Doct. Sir, there is no other way on earth to cure her but this.

Ger. The remedy is worse than the disease. Come from her, Pothecary! I told thee at first I did not like thee. I have a natural aversion against thee. Confess, for I know thou art to do me a mischief. Why were you so concerned to kneel and make such protestations?

Apot. By my life, sir, I did it to please and to satisfy her, for she doubted I was false, and I swore I was not. Alas, sir! we must take these courses to recover her by saying as she says, for physic has the least hand in curing madness. I have cured twenty mad people this way.

Ger. Well, sir, you have a little satisfied me, and with reason too ; but yet there is something within me that hates thee heartily.

Apot. Well, sir, when I have cured your daughter, I hope you'll have a better opinion of me.

Ger. I may of your art, but never of you, I doubt; for thy conscience knows thou art to cozen me. Nay, do not tell the Doctor so.

[*He offers to go to the Doctor.*

Doct. Troth, lady, you are so fine a madwoman, that 'tis a thousand pities you should e'er come to yourself again. Faith, for a frolic, take me by th' ears, and lead me round the room.

Olin. If you will have it so, Doctor, but I shall make you repent it.—I have him, I have him ; and now I'll tear him all to pieces.

Ger. Oh, save the Doctor, save the Doctor !

Apot. Sweet lady, spare the Doctor ! I'm your friend Leander, madam.

Olin. I will do anything for Leander ; but you must stay and live with me, then.

Apot. You see, sir, how very calm the very name Leander has made her. Troth, sir, I doubt you must be forced to send for Leander.

Doct. I doubt we cannot cure her without him.

Ger. She shall die mad first, and I'll die with her. This is a plot. Carry my child to her chamber ! Get out of my house, you villains !

Enter SERVANTS *and* NURSE.

Doct. You shall lay your hands under our feet before we come under your unworthy roof again.

[*Exeunt* DOCTOR *and* APOTHECARY.

Olin. Let me go with Leander! Leander! Leander!   [*Exit* LADY ; *she tears them.*

Nur. You have made a fine hand to make my mistress thus mad. I'll weary you out of your life for this.

Ger. You are very bold with your master, Nurse.

Nur. There's an English proverb says, If you lie with your maid, she'll take a stool and sit down by her master.

Ger. Well, well, I say again, she shall never marry but the Squire.

Nur. She shall never marry your fool Softhead. She shall first merchandise her maidenhead.

ACT IV.—SCENE I.

Enter OLINDA *and* Mrs. NIBBY.

Olin. No, dear cousin, I was not dumb, nor am I mad; I have trusted you with my love, and in that my life.

Nib. Dear cousin, doubt me not; when I am false to you, may I miscarry in my own amours. But pray you, coz, how came you by this lover Leander? for none o' th' house knows him.

Olin. Truly, coz, I never saw him but at church.

Nib. A very good place to make love in.

Olin. Indeed, I have found it so. The first time I saw him was six pews from me; the next time he sat within two, and there he warmed my heart; the next after he sat i' th' same pew with me, and 'twas so ordered betwixt him and the pew-keeper that none sat with us, and there we loved, and there we plighted troth.

Nib. I find a pew-keeper is a worthy friend to love, and for sixpence you may sit with whom you please, and court whom you please, i' th' church. It was handsomely contrived of your lover, though, to come with the Doctor as his apothecary; but what made him persuade you to counterfeit madness?

Olin. He has a design in 't, but had not time to tell me. My father has turned the Doctor off, you see; therefore, coz, you must go to him.

Nib. He'll find some stratagem to see you again, fear not. If not, I'll go to him. But come, coz, now let's laugh at the duel that the Squire's foot-boy told us of his master.

Olin. Ay, he found it safer killing of a sheep than Leander.

Nib. No doubt on 't. Your father's bringing of him in to woo you again; fall to your madness, and let me alone to dispose of the Squire. I'll have him drawn up with an engine, and there he shall hang i' th' air in a cradle till you're married or run away. Here they come; let us withdraw a little.   [*Exeunt* OLINDA *and* NIBBY.

Enter GERNETTE *and* SOFTHEAD.

Ger. But how came your face thus black and blue, and thus black patched? I never saw a lady's face thus furnished.

Soft. They may be thus furnished when they please, but they shall never come so honourably by their black patches as I have done.

Ger. Pray you, how came you by them?

Soft. Do you take these for patches? O dull old age! These are badges, badges of honour.

Look you, my sword is glazed with honour too.
But you shall ne'er know how; it has cost me two
hundred pounds already confessing.

Ger. I know it already, sir; but, Squire, I fear
you did not court my daughter handsomely. What
said you when you wooed her?

Soft. I wooed her with all the fashionable questions of the town. I asked her if she could come
a seven, and she laughed at me; then I asked her
if she would come the caster, and I'd cover her.
No man could say fairer to his mistress, I think.
Then I asked her if she could drink Burgundy and
seal bonds, pay the price of a chine of beef for a
dish of French trotters; and that's all I said to
her.

Ger. I would thou hadst more wit, or I thy
precious acres. Who's there?

Ser. Sir?

Ger. Bid them bring in my daughter if she be
awake. I hope she may take you for Leander, for
she is now out of her dumbness, and is fallen stark
mad.

Soft. How, can she speak? and is she mad?
Heart of a horse, I'll be mad with her for a hundred pound! Oh, I do so love to be mad! And
will she be drunk too?

Ger. Drunk, you brute you? no!

Soft. Why, how can she be mad, then? I cannot
be mad till I'm drunk for my life; but I'll try
what I can do.

Ger. But be sure you humour her, and say
everything as she says.

Soft. Let me alone; here she comes! 'Slid, how
delicately she stares!

Enter OLINDA, NIBBY, NURSE, *and* SERVANTS.

Olin. What's that with the piebald face ?   How camest thou so distracted, thou errant knight ?

Soft. For thy sweet sake, thou devilish damsel.

Olin. Thou art as mad as I am.

Soft. I am stark mad, for my mother was born in March ; therefore let us be married.

Olin. I would not be so mad for all the world.

Soft. And when we are married we'll outdo the Great Mogul for new fashions.   Instead of six Flanders mares, our coach shall be drawn with six centaurs.

Olin. Centaurs !   In the name of madness, what are them ?

Soft. A centaur is a horse born with a postilion on 's back.

Olin. And shall all the footmen ride behind the coach ?

Soft. Yes, o' th' backs of one another, like March frogs in a ditch ; and there they shall spawn young footboys.

Olin. And at the boot of your coach must be running an orange wench, presenting your lady a sweet lemon with a love letter in 't.

Soft. Right !   And instead of points and gilded nails, our coach shall be trimmed round with cartridges.

Olin. And they shall be filled with powder and shot to defend us.

Soft. No ; each cartridge shall have a little tiny page in it, with his head peeping out like *hictius doctius*.

Nib. By 'r lady, I think they are both mad !

Soft. What wonders would I do for my true love !

Nur. There's a verse of a song to that purpose; I'll sing it :

'What wouldst thou do for thy true love,
  If she for help should call?'

Soft. Why, I would fight with a great giant, though he were ne'er so tall.

Olin. Thou fight with a giant? He must be in sheepskin, then.

Soft. Heart of a horse, how came she by that?

Enter CONJUROR.

Olin. Go, bid my conjuror come.

Con. Here, madam!

Olin. Let me see Elysium quickly, and tell me truly what they do there.

Con. Madam, it is so little, and so like what's done in this world, that it is not worth your knowing; but since you command, I must obey. Let idle poets speak their fancies of Elysium, but I that have been there must speak the truth; in short, madam, all the women do nothing but sing, 'John, come kiss me now,' and then the men give 'em a green gown upon the flowery banks, and there they commit love together.

Olin. Do they not dance in Elysium?

Con. Yes, madam, as you shall see. Every one keep their stand. Squire, stand you here.

Soft. Must I see the devil?

Con. Yes.

Soft. Would I were devilish drunk, then.

Con. Why would you be drunk, Squire?

Soft. Because they say when I'm drunk the devil would not keep me company.

Con. You must know my devil scorns to be commanded with canting mountebank words; he is a seafaring kind of devil, that comes when his bosun whistles. Stand fast!

[*He whistles, Elysium opens; many women's voices sing,
'John, come kiss me now;' after that a dance;
they draw up* SQUIRE SOFTHEAD *with a devil,
and he cries out.*

Soft. Save the Squire! save the Squire!

Enter JARVIS *and* ISABEL—NURSE *unseen.*

Jar. Tell my master all the lies you can invent of him, for I know women are good at sudden invention.

Isa. Yes, I could lie sufficiently to do his work; that is, I can lie my part, if you can swear yours.

Jar. If you do not second your lying with swearing, we shall do no good on 't.

Isa. Nay, by my troth, if I lie, I expect you should swear to it; 'tis your revenge as well as mine, and you shall bear your part.

Jar. Troth, I am not very good at swearing.

Isa. Then do you lie, and I'll swear; take your choice, for 'tis all one to me.

Jar. Nay, we must second one another both with swearing and lying as occasion serves.

Nur. That I had but some witness of this villany!

Isa. I'll warrant you, we'll spoil his being a doctor, i' faith!

Nur. You shall not, if I can help it.

Isa. I'll tell your master, first, he is a drunken farrier, and no doctor; a villain not to own his wife.

Nur. How! is this his wife? I dare say 'tis for my sweet sake he does not own her. Poor dear Doctor!

Isa. I'll be revenged to the full.

Nur. So will I, till I am full.

Jar. I'll give you my wife's new gown, and take your revenge my way.

Nur. O rogue ! a cuckold to the ninth degree !

Isa. Sure a new gown and a new gallant are two sweet things, but revenge is sweeter and dearer to me than my children ; therefore let us first go to your master.

Jar. But first let us consider, and lay our story ready.   [*Exeunt* JARVIS *and* ISABEL.

Nur. I'll to the Doctor, and tell him all this. What a slave is this husband of mine ! O rogue, that cannot be content to be a cuckold, but he must be a whoremaster too. Thou shalt have more than an ordinary head, for that at Amboes shall appear but a pricket to thee ; for thou shalt be a monstrous cuckold, if man or beast can make thee one.   [*Exit* NURSE.

Enter DOCTOR *and* APOTHECARY.

Apot. I doubt, Doctor, we shall never win the old man's favour again.

Doct. Troth, I think you were never in 't, for his blood rose at the very first sight of you.

Apot. He finds by instinct the mischief I'm to do him.

Doct. Well, 'tis now come in my head to gain his opinion again.

Apot. O my dear Doctor, how ?

Doct. Why, thus ;—you shall write a love letter to your mistress, as you are Leander, and then deliver it to th' old man, as you're my apothecary ; I'll go with you too.

Apot. What advantage will that be ?

Doct. We'll tell him that Leander, hearing that we gave his mistress physic, offered us a lusty sum to convey a letter to her ; and finding how heartily he resolves against Leander, we thought fit to show ourselves honest by delivering him the letter.

Apot. In troth, this may clear the jealousy he had of us, and bring us in again.

Doct. If this will not, we must find some other trick. What if I continued love to Nurse? She would be very instrumental, if we had so little wit as to trust her.

Apot. It would argue very little wit indeed; but come, let us about the letter. 'Slid, here comes Nurse!

Enter NURSE.

Nur. Oh, Mr. Doctor! I must tell you you're a man of little conscience to make such true love to me as you have done, and have a wife as you have!

Doct. Truly, Nurse, I had thought you had had more honesty than to suffer me to make such love to you, and have a husband as you have.

Nur. But, Doctor, I came to tell you that the woman my cuckold makes love to swears she is your wife, and says you're no doctor, but a farrier, and a drunkard, and a beggar, and they're just now going to my master to tell him so; nay, they're resolved to lie and swear all things they can invent against you.

Doct. There is no great invention in so much truth. A pox on 'em! what shall we do? All our designs are quite spoiled.

Apot. I am undone to all eternity.

Doct. Nay, nay, 'tis I am undone, for I must turn farrier again.—Nurse, I'll come to you presently.

Apot. I'm utterly destroyed if I get not off o' this.

Doct. I have it already! Run you to Bedlam,

and give two of the whippers a piece, and bring them hither, and tell them they own my wife for a madwoman, and carry her to Bedlam, and force her with all violence, and keep her there till further orders.

Apot. I'll instruct them further as they come along.   [*Exit* APOTHECARY.

Doct. Do so; make haste and fly like gunshot. Now, Nurse, this was kindly done indeed to tell me this, Nurse; but be not troubled, for she is not my wife, but a madwoman broke out of Bedlam; and now I am resolved to marry thee, Nurse, for I see thou lovest me truly.

Nur. Ay, but, Doctor, you know I've a husband.

Doct. Hang him! I were a pitiful doctor to suffer anybody to live that I have occasion to have dead.

Nur. If it could be done with a safe conscience.

Doct. Why, if it be safely done, it's done with a safe conscience. I see thou 'rt a fool, and knows nothing.

Nur. You learned men know best; I leave all to you.

Doct. Thou shalt lead the sweetest life, Nurse. First, I will get my son and heir myself, Nurse; and then thou shalt have a brave gallant, with a fine white periwig that cost twenty pound, Nurse.

Nur. O dear Doctor, how sweetly you express your love to me!

Doct. And then your gallant shall carry you abroad, and bring you home o' nights, so well pleased, Nurse!

Nur. O my most obliging Doctor!

Doct. And then thou shalt throw that gallant off, Nurse, and have one with a brave brown periwig, Nurse.

Nur. Did ever man show such true love to a woman? Let all husbands take example by this dear Doctor!

Doct. And then thou shalt have one with a brave black periwig, Nurse, so that thou shalt have children of all colours i' th' rainbow. But why dost thou weep, Nurse?

Nur. I weep for joy to think what a comfortable life I shall lead with you.

Doct. And dare you be true to your young mistress and Leander, and help to bring them together, Nurse?

Nur. I deserve to starve for a true lover else.

Doct. But then you must be true to your master, and tell him when they're together; and then you oblige both parties, you know.

Nur. By my troth, and so I shall; and I'll be sure to follow your directions.

Doct. I dare swear thou wouldst. But, Nurse, I do but jest; I would not wrong the old gentleman for the whole earth.

Nur. Nor I for all the world.

Doct. But, Nurse, go tell your master that the woman is a madwoman of Bedlam; you may swear you have seen her there, for 'tis very true, Nurse.

Nur. I will do it truly, Doctor; but when shall our happy day of marriage be, Doctor?

Doct. As soon as you can persuade your husband to take physic.

Nur. Let me alone for that. O dear Doctor, this fine white periwig does so run in my head.

Doct. And does not the brown one do so too?

Nur. Yes, by my troth, and the black one eke also.   [*Exit* NURSE.

Doct. I dare not trust this jade for all this; yet

for little things, which may be helps to the main,
I shall venture to try her in.

Enter APOTHECARY *and two* OFFICERS *of Bedlam.*

Apot. Mr. Doctor, I have brought you a couple
of officers for your turn; they both understand,
and are ready to serve you for your money.

Doct. But have you given them instructions?

1 Offi. Oh, sir, we have it thoroughly.

Doct. You must be confident, for you'll find a
damned scold of her.

2 Offi. Oh, sir, we that can tame mad folks can
tame a scold, I warrant you.

1 Offi. And though the woman be not mad, we
can make her mad if you please.

Doct. Prithee, how?

2 Offi. With these engines.. Why, people are
not so mad when they come to Bedlam as they are
when they're in 't, I assure you.

Doct. How comes that, I prithee?

1 Offi. Do you think that the food of bread and
water, to lie naked in foul straw, and to be whipped
twice a day, will not make anybody mad? I'll
warrant you, faith.

Doct. But do you give them no physic?

1 Offi. Something they have, but a whip is the
main ingredient; for we whip 'em out of a frenzy
into stark madness, and then whip 'em on till they
come round to their wits again.

Doct. That plainly shows the circulation of the
blood; and this may be cited a consultation.

Apot. Well, sir, you see they know their work;
therefore about it, and there is more money to
encourage you.

1 Offi. You shall hear of her in Bedlam, I'll warrant you.   [*Exeunt* BEDLAM MEN.

Apol. Now, let's about our letter with all speed.

Doct. Come on! and if all fail, we'll fetch your mistress to Bedlam, for she is pretty well entered into madness already.

Apol. No; then people will say, if she had not been mad she'd ne'er been in love with me. Yet anywhere out of her father's house does it.

Doct. Well, if our other designs fail, faith, have at that! [*Exeunt.*

Enter GERNETTE, NIBBY, *and* NURSE.

Nib. Thou wretched old man, first to make thy daughter mad, and then to keep her in't with thy cruelty, when your own conscience knows a husband would recover her!

Ger. But now my mind is altered; for I'm resolved, let her perish, she shall never marry whilst I live.

Nib. At your peril be it, for I'll take my oath before a judge that a husband would bring her to her wits again.

Ger. I renounce and disclaim her.

Nib. A husband, I tell you! Second me, Nurse.

Ger. I'm resolved I'll hear of no husband.

Nur. I tell you once again, a husband.

Nib. And I tell you moreover and above, a husband.

Nur. And I tell you both under and over, and over and under, a husband.

Both. A husband, a husband, a husband!

Ger. I'll stop my ears. I'll hear no more of her.

Nib. But in troth, uncle, consider soberly her sad condition. She is young, and her blood gallops in her veins, and requires the satisfaction of a

F

gentleman. I prescribe her nothing but what I would take myself.

Nur. Alack, she might take it if she were a dying.

Ger. Cannot the comforts of a father recover her?

Nur. Nor of a mother neither, if her heart be set the other way.

Ger. Then let her die mad, for I'll hear of no such thing as husband.

Nib. With all my heart I wish she would marry thy gardener.

Nur. Ay, that she might taste of his apricocks. Nay, nay, nay, you shall hear us out! for look you, master, a husband is such a thing.

Nib. Ay, truly, uncle, a husband is such a thing.

Ger. What a thing is a husband?

Nib. Why, a thing a young woman cannot be without.

Nur. No, nor an old woman neither.

Nib. A husband is a thing that's good for many things.

Nur. A husband is good to father his wife's children.

Nib. Pray you, let him be good at getting them first.

Nur. No matter, that's a thing may be done without him; I see you are a young woman, and know nothing.

Nib. Then a husband is a thing that is a good cloak for a woman's knavery?

Nur. Ay, if a husband could be brought to do the civil office of an orange woman, to fetch and carry, he were worth his weight in gold. I have a husband, my master knows, is the untowardest peevish fellow at it.

Ger. Away, away, you idle woman !

Nib. You mean downright pimping, Nurse; that's a little against the hair, methinks, for a husband. Ben Jonson says, Fathers and mothers make the best bawds.

Nur. Bawds! Your Jonson's an ill-bred, foul-mouthed fellow to call them so. Besides he is a fool, for a husband's worth a hundred fathers and mothers for that office, for then the wife's un-stained ; the world cannot taint her when the husband gives her countenance.

Nib. But will you consider your daughter's madness ?

Nur. Ay, he has turned off a worthy doctor and his apothecary that would have cured her, and now he's jealous of 'em, and will not let 'em come near her.

Nib. 'Slife, I'll indite you for murder ! I'll not see my cousin cast away thus ! Send for this doctor, I say !

Enter JARVIS *and* ISABEL.

Jar. Here is a woman, if it please you, has something to say to you concerning the Doctor.

Ger. Ay, what is it, woman ?

Isa. I would be loth to have your worship abused. This doctor, if it please you, that comes to your house is a very rascal. Swear to it, now.

Jar. Ay, by my feckars-law is he.

Isa. Swear up roundly, and be hanged ! Is feckars-law an oath to pass before a judge ? I say this doctor is a rascal.

Ger. Why, he may be ne'er the worse doctor for that.

Isa. But he is not a doctor, if it please you.

Ger. Why, he may be ne'er the worse rascal for that.

Isa. But, as I said, he is no doctor, but a downright farrier.

Ger. A farrier! by 'r lady, a good foundation to raise a doctor upon. I like him ne'er the worse.

Isa. Besides, he is a beggar, and I am his wife, sir.

Ger. If thou be'st his wife, 'tis an even lay but he's a beggar.

Isa. Besides, we have had five children, and now he will not own me, sir.

Ger. That confirms him a good doctor still, I say.

Nur. This woman is mad, sir.

Ger. She talks sensibly enough, and I believe her.

Isa. I am not mad, sir, and I tell you he is but a farrier. Swear, and be hanged; you leave me sweetly i' th' lurch! I say he can give your daughter a drench, and shoe her before and behind, and that's all he knows of a doctor.

Enter BEDLAM MEN.

2 *Offi.* By your leave, we must make bold with your worship; we have a madwoman broke out of Bedlam, and we understand she is come into your worship's house. Oh, are you there, you mad quean? must we have all this labour to find you, with a pox? I'll scourge you to some purpose, i' faith!   [*He mistakes.*

Ger. What dost thou mean, fellow? this is my servant.

Nur. You rogue! you villain! you rascal!

1 *Offi.* Sir, pray you pardon him; this fellow is a stranger, and come newly to his office since she

stole out of Bedlam. This is the quean, sir; she knows me well enough. Look, look, look, if it please your worship, how the mad whore stares at me now she sees me!

Isa. I mad! I in Bedlam, you rogue! 'Tis that thing, that gentlewoman thing, that looks like a madwoman.

Nib. 'Slight, I'll away and secure my cousin.

[*Exit* NIBBY.

Ger. I hope they do not come for my daughter, Nurse.

1 *Offi.* Nay, nay, nay; come you quean! away with her! Why, sir, we have had this wretch in Bedlam this dozen years; and sometimes she is so well that we let her go about the house; and then she steals out, and 'tis sometimes a week before we can find her again. Fare you well, sir. 'Slid, how I'll lash the whore!

[*Exeunt* BEDLAM MEN *with* ISABEL.

Ger. This woman being mad confirms me the Doctor is wronged.

Jar. The woman is his wife, and not mad, sir; and the fellow is no doctor, but a farrier, sir.

Nur. The rogue is jealous of the Doctor, and that makes him say so, as he is of your worship when I rise a-nights to rub your shins.

Jar. I say again, he is a farrier and no doctor!

Ger. This must be scandal, for I believe he is a learned man. How now? What do you here, sir? Did not I forbid you my house? Are you a farrier, sir?

Enter DOCTOR *and* APOTHECARY.

Doct. Are you a changeling, sir?
Ger. Why changeling, fellow?
Doct. Why farrier, fool?

Ger. He is wronged, sure, by his angry confidence.

Doct. Who told you I was a farrier, sir?

Ger. A woman that said she was your wife; and, truly, I believed it, till two officers of Bedlam fetched her away, and said she was a madwoman.

Doct. Alack, alack! was it she? Why, that poor creature has been in Bedlam this many years; and she has called me husband so long, that of my conscience the poor wretch believes it to be so indeed.

Nur. Ay, but, Mr. Doctor, my husband swears you're a farrier.

Doct. Who? that villain? Why, thou scandalous rogue, how dar'st thou wrong me, when thou hast discovered such strange things to me of thy master?

Ger. Ay, what has the rogue discovered, sir?

Doct. First, he is damnable jealous of you; next, he told me that you got his wife's child; and he desired us of all loves to give you some cantharides, to disable you for getting of children. Ask my apothecary else.

Apot. 'Tis very true, I assure you.

Jar. Sir, they wrong me, and they lie.

Nur. But they do not swear and lie, as thou and the madwoman did. Sir, I'll swear upon a book I overheard them make the bargain; she was to lie, and he was to swear to it.

Doct. 'Pothecary, you overheard that too, did you not?

Apot. I did so, sir, and I'll be deposed upon't. —You put me to hard duty, Doctor.

Ger. You villain, out of my house!

Jar. Sir, they do me wrong; I never said so.

Ger. I know you were always a jealous rascal,

and therefore must believe 'em. So get you out, you villain!

Doct. Sirrah, will you be content to be a cuckold yet?

Jar. I'll be revenged, for I'll cut thy throat.

Doct. I'll be even with thee, for I'll give thee physic!

Ger. Pay him his wages, and let him be gone.

Jar. Give me my wife, then.

Doct. No! I mean to physic her, and make her fit for a gentleman.

Jar. I'll have my wife, if there be law.

Doct. Thou shalt have her before thy suit is ended, for by that time everybody will have done with her.

Nur. Come, sir, I'll pay you your wages; you see what comes of jealousy. Could not you be content to hear and see, and say nothing?

[*Exeunt* JARVIS *and* NURSE.

Apot. But, sir, our business is to present you with this letter, and withal to advise you to look strictly to your daughter, for this Leander is contriving several stratagems to steal her. He offered us I know not what to deliver her this letter.

Doct. But we, knowing it would break your heart, we thought ourselves bound in conscience to bring you the letter, and withal to advise you to be careful of your child, for to my knowledge she'll be gone else. So, having fairly discharged ourselves, we take our leaves. [*Offers to go.*

Ger. Oh, do not go, you are my friends! you have proved yourselves my faithful friends! I beseech you stay and take care once more of my child!

Apot. Not for the world, sir! We came not to that end, sir. We came to show ourselves honest men; and that being now cleared, our credits shall come no more in question.

Ger. I beseech you, leave me not!

Doct. Why, your passion will spoil all our practice; for should it be noised abroad that a doctor of physic carries letters betwixt party and party, 'twere enough to undo us all.

Ger. Good gentlemen, I have received comfort by your fidelity; take it not from me again by your obstinacy. I once more beseech you to take the care of my child upon you.

Apot. Alack, sir, do not weep! We'll do anything to serve you; but our credits are so precious to us.

Ger. Good men, I'll never distrust you more; you have showed such worth in the discovery of this letter, that I weep for joy to think I have found such faithful friends.

Doct. In troth, my tender nature melts too. See, see, my poor Apothecary weeps too.

Ger. Dost thou cry too, Nurse? Alack, poor woman!

Nur. How can I choose but cry, to see my master weep?

Doct. I thought you had cried to part with your husband, Nurse.

Nur. Your own conscience knows I do not love him so well. Pray you, good master, wipe your eyes.

Ger. Good Doctor and Apothecary, weep no more!

Doct. We cannot hold to see your grief so great, sir.

Omnes. Ah—ah—ah—ah.   [*All cry together.*

Doct. Let us cry in four parts, and see how 'twill go.

Apot. I have heard of singing in four parts, but never of crying in four parts before. Come, sir, take comfort, for once more we will undertake your child.

Doct. We must first repair home, to provide things fit for her, and then without delay we come. —Once more we have fastened of him.

[*Exeunt* DOCTOR *and* APOTHECARY.

Ger. Good gentlemen, make haste! Come hither, Nurse; this was kindly done to weep, Nurse.

Nur. I could not choose but weep to see you weep.

Ger. In the middle of my sorrows, there is some comfort in thee yet. Come, kiss me, Nurse. I hope thou hast been true to me, Nurse, and not suffered that rascal thy husband to come near thee.

Nur. Do you think I'd be so false a wretch as to let my husband touch me? I wish the heavy judgment of such a sin may fall on me if ever he so much as kissed me, or ever shall whilst your worship lives; for sure you have been a sweet man in your youth, that is such a comfort to a woman in your old age.

Ger. But am I such a comfort to thee indeed, Nurse? Do not dissemble with me.

Nur. If I do, I wish I may never enter into the —— why am I a woman? But why do you suspect me so?

Ger. Because I thought the Doctor had kissed you when you were in 's arms.

Nur. That you should think such a wicked thing of me, when you saw I'd a fit of the mother.

Ger. Weep not, Nurse! I am satisfied. Come, kiss and be friends. [*He kisses* NURSE.

Enter NIBBY.

Nib. Look, look of that old sinckanter !* Here's a fine mouldy gallant, an old grey badger ! I must play the rogue with him, though I suffer for it.

Nur. 'Slid ! your niece sees you kiss me.

Ger. Alack, I am ashamed for ever, then ! Good Nurse, sound as you did when the Doctor rubbed you.

Nur. Do you think I can counterfeit sounding ? Besides, do you think you are able to rub me as the Doctor did ?

Nib. Oh, woe is me, and woe unto us all ! O this uncle ! this wicked uncle !

Ger. Alack ! what's the matter ?

Nib. O cruel destiny ! O fatal fortune !

Ger. Why, Niece Nibby, what's the matter ?

Nib. That ever I should live to see this day !

Nur. Oh, my dear Mrs. Nibby, what's the misfortune ?

Nib. Oh, where should I find this cursed uncle of mine ?

Ger. Here I am, Nibby ! what's the danger ?

Nib. You are undone and ruined !

Ger. How ! undone and ruined ? Do not delay me !

Nib. Oh, your daughter, your daughter, you wicked wretch ! I am not able to say more for grief.

All. Ah—ah—ah—ah. [*All weep.*

Ger. Tell me quickly what's the matter !

Nib. Why, your daughter's grown desperate mad at your unkindness, ran to the window that stands over the river, and there opening the great casement——·

* Worn-out person.

Ger. Oh, what did she then ?

Nib. Why, lifting up her hands and eyes to that good place where you will never come, uncle, she loudly cried, Since my father has abandoned me, 'tis time for me to quit this life of mine.

Ger. And so threw herself into the river ?

Nib. No ; it seems she did not like that kind of death.

Ger. Why, what then ?

Nib. Why, then she ran like lightning to the table, where your pocket pistol lay.

Ger. And so shot herself with that ?

Nib. No ; it seems there was no powder i' th' pan. But, bitterly sighing and weeping, at last she ran and desperately threw herself upon her bed, and then growing paler and paler by degrees fell into a deadly sound.

Ger. And so died ?

Nib. Stay, stay, you're too quick for your daughter ; but with much rubbing, tumbling, and tossing her, I brought her to life again. So, leaving her at death's door, I came to tell you the news.

Ger. Where are my servants ? Run, bid 'em run ! I'll have a consultation of doctors. And run for Doctor Drench, for he shall join in council with 'em. [*Exeunt. Manet* NURSE.

Nur. I'll to the Doctor and tell him this. I doubt he will not like a consultation with physicians.

If he stand this brush, he's made for ever ;
Luck, if 't be thy will, just now or never.

ACT V.—SCENE I.

Enter DOCTOR, LEANDER, *and* PARSON OTHENTICK.

Lea. Look you, Doctor, this gentleman is my brother, and, though he be young, a minister in orders. I have told him what we designed, and he is to go as my apprentice, and carry our feigned physic.

Doct. Very good! And can you step out of a pulpit into an apothecary's shop, poison a friend or two, and steal to your text again, without scruple of conscience?

Othen. Sir, I shall go as near the wind as a Dutch skipper to serve my brother; but I hope there is no poison in the case.

Lea. No; but there is a little cheat.

Doct. Which I hope you may dispense with.

Othen. Truly, I hope I may to serve my brother.

Doct. Or your sister.

Othen. Yes, sure, to serve any of my relations.

Doct. Or a friend.

Othen. So it be a dear friend.

Doct. Or a stranger with a good living to present.

Othen. That's a good thing still.

Lea. The Doctor's merry, brother; but pray you let me help you off with your reverend weeds, and appear like an apothecary's apprentice, or a disciple of Paracelsus.　　　　　*[Helps him off.*

Othen. Now, Doctor, give me leave to be merry with you. I studied physic, and should have professed it, and an old doctor gave me some rules for a young doctor to observe.

Doct. Pray you, let's hear them by all means.

Othen. First, have always a grave, busy face, as if you were still in great care for some great person's health, though your meditations, truly known, are only employed in casting where to eat that day. Secondly, be sure you keep the church strictly on Sundays, and i' th' middle o' th' sermon let your man fetch you out in great haste, as if 'twere to a patient; then have your small agent to hire forty porters a day to leave impertinent notes at your house, and let them knock as if 'twere upon life and death. These things the world takes notice of, and you're cried up for a man of great practice, and there's your business done.

Doct. Believe me, these are good instructions.

Othen. Nay, I have more. Be sure you ingratiate yourself with the bawds, pretending to cure the poor whores for charity; that brings good private work after it. Strike in with midwives too, that you may be in the council for by-blows; that secures a patient during life. And with apothecaries and nurse-keepers go snips. But above all, acquire great impudence, lest you be out of countenance at your own miscarriages.

Doct. I am so well stocked with that, that if ever impudence come to be worshipped as a deity, they'll set me upon a pedestal for their god.

Lea. But to our business, Doctor! You know we persuaded the old man that we must say and do all things to humour his seeming mad daughter, and by that only way she is to be recovered.

Doct. Right! and the old man believes it too.

Lea. Therefore, when we are there, you shall hold the father in discourse whilst I whisper her; and as she and I will manage her madness, my brother shall marry us to the old man's face.

Doct. By my troth, that would be impudently

done indeed; yet the old gentleman has now so much confidence in us that we may do anything.

Lea. Therefore pack up your pretended physic, and let us cheerfully about it.

Enter NURSE.

Nur. Save you, gentlemen! you are much longed for! My old master does so talk of the Doctor, and my young mad mistress of the Pothecary, that you must come with all speed, for my mistress is so stark mad that my master has sent for three or four learned doctors; and you must make haste, and bring all your learning with you, for you must sit in consultation with them.

Doct. In consultation with doctors? 'Heart, all is spoiled again, and worse than ever 'twas! Tell your master plainly, Nurse, consultation with doctors is not my way of practice,—a company of wrangling fellows, they can never agree. Besides, he undervalues me to think I am not able to cure her without help. But, Nurse, go into my chamber and turn over St. Aratine's book till I talk with my Pothecary.

Nur. With all my heart, dear Doctor!

[*Exit* NURSE.

Lea. This is the unfortunatest cross that e'er befell me!

Doct. The devil hath conspired against you, so farewell for an unlucky wretch. I'll put on my apron and profess farrier again; and then, let the doctors and the devil come, I defy them.

Lea. Nay, nay! stay, Doctor, and let us consider. [*Offers to go.*

Doct. Consider? Do you think I can support an argument with able physicians?

Othen. Come, be not dismayed, for we will go if

there were a whole college of physicians. I am a scholar, and a proficient in physic, and those questions that you cannot answer put them upon me, and doubt not but we will baffle them all; therefore we must be wary, and not talk too much of Padua, for ten to one but some of 'em has been there, and they are strict Galenists; therefore we must be chemists. Now you must not call my brother your apothecary, nor me his apprentice; that will not sound like an outlandish physician. Therefore call him Hurnatio, your operator, and me Stirquilutio, his man.

Doct. Well, boys, you have so encouraged me that I have just now a trick come into my head to baffle them all myself.

Leu. Oh, brave Doctor! What is't? What is't?

Doct. You shall know. But Nurse must be in the plot.

Leu. By no means i' th' earth! She'll betray us all.

Doct. Fear nothing, for I've promised to poison her husband and marry her, and allow her half-a-dozen gallants; and if that will not make her true, I have no art to gain a woman.

Lea. That may go a great way, but——

Doct. But me no buts! Nurse! nurse!

Enter NURSE.

Nur. Here, my dear Doctor!

Doct. Nurse, tell your master that I am resolved to consult with the doctors; but 'tis for thy sweet sake, I'll swear, Nurse. Therefore, my dear Nurse, if thou lovest mirth, and wilt be true to me, we'll put such a trick upon these learned physicians that we'll laugh seven years after it.

Nur. Here's my hand and heart, dear Doctor; I'll be true to you.

Doct. I believe thee. Be sure, Nurse, that you be in the room, and when I bid you fetch your mistress' water, be sure you go out and bring me your own; and then mark what work I'll make with your learned doctors.

Nur. Why, this will please me above all things, most hugely, most strangely!

Lea. Ay, but if Nurse should cozen you, and neither bring her mistress' water nor her own, she would serve you finely.

Nur. I scorn to be so base, sir; and if you think so, sir, you may be by when 'tis made, sir.

Doct. Nay, be not angry, Nurse, for my apothecary—my operator I should say—is to give your husband physic when he is to die, and he knows I'm to marry you; I've told him all. Nay, he is as true as steel.

Nur. Is he so, sir? I crave your pardon for my hasty speech. The Doctor reports you're as true as steel, sir; and I assure you I honour any gentleman that has either truth or steel in him. I shall inform my master of your coming, and I assure you, sir, you shall command my water without fraud or guile. [*Exit* NURSE.

Lea. Let us now consider how to answer these learned doctors.

Othen. That cannot be, for we know not what they will fall upon.

Doct. I find I shall betray myself to be a damned farrier; but, however, I'll brazen it out.

Othen. Doctor, you must be sure you consent not to consult in private, which they will desire; because they never agree. Besides, urge that the father, Nurse, and we may be admitted: it will be a good excuse for your worship not to speak Latin.

Doct. But, by the way, you must furnish me with a snip or two of Latin to save my credit.

Othen. That's easily done; but you must be sure to embroil the doctors first with some strange questions, to prevent their falling upon you.

Doct. Let me alone, I'll do it.
And spite of all their scruples, drams, and ounces,
I will confound these learned Doctor Dounces.

[*Exeunt.*

Enter old GERNETTE *with three learned* DOCTORS.

Ger. Gentlemen, I have made bold to send for you again; and though you could not help my child when she was dumb, I hope you may now she is mad.

1 *Doct.* How! Is she mad? and does she speak?

Ger. Yes, sir. A famous and a learned man, of great skill and wonderful knowledge, gave her something, and in a short time she spake, and fell into raving fits of madness, and has ever since continued so; and this he told me would be the effect of what he then did.

2 *Doct.* This is strange.

3 *Doct.* Most wonderful! What was it he gave her, sir?

Ger. Nay, that I know not; but I assure you he said he could make her speak, and told me her disease would turn to madness, and accordingly it has proved so. Nevertheless, gentlemen, I desire you to join with this learned man, and consider how to perfect her cure.

1 *Doct.* Why, sir, you tell us wonders of him. Where did he study?

Ger. I know not; but he seems to be a great

traveller, for he talked of Tartar Cham, and of Padua, and Greenland.

2 Doct. Tartar Cham and Greenland ? This must be a mountebank and a cheat.

Ger. Upon my credit you will not find him so. for he has seen all universities ; he is but newly come over, and his name is Doctor Drench.

1 Doct. Drench ? Why, that's a fitter name for a farrier than a physician !

Ger. Let his name be as strange as it will, he has also strange humours too, for he'll find out men's ignorance presently.

3 Doct. I think we were best begone, lest he finds out ours.

1 Doct. Why, ay, for if he be a chemist, his opinion and ours must needs differ, and consequently not agree in consultation.

2 Doct. I am, sir, of your opinion, for I think it *infra dignitatem* to hold consultation with mountebanks.

3 Doct. We know not yet, sir, what the man is.

1 Doct. If he be a chemist, sir, he is, *eo nomine,* a declared enemy to the Galenical way, to all truth and learning, and a denyer of principles, and therefore not to be consulted with.

2 Doct. Right, sir ; *contra principia negantem non est disputandum.* He that replies but with submission to *sic dixit Galenus* is not to be looked on as a physician.

3 Doct. Pardon me, gentlemen, I have known some chemical physicians learned and rational men ; and, although not strict adherers to the Galenical method, proceed with great reason and good success, which, I take it, answers all we can say or do.

2 Doct. I profess I think it as bad as murder to

cure out of the methodical way. Oh, what satisfaction 'tis to have a patient die according to all the rules of art !

Ger. But, sure, it should satisfy your conscience better to have them live by rules.

2 Doct. Come life, come death, to follow rules is your satisfaction; and conscience is no ingredient within the rules of physic, sir.

Enter SERVANT.

Ser. Sir, the Doctor is come !

Ger. 'Tis well ! 'tis well ! Gentlemen, to end this dispute, here is a double fee for each ; and, pray you, consult with him his way, and be civil in 't for my sake.

1 Doct. Sir, you and yours here hath prevailed over us.

2 Doct. I profess, to serve so worthy and magnificent a person, I would consult with a farrier.

3 Doct. A farrier ? Nay, for a double fee we would consult with a gunsmith.

Ger. Here he is ! pray you salute him.

3 Doct. We know how to be civil, sir.

Enter DOCTOR, HURNATIO, STIRQUILUTIO, *and* NURSE.

Ger. Save you, sir !

Doct. I thank you.

3 Doct. Save you, sir !

Doct. One save you, sir, is sufficient for all ; we learned men should hate compliment—*verba pauca sapiens sapit.*—Was that true Latin, Parson ?

Stir. Brave ! fear nothing ! At them with some question !

Doct. I shall fall into the farrier.—Well, I find.

gentlemen, you are professed doctors of physic, and are met to consult the health of a distracted lady; therefore to the point, and avoid your canting words that would stick in a wise man's throat and choke him.

2 Doct. But, sir, 'tis necessary we deliver ourselves in proper and learned phrases when we discourse either of physic or distempers—*in arte artificialiter loquendum;* and withal, sir, 'tis fit that we of the consultation should withdraw.

Doct. No withdrawing, sir; 'tis not my way. I love persons concerned should hear and see what's done, that they may judge who are doers and who are talkers; and if you affect the vain-glory of learned phrases, my operator Hurnatio and his man Stirquilutio shall dispute you, for with great pains I have enabled them to argue in all tongues, because they know I hate the trouble on 't myself.

Stir. Start a question quickly.

Doct. I shall only trouble you with one question or two myself. First, I ask you whether you know the practice of before behind, behind before?

2 Doct. Before behind, behind before? Why, that is something belongs to a horse! A farrier or a blacksmith must answer that question.

Doct. I know where you'd be presently. In some sort 'tis true that you say; yet in Italy both women and boys have their before behind, behind before, as well as your horses have here.

Stir. Bravely come off, Doctor!

Doct. I know not well your way of practice, but the cost you put the people to in that common disease called the mourning of the chine, I do abominate you for.

3 Doct. Mourning of the chine? With your

favour, sir, that is the disease of a horse, and the phrase of a farrier.

Doct. And, sir, I say again, I call it the mourning of the chine, for the word pox is a phrase of ill manners; and therefore I think it proper to call it the pox in a horse, and civil to call it the mourning of the chine in a man.

Stir. You'll have no need of Latin, Doctor.

Doct. Look you to that, Parson.—And I must tell you I shall spoil the benefit you get by that disease; for I'll advise every man to plant a guaiacum tree in his orchard, and a leaf of that at any time will cure infallibly; and that's one of the secrets I will reveal to the world, to spoil the practice of mountebanks, clap doctors, and bill men.

2 Doct. But will that disease be cured with the leaf of a guaiacum tree?

Doct. Ay, sir, as I can order it.

1 Doct. Pray you, sir, how will you order it?

Doct. Why, first, sir, I will make you a mash.

3 Doct. How, sir, that's a farrier's phrase again. What mean you by a mash, sir?

Doct. Tell 'em, tell 'em, Stirquilutio, and let not me be troubled to interpret.

Stir. Why, sir, the Doctor is so much read in the Arabian physicians that he often uses their terms. *Masha* in the Arabic is what *quinta essentia* is in the Latin.

Doct. Well helped, Parson.—You wonder at my phrases, and I at your want of Arabic. Now, sir, when any man is troubled with the staggers, we do not cut him and slash him in the forehead as you do your horses.

2 Doct. Staggers in a man? With your favour, sir, you have talked all this while liker a farrier

than a physician; and I begin to think you are
one, sir.

Doct. How shall I get off now ?

Stir. Yes, sir, he is a farrier, and an able farrier
too; for if you be not good farriers, and good surgeons too, you deserve not the name of doctors.

Hur. And pray you, come to the point concerning our mad patient.

Doct. Ay, there's the best trial of our judg-
ments; therefore, Nurse, run and fetch your young
mistress' water presently.

Ger. Ay, that the gentlemen may the better
judge what to apply; and I beseech you, gentlemen, agree, that I and my child may find comfort
from you.

3 Doct. Sir, you shall be sure of all the aid our
art can show.

Doct. And likewise our endeavours, sir.

2 Doct. But, sir, amongst all signs of sickness or
health, whereby the skilful physician is led into
the knowledge of the state of the body, two above
the rest are most certain, which are the pulse and
urine.

3 Doct. Ay, whereof the pulse shows the state
of the heart and arteries, and urine the state of
the liver and veins.

2 Doct. Therefore the question is, whether of
these two severally considered does give the most
certain signification ?

Doct. Urine, urine, urine ! which makes me send
for her water.—Still, I say, Stirquilutio, give 'em
reasons, and let not me be troubled.

Stir. Then, I say, *Montanus de excrementis* says—

Doct. I say, give them reasons in their own
mother tongue.

Stir. Then, I say, the urine above the pulse

gives the most manifest, certain, and general
signification of all diseases, because with the blood
it is conveyed into all parts of the body, and from
thence returns back again in the veins to the liver
and vessels of urine, and so brings some note of
the state and disposition of all those parts from
whence it comes.

3 *Doct.* 'Tis wonderful that an under-servant to
a doctor should have this learning!

2 *Doct.* I doubt whether the master understand
so much.

Doct. Say you so, sir? I'll be even with you.—
Parson, I'll tell that Doctor he is not well,
and whilst I feel his pulse, convey you this cow-
itch down his neck. Come hither, sir, I pray you.

2 *Doct.* Your pleasure, sir?

Doct. You are not well, sir.

2 *Doct.* As ever I was in my life, sir.

Doct. Let me feel your pulse. You accuse me
of farrier's phrases; I've another farrier phrase for
you. You are not well; you are foundered in
your body, and it will fall upon your shoulders.
First, it will begin with a kind of itching, then
into inflammations and catarrhs; therefore, look
to't, be rowelled betimes.

2 *Doct.* I slight your opinion, sir.

Doct. Well, mark the end on 't, sir.

Enter NURSE *with water, and* NIBBY.

Nur. Gentlemen, my mistress presents her service to you, and desires you to be civil to her
water, and use it with as much modesty as you
may, for I assure you her virgin water was never
exposed to public view before.

3 *Doct.* Pray give it the stranger.

Doct. By no means, gentlemen; I must have your opinion first.—Nurse, art thou true to me?

[*The* DOCTORS *take the water.*

Nur. By my little life, it's my own water, Doctor!

Doct. By my great life, I'll marry thee to-morrow, then. But, Nurse, when I wink at you, you must own the water to be yours.

Nur. I'll do it, dear Doctor!

2 Doct. Here is dangerous water, it does not show the three regents; neither is here colour, substance, perspicuity, darkness, contents, or smell.

3 Doct. Therefore, the urine being obstructed, must needs fly back upon the parts, as to the stomach in vomitings, to the belly in dropsies.

2 Doct. Or to the head in frenzies. Here we find plain madness.—'Slife, I itch most terribly; this fellow, sure, can conjure.

Hur. The cow-itch works, he is at it already.

Doct. Come on, let me see the water! Hum, ha, here is no madness, nor the least sign on 't. Come hither, sir; is your daughter married?

Ger. No, sir; why do you ask?

Doct. Then I say she is a baggage! She had a child lately, and counterfeits madness to keep the knowledge on 't from you.

Ger. Gentlemen, I beseech you believe not this scandalous Doctor. Sir, I'll have you punished for this defamation. My daughter had a child, you wretch?

Doct. Come, you're a weak old man. I say again that she that made this water has had a child lately, therefore let search be made to find it out.

2 Doct. You will do well to examine it, for 'tis

possible it may not be her water, for doctors have had such tricks put upon 'em ere now.—This itching makes me mad.

Doct. But they can put no such tricks upon me, for my judgment cannot fail me; therefore, I say, look to 't, for there's a child in the case.

Ger. Call all my servants! Where's my daughter's women? Here must be treachery, and, Nurse, you must need know it!

Nur. Sir, I do know it indeed, and I crave your pardon.

Ger. What! Has my daughter had a child, then?

Nur. No, sir, but you know I have had one.

Ger. But the Doctor says she that made the water has had a child.

Nur. The Doctor says very true, for 'tis my water, sir.

Doct. I was sure I could not be deceived.

Ger. Are you sure you speak truth, Nurse?

Nur. By my little life do I. Mrs. Nibby can witness.

Nib. Nurse speaks very true, sir.

Ger. Why did you so bold a thing as this, Nurse?

Nur. If you'll have the truth, I did it to find out which would prove the ablest doctor, and the stranger, it seems, is the doctor of doctors, i' faith.

2 Doct. I believe he is, for ever since he felt my pulse my back has played the devil.

Ger. Worthy sir, I once more heartily crave your pardon, and must acknowledge you an able and faithful gentleman; and, Doctors, I beseech your leaves to make use of this worthy stranger as to the cure of my child.

2 Doct. He must cure me too, for the vengeance has got into my back parts.

3 Doct. Sir, we consent, and think you have made a worthy choice ; so we take our leaves, sir.

Doct. Nay, gentlemen, I hope you'll stay and see our way of practice. Alas ! we cure madness with as much ease as you do fevers, and merely with humouring them.

2 Doct. I believe every word he says.

Hur. 'Tis well you're convinced. O brave cow-itch !—Pray, sir, let your child be brought forth, that we may despatch.

Ger. Go, Nurse, prepare her quickly.

Nur. She is ready, sir.

[*Exeunt* NURSE *and* NIBBY.

Doct. Stirquilutio, go get me a parson's cassock.

Ger. Why so, sir? why so?

Doct. Because, sir, you saw in her madness she fancied my apothecary, my operator, to be Leander, and was much in love with him.

Ger. She was so, to my grief. But what then, sir?

Doct. Why, then, sir, if she take him for Leander again, you shall see how finely I'll fool her into her wits again.

Ger. Here she comes !

Enter OLINDA, NIBBY, NURSE, *and* SERVANTS.

Olin. What ! is all the world got together? Then I hope I shall find Leander amongst them.

Ger. Again Leander? A pox on him ! Who knows him, or ever saw him?

Nib. None of your household. We have only heard well of him ; and I believe she never saw him but at church.

Ger. Like enough ; that's one o' th' ends people

go thither for. I'll take warning how I ever send my child to church again.

Olin. Are you Leander, sir?

Doct. Say ay, say ay, Doctor!

2 Doct. I am Leander, madam, at your service, if my back would give me leave.

Olin. Thou Leander, beast? Why, thou shruggest as if thou wert lousey, and wanted a clean shirt. Oh, Doctor Devil, have I catched you? Where's my Leander? Find him, or I'll tear thee into air!

Doct. Here! here, is your Leander, madam.

[*Presents the* PARSON.

Olin. Oh, you devil, would you put a false Leander upon me? Find me out the right, or I'll throw thee headlong to that dismal place prepared for doctors.

Doct. Here! here, madam, is your right Leander!

Olin. Ay, this is he indeed; now I thank you, Doctor — nay, sir, I'll take a course with you! Why, Leander, would you torment me with your absence thus?

Hur. It was not my fault, Heaven knows; it was your cruel father kept me from you.

Ger. Why, rascal Apothecary! Why say you so, you villain?

Doct. 'Tis you are mad! Gentlemen Doctors, you saw how fine and calm she began to be upon humouring her. 'Tis you that keeps her mad; I'll justify it.

Ger. Nay, I have done! I have done! But here is something here that will not be removed.

Olin. Nay, sir, I'll fetter you from running. Doctor, get me a parson. Does none of these grave men belong to the clergy?

2 Doct. No, madam.

Olin. Run, run and fetch me one ; they're never i' th' way when they should do good.

Doct. Stirquilutio, put on the parson's coat quickly. Madam, have patience ; the parson will be here presently.

Ger. Why so ? Why so, Doctor ? Why so ?

Doct. To bring your child to herself again. Ask these doctors else.

2 Doct. Nay, no doubt they are right, sir, if you obstruct them not. I must have his opinion for my disease too.

Doct. Look you ! here is the parson, madam.

Olin. Oh, welcome, sir ! Nay, not a word out of your book, but turn to your text of matrimony, and marry us presently ; and pray you, let not that old man know we are married.

Doct. No, no, by no means. You must not know, old man, your daughter's to be married.

Ger. Nay, nay, nay, Doctor ; Doctor, no jesting with marriage.

Doct. Why, are you jealous of my operator ? Alas, poor wretch ! Why, gentlemen, the man has a wife and four children.

Ger. Has he ? And art thou sure of that, Doctor ?

Doct. Why, sir, before these gentlemen, if I speak false, degrade me of the dignity of a doctor.

Ger. I believe you and am satisfied, and now I am as light and airy as a boy.

Olin. Who will be my father, and give me to Leander ? I have a mind to this grave gentleman. Do you refuse me, sir ?

Doct. No, no, no, madam ; go and give her, sir, go. Bless us all, you see what a raging fit she had like to have fallen into.

Ger. Ay, but I do not like ; I do not know—I
do not like—I do not know what to say to it.

Doct. The devil's in you ! Why, you have forgot
the fellow's married.

Ger. I had forgot, I had forgot ; in troth, I
should laugh to see her thus recovered. Why,
gentlemen, is not this a strange way to cure madness ?

3 Doct. It is so, sir ; but it seems they have the
experience, the practical part, and truly it seems
rational.

Doct. Why, sir, if we can but get her to sleep in
the belief that she is married to Leander, my life
for yours she wakes i' th' morning in her right
senses.

2 Doct. And sure this back will put me into my
wrong senses.

Ger. Ha, ha, ha ! I laugh to think, poor girl,
how she'll be cozened into her wits again.

Nur. Master, as I live, they're married in
earnest ! I'll be sworn, with the very same words
that I and my husband was.

Ger. Let them alone ; 'tis all but jest, Nurse.
Why, the apothecary's married, fool, and has four
children.

Hur. 'Tis true that he is married, but no four
children, sir ; but we will have four and four to
that girl.

Olin. What ! shall we have but eight, Leander ?

Hur. Fifty, fifty sons, to vie with Priam ! Besides girls shall be reckoned but as by-blows.

Nur. Fifty, besides girls ! When shall a poor
woman get such a husband ?

Hur. Olin. Now, sir, we both crave your blessing.

Ger. Well said, Apothecary ; thou acts it to the

life, i' faith! Gentlemen Doctors, does he not do it well?

Hur. I shall do it better yet. Nurse, make a sack-posset, and let's to bed presently.

Ger. No, no, no, no, Nurse; no going to bed! There you overact it, 'Pothecary.

Olin. Sir, he is no apothecary, but real Leander, and my lawful husband; therefore we must of necessity go to bed, sir.

Ger. Why, Doctor, this girl is stark mad still.

Doct. No indeed, she speaks sensibly. What would you have a young woman do but go to bed when she is married?

Ger. Why, Doctor, thou overacts thy part too!

Doct. In troth, sir, this is neither apothecary, operator, nor Hurnatio, but very Leander; neither is this his man Stirquilutio, but his brother, and a minister in orders, who has lawfully made 'em man and wife.

Ger. How, villain! Didst not thou say he was married and had four children, and bid me degrade thee of the dignity of a doctor if it were not so?

Doct. I did so, sir, and therefore I'll degrade myself. There goes the doctor, and here's honest Robin Drench, the farrier.

All. How! a farrier?

2 Doct. Did not I tell you he must be a cheat?

Hur. You have found him so, 'tis much that a Doctor wedded to rules and method should be cozened by a farrier; for you have no disease, 'twas only a little cow-itch put down your back.

2 Doct. A pox upon you and all your cheats!

Ger. Oh, this cursed farrier! this cursed villain! Then you are not mad, lady?

Olin. No, sir; neither was I mad or dumb, but

counterfeited both to cozen the Squire and you, sir.

Ger. And you, sir, were Leander when you brought me the letter from Leander?

Lea. Yes, sir.

Ger. And you told me that Leander would steal my daughter, and gave me good counsel to look to her?

Lea. I did so, sir.

Ger. 'Twas good counsel, if I could have taken it. That cursed letter feigned from Leander cozened me; that got them credit with me, spite of my jealousy. Thou art a pretty fellow, I confess, but the most impudent and audacious villain to marry my child against my will, and before my face too, gentlemen.

Olin. Do you think I'd have been married but in my father's presence? Not for all the world.

Lea. 'Twas love forced us to make this shift, sir.

Ger. A pox of love, for that's the end on't! Did not I tell thee all along that thou wouldst cozen me?

Lea. You did so, sir, but love can take no warning.

Ger. For my revenge, I'll to bed and fall desperately sick, make my will, and die, and leave thee ne'er a groat, that thou and thy issue may starve and perish.   [*Exit* GERNETTE.

Olin. Fear not, Leander! When this fit is over, he's to be reconciled, fear not!

Doct. Gentlemen Doctors, I hope 'tis no disparagement to you that a poor farrier, by a combination with Nurse, has cured a madwoman.

Nur. Ay, but where is my reward for it?

Doct. Faith, Nurse, if thou wilt accept of a farrier instead of a doctor, I'll love thee still.

Nur. A pox on you for me! My heart is so set upon the white periwig that I shall ne'er be my own woman again.

Enter JARVIS, ISABEL, *and many* NEIGHBOURS.

Jar. Where is my master? Here is witness enough now that he is no doctor, but a drunken farrier. These are all his neighbours, gentlemen!

Doct. I confess I am a farrier; they all know it too. But can my neighbours bear witness thou'rt no cuckold?

Isa. No; but here is witness that I am thy wife, and that I am not mad.

Doct. I'll own that too; thou art my wife, and not mad—nay, more than that, I'll go home and live with thee.

Lea. Well, I'll give you a pension of fifty pounds a year for the good service you did me in your reign of Doctor.

Doct. I thank you, sir. And, Jarvis, thou shalt have thy wife again, that thou mayest have a foundation for thy jealousy; for I find when thou art not jealous thou'rt a dead man.

Soft. Save the Squire! Save the Squire! Save the poor Squire!

[*The scene opens, and the* SQUIRE *is discovered hanging in a cradle.*

Olin. Is not that the Squire's voice?

Nib. Yes, and 'tis high time to let him down now. Open! open! Come, Squire, will you quit your interest in your mistress now to be set free?

Soft. Ay, with all my heart, and the devil take her to boot!—[*Let him down.*]—I have hung so long in the air that the household took me for Mahomet's tomb, and paid my worship with their piss-pots out of the garret, I thank 'em.

Nib. I caused it to be done !

Nur. I was joined with her in commission of the member vessels.

Nib. But, Squire, since you ha' lost your mistress, what think you of marrying the wild Irish chambermaid ?

Soft. Who ? Madam Pogamihone ? I'll marry my mother's sow first.

Lea. But, Squire, when shall you and I fight another duel ?

Soft. Sir, if I were a man that were given to quarrelling, as sometimes they say in my drink I am, I'd have you know that I am able to beat and cudgel half-a-dozen such fellows as you are ; ay, and make you creep under the tables and joint-stools, sir. Nay, I could cudgel you under a candlestick, sir ; that is, if I were a man that were given to quarrelling.

Lea. I am very happy that you are a man not given to quarrelling.

Soft. So you are, sir ; but if I were given to quarrelling, here's a leg that is four and twenty inches about, that's three inches more than any of the King's cables, sir ; and I'd have you know, sir, that I am able not only to kick you downstairs, but kick you upstairs again, sir. Still, that is, if my leg were given to kicking, or I to quarrelling.

Lea. Well, sir, we are all blest, that your leg of four-and-twenty inches about is not given to kicking. Nurse, let the sack-posset be made. In the interim we'll dance, and have the song of Arthur O'Bradley, where Christopher carried the custard.

Duet. And Bartle the beef and the mustard.

DANCE.

Lea. Come, my Olinda, let us in and prove
The sweet rewards due to our virtuous love.

[*To* OLINDA.

Othen. Ay, ay, to bed! you now need fear no
proctor,
But thank your farrier cudgel'd to a doctor.

EPILOGUE.

You that are learn'd, expect honour for it;
We that are unlearn'd slight and abhor it.
The rich does look with scorn upon the poor,
But give no alms; the beggar scorns you more.
Thus does the wretch your wealth disdain; nay
    worse,
For each proud look the beggar gives a curse.
But give him alms, as I believe 'tis rare,
The beggar gratefully returns his prayer.
So when the unlearn'd by the learn'd improve,
They'll give them honour for their learned love.
But stead of that, the unlearn'd they indite,
And proudly ask us how we dare to write?
We humbly answer our indictment thus,
If poetry be fancy, the right's in us;
For you with authors are so deeply read,
Invention has no room in learned head;
Borrowing what you read, and authors citing,
Is your invention, and your writing.
Now th' illiterate are for fancy bent,
Having no learning they must needs invent.
Thus poetry is ours to inherit
As much as yours with your learned merit;
For as Quakers preach, we write, by the spirit.

THE OLD TROOP:

OR,

MONSIEUR RAGGOU.

The Old Troop; or, Monsieur Raggou.   As it was acted at the Theatre Royal. By John Lacy, Gent.   London; Printed for William Crook and Thomas Dring, within Temple-Bar, and at the White-Lyon next Chancery Lane end in Fleet Street.   1672.   4to.

The Old Troop; or, Monsieur Raggou.   As it is acted at the Theatre-Royal. By John Lacy, Gent.   London; Printed for Benj. Tooke, at the Middle-Temple Gate in Fleet Street.   1698.   4to.

OF this piece Langbaine affords scant information. He "fancies by the style it is founded on some French original," like the *Dumb Lady*, "tho' my small acquaintance with French poets makes me speak only on conjecture. Both it and the *Dumb Lady* were acted with universal applause."

Sir Walter Scott, in his novel of *Woodstock*, vol. ii. chap. 2 (12mo, 1832), has taken a hint from our author. Sir Henry Lee, addressing Captain Wildrake, the cavalier, says : "I am glad this dilapidated place has still some hospitality to offer you, although we cannot treat you to roasted babes or stewed sucklings—eh, Captain?" Wildrake replies : "Troth, Sir Henry, the scandal was sore against us on that score. I remember Lacy, who was an old play-actor, and a lieutenant in ours, made drollery on it in a play which was sometimes acted at Oxford when our hearts were something up, called, I think, *The Old Troop*."

To these passages Sir Walter appends an interesting note, which he titles *Cannibalism imputed to the Cavaliers*. He says : "The terrors preceding the Civil Wars which agitated the public mind rendered the grossest falsehoods current among the people. When Charles I. appointed Sir Thomas Lunsford Lord-Lieutenant of the Tower, the celebrated John Lillburn takes to himself the credit of exciting the public hatred against this officer and Lord Digby, as pitiless bravoes of the most bloody-minded description. Of Sir Thomas in particular, it was reported that his favourite food was the flesh of children, and he was painted like an ogre in the act of cutting a child into steaks and broiling them. The Colonel fell at the siege of Bristol in 1643, but the same calumny pursued his remains, and the credulous multitude were told—

> "'The post who came from Coventry,
>   Riding in a red rocket,
> Did tidings tell how Lunsford fell,
>   *A child's hand in his pocket.*'"

Many allusions to this may be found in the lampoons of the time, "although," says Dr. Grey, "Lunsford was a man of great sobriety, industry, and courage." Butler says that the preachers—

"Made children with their lives to run for't,
As bad as Bloodybones or Lunsford."

"But this extraordinary report," Sir Walter goes on to observe, "is chiefly insisted upon in a comedy, called *The Old Troop*, written by John Lacy, the comedian. The scene is laid during the Civil Wars of England, and the persons of the drama are chiefly those who were in arms for the King. They are represented as plundering the country without mercy, which Lacy might draw from the life, having, in fact, begun his career as a lieutenant of cavalry in the service of Charles I. The troopers find the peasants loath to surrender to them their provisions, on which, in order to compel them, they pretend to be in earnest in the purpose of eating the children. A scene of coarse but humorous comedy is then introduced, which Dean Swift had perhaps not forgotten when he recommended the eating of the children of the poor as a mode of relieving the distresses of their parents." Here he quotes largely from *The Old Troop*, Act iii., which see at page 173 of the present volume.

"After a good deal more to this purpose, the villagers determined to carry forth their sheep, poultry, etc., to save their children. In the meantime, the cavaliers are in some danger of being cross-bit, as they then called it—that is, caught in their own snare. A woman enters, who announces herself thus :—

Wom. By your leave, your good worships, I have made bold to bring you in some provisions.

Fer. Provisions! Where is thy provisions?

Wom. Here, if it please you; I have brought you a couple of fine fleshy children.

Cor. Was ever such a horrid woman? What shall we do?

Wom. Truly, gentlemen, they are fine squab children! Shall I turn them up?—they have the bravest brawn and buttocks.

Lieut. No, no; but, woman, art thou not troubled to part with thy children?

Wom. Alas, sir, they are none of mine—they are only nurse children.

Lieut. What a beast is this! Whose children are they?

Wom. A laundress,* that owes me for a year's nursing. I hope they'll prove excellent meat; they are twins, too.

---

* The word in the original play is "Londoner's."

Rag. Aha! but—but begar we never eat no twin shild; the law forbid that.

"In this manner the cavaliers escape from the embarrassing consequences of their own stratagem, which, as the reader will perceive, has been made use of in the preceding chapter."

This play was produced at the Theatre Royal on 31st July 1668, and Pepys went to see it. "To the King's house, to see the first day of Lacy's *Monsieur Raggou*, now new acted. The King and court all there, and mighty merry—a farce. Thence Sir J. Minnes giving us, like a gentleman, his coach, hearing we had some business, we to the Park, and so home."

Geneste, in noticing it, says: "This farce in five acts was written by Lacy, who no doubt acted Raggou; the piece, however, is printed without the names of the performers. Most of the characters are officers or privates in a troop of horse in the service of Charles the First, at the time of the Civil Wars; some Roundheads are also introduced. It is remarkable that Lacy should represent the subalterns in this troop as plundering the country in a shameful manner." He further says: "*Old Troop* was not published till 1672, but it is sufficiently clear that it was acted before *The Vestal Virgin*, as in the first epilogue to that play Lacy speaks of himself as having been *once* a poet; in the second he says:

"' Well, if nothing pleases but variety,
I'll turn Raggou into a tragedy.
When Lacy, like a whining lover, dies,
Tho' you hate tragedies, 'twill wet your eyes.
Letters of Marque are granted everywhere,
  *   *   *   *
Which makes poets and Dutchmen certain prize;
All that I wish is, that the Dutch may fight
With as ill fortune as we poets write.'

"These lines," he remarks, "must have been written soon after the declaration of war against the Dutch, which was made the beginning of 1665, N.S." He therefore assumes that *The Old Troop* appeared upon the stage in 1665.

The Vestal Virgin, or the Roman Lady, just referred to as to its epilogue, is a tragedy by Howard. "In this play,

as originally acted," Geneste observes, "all the principal
characters but two are killed, and, just as the tag is spoken,
Lacy entered to speak the epilogue :—

> "'By your leave, gentlemen,
> After a sad and dismal tragedy,
> I do suppose that few expected *me*.'

"An alteration was afterwards made in the conclusion
of the 4th act, and almost all the 5th was written afresh.
According to this change, only one of the characters dies.
Lacy came on as before, but, finding most of them alive, he
said there was no use for him, and that the poet had spoiled
his epilogue."

The Old Troop was performed on 30th July 1707 with
this cast :—"Raggou, Bowen ; Captain, Keen ; Lieutenant,
Verbruggen ; Cornet, Booth ; Lancashire Trooper, Johnson;
Ferret-Farm, Bullock ; Two Neighbours, Norris and Pack ;
Biddy, Mrs. Pater." The piece was represented at intervals
over the next ten years, but there is no record of it beyond
that.

The young Prince George, to whom the play is dedicated,
was the youngest son of Barbara Villiers, daughter of the
accomplished and amiable Viscount Grandison. She became
the wife of Roger, Earl of Castlemain, of the kingdom of
Ireland, and one of the mistresses of Charles II. Banks
observes, in his *Dormant and Extinct Baronage of England,**
that "she was a lady of great beauty and personal accom-
plishments ; Collins says, 'of personal virtues,' which
seems difficult to accredit, when the fruit of her illicit
amours with the amorous King evidenced that she had no
virtue at all."

So high an opinion had the monarch of her "personal
virtue," that he was graciously pleased in 1670 to create
her Duchess of Cleveland, Countess of Southampton, and
Baroness of Nonsuch, with remainder to Charles Fitzroy,
the eldest of his natural children by her, and, in default of
issue male, to his brother George, "the young prince," who
was in 1674 created Earl of Northumberland, Viscount Fal-
mouth, and Baron of Pontefract. In 1682 he was created
Duke of Northumberland. He married Catherine, daughter
of Thomas Wheatly, Esq. of Breknol, in Berkshire, the
widow of Thomas Lucy of Charlcote, in Warwickshire. He

---

* Vol. iii. p. 197. London, 1809. 4to.

died in 1716, leaving no issue. According to Evelyn, this marriage was a very mean one, and he, "with the help of his brother Grafton, attempted in vain to spirit her away."*

His virtuous mother surviving her husband, the Earl of Castlemain, who died in 1705, took as a second husband Robert Fielding, commonly called Beau Fielding, from whom she was very speedily separated judicially. Her Grace departed this life at Chiswick, 1709.

Evelyn met the Duke at dinner in the house of Sir Stephen Fox (24th July 1684). "He seemed to be a young gentleman of good capacity, well-bred, civil, and modest, newly come from travel, and had made his campaign at the siege of Luxemburgh. Of all his Majesty's children, of which he had now six Dukes, this seemed the most accomplished, handsome, and well shaped. What the Dukes of Richmond and St. Albans will prove, their youth does not yet discover; they are very pretty boys." The same writer, in another part of his diary, 18th November 1685, describes the Duke as "a graceful person, and an excellent rider."

The immediate elder brother of the Duke of Northumberland, Henry Fitzroy, was born on the 20th September 1663, and was created by his father, 16th August 1675, Viscount Ipswich and Earl of Euston, and in the month of September following Duke of Grafton. "From his youth he evinced," says Collins, "a brave and martial spirit, addicted himself first to the experience of maritime affairs, serving in several naval engagements under Sir John Bury previous to his elevation to the peerage. Subsequently he turned his attention to military affairs, and commanded a part of the forces of King James against the Duke of Monmouth, receiving at the siege of Cork a shot which broke two of his ribs on the 21st of September 1690. After lingering for a fortnight, he died at the early age of twenty-seven, and his body was taken to England, and buried at Euston, in Suffolk. He was in this way not older than twenty-four when he assisted his younger brother of Northumberland, three years his junior, to spirit away his Duchess."

It is evident that the youthful Northumberland had been entrapped by the widow of Charlcote, whose wiles, based on past experience, he had found it difficult to resist. From the character previously given by Evelyn of this prepossessing

---

* *Diary*, vol. ii. p. 251. (29th March 1686.)

youth, it is matter of regret that he ventured to enter the lists with a widow. "Ware hawk," said Dirk Hatterick; "Ware widows," the Duchess of Cleveland should have said to her son.

The Duke of Northumberland had no children by these inauspicious nuptials. He held the office of Chief Butler of England, in which he was succeeded by his brother, the Duke of Cleveland, upon his death at Epsom, in the 51st year of his age, 28th June 1716.

TO THE YOUNG PRINCE GEORGE, THIRD SON TO HER GRACE THE DUCHESS OF CLEVELAND.

SIR,—I acknowledge that I am no less unworthy to appear before you than I was before your elder brother, having in me the same duty and reverence for your high blood, and the same equal regard for your person. Yet I come with confidence to you; for, having found so affable and sweet a reception from your dear brother, I ought not at all to doubt of yours. Since his great blood runs in your veins, you must also retain his virtues; and in you they are justly called so. Yet they are not so in all men; for if slaves and servants and meaner men prove affable and humble, it is not virtue in them, because it is their duty; but in you, being adorned with all your greatness, it shows so rich a goodness in you that all men are obliged to return you honour for it, which I do with my heart and all my faculties. I also present you, Sir, with a poor Frenchman, Monsieur Raggou, being party perpale trooper and cook. I tender him to you in his own equipage, just as he landed, with not so much as a shirt to his back; but that is no new thing to the English nation. Therefore, Sir, receive him as an object to exercise your charity upon; being naked, clothe him; let him but wear your livery, and he will not only be received, but be made welcome to all men. Lay your protecting hand upon him, and he

is safe from the malice of his enemies. And, Sir,
as I am bound, so I pray that you may want no
one virtue that may make you up a miracle. May
your great blood appoint you to cut your own fortune out, and may you do it with such success
and valour that all men of courage may honour
you, and the rest of the world fear you.—And this,
Sir, shall always be the prayer of your obliged
and most obedient servant,

JOHN LACY.

EPISTLES, 'tis true, are customary, but I think as unnecessary as funeral sermons, for they must either insinuate and flatter grossly, or else say nothing to the purpose. For my part, I cannot imagine, reader, what to say to thee, unless, like a raw preacher, I swerve from my text, and instead of a modest apology for my bold printings, tell thee a tale of Maestricht being taken, or the Dutch bang'd at sea; and to do that were to rob the *Gazette*, and so be called in question for intrenchments. What then shall I say? Shall I praise my play to thee? No; that were to be a vainglorious ass, and in thy power, reader, to prove me so. What, then?—shall I decry it? No; that were to break the stationer, that perhaps has paid too dear for it. What, then?—shall I discover the plot and intrigue of the play to thee? No; to speak of the plot in the epistle were to forestall the reading of the play, and so damn the sale of it. Instead, then, of an ingenious epistle to divert, I beg a crafty boon, reader, that some one eminent leading voice amongst you will be for once so kind as to give an excellent character to the world of this my play, and by that decoy people may be drawn in to buy it off; so that, as I have cozened the stationer, by this means the stationer may overreach you; and in so doing, reader, you will most highly oblige your humble servant,

JOHN LACY.

PROLOGUE.

To you that judges are i' th' public street
Of ballad without sense, or even feet ;
To you that laugh aloud with wide-mouth'd grace,
To see Jack Pudding's custard thrown in 's face—
To you I do address ; for you I write ;
From you I hope protection here to-night.
Defend me, O my friends of th' upper region,
From the hard censure of this lower legion.
I was in hope that I should only see
My worthy crew of th' upper gallery.
What made you wits so spitefully to come ?
To tell you true, I'd rather had your room.
Order there was, and that most strictly gi'n,
To keep out all that look'd like gentlemen.
You have e'en bribed the doorkeepers, I doubt,
Or else I'm sure they would ha' kept you out.
You must nor censure poet nor his play,
For that's the work o' the upper house to-day.
Deal you, Sirs, with your match, your Dryden wit,
Your poet-laureate both to box and pit.
It is some conquest for to censure him
That's filled with wit and judgment to the brim :
He is for your censure, and I'm for theirs,
Pray therefore meddle with your own affairs.
Let wits and poets keep their proper stations ;
He writes to th' terms, I to th' long vacations.

THE PERSONS' NAMES.

CAPTAIN,
LIEUTENANT, } *Of the Troop.*
CORNET,
TOM TELL-TROTH.
RAGGOU.
FLEA-FLINT, *Plunder-Master-General.*
Captain FERRET-FARM.
Quarter-Master BURNDORP.
BIDDY, *the Cornet's Boy.*
DOL TROOP.
TROOPERS.
CONSTABLES.
PAINTER.
CARPENTER.
SERVANTS.
WOMEN and CHILDREN in abundance.

ROUNDHEADS.

GOVERNOR of a Garrison.
Captain HOLDFORTH.
Captain TURTEXT; and his two holy Sisters.

I

AN OLD TROOP;

OR,

MONSIEUR RAGGOU.

———◆———

ACT I.—SCENE I.

TELL-TROTH *and* DOL TROOP.

Dol. I have heard your story, and much pity you. But in truth I am a wicked, a very wicked woman, for I never did one good deed in all my life; and I doubt you're unlucky, that your fate directs you to me.

Tell. I find you have opportunity to do good, and will, to serve me; and for reward, if that——

Dol. Nay, y' are liberal enough; you understand the world, for money creates good and evil; and I, that never thought of doing good, will now heartily endeavour it. Go to my quarters, for I have a great deal of roguery to act for myself, besides the good I am to do for you.

Tell. Inquire all you can into the last thing you spoke of, for I confess that troubles me. If she proves but honest, I'll forgive her wildness.

Dol. I'll do it with all the craft I can.

[*Exeunt.*

Enter LIEUTENANT, FLEA-FLINT, FERRET-FARM, *and* BURNDORP.

Flea. Good morrow, good morrow, Lieutenant.

Lieut. Precious rogues! what brave honours and titles you have arrived at in the wars, rascals! Plunder-Master-General Flea-Flint! What Prince can give thee so great a title?—a great credit for my colonel, rogue. Then here's Captain Ferret-Farm, an honourable gentleman; for always, when we are fighting, you are ferreting the farms, and searching the women for letters of intelligence, you damn'd rogue! Then here's the Quarter-Master Burndorp, a rogue that, when we have brave large quarters assign'd, you sell half of 'em, and then truss us up nine or ten in one house together. A pox on you, rascal!

Burn. But why are you thus cruel, Lieutenant?

Lieut. Hang you, dogs! Did not I know you at first to be three tatter'd musketeers, and by plundering a malt-mill of three blind horses you then turn'd dragooners; and so, quartering in a farm where a good team was, you chang'd your blind horses for better, and then you commenc'd troopers at Oxford; and when you had plundered yourselves into good clothes, you impudently called yourselves major, and captain, and quarter-master, and then you ran away from your own troop, and I entertained you for reformado-officers? you know I know this, and yet, you dull, ungrateful rascals, you will not know why I am angry!

Fer. Why are you angry?

Flea. Why?—I'll tell thee why. He wants twenty pounds and a good gelding, coxcomb. He must have it, too; I know him well enough.

Burn. Is that it? He shall have it, and thank

him, too. Pray, accept of this twenty pounds, Lieutenant.

Fer. And we have a good gelding for you, Lieutenant, as ever you laid leg over.

Lieut. Why so? Why will you put me to't to give you ill language? Cannot you understand me without scurvy usage?

Fer. I did not understand you, by my troth, Lieutenant.

Lieut. Pray, understand me hereafter. Now are you three as honest, harmless fellows! How dost thou do? Who dares say that thou wilt flea a flint? or he search for letters in a wench's placket? or the Quarter-Master burn a town? I'll set 'em by the heels that say it. Honest Robin, Tom, and Dick, when shall we drink a tub of ale together?

Burn. When you please, worthy Lieutenant.

Lieut. Get a tub at one of your quarters, and I'll come to you. And pray, understand me thoroughly hereafter. I believe I shall be very angry within this week again; therefore, pray, take care to prevent it.   [*Exit.*

Flea. It were a good deed ne'er to plunder more.

Burn. Why, prithee?

Flea. No thriving on't for these damn'd officers. To put excise and custom upon plundering!—to put toll upon fleaing a flint! I hold my own quarters to be my lawful inheritance as much as any man's land or office that is held by old custom and time out of mind.

Fer. Nay, I hold my quarters to be so much my own, that the wife, the daughter, and maid-servants ought to be in my occupation.

Burn. I deny that; for the man of the house ought to have his wife himself, in case he have a

daughter to furnish you. Nay, the strictness of
the statute of plundering says, that in case he
has but barely a maid-servant, you ought not to
meddle with his wife, or indeed his daughter.

Flea. I am of the opinion of the gentleman that
spoke last; for I am, in my own quarter, lord of
the manor, and all wefts and strays are mine.

Burn. I'll say that for thee, a maid cannot go
a-milking but thou mak'st a weft or stray of her.

Enter CORNET.

Cor. Here's the faithful fraternity!—a league of
knaves that's never to be broke! It is a joyful
thing when brethren plunder together in unity.
How d' ye, Plunder-Master General?

Flea. We have all arrived at excellent nick-
names, to say truth, according to our several
degrees and ways of plundering; but you, Cornet,
have a name that's proper for all cornets to be
call'd by, for they are all beardless boys in our
army, for the most part of our horse were rais'd
thus: The honest country gentleman raises the
troop at his own charge, then he gets a low-
country lieutenant to fight his troop safely, then
sends for his son from school to be his cornet, and
he puts off his child's coat to put on a buff coat;
and this is the constitution of our army: so I salute
you, Cornet Beardless. Thou art called Ferret-
Farm because thou art so terrible valiant amongst
the country bumpkins, and Aspen because thou
shakest and tremblest in a day of battle.

Fer. Whoo, pox! this is absolute malice.

Cor. There thou art out, for this is neither
malice nor anger, but downright truth.

Flea. You abuse him, i' faith! I have seen him
up to the chin in blood.

Cor. 'Twas in a saw-pit, then; yet, when the armies meet, I'll say that for him, he will draw up as confidently as if he would take a general by the beard; and he will as confidently ride out of the army before the battle joins; and if any man ask him whither he goes, he says he is sent for orders; so you hear of him no more, and the next day you find him as sure in a saw-pit.

Fer. Pray let the saw-pit alone, and provoke me not; good men have done the like, therefore be not too bold with your betters.

Flea. Provoke him not, for he's a devil at a sword, though he tremble at a gun.

Fer. A gun, I confess, is as terrible to me as thunder and lightning; they 're out of my element. Well, but leave this discourse, and, so you do not laugh at me, I'll tell you a story.

Flea. What is 't?

Fer. Why, faith, our Dol's with child, and lays it to me.

Burn. Pox on her! she was with me this morning, and I compounded with her for five pound.

Fer. The whore had seven of me, by this light.

Cor. An excellent cunning quean! She knows the family of the Flea-Flints are ever the monied men of the troop. I'll make use of my time too: give me ten pound to keep counsel, or I'll make you the laughingstock o' th' army.

Flea. Thou wilt not turn treacherous rogue, now, sure?

Cor. 'Tis no treachery. Show me a soldier that will not take advantage.

Flea. Ay, of the enemy.

Cor. For ten pound any man's my enemy or friend. There's another principle for you, and very fit for the Flea-Flints to make use of.

Burn. We scorn to compound; but we will lend you so much money if you will mortgage the next fresh quarters.

Cor. I'll do 't.

Burn. Then there's your ten pound.

Cor. Now are you men of inheritance; now you have a good title to every man's goods and chattels; and for ten pound more I'll help you to a lawyer shall plead it, and make it good to you and your heirs for ever.

Enter TELL-TROTH.

Tell. God give you good morn, sirs; I pray you, which of you is the Captain Commander ?

Flea. Why, friend, we have ne'er a captain here; he lyes leaguer at Oxford, to give the King intelligence when his troop beats or is beaten.

Cor. There y' are a scandalous rascal. Some captains, I confess, have that trick, but our captain always fights his troop himself. But we have a good lieutenant here, if that will serve your turn.

Burn. Ay, he's too good for us; I would the devil had him!

Cor. What's thy business ?

Tell. I'd be a trooper.

Fer. And canst thou fight ?

Tell. Wilt thou try ?

Fer. No; faith, friend, I believe thee. Wast ever a soldier ?

Tell. Ay, a Parliament one.

Flea. What ! and didst thou run away ?

Tell. No, I walked this pace; I scorn to run.

Burn. I believe this fellow's a spy.

Tell. You lie; I am very honest ! Now, dare you fight ?

Burn. No, by my troth, not with thee.

Tell. Then remember, if anybody want the lie, you had it last.

Flea. This is such a fellow as I never met with. Yet why didst thou leave the Parliament ?

Tell. For the same cause that I believe I shall leave you.

Flea. What's that ?

Tell. Because I liked 'em not.

Fer. Who was thy captain ?

Tell. One Captain Verily Rett.

Fer. Of what profession was he ?

Tell. Of every one's profession, I think.

Fer. What's that ?

Tell. An hypocrite.

Burn. And dost thou come out of love to the King ?

Tell. No ; I come to see fashions.

Burn. But why didst thou leave thy captain ?

Tell. Because he is an hypocrite — a yea-and-nay knave. He cannot endure to plunder, but, in a godly manner, he will take all he can lay his hands on.

Cor. But wilt thou fight for the King out of stark love and kindness ?

Tell. No ; I'll fight for him as all men fight for kings—partly for love, partly for my own ends. I'll fight bravely for a battle or two, then beg an old house to made a garrison of, grow rich, consequently a coward, and then, let the dog bite the bear, or the bear the dog, I'll make my own peace, I warrant you ; and, in short, this is my business hither.

Enter LIEUTENANT.

Lieut. Where are you, sirs ? The Captain has brought orders to march, but whither I know not ;

and, better news than that, he has brought pay, boys!

Flea. I hope you are not angry, Lieutenant?

Lieut. I am not yet, but I shall be very suddenly, therefore provide against it; the next fresh quarter you will have advantage enough. I hope we understand of all hands?

Flea. 'Tis sufficient, Lieutenant.

Cor. But here's the strangest fellow come to be a trooper.

Lieut. He's welcome! Hast thou a good horse, friend?

Tell. No, but I've a bridle; and if you'll entertain me, I shall quickly have a horse. Are you the Captain?

Lieut. I am but lieutenant, friend.

Tell. Ho! I thought you had all been captains. I'm sure you are all call'd so.

Enter CAPTAIN.

Lieut. But here comes one that is so; this is a very captain.

Tell. I tell thee that's very much. What's his name?

Lieut. Captain Honor.

Tell. Ay! have you such a thing as honour amongst you?

Capt. Lieutenant, get your corporals together, and give 'em orders to make ready for a march; and be sure you charge 'em to see every horse in their squadrons shod, otherwise we shall have 'em lye behind drinking and plundering, and then pretend they stay to shoe their horses. Let me hear no more on't!

Tell. 'Tis possible a very captain may be honest.

Lieut. But, sir, before you do anything, talk with this fellow; he would fain be a trooper.

Capt. Now, friend, would'st thou be a soldier?

Tell. Yes, if I could light of a good side, a right cause, and good men to manage it.

Capt. On my word that's shrewdly put! Well, I'll promise thee a good cause, and some good men; in multitudes all are not virtuous nor valiant.

Tell. That's well said; I think I shall begin to take a liking to you. But, Captain, I hear a man may learn to flea a flint amongst you, to drink and plunder.

Capt. D'ye hear that, rascals? But where did'st thou hear this report of us?

Tell. In a London pulpit. But another sort of people told me they preach'd interest more than gospel, so that a man knows not which side to take.

Capt. Nay, upon my word, thou art come to the right side.

Tell. I guess as much; for you talk worse than you do, and they do worse than they talk.

Capt. This is an odd kind of fellow, and I believe a dangerous. Friend, withdraw, while I read my orders to my officers.

Tell. A word in your ear first: are you wonderful honest?

Capt. Thou art a strange, blunt fellow. Yes, I am honest.

Tell. But are you wise too? For else the want of wit to manage your honesty may make you a knave. I know 'tis some men's cases.

Capt. Thou dost surprise me! Sure, thou hast more business than to be a trooper?

Tell. I have so, but I must ask you another question ere you know it. Are you staunch enough to keep a secret? Be not angry—many of your party cannot hold; for tell you news, and you fly like lightning to the next man to disgorge it; and so it goes round till it comes to the enemy, and thus you betray your business, and intend it not neither.

Capt. I have not heard so dangerous a man. Pray, friend, think me worthy to know your business.

Tell. You shall. And to show you that I have business, I know what your orders are.

Capt. Why, 'tis impossible!

Tell. Nothing impossible; you are to remove your troop to Cilstow, there quarter till further orders, but not to go to bed, for you are within three miles of a little house call'd Thievesden Garrison; and you are to expect a company of foot to quarter with you—is this your orders?

Capt. You amaze me! How came you by this intelligence?

Tell. It came to Thievesden House this morning, and so to me. I am their confidant, and would fain be yours.

Capt. Do you not know who sent it?

Tell. No, nor they neither; there's the subtle carriage of the thing.

Capt. But pray, sir, let me ask you who you are?

Tell. I am a plain, honest-meaning man, a neighbour to that garrison of Thievesden, and one that has div'd into the bottom of both your parties, and find that you have faults, but the other great wickedness.

Flea. I do not like this fellow; he had a fling against drink.

Fer. And plundering; but twenty to one he hath paid for 't.

Flea. He had a plaguy jerk at flaying of flints too.

Capt. What if you went to Oxford with me?

Tell. So I may be hang'd when I come home again? for they will know it as sure. Pray let me eat and refresh myself, and then conclude of something. [*Exeunt.*

Enter DOL, *and calls* LIEUTENANT *back.*

Dol. Lieutenant, I'd speak with you.

Lieut. Dol, I'll come to thee presently. [*Exit.*

Dol. I cannot say I am with child, but with children; for here has been all nations, and all languages to boot. If the several tongues should work upwards now, and I speak all languages? Why, I am not the first learned woman, but I believe the first that ever came by her learning that way. If I should have for every man that has been dealing here a child, and if the children should be born with every one a back and breast on, as they were got, bless me, what hard labour should I have! But, for all this, I hope I do not go with above a squadron of children. But to my business. I mean to lay this great belly to every man that has but touch'd my apron strings. I thank the law, 'tis very favourable in this point; for when I have played the whore, the law gives me leave to play the rogue, and lay it to whom I will.

Enter LIEUTENANT.

Lieut. Why, how now, Dol? How go matters with you, good Dol?

Dol. I desire you'd stand my friend, sir; you see my condition?

Lieut. Thou wilt not lay thy child to my charge. I hope?

Dol. No, sir, I have more wit; my drift is to lay it to more than one man or one squadron. Sir, I understand there's a month's pay in your hands; and I am resolv'd to lay this great belly to every man round the troop. Some I have struck already, and they have very fairly compounded with me. Some, I suppose, may bustle and stand out; but if you will countenance me, then they must compound at our rates.

Lieut. But, Dol, what benefit is this to me? For I profess no friendship, but follow the general principle of mankind, Dol, which is to pick the money out of thy pocket to put it into mine. So, Dol, in plain terms, what will you give me?

Dol. Why, Lieutenant, you shall go snips.

Lieut. Why, Dol, we are agreed. But after we have struck the troop round, who dost thou pitch upon to father it?

Dol. Why, faith, I did design to marry Monsieur Raggou, the French cook that rides in your troop.

Lieut. Thou wilt never endure to live with him, 'tis such a nasty slovenly rogue.

Dol. 'Tis no matter for living with him; I want a husband.

Lieut. He stinks above ground. He has not had a shirt on's back time out of mind.

Dol. That makes it a fit match, for, by my troth, I do not deserve a man that's worth a shirt.

Lieut. Well, Dol, upon the aforesaid terms you're sure of me; play your game with all confidence.

Dol. Well, I'll to work amongst 'em presently; or if I might gain you to advance my greater desires, which is my cornet's boy that waits on him. I am foolish, for I love him strangely, desperately. A hundred pounds, in plain terms, make him mine.

Lieut. But, Dol, where is this hundred pound ?

Dol. I have shark'd these four years, and made a shift to scrape four hundred pounds together.

Lieut. Still, I say, you're sure of me with ready money.

Enter MONSIEUR RAGGOU *and his* LANDLADY.

Well, Dol, away! here comes Monsieur Raggou —step aside !

Dol. Oh, let him have his money. If our cornet's boy fail, I'll have him, or he shall certainly keep the child.   [*Exit.*

Rag. Landlady! come, take a my pistol and lock in your trunk very safe.

Land. Yes, sir.

Rag. Take heed, for begar you will be hang if my pistol run away !

Land. O Lord, I'll take no charge on 't !

Rag. You Roundhead whore, lock it up, or me will kill you, begar !

Land. I'll take all the care I can on 't, sir. [*Exit.*

Rag. So, me will steal my pistol from her trunk, and say she carry it to de enemy, and den me will so plundra de dam whore.

Enter BUMPKIN.

Stand ! who are you for, Bumpkin ?

Bum. O Lord, sir, I am for nobody !

Rag. You dog, be you for de King or de Parliamenta ?

Bum. Why, I am for——pray, sir, who are you for ?

Rag. Tank you for dat ! Begar, you be very full wid cunning. You will be of my side if me name myself first. Speak, you dam dog ! who be you for?

Bum. In truth it is not good manners to say who I am for; your worship ought to speak first.

Rag. Pox take you! Me be for de Parliament, you dog!

Bum. Oh, the Lord bless your worship, I am for the good Parliament too.

Rag. Je'rny, I am for de King, you Roundhead dog! Begar, me will plundra you, soul and body.

Bum. Oh, good sir, spare me; I am for the King!

Rag. Diable, me will plundra you for being Jack of both sides. Diantie, he have but one silling about his soul and bodee. Get you gone, you dog!

[*Exit* BUMPKIN.

Begar, me have no luck. Zoun, me plundra every day dis tre years, and begar me never get but one silling or one sixpenne, begar. Ha! Monsieur Lieutenant, me hear very brave ting of you.

Lieut. What's that?

Rag. Me hear you have some largion for Monsieur la Soldier; pray, how much will come to Monsieur Moy?

Lieut. Faith, Monsieur, some three pounds.

Rag. How!—tre pone! Whar be de tre pone? How much be tre pone?

Lieut. Why, here 'tis, Monsieur; so much as you see.

Rag. Begar, sure you mock a de moy; begar, me never see so much money togeder in my life! Me will lye down and tumble in my money, like de dog dat tumbla in de carrion; it is so sweet. O brave Capitain! O brave Lieutenant! Gad a bless de King of England, and de King of France too, when he give me tre pone! Lieutenant, be to be mad a dangerous ting?

Lieut. Oh, very dangerous.

Rag. Begar, dere be your tre pone again! It will

make a me tark a mad; me no know vat me sall do with all dis money. Begar, me admire tre pone of all de ting in this varle; it vill make de great Turk de Christian, or de Christian de Turk, better den all de argument in the varle. Pray, Lieutenant, keep dis money for me, one, two, tree year, till me take counsel of all my friend in France vat me sall do wid dat.

Lieut. Go to Oxford, and buy some necessaries with it; you are so nasty, nobody is able to come near you. Buy some shirts, to keep you sweet and clean.

Rag. Buy some shart! Me love you very well, Lieutenant, but you no understand; for vat sall me have some shart?

Lieut. To keep yourself sweet, and from being lousey.

Rag. Who can see my shart? Here be my doublet come close, my coat come over all dat, den who de devil see my shart? For vat sall me have a shart, when nobody see my shart?

Lieut. But then you want stockings and twenty necessaries.

Rag. Me pull up my boot, who see me have a stockin? You vill have a little English tricka, and never understand; for vat will you have more ting about you den vat vill make a show in de varle and everybody can see? Pray, let me lay out my money to please my own fancee.

Lieut. With all my heart.

Rag. Den me will lay it out for my honour, and for de honour of de King and my Lieutenant. So adieu. Buy shart!—who see my shart? [*Exit.*

Enter DOL.

Dol. Faith, Lieutenant, I'll at him and some of

K

the rest presently; therefore leave me to work. I am asham'd I am such a fool to doat on a boy; but no remedy. Remember, therefore, and about it.

Lieut. Do you remember the hundred pound, I'll work him; fear not.   [*Exeunt severally.*

Aст II.—Scene I.

Enter Dol Troop.

Dol. Now to my business. My Flintflayer compounded with me very civilly, that I did fear would have outwitted me. I am afraid of nothing but an impudent rogue that has no shame in him, that will father the child rather than part with his money, and so spoil my compounding with the rest of the troop. I'll be as wise as I can, so have among 'em!

Enter a Trooper.

Troop. What a pox makes she here?
Dol. How d'ye, Mr. William? I'm come to tell you I am gone half my time, that you may provide; for I am quick.
Troop. Art thou? Faith, I'll be as quick as thou art, for I'll be in Holland, if the wind serve, to-morrow.   [*Exit.*
Dol. 'Slife, if they should all boggle thus, I should make a thin troop on't.

Enter Raggou.

Rag. Oh, Madam Dol! Ow dee? ow dee?
Dol. You see how I do. I am near my time; I

desire you to provide. You swore a thousand oaths to me you would keep the child.

Rag. But me did but swear in French, Madam Dol, and dat vill no stand good in English law, Madam Dol.

Dol. Come, sir, come; I'll make you father my child, or I'll make you do worse. Will you compound?

Rag. Me scorn to compone, and scorn to fader your shild! You be a dam whore, Madam Dol.

Dol. You are a rascal, Mr. Monsieur, and I'll make you father the child in spite of your French teeth.

Rag. Begar, Madam Dol, you be de great whore de Babylon! Begar, me vill make appear noting can get you wid shild but de maypole in de Strana; and den me can make appear by good vitteness dat me have no maypole abouta me. So adieu, Madam Babylon! Pox take you!—me fader your dam son of a whore's shild? [*Exit.*

Dol. You fickle Frenchman, I shall be reveng'd on thee! I'll marry thee, but I'll be reveng'd on thee!

Enter CORNET, LIEUTENANT, *and* BIDDY.

But here comes my Cornet and his boy, and the Lieutenant. I see he is mindful of my business.
[*Exit.*

Lieut. Cornet, I have an earnest, and, by my troth, a most pleasant suit to you.

Cor. You cannot miss the grant of it. What is 't?

Lieut. But first, do you love money?

Cor. By my troth, I know not, for I never had a sum worth loving in my life yet.

Lieut. Will fifty pound do any hurt?

Cor. But what must I do for it?—betray the troop to the enemy, or some garrison? for under that I cannot deserve fifty pound.

Lieut. Towns are not so cheap yet; though treason be plentiful, 'tis not grown a drug. But to my suit : you are to know that our Dol is desperately in love, and with whom?

Cor. Not with me? I find I must earn this fifty pound.

Lieut. No such matter; you have too great a conceit of your good face.

Bid. Indeed you lie, Lieutenant, for he can never think too well of that face. [*Aside.*

Cor. Who is it she is in love with?

Lieut. By my troth, with thy boy here; desperately in love with thy boy.

Bid. The devil take her for her pains! But why do I curse her, that am so desperately in love myself? [*Aside.*

Cor. Why, this story is very pleasant, if you knew all.

Bid. O Lord, you will not tell him what I am, I hope?

Cor. Lieutenant, I must deny your suit, for it must not be a match; for the boy is, in plain terms, a girl.

Bid. The devil take you for telling him!

Cor. Why so? My lieutenant's very faithful.

Lieut. A girl! Let me see your face.

Bid. O, you unworthy man! Good sir, forgive me, for I am even ready to scold.

Lieut. This is the pretty young daughter that belong'd to your winter quarters, and so came away for love?

Bid. Yes, sir; but if your cornet had been true, I had been past love by this time—I had been married.

Lieut. Why, are all married people past love?

Bid. Yes, sir, of the men's side especially; but, sir, I am naturally very merry, and shall be if you will but do me the favour to think me very honest.

Lieut. I shall do you a great favour if I do, for I never thought anybody so yet; but if it please you, I'll try your honesty, and then I'll give you my opinion.

Bid. Be not rude when you try me. If you be, you were better venture on a maiden cat at midnight, for I shall scratch worse, and so mark you, not for my humble servant, but my humble caterwauler.

Lieut. I could meet such a creature o' th' housetop at any hour, and scratch and squeak, and tumble down together, and get the prettiest kitlins as we fall.

Bid. I am glad to see you merry, sir, for merry people are likely honest.

Lieut. Well, we'll try; but if you love mirth, consent to marry with this Dol. There's money for us all. [*Exit.*

Bid. Content, i' faith! 'Twill be excellent sport to marry her, for I love roguery well enough; but, the devil's in 't, she'll know me to be a girl!

Enter DOL *aloof.*

Cor. No, no; she shall not come near you, nor touch you, till she's brought to bed. Then two to one but the troop marches away and leaves her behind; then I'm sure the country bumpkins will knock her o' th' head.

Dol. There's a cornet in grain, i' faith.

Bid. Troth, you are very charitable. Well, since my hand's in at wearing breeches, I'll do all the offices of a man. I would I had wherewithal to perform, for, by my troth, I am weary of our own sex.

Dol. She cries, i' faith ; I like that well.

Cor. You little fool, you do not cry, I hope ?

Bid. No, faith, that was but a tear by chance. You made me leave my friends, you know, when you talk'd of marriage to me ; but not one word on 't now you have made me your be-de-boy.

Dol. I know not what to say to that !

Cor. We'll talk of those things when we are settled.

Bid. By my troth, you have put me in such a gog of marriage that it will not out of my head ; and yet I scorn to ask you to marry me, and I scorn to crack a commandment with you. Was not that basely done of you to tempt me ? But I shall scold, which is a thing I hate. O base fellow! you would be going o' th' score with me for my virginity ! Faith, sir, I'd have you know 'tis worth ready money at any time ; and, faith, I'll swear it shall ne'er go under matrimony.

Dol. She is honest, i' faith ! I love a virtuous woman, though I am none myself; like him that lov'd the sound of Greek though he understood it not. She is right honest, i' faith !

Bid. Marry me, and then halloo, dog, for thy silver collar; but till then I'll gnaw my under-sheet to the bedcord before you shall have your will of me. I am sometimes mad when I think how I left my friends. Sometimes I could scold, and sometimes I could cry ; and the devil take that good face of yours, I can do neither for it !

Cor. Come, come ; you trust your person with me, and why not your virginity ? How long do you think you can hold out at this staunch rate ?

Bid. Faith, sir, I can hold out till it's fit for nobody—till I'm past the use of man, before thou shalt have it, shameless wretch!

Dol. She is certainly honest, and that's half our work done!

Cor. Come. prithee let's think of our mock-marriage with Dol, and after we'll be serious.

Bid. Why, I'm for that too; but yet I cannot choose but cry to see how false you are, and how they talk at home of me, She's run away with a soldier, and that rascal will not marry her. Oh, the devil take you! I shall never recover that credit again.

Cor. Come, we'll cozen 'em all at last.

Bid. Nay, I believe thou'lt cozen more than me; for what woman can forbear running away with thee that sees those leering eyes, thou bewitching devil, thou?

Cor. Oh, remember you hate scolding, Biddy.

Bid. I had forgot that, indeed.

Cor. Nay, prithee, no more of this story.

Bid. Well, I will not : but truly I grow weary of your unkindness, and I am serv'd well enough for scorning a man that doated on me!

Dol. A ha! Ay, marry! That's somewhat, indeed.

Bid. But I see, a cornet with his flying colours, and his word, "Have at all," goes a great way with a virgin. Who can resist it ? [*Exeunt.*

Enter CAPTAIN, LIEUTENANT, *and* TELL-TROTH.

Capt. Lieutenant, stay and receive orders. But, sir. how many companies are there in Thievesden garrison?

Tell. Ne'er a company; for not one of 'em will be call'd captain of a company, but captain of a

congregation. One is call'd Captain Holdforth ;
another Captain Tubtext ; rogues marked at the
font for rebellion.

Capt. Rebellion is the first point of reformation
always.

Tell. They are form'd to a new stamp of villany,
the last impression—that which put the devil into
a cold sweat. Take the wickedest and worst re-
puted men you have, and turn them loose to
plunder, and I defy 'em to make the tithe o' th'
spoil these hypocrites have done !

Capt. You are very bitter.

Tell. Malice cannot lay 'em open. They lecture
it thrice a week, and summon the country to come
in. They that refuse, they take their goods and
leave 'em ne'er a groat ; and then they say they
took but their own, for the good creature is the
inheritance of the people of God.

Capt. It seems every captain is a teacher, and
his own company is his congregation, so that they
hang and draw religion among themselves. No
doubt most blasphemous villains !

Tell. Well, sir, I'll home to-night. March your
troops to Lavel to-morrow ; stay till I come to you !
So fare you well, and I wish a blessing upon your
good meaning !   [*Exit.*

Capt. Lieutenant, be careful how you march to-
morrow, and take heed I hear of no complaint.
I'll to Oxford in the morning, to give an account
of this fellow !

Lieut. I hope you'll allow us our old harmless
drolleries.

Capt. Ay, most freely.   [*Exit.*

Enter CORNET.

Cor. Lieutenant, half the troop will be gone.

Dol has laid her child to 'em all, and they're for horse and away!

Lieut. What shall we do?

Cor. Endeavour to prevent it, that is all that's to be said.   [*Exeunt.*

Enter a TROOPER *with his arms, and* MONSIEUR RAGGOU *meets him.*

Rag. Ow dee, ow dee, Monsieur Lancashire? Vat make you have your arms so late at night? Is dere alarm? Be de enemy in de quarteer?

1 *Troop.* Worse than the enemy—the devil's in the quarter! Our Dol is with child, and would lay it to me; but I'll lay down my arms and go home.

Rag. Begar, me vil lay down my arms and go home too. Ha! begar, now I tink, me have no home.   [*Exit.*

1 *Troop.* Captain! Captain!

Within. Who's there?—what's the matter?

1 *Troop.* Thomas, 'tis I, the old mutineer. Tell the Captain I must speak with him.

Within. He is but just laid down on the bed to sleep a little. Come i' th' morning!

1 *Troop.* Flesh and blood, I will speak with him!

CAPTAIN *above.*

Capt. What's the matter?—an alarm?

1 *Troop.* Ay, marry is there, Captain; there will be a whole squadron upon you presently.

Capt. 'Sdeath, my horse presently!

1 *Troop.* The enemy, Dol, is fallen into our Lancashire quarters, and has laid her child to our squadron. So here is your back and your breast, Captain, and I'll go home.

Enter four TROOPERS *and* RAGGOU.

2 *Troop.* Flesh ! we'll father no child, not we !

Rag. Begar, me vil fader no shild too.   Hey !
Monsieur Capitain, here be your one pistole !

3 *Troop.* Captain, we have brought you some
Lancashire arms; here is some ten or eleven sowze
kidgiors for you.

Capt. What the devil ails the fellow ?   [*Above.*

Rag. Begar, Capitain, me vil keep no shild ;
your dam Madam Dol have get us all with a
shild !

Capt. Run for the quean to come to me.—I shall
have all my troop forsake me.   Stay, sirs; I'll come
to you.   I must as well humour 'em as be severe,
or else no soldiers.   [*Exit from above.*

Rag. Vell, me do know very well how it sal be
my shild or no.

4 *Troop.* Well, monsieur, and I have a mark
to know whether it be mine or no as well as you.

2 *Troop.* And so we have all.

Enter CAPTAIN *and* CORNET.

Capt. My masters, you might have had so much
manners to have held your complaints till morning;
but, however, I have sent for Dol, and I'll do you
justice before I stir now.   How now, Raggou?
what are thy sleeves stuff'd withal so ?

Rag. Begar, dis sleeve be my stabla—dere be
good oata for mine arse ; and dis sleeve be my
kitchin—dere be meat for myself!   Vill you eat
dis morning, Capitain ?

Capt. Foh ! your sleeves stink abominably !

Rag. Zoun, do you call dat a stinka ?   'Tis true,
it have a little huggo ;* begar, dis sleeve keep your

* Haut gout.

troop alive—dis sleeve is de physician to all de troop. When any man be sick, me set on some hot vatera, dere let my sleeve boil one hour in it, and dat make de comfortable pottage in de varle. Have me not cure you all?

4 Troop. Yes, indeed, Captain, he has cur'd us twenty times!

Rag. Begar, Capitain, me have cure that dam whore Madam Dol, and yet for all dat she lay her shild a top upon me!

Enter DOL.

Capt. Oh, here she is! Now, you audacious quean, what makes you alarm these people thus? Who got you with child? Speak, and speak truth, I charge you!

Dol. Why, then, I will speak truth, an't please you. Good Captain, do not fright me!

Capt. Well, then, is it his child? did he get it?

Dol. I cannot say absolutely 'tis his, Captain.

Capt. Why, is it this fellow's?

Dol. I cannot say directly 'tis his neither.

Capt. Is it Monsieur Raggou's?

Dol. I cannot say, to speak truth, 'tis his in particular.

Capt. Death! you abominable quean, say whose 'tis, or I'll slit your nose!

Dol. Why, truly, I cannot lay it to any one man; but, Gad is my judge, 'tis the troop's child, Captain!

Capt. Was ever such a slut heard of?

Dol. I desire your worship to believe me in one thing. Truly, Captain, and as Gad's my comfort, I have been as true and faithful a woman to the troop, as ever wife was to a husband, Captain.

Rag. Oh ho! are you so? Me tink now, Madam

Dol, you are de whore de Babylon ; for one whole troop may make a maypole.

Capt. Why, this is some honesty yet, that she is true to the troop.

Rag. Ould, Capitain! for ought a me see, dis shild be your shild !

Capt. How prove you that, sir ?

Rag. Begar, she say de shild belong to de troop, and you say de troop belong to you ; derefore de shild is your shild, begar !

Capt. But I'll make some of you father it. There is none of you but have some private mark to know it to be your own by.

4 *Troop.* Faith, Captain, if it be born with a gauntlet and a headpiece on, I'll own it.

2 *Troop.* Troth, Captain, if it be born with a bridle in its hand, and boots and spurs on, I'll own it.

1 *Troop.* Troth, Captain, I ne'er touch'd her. I was about it once, but the jade laid herself so like a constable tied neck and heels together, that I went to plunder her, and she up and beat me like a dog.

3 *Troop.* And by my troth, if it be born leading a horse into the world, 'tis my child, Captain.

Rag. Ould ! you every one have a mark to know your shild. Madam Dol, before my Capitain, if your shild be born wid never a shart, den it be my shild, for me have had no shart dis forty week.

Enter FERRET-FARM.

Fer. By your leave, Captain.

Capt. What want you, Aspen ?

Fer. I come to free all these men, and to own the child, Captain.

Dol. How! own my child? The rogue never touch'd me in his life, Captain!

Fer. Ha, Dol! confess, confess! Will you have the truth, Captain?

Capt. Ay, prithee, with all my heart.

Fer. Why, then, I must confess she goes with two children; one I got on the great trunk's end, and the other on a staircase—by my life, Captain.

Capt. I never heard of staircase children before.

Rag. But vat if de shild be born wid no shart? You sall be hang before you fader my shild!

Dol. Captain, if I were to die to-morrow, the rogue never touch'd me.

Fer. I'll cudgel the rogue to death, Captain.

Capt. Hold! hold!

Rag. Let him come, Captain! Me vill kill him, begar! [*Draws, and throws off his coat.*

Capt. Hold, Dol! I charge you to put up, monsieur!

Rag. Me vill put up, den.

Capt. Not one word more, I charge you, but all to your quarters! Begone! Cornet, 'tis time to sound to horse; and take heed I hear of no complaints.

Rag. Begar, me never see all dat before! Diable, me be Monsieur Raggou indeed! Me vill put on my coat presan, for, begar, if Monsieur Dunghill-raker see me, begar he vill put me in his sack.
[*Exeunt.*

Enter twelve TROOPERS *at six doors—two at a door.*

1 *Troop.* Pox of this French fool! What! does he mean to give us all ribbons? We do but laugh at him.

3 *Troop.* His business is to be admir'd. I admire he has bought him ne'er a shirt.

2 Troop. He is like the hypocrites that will not sing psalms ; because they've ne'er a room to the street they cannot be heard.

4 Troop. And so he'll have ne'er a shirt because it cannot be seen.

Enter LIEUTENANT, FLEA-FLINT, FERRET-FARM, *and* BURNDORP.

Lieut. Come ! to horse, to horse !

Flea. Lieutenant, pray let Monsieur Raggou ride before, and make the quarters to-night.

Fer. Pray do, sir ; for every fresh quarter we know you expect, and therefore you must wink.

Lieut. But, sirs, I dare not own you ; for my captain is so severe that I protest he'll hang any man that plunders, especially you flint-flayers, that he has forgiven so often.

Burn. Why, sir, we'll venture that, for we have a way to come off.

Lieut. Pray, how ? for if the country complain, and they discover you, the world cannot save you.

Flea. Why, sir, you know Monsieur Raggou has a remarkable coat, with one sleeve always full of meat for himself, and the other full of oats for his horse ?

Lieut. Well, what then ?

Flea. Why, I have such a coat, and I will stuff up the sleeves and rob like him. I can spatter French, and have everything so like him that yourself cannot distinguish.

Lieut. Well, and how rob the rest ?

Fer. To satisfy you, in such disguises as the devil cannot find us out in.

Lieut. You'll do well to keep in those disguises still, for, i' faith, he'll find you at the long run else.

Well, if you will venture, do ; I'll aid you in what I can.

Burn. If the country complain, they come directly to you, Lieutenant.

Fer. Then you bid 'em describe the men, and without peradventure they fall upon the Frenchman with his remarkable sleeves.

Lieut. But suppose he stand it out, and make it out where he was in the time of plundering ?

Flea. That's shrewd, I confess.

Lieut. Come, I'll help you ! If the countrymen come in and describe him, I'll go directly to him, and tell him I have orders to seize him, for my Captain is resolv'd to hang him. So, out of my kindness to him, I'll let him make his escape, and I'll warrant he'll away as if the devil drove him !

Fer. But suppose he will not go at that neither ? for he's impudent enough.

Lieut. Ha ! if he will not—let me see—I'll write a letter and have it ready in my hand, and we'll pretend to search him for letters of intelligence, and so clap the letter into his pocket and pull it out again, which shall be as if it came from the enemy, and that, according to his promise, they hope he will betray the troop.

Fer. Ay, marry, this is something ! Needs must he go that the devil drives.

Flea. Then much more must he go that the Lieutenant drives. I warrant he goes to some purpose.

Fer. Good ; and when he is gone and fled for 't—

Lieut. The case is plain, he's guilty. None but he could do it.

Burn. Why, this is plot and intrigue, Lieutenant ; bravely laid, i' faith !

Flea. Why, then, *esperanza*, Flea-Flint.

Fer. What work we'll make !

Enter RAGGOU *and his* LANDLADY.

Lieut. Here comes the poor rogue and his land-lady! He little thinks of our tragical design against him. I'll step aside and see what work he'll make.
[*Exeunt.*

Rag. Come, landlady, bring me my pistole! me must march.

Land. Ay, sir, I'll fetch it you; 'tis safe enough.
[*Exit.*

Rag. Begar, me have steal my pistole! Me vill make her believe she vill be hang, and den she vill endure plundering de betra. But, pox take her! me have search, and she have noting to plundra.

Enter LANDLADY.

Land. O Lord! what shall I do? Monsieur, your pistol's gone!

Rag. Ha!

Land. It is gone—it is stolen!

Rag. Ha! you have carry my pistole to de enemy, you dam whore! Begar, you sall hang tre pair of stair higher den Haman.

Land. Truly, I know not what's become on 't. I hope you have it yourself.

Rag. Oh, you dam whore, me vill plundra your house for slander a moy.

Land. Good sir, I have nothing worth plunder-ing but a great cheese.

Rag. Give me your sheese, you devil, you!

Land. Here it is, sir, and all I have in the world.

Rag. Pox take you! give me one silling for my sheese!

Land. With all my heart. Truly it's all the money I have!

Rag. Now give me my sheese agen, you dam

whore! Vat sall me do wid dis sheese?—it vill not go into my kitchin sleeve. Begar, for one silling more you sall have the sheese indeed!

Land. You'll plunder it again!

Rag. Begar, it go agen my conscience to take your sheese, because it vill no go in my kitchin sleeve!

Land. I have not a penny to save my life!

Rag. Begar, me sell it to your neighbour!

Enter NEIGHBOUR.

Vat vill you give me for my sheese?

Land. It's my cheese!

Rag. Begar, she lie; me plunder it very fair from her.

Neigh. Then I hope I may buy plundered goods as well as other people. What's your price?

Rag. Begar, dog sheap—one silling!

Neigh. There's your money.

Land. Will you offer to buy my cheese?

Neigh. 'Tis my cheese.

Land. I'll try that.   [*Fight and exeunt.*

Rag. Begar, fight till de devil part you!

Enter LIEUTENANT *and all the* TROOPERS.

Oh, Monsieur Lieutenant!

Lieut. What dost with that cheese?

Rag. My landlady love me vera dear, and she give me dis sheese as a token to wear for her sake.

Lieut. Raggou, you must needs go make the quarters for the troop.

Rag. Wid all min heart! But, Lieutenant, dere be a favour for you.   [*Gives him a knot of ribbon.*

Lieut. But what is the meaning of this?

Rag. Begar, it be for my honer; me have lay out all my tre pone in ribbon, and give all de troop my favour to wear in de hat.

L

Lieut. What! and is all thy three pound gone in ribbon, and bought never a shirt? 'Tis very fine.

Rag. Begar, and so it be very fine. As me tell you before, who de devil see my shart? All de varle see Monsieur Raggou in de hat; every man vill admire, and ask, Who gave all that favour to de troop? den dey cry, Monsieur Raggou, de French cook. Begar, dat sall be more honer for me den ever you sall get by your shart!

Lieut. Thou art a right Frenchman. My horse there, groom! Let's march away.   [*Exeunt.*

ACT III.—SCENE I.

Enter FLEA-FLINT, FERRET-FARM, *and* BURNDORP.

Flea. Is not this like him as can be?

Burn. 'Tis like enough to delude the people with.

Flea. I'll rant and tear the ground, boys. I will so plundra all de dam bumpkin dog!

Fer. That will pass; that's his word; 'tis like him.

Flea. Be you pretty modest, sirs, and let me play the devil among 'em. I will so terrify 'em with French gibberish, that you shall appear nobody amongst 'em.

Burn. Good! for, the more active and terrible thou art, they will the more remember thee when they come to complain, and so we shall be sure to escape.

Flea. Come away, sirs; we must be quick, and ride hard for 't.   [*Exeunt.*

Enter RAGGOU, *like* FLEA-FLINT.

Rag. Begar, me have maka myself like Flea-Flint, and me vill burn one two town as me go to make a de quarter; and me vill speak English, and me vill call myself Flea-Flint. Let me see. Come, where is this constable? where are all these damn'd dery damn'd rogues and whores? I'll slay your very souls, you beastly bawds! Begar, all dat be very good English, and it be very much like Monsieur Flea-Flint; and begar, me hope he vill be taken and hang for dat, for begar me vill plundra de devel if me catch him! [*Exit.*

Enter CORNET *and* BIDDY.

Cor. Come; let me see, Biddy, how finely you'll court your mistress, now.

Bid. I can court her as all men court women. You shall lend me two or three hundred oaths, your dissembling tongue, and your false heart, and then I cannot miss the right way of wooing her.

Cor. This comes very near scolding, Biddy.
  [*Takes her by the chin.*

Bid. You make me forget myself. Look you, now, would any honest man take a maid so kindly by the chin, and yet not mean to marry her?

Cor. Thou little fool, at that rate every man i' th' kingdom would have ten thousand wives. If you'll part with your maidenhead, have at you, Biddy. Come, come, you loving worm; I know I shall have it at last.

Bid. Nay, o' my conscience, I believe thee; yet I have held fast hitherto.

Cor. I am glad to hear that, i' faith!

Bid. But I find I must look no more on those eyes; if I do, i' faith, I shall flutter so long about the candle that I shall singe my virgin wings at last. I will therefore now conclude that I am a man, and must go court my mistress.

Enter LIEUTENANT *and* DOL.

Cor. Here's the Lieutenant and Dol; now behave yourself like a man.

Bid. Could you show me how to behave myself like an honest man? That's out of your way, I doubt.

Dol. Still better and better! This confirms me.

Bid. Well, give me thy hand. I'm resolv'd to be very virtuous and very merry, and never think more of thee.

Cor. Well, Mrs. Dol, here's one has consented in part to marry you.

Dol. Pretty creature!

Bid. Ugly toad! [*Aside.*

Dol. Well, and will you be content to ride before me lovingly a days?

Lieut. Ay, and behind thee, too; ride thee all points o' th' compass, wench, fear not!

Bid. O Lord! but is there so many ways of riding, Lieutenant?

Lieut. Hast thou liv'd to these years and not known that yet?

Cor. Well, but when will you marry?

Bid. Nay, by my faith, let us woo first and then marry, because I believe there is more pleasure in wooing than in the effects of it.

Cor. Why do not you begin and court her, then?

Bid. Nay, by my faith, let her begin first.

Lieut. That's not the mode, for the woman to woo the man.

Bid. That is if the man love the woman; but that's not my case, for 'tis she loves me, not I her.

Lieut. Oh, but in complaisance you must begin. It is not civil to put a woman to 't.

Bid. Not I, faith. Pray, forsooth, do you begin.

Dol. Indeed it shall be yours.

Bid. I protest it shall be yours; therefore begin, or I vow I'll break off the match.

Dol. Nay, rather than so, I'll begin. Sweet sir, I am much and greatly asham'd.

Bid. Were you ever so before, mistress?

Dol. Yes, truly, I have been asham'd, but it is so long since——

Bid. That you have forgot it, I suppose. But I disturb you, forsooth?

Dol. No disturbance, sweet sir; I want fine words to express my love in. I am sorry that the cart-wheel of fortune should drive me into the coach-box of your affection.

Bid. Fortune will take it scurvily to call her wheel a cart-wheel; besides, coach-box and cart-wheel did never agree in this world yet.

Dol. I am not able to express my love as it deserves; but I have four hundred pounds in gold, if that will do it.

Bid. By my faith, you express yourself very well, and I will woo you heartily for it. Madam, you have struck me with such a desperate dart from those fair somewhat or other that you have about you. Are you sure you have the gold you spoke of?

Dol. Yes, my dear heart, very sure.

Bid. Then if I do not love you above all woman-kind, perish me, and sink me, refuse me, rot me, and renounce me!

Cor. Hold, hold, hold! do you call this wooing?

Bid. Yes, faith; I had a sister cast away with the very same speech, therefore do not interrupt me, for I know all mankind woos thus.   And as I was swearing, madam, the devil take——

Lieut. Enough, enough, enough, enough!

Bid. But, madam, are you satisfied?

Dol. I am, to the full, and do believe you.

Bid. But if you please, madam, now my hand is in, to accept of a hundred or two of oaths more.

Dol. No, no, no—by no means; I believe you without 'em, and I am yours.

Bid. I have not sworn out half my alphabet yet.

Dol. You have done sufficiently, indeed.

Bid. Well, give me your hand, then.   You are the first woman, certainly, that was ever gain'd with so little swearing.

Cor. Thou hast wooed her and won her most bravely!

Bid. Have I? Why, then, I'm thine.   But hark you, Lieutenant and Cornet, we will be married privately, and in the dark, because her face shall not turn my stomach.   Madam, I have one ill-humour—I cannot abide a woman with a bare face; therefore, if I could buy you a masque that would stick to your face and never come off, I believe I should love you very well.

Dol. I'll have a masque, or what you please, my
          dear;

          Next bout, I hope, will be my turn to jeer.

Lieut. Come! let's in, and visit our new quarters.   [*Exeunt.*

Enter RAGGOU *making quarters,* CONSTABLES,
          and NEIGHBOURS.

1 *Neigh.* I beseech your worship do not quarter so many upon me; I'm but a poor man.

2 *Neigh.* Alas, poor man! you have overcharg'd him.   Rogue, he has more money than half the town!

Rag. You be a dam dog to betray your neighbour. Who would tink to find de devel in a
country bumpkin? Begar, me vill make use of
your devilry.

1 *Neigh.* I pray your worship, take four horse
from me.

Rag. You be a dam rich dog; begar, you sall
have a squadron upon you if you no understand
me.

1 *Neigh.* How should I understand you?

Rag. You be a dam dog; begar, me vill put
twenty horse upon your back till you understand
a moi! Vat vill you give me if I take all de horse
from you?

1 *Neigh.* Indeed I'll pray for your worship.

Rag. O ho! be dat all? Do you understand noting but prayer? Divel, you fool! vat be prayer to
de quarteer-master? But can you pray in French?

1 *Neigh.* Alas! not I, an't please you.

Rag. Den, begar, your English prayer will no
save a Frenchman; you sall have ten arse more fo
dat.

2 *Neigh.* An't please you, monsieur, I understand you.

Rag. You sall have no arse upon you.

3 *Neigh.* And I understand you very well, sir.

Rag. Begar, you have very mush, a great deal of
understanding!

3 *Neigh.* Here are more of our neighbours that
understand you, sir.

Rag. Begar, den me undestand too! Get all your
money togedra, and put in my pocket yourself; den
me can swear, begar, me never take no penny of
you, aha!

3 *Neigh.* We will do it gladly, sir, and pray for
you too.

Rag. Begar, me no care for dat. But you dam
dog that no understan a moi sall quarteer all de
troop; and den look to your wife, for, begar, Flea-
Flint vill so get your shild for you.   [*Exeunt.*

Enter FLEA-FLINT, FERRET-FARM, BURNDORP,
    LIEUTENANT, CORNET, RAGGOU, *and* DOL.

Burn. Lieutenant, we have done the work.
Fer. We have burnt seven towns.
Flea. We have rais'd fourscore pound.
Lieut. Y' are dexterous at your trade—you have
made quick despatch ; but peace, we'll share anon!
                                            [*Aside.*
Now you're welcome. Come, where's the boors o'
th' house ? We'll see what my quarters can afford.
Where are you all ? What house here, ho ?

Enter WOMAN *and* MAID.

Wom. What want you, sir ?
Lieut. Art thou the woman o' th' house ?
Wom. Yes, sir ; a poor woman.
Lieut. Art thou poor ?—what a pox do I in such
a quarter ? Why, Quarter-Master Raggou, is this
the best house in the village ?
Rag. Zoun! hang 'em, they're very rich dog; but
you sall have no meat for yourself, no oat for your
arses, but her dam husband vill feast you all wid
pray for you.
Lieut. Diable, you Rotterdam whore, I'll make
you bring out your things ! Where's your cows,
your calves, and your sheep ?
Wom. Alas ! we have none, sir.
Cor. Hast thou any drink, good woman ?
Wom. No, truly, we have none.
Flea. Nor hast thou no wine nor strong water,
good woman ?

Wom. No, indeed, we have none.

Rag. Why, den, a pax take you, good woman!

Lieut. No hens, nor turkeys, nor swine, nor nothing?

Rag. Hang her! begar, she hide everyting when dey hear me come to make a de quarteer.

Fer. Send to the market town and buy provisions, and be hang'd, or I'll set fire o' your house, you damn'd dery damn'd whore!

Rag. Zoun, dis dam coward, how he domineer over de bumpkin woman!

Woman. Alas, we have no money, sir ;—not we.

Fer. What dost thou tremble and shake so for? What a pox ails thee?

Cor. What shall we do? Threat'ning will not serve the turn.

Lieut. Do but second me, and I'll make 'em bring out all they have, I warrant you! Do but talk as if we us'd to eat children.

Fer. 'Tis enough!

Lieut. Why, look you, good woman ; we do believe you are poor, so we'll make a shift with our old diet. You have children i' th' town?

Wom. Why do you ask, sir?

Lieut. Only have two or three to supper. Flea-Flint, you have the best way of cooking children!

Flea. I can powder 'em to make you taste your liquor. I'm never without a dried child's tongue or ham.

Wom. Oh, bless me!

Flea. Mine's but the ordinary way ; but Ferret-Farm is the man : he makes you the savouriest pie of a child's chaldron that ever was eat.

Lieut. A pox! all the world cannot cook a child like Monsieur Raggou.

Rag. Begar, me tink so ; for vat was me bred in

de King of Mogul's kitchen for? Tere ve kill twenty
shild of a day! Take you one shild by both his
two heels and put his head between your two leg,
den take your great a knife and slice off all de
buttack, so fashion; begar, dat make a de best
Scots collop in de varle!

Lieut. Ah! he makes the best pottage of a child's
head and purtenance! But you must boil it with
bacon. Woman, you must get bacon!

Fer. And then it must be very young.

Lieut. Yes, yes. Good woman, it must be a fine
squab child, of half a year old; a man-child. Dost
hear?

Wom. O Lord! yes, sir.

Rag. Do you hear? Get me one she-shild, a
littel whore-shild, and save me all de lamb-stone
and sweetbread, and all de pig-petty-toe of de
shild. Do you hear, you Roundhead whore?

Wom. Ay, sir, ay. O that ever I should live to
see such men!   [*Exit.*

Lieut. I warrant you it works. If there be provision in the country, we shall have it.

Flea. How the whore trembled for fear!

Cor. We shall have all the women in the village
about our ears. Hide-bound whores! it's a question whether they'll part with their meat or their
children first.

Lieut. This foolery will be noised about the
country, and then the odium will never be taken
off.

Cor. Why, what can they make on't? All understanding people will know it to be mirth.

Lieut. I know they will; but the envious priests
will make fine talk on't, and make a great advantage on't too. Though they know it to be nothing
but mirth, they'll preach their parishioners into a

real belief of it, on purpose to make us odious. They'll preach against anything. I heard a scandalous sermon of two hours long against Prince Rupert's dog.

Cor. Come! 'tis no matter what hypocrites preach; let us see what the event will be!

[*Exeunt.*

Enter WOMEN *in a fright, alarmed by their Neighbour.*

Wom. Look to your children! If ever you mean to see your children alive, hide your children: they'll eat your children!

1 *Neigh.* Woe is me! what's the matter, neighbour?

Wom. I say, hide your children.

2 *Neigh.* Ah! good neighbour, what's the matter?

Wom. Why, run away with your children!

3 *Neigh.* Why, that ever we were born! What's the matter?

Wom. They will eat our children.

4 *Neigh.* Oh, these bloody cavaliers! How! eat our children?

Wom. They talk of boiling your children.

All. Oh, mercy on us!

Wom. And roasting your children.

All. Oh, bloody villains!

Wom. And baking your children.

1 *Neigh.* Oh, hellish cavaliering devils!

Wom. There's nothing to be thought of but hiding your children.

1 *Neigh.* I would mine were in my belly again!

Wom. That's not safe; they'll search there in the first place, to be sure.

2 *Neigh.* I'll hide mine in the straw.

Wom. And so we shall have one of 'em lay you down a-top of it, and smother one child whilst he is getting another. I say, run away with your children !

3 *Neigh.* Oh, bloody wretches ! I have heard much of their getting children, but never of their eating children before.

4 *Neigh.* Neighbour, their getting of children might be borne with ; but eating 'em was never heard of.

Wom. They have got a cook from the Great Mogul on purpose to kill children ; and they talk of roasting their haunches, and baking the chaldron, and broiling the chine.

Maid. And making pottage of the child's head and purtenance.

All. Oh, deliver our poor children !

Wom. Do you stand whining and crying? Fetch out your sheep, and your calves, your hens, your pigs, and your geese, and your bacon ; for there's no other way to save your children.

All. Ay, with all our hearts !

1 *Neigh.* I'll bring two fat sheep.

2 *Neigh.* I'll bring turkeys and hens.

3 *Neigh.* I have a brave fat calf, worth eleven nobles ; by my troth, I had as lieve part with one of my children.

Wom. Oh, you uncharitable beast ! Go fetch your calf. Run, everybody, and bring your things to my house as fast as you can drive ! [*Exeunt.*

Enter LIEUTENANT, CORNET, FLEA-FLINT, FERRET-FARM, BURNDORP, *and* RAGGOU.

Lieut. Meat or children to supper, for a wager, gentlemen?

Cor. Meat, for a wager, if they have it.

Lieut. Ay, without doubt ; for never was woman and children so alarmed in this world.

Flea. When they were got together, and told their children would be eaten, they set up their throats and made a more horrid noise than a Welsh hubbub, or an Irish dirge.

Enter NURSE *with two children.*

Fer. How now ! what think you if we be put to eat children indeed? By this light, here's a woman with two children !

Lieut. We shall be crossbit with these country whores. What shall we do ?

Rag. Begar, me vill help you off; you sall eat no shildren !

Nurse. By your leaves, your good worships, I make bold to bring you in some provisions.

Fer. Provisions ! Where—where is thy provisions ?

Nurse. Here, an't please you. I have brought you a couple of fine fleshy children.

Cor. Was ever such a horrid whore? What shall we do ?

Nurse. Truly, gentlemen, they're as fine squab children—shall I turn 'em up ? They have the bravest brawny buttocks !

Lieut. No, no ! But, woman, art thou not troubled to part with thy children ?

Nurse. Alas ! they are none of mine, sir ; they are but nurse-children.

Rag. Dere be a dam whore for you !

Lieut. What a beast is this ! Whose children are they ?

Nurse. A Londoner's, that owes me for a year's nursing. I hope they'll prove excellent meat. They're twins, too !

Rag. Aha! but, begar, we never eat no twin-shild; de law forbid dat. But, hark you! have any woman with shild in de town?

Nurse. Yes, half a dozen.

Rag. Lieutenant, it be de best meat in de varle! Begar, a woman with shild is better meat den one hen with egg at Shrovetide.

Enter LANDLADY *and* WOMEN *with provisions.*

Lieut. How now! what news, landlady?

Wom. Here is a great many poor women that have brought in provisions, in hope you'll spare their children.

1 *Neigh.* We beseech your worships, spare our poor children, and you shall want for nothing our country can afford!

Lieut. Good woman, we are content to spare your children, but you must get us some strong drink.

2 *Neigh.* Ay, ay; we'll get you everything you want.

Lieut. Why, then, go all home, and be contented; for we promise you, if we eat any children, it shall be the two nurse-children.

All. Ah, —— preserve you all, gentlemen!

Rag. Take some comfort, for if we should eat your shildren you sall no be a loser by dat; for look you, good woman, how many shildren we eat in a parish so many shild we are bound to get before we leave it. Dat is very fair.

[*Exeunt* WOMEN.

Lieut. Why, is not this better than fasting?

Flea. Well, and what harm is there in all this?

Cor. None i' th' world. Come, let's in and dress our supper!

Rag. Me will go eat at my own quarteer. It be

a brave ting to be in office. Begar, de clowns
worship me as if me were deir great god Bumpkin !

[*Exeunt.*

ACT IV.—SCENE I.

LIEUTENANT, FLEA-FLINT, FERRET-FARM, *and*
BURNDORP.

Flea. Lieutenant, here's all our country crew
that we plundred yesterday.

Fer. But our comfort is they know us not, but
cry out of a Frenchman, with two coat sleeves
stuffed like two country bag-puddings.

Lieut. This cunning rogue has crossbit you all.
He has been plundering as he went to make his
quarters, and in a buff coat too ; for here is a
dozen fellows at my quarter, and they all describe
a rogue so like thee that I protest thou wilt
suffer for it. Nay, the rogue called himself Flea-
Flint too !

Flea. Ouns ! what shall we do, sir ?

Lieut. Upon my word, this is no jesting business.

Fer. 'Sheart, over-reached thus !

Lieut. You must e'en think of over-reaching
him again. You must first think of stopping the
clamour of the bumpkins ; that's your first point
of security.

Flea. But, Lieutenant, how should we do't ?
Faith, you must try your wits, and stick to us.

Lieut. I knew you would venture so far 'twould
come to my turn to fetch you off at last, rogues.

Flea. Why, sir, my man and his both shall
swear Raggou borrowed a buff coat of them.

Lieut. Let him be gone first, and then you may swear anything. One of you go, tell the bumpkins I am searching for the rogue; the rest go with me to Raggou. [*Exit* FERRET-FARM.

Burn. This is his quarter.

Lieut. This? Knock! It seems to be the best house i' th' town. [*Knocks.*

Maid. Who would you speak with? [*Within.*

Lieut. With Monsieur Raggou.

Maid. Sir, he gave us strict charge to let nobody speak with him.

Lieut. But I must and will speak with him.

Maid. Indeed, sir, he charged us, upon pain of his displeasure, not to disturb him.

Lieut. Pain of his displeasure! What an impudent rogue's this! Show us, show us!

[RAGGOU *is discovered in a taffata bed, with a back, breast, and head-piece on.*

How now!—what! in taffata curtains? The impudent rogue makes me laugh. You rascal, Raggou! Look, in his head-piece, too!

Rag. Who de devel disturb me? You dam whore, you know vat me do to you last night!

Lieut. Why, what was that you did to her last night?

Rag. Begar, me lie with her at three motion, as de musketier shoot off his gun—make ready, present, and give fire.

Lieut. O' my word, that's good discipline!

Rag. Begar, she sall make ready for you, if you will present and give fire.

Lieut. But how came it that I had not this good quarter?

Rag. Because me knew me should make a de quarter but one night; and so, begar, me make a de best use of my time, as all the whole varle do too.

Lieut. But what a rogue art thou! Why dost thou lie in such a bed in thy arms?

Rag. For two gran reason, sir. First, because my French louse sall go great way about before he come to de clean sheet; next, because a de dam English flea shall not bite a my sweet French body.

Lieut. Well, maid, go down; I must speak with him. [*Exit* MAID.

Rag. Vat you have wid me, Lieutenant?

Lieut. Faith, out of my love I would save thee from hanging.

Rag. Hang! For vat? Begar, hang me if me deserve, so you hang all dat deserve a de hang. Begar, dat is de whole troop—Lieutenant and all!

Lieut. Here you plunder in one shape, and there in another—sometimes, like Flea-Flint, in buff; sometimes like yourself,—that here is all the country come in with such horrid complaints. Nay, they say you ravish women too!

Rag. Lieutenant, begar, me never ravish but one old woman, and she give me five shilling for my pain.

Lieut. Nay, here is worse than all that; my Captain has intelligence you're a dangerous man, and hold correspondence with the enemy.

Rag. Me sall be hang, Lieutenant, if you tink so.

Lieut. Nay, 'tis so; I have orders to search you. Put that in his pocket, and pull it out again.
[*Aside.*

Rag. Ah, begar, me have no long life before me be hang!

Burn. Oh, sir! are you good at that? He was going to convey letters out on 's pocket.

Rag. Begar, he lie, Lieutenant; me have no

M

lettra! Begar, hang a me if me can write an read! De hornbook be de Hebrew to me, begar!

Lieut. Search him, search him.

[*Search, and pulls a letter out and an engine.*

Burn. Here's a letter, Lieutenant, and an engine, I think.

Flea. What's this?

Lieut. Oh, you need not write and read if you have this. I'll be hanged if this be not the key of his character he writes to the enemy with.

Rag. Dat make a de French pie, and make a de garniture for de dish; dat be all!

Lieut. Let's see. The case is plain; he sent his intelligence in characters of paste. This very thing will hang him. But let's read the letter.

Rag. Begar, me have no lettra! De devil send it in my pocket!

Lieut. (*Reads*) "Monsieur Raggou, in hope that under this poor disguise of a French cook you will show a rich faith"——

Rag. Vat he mean by fait? Begar, me have no fait!

Lieut. (*Reads*) "And when you have delivered up your troop to us, the Parliament will own you as yourself, and give you the respects due to your great and honourable family."

Rag. Devel, me have no honourable, nor family neider, begar!

Flea. The case is plain; you are of some great family.

Rag. Lieutenant, me confess me come of de King of France kitchin, of de honourable family of de Turn-spit. Begar, me tell you true, dere be all my family, and my honourable too.

Burn. Oh, sir, 'tis a very cunning fellow. My Captain sends word he used to be conversant with the Roundheads, and pray with them.

Rag. The devil take a me, me never pray in my life! Me swear altogedra in de King of France kitchin!

Lieut. I love you so well that I'd be loth to hang you, monsieur; therefore I'm content to let you 'scape. But be sure you be not taken.

Rag. Begar, den hang a moi, for my arse vill no go very far.

Lieut. Well, pray be gone, and say you found a friend.

Rag. Gad a bless you, Lieutenant. Ven me come in France, zoun, me vill so pray for you!

Flea. And yet you say you never prayed in your life.

Rag. Begar, me tank Gad me never have occasion to pray till just now. Adieu, adieu—a—— Who send me dat dam lettra in my pocket?
[*Exit.*

Lieut. Well, now we must keep the bumpkins here till he is gone, and then give 'em orders to search the countries for him.

Burn. And that will whidle them as well as if you had given them their money again. [*Exeunt.*

Enter GOVERNOR, CAPTAIN HOLDFORTH, MR. TELL-TROTH, *and* CAPTAIN TUBTEXT.

Hold. In truth, drinking is a harmless recreation so we proceed not to drunkenness.

Tub. Pray, how far forth may we proceed in drink? for I would take no more than is fit to be taken with a safe conscience.

Tell. Why, Captain Tubtext, if thy belly were as large as thy conscience, by that computation the great tun at Heidelberg would be just thy morning's draught.

Tub. Here is old Tom Tell-Troth! ha, ha, ha!

Hold. In truth, if he were not very faithful, we should never away with his boldness.

Tub. Well said, Captain Holdforth! But to the question: How far may we proceed in drink?

Gov. As far as the innocent recreation of knocking one another down with cushions come to. It is the exercise of our superior officers.

Hold. I have observed, indeed, they do three things together: they drink, then practise pulpit faces——

Tell. To cheat the people with!

Tub. Ha, ha, ha! In truth, you hit so home!

Hold. And the third is throwing of cushions. The practising and dissembling of holy looks is of great use and design.

Tub. And drinking and throwing cushions a great refreshment to the body.

Gov. As, for example.   [*Throws a cushion.*

Hold. Ha, ha, ha! I have seen our grandee throw a cushion at the man with the great thumb, and say, "Colonel, wilt thou be a cobbler again?"
          [*Throws a cushion.*

All. Ha, ha, ha!

Tub. Come, here's to you, Governor! you, Colonel *Goldsmith*, with a conscience as dirty as a blacksmith, will you sell thimbles again?
          [*Throws a cushion.*

All. Ha, ha, ha!

Hold. Noble Colonel, wilt thou brew ale again?
          [*Throws a cushion.*

What an everlasting cheat is reformation and false doctrine! It has raised us from cobblers to commanders.

Tub. There is no other way to raise rebellion but by religion.

All. Ha, ha, ha!

Gov. I never knew the use of religion before.

Tub. The women tickle like trouts at it. Ha, ha, ha! [*All laugh.*

Tell. I believe the country will find it so, for I hear of twenty wenches with child.

Gov. In truth, I wonder at the witchcraft of it; for, notwithstanding the people have been bit through the chine-bone with it, yet, for all that, before the old wound is healed, they are ready to run after the lanthorn of new lights again. Ha, ha, ha!

Tell. Well, sirs, since you are in such an ingenious way of confessing, tell me one thing. Do not you wish your garrison a-fire, so you were at home with all the wealth you've got?

Tub. Thought's free. But talk no more of that; these are both treacherous rogues; I dare not trust 'em.

Tell. Well, you are merry, sirs; but faith, be plain, sirs. What says my seeming saint that drinks by the conscience? Dost not wish thyself at home, wallowing in thy plunder?

Hold. You might find a better name for it. Hark in your ear! we are all such treacherous rogues, we dare not trust one another, but we'll talk in private.

Gov. But our contribution women will come in anon.

Hold. Ha, ha, ha! In truth, they edify as one would have 'em.

Tell. Well, now, you ought to be serious, and consider the enemy's approaching.

Tub. In truth, a good occasion to fetch in all the goods and chattels of the country, upon pretence of securing them, and so make conditions with the enemy to march away with them. I see we shall be rascals to the last gasp.

Hold. And so we shall have provisions for a long siege.

Gov. I'll make your siege short enough.

[*Exit* GOVERNOR *and one* CAPTAIN.

Tub. You are faithful; they are rogues. Read that, and tell me whether you will undertake or no.   [*Gives* TELL-TROTH *a letter, and exit.*

Tell. How very good! Is't possible? This is a greater rogue in his own nature than the devil's invention can make him. He would not only betray his trust, but deliver up all the rest of the garrison to mercy, conditionally that he may have all their wealth, and safe convoy to his own house. I need lay no plot; 'tis done to my hand. I love the King well; yet my own ends are mingled, because I have a mistress among 'em, and cannot have her but by serving the King. And I believe most men have their reasons for their loyalty as well as I; so that, good king, wheresoe'er you see me, trust to yourself. Yet I will do something. What if I betrayed this rogue and his letter to the Governor, to secure myself? But then, if they have a mind to deliver up the garrison, 'twill make 'em shy of me. I find I have a hard task on't.

Enter GOVERNOR.

Gov. O, Tell-Troth, I came to ask thee a question; and what thinkst thou?

Tell. Troth, I know not.

Gov. To know whether thou lov'st me truly or no.

Tell. If you be serious, I could be angry with you for raising such a doubt. To show you that I love you (I do not say your cause, but you), read there. Look you, one of your Captain Rogues gave me that letter; and the other gave me a whisper to the same purpose, too.

Gov. Is 't possible? What 's to be done with these villains?

Tell. Something must be done; they 'll betray you else.

Gov. I thank thy honesty; I find it so.

Tell. Shall I speak boldly? Serve 'em in their own kind.

Gov. In troth, I had it in my head before to betray 'em, for the rogues are rich.

Tell. Come! let not you and I be shy of one another. Do it yet! ,

Gov. Art thou in earnest?

Tell. By my life; and I will put you in a way, too.

Gov. Let 's in, and consider how. Had we best secure 'em?

Tell. No. First command their two companies out, then draw 'em into several parties, and then with your own company disarm 'em, and so clap them up and their officers; then show 'em the reason (this letter). When that's done, send the letter to the Parliament, and write how you have secured 'em; which will so ingratiate you with them that you'll never be suspected for betraying on 't yourself.

Gov. My worthy friend, shall I fall on my knees and worship thee?

Tell. Let 's be wise, and about our business.

[*Exeunt.*

Enter CORNET *and two* TROOPERS.

Cor. Where have you been, sirs?

1 *Troop.* Why, we have been to take Flea-Flint. My captain is resolved to hang him.

Cor. For what?

2 *Troop.* For plund'ring, and so forth. But the rogue has intelligence of it, and is gone; but he is in as bad a case as Raggou, for we must send hue and cry after him.   [*Exeunt.*

Enter RAGGOU.

Rag. Ah, *jan povera de moi!* my arse can no carry me from de danger of de hang a de moi; and yet me have spur two such great hole in his rib dat you may creep quite trow him. Me must go change mine coat and mine hat; begar, me sall be known by dat! Vat come here now?

Enter FRENCHMAN *with a Show.*

What come?

French. Come! who see my fine shite, my rare shite? Who see my fine shite, my rare shite?

Rag. Monsieur, where you go wid your shite?

French. To de Bristol Fair, monsieur.

Rag. Dis Frenchman look as if he will be hang. Begar, me vill put a de sheat of de hang upon him! Monsieur, begar me have de very fine shite too, and it vill come de Bristol Fair too. It be de great vonder of de varle; it be de great fat dromadory. You hear of dat?

French. Wee, wee; all de varle know de fat dromadory.

Rag. Begar, you and me vill join partiner in de Fair, because you be my countryman.

French. Ay, monsieur, and tank you too.

Rag. We vill give out in de bill of de two famous Frenchman; one inventra de show of all trade, and de oder make a de invent of de fat dromadory.

French. Monsieur, wid all my heart!

Rag. Very good. You sall go take a de best house in de town. Dere be two piece, two jacoby for you ; get some vera good dinner. You sall take a my coat and de hat, and leave your show wid me, for my waggon will come wid my dromadory presan.

French. I had good luck to light o' this Frenchman. [*Aside.*

Rag. Begar, me have betra luck to light o' dis Frenchman ! So, help me wid your wastcoat— vera good. So, now, make all de haste in de varle. Adieu, adieu ! [*Exit* FRENCHMAN. So now, begar, me be very safe ! But how de devil sall me show mine shite ? Begar, me forget to ask vat language all de puppet in de show speak. *Parla Francois, Monsieur Puppey ? Owieda.* Aha ! very good !

Enter CONSTABLES.

1 *Con.* Sure we shall catch this fellow at last, for we hear of him everywhere.

2 *Con.* Ay, his two sleeves stuffed, and his French hat edged with ribbons, will discover him.

Rag. Diable, dere be de constable and Mr. Hue-Cry come to catch a me.—Who see my shite, my rare shite, my fine shite ? Begar, me sall shite myself indeed !

1 *Con.* What a pox does he mean ?

2 *Con.* He would have you see his show.

1 *Con.* Come, faith, let us. You, fellow, come, let's see your show !

Rag. How sall me do now ? Begar, me must show it as well as me can.

2 *Con.* Sirrah, did not you see a Frenchman pass by ?

Rag. Frenchman ? Vat have he upon him ?

1 *Con.* Why, he has a greasy coat with the sleeves stuffed out.

Rag. A pox take him! Begar, he rob me just now of two piece—all me have in de varle! Dat make a me cry.

2 *Con.* O rogue, rascal!—alas to-day! Give him a crown, churchwarden; we are at the parish charge.

1 *Con.* Come, do not cry, poor fellow; let's see thy shite. There's a crown for thee!

Rag. A Gad bless you! Here be de brave shite of de varle!—here be de King of Spain play on de bagpipe to his Privy Council. Dat's a very good jest. Den dere be de King of Solomon; he give judgment upon de wise child. Dere is de first act. Now, put on your hat, and look upon all de lady. [*Plays and sings.*

> "Jam more cum povera bla cum povera,
> Jam, jam, jam, jam tomba nette,
> Jam, jang tombe nette equbla."

Now, here be de Queen of Swiveland. She sit in great majesty; her leg hang over de chair, vera full of temptation—make your chops watra. Vera good jest. Den dere be de whore of Babylon; she make great love to de May-pole in de Stran. Second act.

> "Jam more cum povera," etc.
> [*Plays and sings.*

Dere be de King of Denmarks and Norvay learning to juggle of de Bishop of Munsera. Dat's a very good jest. Dere be de silent ministra; he make a de long preach in de play-house. Dere is tre act; dat is all.

2 *Con.* I thought your plays had always had five acts?

Rag. Dey be de great puppet have five act; de little puppet have but tre. Vill you go catch dis dam dog for me, and get a my money for me agen, my two jacoby? Begar, me be undone if you no catch dis dam dog for me!

1 *Con.* We'll away. We'll have him, I warrant thee! [*Exeunt.*

Rag. Begar, me be very fine sheat, if it vill hold out. But hold a—vat if dey catch my coat? Begar, den dey vill hang a my coat. But dam dog vill confess me have his show, den. Begar, me sall be hang wid mine coat. Begar, me vill put away mine show!

Enter FLEA-FLINT, *with Hue and Cry after him.*

Who de devil is dat?

Flea. A pox on't! I must be robbing alone, and without my Lieutenant's advice. I must be careful, or suffer for it. The rogues follow me with hue and cry; I am not able to go farther; I must change my clothes. How now—what fellow's this? 'Sheart, would I could persuade him out of his show, and take my cloak for it!

Rag. Begar, would me could persuade him to take my show, and give me de cloak for dat!

Flea. Come hither, honest fellow.

Rag. Devil, it is Flea-Flint! Ah, me be povera de moy; begar, me be half-hang already. Me vill no speak French, begar, den he vill know me; me vill belch Dutch at him. Yaw, *min heer.*

Flea. Come hither, honest man. What's that? —a show?

Rag. Yaw, *min heer.* Begar, me vill slit my mouth from one ear to de odra to speak good Dutch; and den when me speak French, begar,

me vill sew it up again.   Dere's a vera good trick
to save a my life !

Flea. Fellow, wilt thou sell thy show ?

Rag. Yaw, *min heer.* Begar, dis Dutch make me
vera sick.   Look ! begar, every time me cry *Yaw,
min heer,* dere come up a pickle herring with it.
Yaw—look, dere it go !

Flea. Art thou a Dutchman ?

Rag. Yaw, verathticke.

Flea. Where hab you de neder lands go Weston ?

Rag. Diable, vat sall me say ?   Begar, me have
no more Dutch !

Flea. Hab you de neder lands go west Lanceman ?

*Rag. Ich haben de Hoigh Dutch lander goe weston
Lanceman.*

Flea. Nay, it may be what Dutch it will, for I
can speak no more.

*Rag. Ick maken weel vander slapan can helder
hought.*

Flea. But wilt thou sell thy show?

Rag. Yaw, yaw, ick vill van hundred gilder haben.

Flea. That's ten pound ; that's too much.   I
would I had it at any rate !

Rag. Begar, never fear ! you sall have it.

Flea. Wilt thou take five pound ?

Rag. Neave ick ; ick maken de show myself,
and ick maken dat better as dis, and dat's better
as dat, and dat's better as all, begott.

Flea. I hear 'em coming.   Here's ten pound
for thee, and I'll give thee my cloak to boot,
and hat.

Rag. Dere be my show and my cap.   Me tank
you, Lanceman.   So, dis dam rogue never do no
good in all his life before ; and me hope, begar, he
vill be hang for dat !   [*Exit.*

Flea. Now, what shall I do with this show, for

I cannot show it ? Why, if anybody would see it, I must say it's locked up, the key is gone before to Bristol Fair; that's all I have for't.

Enter CONSTABLES, *looking for* FLEA-FLINT.

4 *Con.* Come, sirs, we shall have him at last.

3 *Con.* Stay, sirs—what fellow's this ? Who are you, sir ?

Flea. A poor man, master, going with my show to the Fair, to get a penny; and a rogue has robbed me of all I have, almost ten pound !

4 *Con.* O damned rogue ! Had he not a gray cloak and hat ?

Flea. Ay (wicked villain !), the same, master.

3 *Con.* It's the same rogue we are looking for; we shall have him i' th' Fair, I warrant you. Let's away ! [*Exeunt* CONSTABLES.

Flea. This rogue thinks himself so safe now, and he'll be hanged sure enough if they catch him.

Enter the first CONSTABLES *with him that had* RAG-GOU'S *clothes.*

1 *Con.* Look you, there's the notorious rogue with the show. Take him !

Flea. What would you have with me, gentlemen ?

French. Begar, me vill have my show from you !

Flea. Pox take you and your show ! A damned rogue that had it has robbed me of ten pound and my hat and cloak.

1 *Con.* Come, these are both rogues ; bring 'em away !

1 *Watch.* Hold ! it will do us no good to have them hanged ; what if we plunder them, as they use to do us ?

Con. 'Tis a very good notion. Do you hear ?

We are to ask you a question. Will you be hanged or be plundered ?

Flea. I'll be hanged before I part with my money.

2 *Watch.* Then let's hang him; we can take his money when he is dead.

Con. Then do you hang him.

Enter BUMPKIN, *passing over the stage.*

1 *Watch.* Not I; I know not how to hang him.

2 *Watch.* Troth, hang him yourself, if you'll have him hanged.

Con. Dost hear, brother Bumpkin? I'll give thee an angel, and hang this fellow.

      [CONSTABLE *calls to the* BUMPKIN.

Bump. It is not worth while for one, but I'll take angels apiece to hang you all.

Con. Hang you, rascal! Come, there, fall on, boys, and plunder him.   [*Plunder* FLEA-FLINT.

Flea. Pray you, gentlemen, give me some money again to bear my charges home.

Con. There's a crown for thee, and farewell !

      [*Exeunt all but* BUMPKIN.

Bump. Hey day ! this will prove a very wonder,
  That Bumpkin should soldier plunder.

ACT V.—SCENE I.

Enter a JOINER, SERVANT, *and a* PAINTER *at one door, and* RAGGOU *at another.*

Serv. Joiner, make haste, and set your t'other post up; and painter, fetch your colours, your pots, and pipkins, and paint this post in the mean-time. It must be despatched before the people are stirring.

Paint. My things are all ready, sir, at the next house. We can scarce see to work yet.

Serv. And be hanged, then! Go, get some ale to clear your eyesight; I'll warrant you'll see the bottom of the pot well enough without daylight.

Join. Make what haste you can ; I'll bring my post as soon as you'll be ready to paint it. [*Exit.*

Paint. I'd laugh at that, i'faith ! But, friend, what noise was this all night ? I think the watch was searching for somebody.

Serv. Ay, ay ; hark, you may hear 'em searching still. Why, it seems 'tis a kind of outlandish Frenchman that they look for ; he has a gray hat and a gray cloak. But come, let us mind our business, and make haste. [*Exeunt.*

Rag. Dat be· me. Dey slander a moy ; me be no outlandish Frenchman—begar, me be a French Frenchman ! Hark, dey come ! Vat sall me do ? Begar, me vill stand for de odra post till de dam bumpkin be gone. A pox take 'em !—de devil could not hue and cry me so close. How sall me do to be like a dat post ? Hark, dey come now !

[RAGGOU *gets upon the post, and sits in the posture of the other post.*

Enter CONSTABLE *and* WATCH.

Con. Pox o' this outlandish French fellow for me !—I 'm as dry as a dog.

1 *Watch.* So we are all ; let's go and knock 'em up at an alehouse, and eat and drink a little.

2 *Watch.* With all our hearts.

Enter PAINTER.

Honest painter, canst tell where we may have a little ale ?

Paint. Ay, sure; two or three doors off you'll find 'em up, and a good fire, where you may toast your noses, boys.

Con. Thou did'st not see an outlandish Frenchman this way?

Paint. No, I saw no Frenchman.

[*Exeunt* CONSTABLES *and* WATCH.

Why, what a devil!—this joiner has been here, and set up his post before I came. How time slips away at an alehouse!

Rag. Begar, would a good rope would slip away you too!

Paint. Now to work. [*Whistles and paints him.*

Rag. He vill paint a me; vat sall me do?

[*As he stoops,* RAGGOU *throws a stone at him.*

Paint. A pox o' these roguing prentices! Sirrah, I'll have you by the ears! A company of rogues; a man cannot work for you! If you serve me such another trick, I'll break all your windows.

Rag. De pox break all your neck!

[*Throws the pipkin at him as he stoops.*

Paint. Why, you damn'd rogue, you have broke my head. 'Sheart, I'll complain to your master. Spoil'd all my colours, too! I'll not endure it; I'll be reveng'd, whatsoe'er it cost me. [*Exit.*

Rag. A pox dis rogue!—he murder mine face wid his dam paint. Now de coast be clear, me vill take a de coat of Monsieur Jack Painter and go; for begar, dere be no stay in dis town for moy.

Enter JOINER *with his post.*

Hark! dere be someting; me must be de post agen. A pox on dat!

[*He stands up for a post again.*

Join. Why, how now?—what a devil! another post, and none of my work? 'Sheart, do you em-

ploy two men at once? I'll not be used thus; I'll
be paid for my work, and then let the devil set up
your posts. [*Exit.*

Rag. So, now, begar, me vill take de coat of de
Jack Paintra, and de post of de Jack Joiner, den
no man will suspect a moy. [*Offers to lift the post.*
Diable, it is too much heavy for moy; begar, me
betra he hang den have all dis dam joiner sit upon
me. Diable! and vould me vere in bed wid all
de king of France army. Begar, me vould fain see
vat dam English bumpkin, Mr. Hue-cry, come fetch
me from dem. [*Exit.*

Enter SERVANT, PAINTER, *and* JOINER.

Serv. Why, what a foolish fellow art thou to be
so angry! I employed no joiner but thyself.

Join. 'Sheart, there were two carved posts up,
and I'm sure I brought the third.

Serv. Thou art mad, and so is this fool too. To
complain of throwing stones at thee, when we
have ne'er a prentice, nor none within six doors
of us!

Paint. I'm sure my pipkin's broke, and my head
too; pray, look here!

Serv. Why, what's here? Here's a broken pipkin
indeed, but where's the three carved posts?

Join. There were two stood up when I came to
the house, and I set the third down here. Ouns!
my post and my tools and all's gone!

Serv. I believe you are both drunk.

Paint. Heart, man, I painted the post that stood
there.

Join. Well, and heart, man, I brought the
t'other, an' you call it heart man; and all's gone,
you see.

N

Serv. My masters, go look after your things, and make an end of your work.

Paint. Let's go search for this fellow that stole our goods here. [*Exeunt.*

Enter TELL-TROTH *and* DOL.

Tell. Oh, Dol, d'ye hear? Put her off till your friend come as before you pretended, and say you'll marry when the garrison is delivered up.

Dol. The Lieutenant and Cornet are very eager to have it despatched, that they may have the money I promised; and then they are resolved to laugh me to death.

Tell. Well, but you know it will be our turn to laugh at them, if all be right you have told me.

Dol. Upon my life, I have been faithful in all points; and I find I shall take pride in doing good since I have prospered so well in serving you.

Tell. Your reward shall answer your service. I must to the Captain, and give him an account of all I undertook, which will meet his expectation.

Dol. Let me alone to manage my undertakings.

Enter CAPTAIN *and* LIEUTENANT.

Tell. Here's the Captain. Be you gone, therefore; I would not be seen with you till I make him acquainted with everything. [*Exeunt.*

Lieut. But pray, sir, why are you thus severe now, to banish the flint-flayers?

Capt. The King's honour and interest is so abus'd with these scandalous fellows that I'm resolv'd to cashier 'em.

Enter TELL-TROTH.

Oh, friend Tell-Troth! Look you, Lieutenant, my opinion seldom fails me.

Tell. So you had some dispute, then, concerning me? Look you, sir, it's now in my power to do more than ere I hop'd for. You have a foot company?

Capt. Yes; they are now marching into the quarter. Lieutenant, see they march fair, and do no wrong. [*Exit* LIEUTENANT.

Tell. Read that! Upon my life there is but three companies, and two of 'em are disarmed and prisoners, officers and all. I laid no plot to do it. I found 'em all ready to betray one another to get the wealth; the manner how, hereafter. The governor has commissioned me to make his conditions, which must be a convoy, with all his wealth, to his own home. The country bring in their plate and goods to secure 'em from your party, and he'll make conditions with you to march away with them and so cheat the people (precious rogues!), besides what they preach the women out of.

Capt. That must not be, for the King has intelligence that they have great treasure there.

Tell. Does he know how they came by it?

Capt. Yes, very well; with the cheat of preaching; I mean tub-preaching and lectures. The lectures your wives read you never awed you so.

Tell. But faith, sir, give him his conditions!

Capt. I'll storm it first.

Tell. I intend not to have you keep conditions when you have made 'em.

Capt. That's base! I scorn that; my honour is at stake.

Tell. What! for breaking articles with a rebel? Had it been a fair enemy, I grant you. Suppose you storm it, and be beaten off? The King would give you little thanks for the punctilio of your own private honour. Let your lieutenant do it; the captain may with his honour break the conditions that his lieutenant makes.

Capt. I may approve of that; I would not have my own hand appear against me. But I am glad to see you thus earnest for the King. Sure you have some design?

Tell. By my troth, I have, but so small a one it is not worth this labour; you shall know it, for you must assist me.

Capt. With all faithfulness.

Tell. Come, then, let's sign articles! So, march and take possession. [*Exeunt.*

Enter RAGGOU *like an old woman.*

Rag. Me vill make a me nose of wax like de old woman, and vill go to Madame Dol and tell her me come from Monsieur Raggou. Vera good! And if she vill beg his pardon of de Capitain, he vill come and marry her, although her shild be born wid a shart, and back, and breast too; for, begar, me find in my conscience me had betra marry a dam whore dan be hang. [*Exit.*

Enter TELL-TROTH, CAPTAIN, LIEUTENANT, CORNET, etc., *with the* GOVERNOR *prisoner.*

Tell. Now, sir, are you satisfied in my faith?

Capt. I am so; and I have found you a worthy person. Command me to anything.

Tell. Then I'll make you merry till I go about my design. Captain Tubtext, that got the two sisters with child, is now in bed with them eating a sack posset; and that we may both shame and fright 'em, there are bears i' th' town, and other shows that are going to Bristol Fair. Now, I'll speak to the bearward to muzzle a bear, and turn him loose into the room, and I'll bring you where you shall see the sight.

Capt. Content, for I am a great lover of sports. Let not the shows go away, for I mean to celebrate Dol's wedding.

Lieut. That's kindly done. You'll need no other sport than to see Dol rant and tear when she finds she has married a girl.

Capt. But the sport will be when you and the Cornet receive your fifty pound a-piece you told me of.

Lieut. Yes, faith, we shall have it sure enough.

Capt. Yes; for 'tis deposited in my hands.

Cor. Never was jade so deeply in love; but the jest is, the girl has made conditions with Dol to put on a mask when she is marrying, for her face is so bad she cannot away with it.

Capt. Give all the troop favours; let 'em despatch, and bring them in to the baiting of the sack posset, and let the country be summoned in!

[*Exeunt.*

[TUBTEXT *and his Sisters are discovered in bed eating a sack posset.*

Enter CAPTAIN, LIEUTENANT, CORNET, *and* FERRET-FARM, *above.*

Tub. Here is this spoonful in remembrance of our sweet sister's precious fruit she goes with.

[*He puts a spoonful in each of their mouths.*
1 *Sister.* My tender and most shame-faced thanks be returned you.

Tub. Now, here is to the maiden-fruits of this our weeping sister. Wipe your tears. If they were cavaliering burthens you went with, your case were mournful ; but as they are my offspring, repent not, for your infants, be assured, will be babes of grace.

Capt. What a damn'd rogue is this !

1 *Sister.* Why, then, it seems we religious lambs may play with one another without sinning ?

Capt. Was ever such blasphemous rogues and whores ? I tremble to hear 'em. Let in the bear upon 'em !

1 *Sister.* Here is to this our sweet comforting man !

2 *Sister.* I am overjoyed to hear that religious lambs may play, and yet not sin.

[*Put their spoons in his mouth.*

Enter BEAR.

Tub. What's here ?—a bear ! Mercy upon us !

All. Help, help, help, help !

Tub. Shift for yourselves, sweet sisters.

Capt. Now bear ! now saint !

Lieut. Halloo, saint !—halloo, bear ! I'll hold a ——

Cor. Hundred pound of the bear !—thou boy bear !

Lieut. A hundred pound of the saint ! So, now, take off your bear.

Fer. By my faith, we must stave and tail him off for aught I see, Captain. I have been at many a bear-baiting, but never at a saint-bear-baiting before. [*Exit* BEAR, etc.

Capt. Now, sir, is your name Tubtext ?

Tub. Yea !

Capt. And do you think your two whores are with child with two babes of grace ?

Tub. Yea, foul mouth !

Capt. What an audacious rogue is this ! And dost thou really believe thyself in such a degree of perfection that thou canst not sin, and so need no repentance ?

Tub. Yea, sure, we are past repentance.

Capt. Thou damn'd villain, I believe thee. Blasphemous rogue ! how many poor souls hast thou deluded ? Sirrah, it were just to make thee marry these two women, and then hang thee for having two wives !

Enter FERRET-FARM.

Fer. Sir, our wedding folks are coming, and are so merry and so pleas'd that, if their joy continue, the example will make us all marry.

Enter BIDDY *as bridegroom*, TELL-TROTH *in her hand dressed in* Dol's *clothes, and* DOL *in other clothes, and* RAGGOU *dressed like an old woman with a muffler.*

Look you ! here they are, pleased as you see !

Dol. Now stand you here till I beg your pardon of my Captain.

Bid. By your leave, Captain, I have made bold to espouse your old handmaid, Dol. And give us leave to laugh, for faith my Lieutenant and Cornet has cheated her, Captain, for they have matched her to a girl. I am a very girl; and yet I have not wrong'd you, for I told you before I could not get your children.

Tell. And we laugh to think how we have cheated you; for though you cannot get my children, if I can get yours we shall do well enough.

Bid. O Lord, what's that ?—that is not Dol's voice !

Dol. Y' are i' th' right ; it is not Dol's voice, nor Dol that has married you—keep the money, Cap-

tain—but your old love, Tell-Troth. Pray have
your money, Lieutenant, before you laugh me to
death.

Bid. What! my old lover, Tell-Troth?

Tell. Now the laugh is on our side, gentlemen.
Come, be not troubled, for I am the same honest
lover that e'er I was.

Bid. Nay, I'll swear thou deserv'st me; thou art
a desperate lover to venture on a wench that has
troop'd so long under such a handsome cornet.
But he's a fool too, for if he had followed his blow
close at one time, he had had all that I could have
given him.

Tell. I had spies upon you, and am well assur'd
of your honesty. Ask Dol!

Dol. Yes, faith, I watched your water at every
turn. Do you remember he would have gone
o' th' score for your maidenhead? But you cried
'twas worth ready money at any time; but marry
me, and then halloo dog for thy silver collar. You
remember this?

Bid. Ay, to my shame I do.

Tell. What, are you ashamed that you are
honest?

Bid. No; but I'm ashamed that I lost so much
time, for I'm sure thou would'st ha' had me,
honest or not honest.

Tell. Come, be not troubled; I pass by all.

Bid. I love thee for thy confidence; give me thy
hand. By my life, I'm very honest; but I have
had as much ado to keep myself so as ever poor
wench i' th' world had.

Cor. But I hope, Biddy, you and I shall not lose
our acquaintance?

Bid. If my husband will have it so, I cannot
help it. But I hope he has more wit than ever to

let me see you again ; if you have not, husband, in good faith, at your own peril.

Tell. I'll have wit enough ; fear not !

Enter FERRET-FARM.

Fer. Sir, here's the country gentlemen come.

Capt. Pray, let 'em come in !

Enter COUNTRY GENTLEMEN.

Gentlemen, 'tis not unknown how publicly you have appeared against your Prince, and how secure you thought yourselves under the protection of these hypocrites. But, to show you what rogues they are, all the wealth that you brought hither to be secured from us, they would have made conditions to have marched away with, and so cheated the whole country ! Look you, there's their articles !—there's reformation for you !

1 *Gent.* We are deceived indeed in them—to have used us thus !

Capt. You must own, gentlemen, that all the wealth that's here is justly forfeited to the King.

2 *Gent.* We grant it, worthy Captain, and our lives to boot.

Capt. Although the wealth that's here be great, and the King's wants require it, yet, to show that he had rather have his subjects' hearts than money, he has commissioned me to return every man his own again.

1 *Gent.* Sir, this gracious act of the King, and your readiness to perform it, shall turn us all faithful subjects to the extent of our lives and fortunes.

Capt. Now, you deserve his mercy.

Dol. Sir, will you grant me a request ? Poor Raggou has sent me word, if I can beg his pardon of you, he'll marry me.

Capt. Dol, you have been instrumental to our friend Tell-Troth; I must grant you anything.

Dol. Then pray, sir, let's make a little sport with him. Who do you think that old woman is ?

Capt. I know not.

Dol. 'Tis Raggou himself. Pray, fright him a little before you seal his pardon.

Capt. What a devil has he done to his face ?

Dol. I know not. I believe he has clapt wax upon 't.

Capt. Now, good woman, what would'st thou have ?

Rag. Me come in de crowd, in hope to see a soldier hang. It would be great satisfaction to de country, truly.

Capt. Well, good woman, where dost thou dwell?

Rag. Begar, me have no dwell; vat sall me say to him ?—I live at Bristol town's end, an't please your worship.

Capt. But, woman, if thou would'st tell me where to find a plundering Frenchman called Raggou, the country should hang him with all my heart; for that's a notorious rogue, and he shall be hanged if he live above ground !

Rag. Begar, he serve a me vera well to hang me ! Vat a devil make a me come here ? Dis be my vit ! A pox on mine French vit !   [*Aside.*

Capt. Woman, find out that rascal for me. Here is ten shillings in earnest; and when thou takest him I'll make it ten pound.

Rag. But will your worship secure me that I shall have no harm if I find him ?

Capt. Ay, upon my honour, before all this company, thou shalt have no harm.

Rag. Bear witness, gentlemen. Now give me ten

pound, for, begar, me be de man ; me be Monsieur Raggou !

All. How ! Monsieur Raggou !

Rag. Wie, mafoy, ha, ha ! Me have sheat a my capitain of ten pound, and save a my life too ! Dere be de French vit ! Begar, me honour my vit very much for dat !

Capt. Call the Marshal. Take him, and hang him upon the next tree.

Rag. Hang a moy ? Did not you before vitness engage your honour dat me sall have no harm ? Begar, you vill do me great deal wrong if you hang me now !

Capt. I promised, indeed, that the old woman should have no harm ; but Raggou shall certainly be hanged.

Rag. Aha ! dere be a dam English trick vill hang a Frenchman ! But hold, hold ! if you hang Raggou, how can you save de old woman ? Dere be law case for you ! Let me have fair play for my life.

Capt. Take the old woman's garments and lay them up safe, and then they have no harm ; then my honour is clear, and here is Raggou fairly to be hanged.

Marsh. Come, come away ! 'Tis a plain case ; you must hang for 't.

Dol. Why were you such a fool as to come hither ?

Rag. For love of you, you dam whore, you !

Dol. Why would you betray yourself for ten pound ?

Rag. Dat be my cunning. De hangman sall have de ten pound because he sall no hurt a me when he hang me ! But, Capitain, begar you can no hang me in justice ; for de old woman is Raggou, and Raggou is de old woman, and de devil

can no part us.   So, if you hang Raggou, you hang
de old woman, and you hang your own honour too,
begar !

Capt. Well, sir, you have pleaded so well for
yourself, that, conditionally you will marry Dol,
I'll pardon you.

Rag. If you tink it better to marry den to be
hang, Capitain, me leave all to your judgment.

Capt. Why, then, marry her.

Rag. But who sall keep de shild ?

Capt. The troop shall keep it.

Rag. Why may not de troop as vell marry her,
and me vill make one ?   Dat's very fair, me tinks.

Capt. Nay, you may be hang'd yet if you will.

            [*He takes the woman in one hand, and the
                halter in the other.*

Rag. Let a me see.   Here be whore, and here
be halter—vera fine shoice, begar !   Me can no
tell which to shuse ; but me vill e'en stan to mine
fortune, and cross and pile for it.

Capt. By my troth, it shall be so !   And take your
choice—cross or pile ?

Lieut. Why, cross he shall 'be hanged, and pile
he shall be married.

Rag. No, begar !   It shall be cross if me be
married, and pile if me be hang.

Lieut. Now it's an even lay whether this farce
be a comedy or a tragedy.

Cor. Come, gentlemen ; whore or halter for a
wager ?

Lieut. Whore, for a wager !

Cor. Halter, for a wager !

Rag. Hold, hold !   Vat if it be nedra cross nor
pile ?

Capt. If it be neither cross nor pile, thou shalt
neither be married nor be hanged, upon my honour.

Come, here is your fortune for you. I' faith, 'tis cross! Thou art to be married.

Rag. Den dere be your halter again, and me tank you.

Capt. Come, take your beloved wife, and strike a match.

Rag. Den let her take me, and de devil in hell give her good of me!

Capt. Then you have my pardon, and all is well.

Enter FERRET-FARM.

Fer. Sir, here are two of Queen Elizabeth's tilters, going to Bristol Fair, desire to dance before you.

Capt. With all my heart. Call 'em in!

A dance of two hobby-horses in armour, and a jig.

You have done well. Where's my man? Give 'em half a piece. You have done prettily indeed. Lieutenant, cashier the flint-flayers. As for these hypocrites, I'll keep them prisoners till the King dispose of 'em, which will be but too mercifully, I'm sure.

Cor. I suppose, Governor, the Parliament will reward you with some Bishops' lands for being so honourably pulled by the ears out of your garrison?

Capt. Come, upbraid 'em not; I hate that. To-morrow, sirs, summon in the country, and every man shall have his right.

All. God bless the King, and all his good soldiers!

Capt. You see, Lieutenant, how with good usage the people return to their loyalty. I know you are a brave fellow; but you have been to blame in the country, and that dis-serves your Prince more than your courage can recompense.

Lieut. Sir, you shall never have occasion to say this again.

Capt. I believe you ; and I wish that the great timber, the pieces of state, that lie betwixt the King and subjects—

I wish that they would take a hint from hence,
To keep the people's hearts close to their Prince !

[*Exeunt omnes.*

EPILOGUE.

PROLOGUES and epilogues should something say,
In order to the excusing of a play;
But things to the purpose being laid aside,
We shoot at random at least six bows wide,—
Speaking of this or that, of sea or land,
Of any matter but the thing in hand.
If men with such faults poets do commence,
I may put in with my impertinence.
And though my dull Muse cannot make y' a feast,
I'd fain be thought a poet at the least.
I find I am one ; I can prove it plain,
Both by my empty purse and shallow brain.
I've other symptoms to confirm it too ;
I've great and self-conceit of all I do.
I have my little cullies, too, i' th' town,
Both to admire my works and lend a crown.
My poet's day I mortgage to some citt,
At least six months before my play is writ ;
And on that day away your poet runs,
Knowing full well in shoals come all his duns.
If these things make me not a perfect poet,
He that has better title let him show it.

SIR HERCULES BUFFOON.

Sir Hercules Buffoon ; or the Poetical Squire. A Comedy. As it was acted at the Duke's Theatre. Written by John Lacy, Com. London: Printed for Jo. Hindmarsh, Bookseller to His Royal Highness, at the Black Bull in Cornhill. 1684.

LANGBAINE says: "This play was brought upon the stage, and publisht after the author's decease. The Prologue was writ by Mr. Durfey, the Epilogue by Jo. Heyns the comedian, and both spoken by the latter. I know not how this play succeeded in the theatre; but I am confident had the author been alive to have grac'd it with *his* action, it could not have fail'd of applause. This Mr. Durfey has observed in the beginning of his Prologue:—

" ' Ye scribbling fops !—Cry mercy, if I wrong ye,
But, without doubt, there must be some among ye ;—
Know that fam'd Lacy, ornament o' th' stage,
That standard of true comedy in our age,
Wrote this new play :
And if it takes not, all that we can say on't
Is, we've his fiddle, not his hands to play on't.' "

Geneste remarks : " This is a posthumous comedy by Lacy. It was acted at Dorset Garden." He speaks disparagingly of the play, and ends with " Lacy's friends should have buried his fiddle with him."

Jo. Haines or Hayns, who spoke the Prologue, and who wrote and spoke the Epilogue, was an actor in great repute. His life was a roving, and consequently a varied one, and he constantly aimed, but very frequently fell far short of his mark, at carrying out the comedian, or rather buffoon, off the stage as well as on it. An account of him will be found in the prefatory memoir to Tom Killigrew's Dramatic Works in the present series ; but as more immediately in connection with the author of the present volume, it may be well to notice the following incident here. On the dissolution of the play-house in Hatton Garden (1672), Hayns obtained an engagement at Drury Lane, "at which time the Rehearsal, writ by His Grace the Duke of Buckingham, was to be acted. The famous Lacy, whose part was that of Bays, unseason-ably falls sick of the gout, and consequently is incapable of appearing on the theatre. Hayns is looked upon as the fittest person to supply the place of the distemper'd, his Grace himself being pleased to instruct him in the nature of the part, and Mr. Lacy, by his Grace's command, took no small

pains in teaching it him ; nor did Lacy gain less reputation
by this his suffragan and schollar than if he had acted it
himself.   So well did Hayns perform it, that the Earl of
R[ochester], Lord B[rouncker ?], Sir Charles S[edley], and
several of the most ingenious men, ever after held him
in great esteem, which increased more and more with his
conversation." *

The dialogue of the present comedy is indued with no
inconsiderable amount of wit, and the characters are well
drawn—more especially those of the hero, and of the un-
principled Sir Marmaduke Seldin and his daughters twain.

* *Life of the late famous Comedian, Jo. Hayns.* Lond. 1701. 8vo.

PROLOGUE.

*Written by Thomas Durfey, Gent.   Spoken by J.
Haynes, Com.*

YE scribbling fops!—Cry mercy, if I wrong ye,
But, without doubt, there must be some among
   ye ;—
Know that famed Lacy, ornament o' the stage,
That standard of true comedy in our age,
Wrote this new play ;
And if it takes not, all that we can say on 't
Is, we have his fiddle, not his hands to play on 't.
Against our interest he, to do you right,
Your foes the poets has abused to-night,
And made us like rude birds our nest besh—te.
We know,
If you would write us plays, they'd lose their
   ends,
Kind parties still would make your pains amends :
For there's no fop but has a world of friends,
Who will like city whigs help one another,
And every noisy fool cry up his brother.
No more, then, rack for prologue or for song ;
Such trifles to dull quality belong.
Nor lampoon ladies that your virtues trust,
That bask in the hot Mall's pulvillio dust ;
Whose low-hung fringes, with attractive arts,
Sweep heaps of straws 'mongst crowds of lovers'
   hearts.

Subjects like these will never get you fame;
Nor can you write, if this be all your aim,
More than a rogue can sing that sets a psalm.
But if, like wits, you would the town oblige,
Write a good comedy on some famed siege,
But not in rhyme ; and if to please you mean,
Let Luxemburg be taken the first scene.
Yet, now I think on 't, choose another story ;
Some sparks that late went o'er to hunt for glory
Have spoiled that jest, and ta'en the town before
    ye.
No wonder, too, for who could stand their rage,
Since they with Coningsmark broadswords engage?
I fancy you'll turn butchers the next age ;
For these new weapons look, that guard your lives,
Like bloody cousins-german to their knives.
I'll put a question t' ye, Pray does the writer,
As times go, get most credit, or the fighter?
Wit is applauded when with fancy dressed ;
But to be knocked o' th' head's a cursed jest,—
A fate in which your forward fool miscarries.
No, 'tis much better to lie sick at Paris,
Where we can write what the French king intends,
And storm a town in letters to our friends.
Another inconvenience we must own ;
There's many a fool is by a bullet known,
That once passed for a wit of high renown.
The proof of sense lies hid in safety here,
But when the skull is broke the brains appear.
Ah, sirs, if you to the rough wars should follow,
How many pates, like mine, would be found
    hollow?
Faith, then, take my advice, stick to Apollo ;
Write, and be studious in dramatic rules ;
For should our poets sound your shallow skulls,
You were undone for wits, and we for fools.

THE ACTORS' NAMES.

LATON,   .   *Two Gentlemen.*
BOWMAN,
AIMWELL.
LORD ARMINGER.
SIR MARMADUKE SELDIN,   *Uncle and guardian to the two heiresses.*
SIR HERCULES BUFFOON,   *A lover of wit and lying.*
ALDERMAN BUFFOON,   .   *His uncle.*
SQUIRE BUFFOON,   .   .   *Son to Sir Hercules.*
OVERWISE.

A JUDGE, a CLERK, a FRENCH TAILOR, and WOMEN.

MARIANA.   *Eldest daughter to Sir Marmaduke.*
FIDELIA, . .   *Youngest daughter to Sir Marmaduke.*
BELMARIA, .   *The two heiresses.*
INNOCENTIA,
LYDIA, ...   *A servant to Mariana.*
A FRENCH WAITING WOMAN.
A SEAMAN, . . .   *Lover of Lydia.*

SERVANTS, CONSTABLE, WAITERS, and FOOTBOY.

SIR HERCULES BUFFOON.

—————◆—————

ACT I.—SCENE I.

Enter LATON, BOWMAN, *and* AIMWELL.

La. Dear Bowman, well met! Aimwell, thy servant!

Bow. Oh, Mr. Laton, I was told you were in a gay humour last night,—good company, and very witty.

La. An easy thing for any man to be witty, or a wit at my rate ; for we that make the greatest bustle, the loudest noise, and are rudest to the women, are called wits.

Bow. Then you conclude rudeness and ill-manners to be the ingredients of wit ? I see thou understand'st some wit.

La. Yes, the wit of this age I do ; for to be witty now is to be more troublesome in a playhouse than a butcher at a bear garden. That's wit to tear women's clothes and linen off in the house ; that's wit to see plays for nothing,—one act in the pit, another in a box, and a third in the gallery,— that's wit. And lastly, to cheat your hackney-coachman, link-boy, and your whore, and give 'em nothing—oh, that's mighty wit !

Aim. Hang 'em, those are sherks, not wits!

La. They go for wits, I assure you, sir. When
a poor coachman has driven me all day, and I not
knowing how to pay him, I have bid him drive to
such a place, and there I tell him he must wait
till I have supped. Under that pretence I slip out
at a back door, and there, your coachman's paid !

Aim. This is a very ungentleman-like wit, I
assure you.

La. Take heed what you say, for I always do it
when I am drunk.

Bow. Ay, and when you are sober too, I doubt.

La. Faith, when I want money ! but now they
all know me so well, that when I call a coach they
drive away from me as the devil were i' th' wheels.

Aim. If thou call'st this wit, prithee be witty
no more. But, waiving all this, what news ?

Bow. All the discourse o' th' town is of the two
great heiresses of the city—three hundred thousand
pounds betwixt two sisters !

Aim. 'Tis almost incredible that a merchant in
his lifetime should raise so vast an estate.

Bow. 'Tis no wonder. Several aldermen have
left greater sums, whose sons to this hour wallow
in wealth, and honour too.

La. Has their father left them orphans to the
city ?

Bow. No ; but he has fetched his elder brother
out of prison, and made him their guardian.

La. If he be poor, they will as certainly be
bought and sold as soap and hops are at Sturbridge
Fair.

Bow. Maybe not, for he's of great education ;
and, though he be a man of parts and wisdom, yet
his pride would never suffer his high spirit to
stoop to his low fortune, but still spent on till he
was clapped in prison.

Aim. 'Tis strange his brother should trust him in that low condition.

Bow. 'Tis so ; but to encourage him to be just, he has left him a thousand pounds a year for his life.

La. For all that, they that bid most shall have em.

Bow. He has two daughters of his own, indeed. What his love to them may tempt him to I know not ; but this men say of him,—he is the devil in his anger, and in his temper the most airy, jocose, and civil gentleman in the world.

Aim. So much for him, now for ourselves. How design ye the day?

La. My business is to visit the famous Norfolk knight, Sir Hercules Buffoon. They say he is come to town.

Bow. I am glad to hear it, for he is a man of great divertisement.

La. To most men he is a pleasant creature. His ambition is to be a wit, but he wants materials. All the tools he has towards it is lying ; and that he does so well, that 'tis hard to know when he lies and when he does not.

Aim. I have business with him ; let us all go.

Bow. Faith, let us call on my Lord Arminger, for he loves such divertisement.

La. With all my soul, for I value him above all mankind.

Aim. He deserves it, sir, for he has all points of honour in him to perfection.

Bow. I am not the least of his admirers, and so let's go wait upon him. [*Exeunt.*

Enter SIR MARMADUKE SELDIN, MARIANA *and* FIDELIA, *his daughters.*

Sel. Fortune, Mariana, has bailed me out of the jaws of prison, and made me guardian to my brother's daughters. Three hundred thousand pounds they have, which shall lodge you both in the arms of honour. But you must follow my instructions, and subtlely act your parts in my design.

Mar. So your design be just, sir.

Sel. Just! Dare you question the actions of your father? Does your conscience scruple to be great, Madam Precision?

Mar. No, sir, if that greatness be fairly purchased; but where have we fortunes to expect such blessings?

Sel. Is not three hundred thousand pounds enough to invite the best of subjects to your bed, madam?

Mar. Bless me! that's your brother's money, left for his own dear children. I hope, then, you'll not betray your trust, and strip yourself of that honest fame you have ever lived in?

Sel. Who would not be a knave, a damned one, rather than a beggar? Who can withstand this great temptation? The fools, the wise, the learned, nor the religious, have power to resist such a blessed occasion; why, then, should I be styled, That honest fool? No!

Fid. Sister, can you forget that our wants made our landlady attempt our virtues, saying she would help us to a kind gentleman that would pay our rent for us, if we would be kind to him again?

Sel. A bawd, by my life! Oh, damn her! But landladies are licensed bawds; for paying scot and lot they have vestry commissions to corrupt the daughters of each parish. But say, Mariana, resolve you to obey?

Mar. Sir, on my knees, I beg I may retire from the mischiefs I foresee. Your honour and my cousins' ruin are at stake, and must be lost. I'll beg some heavenly guide to direct me where virtue dwells.

Sel. That's where no mankind inhabits. Virtue is a meagre, starved old woman, that lives in a cellar on the alms of a parish; and that's the best preferment virtue ever purchased.

Fid. And will you be one of those virtuous old women, sister?

Mar. Yes, and from my heart I wish you were so too.

Fid. Thank you, sister; but I hope 'tis time enough to think of virtue when one's teeth are out. To be a virtuous young woman and a virtuous old woman too is too much. I think 'tis fair, father, for a young woman to resolve to be virtuous when she's old.

Mar. Would you not be virtuous whilst you're young, sister?

Fid. Yes, dear sister; but one would not make it their business. If it come, 'tis welcome; if not, by my troth, I'll not break my heart about it.

Sel. Thou art my own child, by heaven! For thee, Mariana, though thou art the treasure of my heart, I'll tear thee from it, for it must be torn, thou art so firmly rooted; but henceforth I'll hate thee for thy disobedience. Therefore, be gone!

Mar. 'Tis the only thing my soul desires; for I had rather be the offspring of a monster than the child of him who means such horrid wrongs to those that trust them.

Sel. 'Sdeath, her saucy zeal has made her impu-

dent! You fanatic devil, dare you talk to me
thus and not shake and tremble? Has virtue be-
reft thee of modesty and manners? A curse upon
the errors of the age, when children grow precisely
obstinate! The damned ignorant call that virtue.

Fid. Prithee consider, sister, virtue cannot maintain thee; and when once 'tis known a handsome woman is in want, then, as the poet worthily
says, the powerful guinea cannot be withstood.
Pray you, sir, let me but have her one hour, I'll
make her sensible what destruction virtue brings
to womankind. But, pray you, tell her how great
she shall be; I fancy an honourable title may prevail with a tender conscience.

Sel. She shall be sure of the highest, or, if subjects can arrive at greater dignities, we will still
fly higher.

Fid. But hark you, father, what shall I be all
this while? This tempting honour has kindled
such a fire in me that I'm ready to break out into
dignities, and cannot be quenched till I'm refined
and purified fit for empire. There's noble pride
for you, father!

Sel. My own spirit dictates to thine, and makes
our hearts strike time and thought together.

Fid. Sister, look here. Farewell conscience! for
greatness' sake I'd make no scruple to poison my
very father.

Sel. How! how?

Fid. If you stood betwixt me and honour,
father.

Sel. Oh, my genius! my own dear genius!

Mar. Was ever thing so very young so very
wicked? Thou should'st ha' ta'en thy leave of
heaven fairly, and not suffered the society of devils
to have entered thee so soon.

Fid. Alack, father, she'll preach anon! I dare swear a great pew in a fanatic church is her *non ultra.* She has no honourable pride in her; she is not of our family.

Mar. From my soul I wish I were not.

Sel. That shall be granted, never doubt. The thing I doat on more than heaven proves my greatest hell. Thy virtue makes thee thy own angel and my devil.

Mar. Well, I'll go where nothing of religion is professed, and there, perhaps, may be no wickedness; for heathens, sure, have no sins of your monstrous growth.

Fid. I had rather be a rich and honourable monster than a virtuous beggar, sister.

Sel. Is greatness, then, a monstrous sin? That's like those malicious brutes who call coaches hellcarts because they go afoot; so you think wealth monstrous because you are a beggar. That ever we should bring our children up to be religious! It only teaches them to rebel against their Prince and parents. Then Dame Nature, that cunning jilt, commands and orders us to doat on them, when they return nothing but ingratitude. Would nature had let that subtle knack alone, for 'tis the chiefest curse that mankind has, loving and providing for our brats. Come, minion, I'll provide for you; for, by the life that's lent me, if within this hour you comply not, I'll ease your troubled mind with this——

Fid. Let me, father, but have her to my chamber; if I do not charm her to obedience, and, like a twig, bend and supple her fit for all your projects, then disown me too.

Sel. Thy words come from thee with an angel's voice.

Mar. A devil's or a peacock's rather.

Fid. You bray like an ass, lady, and may come into the concert. What harmonious music would a peacock, a devil, and an ass make? The peacock should chaunt the treble, the ass should bray the tenor, and the devil should roar the bass. And to these add but a sow-gelder, and say they are come out of France, and they would pass for the best music in Christendom. Come, foolish sister; come, angry father; I'll confute your she lay elder, never fear me! [*Exeunt.*

Enter Sir HERCULES BUFFOON *and* Alderman BUFFOON *at different doors.*

Ald. My worthy nephew, Sir Hercules Buffoon, I rejoice heartily to see you at London! And pray you, sir, what news does the country afford?

Her. Why, all the news in the country is that there's no news at London.

Ald. What! and the Gazette bawling in the streets twice a week?

Her. Burn the Gazette! we know what news there's in 't before it comes out. There's my lady's little dog, with liver-coloured spots; then a horse stolen or strayed, fourteen hands high, they that can bring tidings of him shall be well rewarded. Then there's the old stop-gap ditto; and these are for ever and ever the news of the Gazette. I'll be better informed in the country at a thatched alehouse, where the gentry meet twice a week to communicate news.

Ald. But prithee, nephew, tell me what news i' th' country?

Her. They say for certain that London and Westminster are grown so godly that in a whole week there's scarce a cuckold made.

Ald. You found not that in the Gazette, I hope ?

Her. A pox on the Gazette! They have got a trick now to expound it, and they make as many false interpretations as thou makest, uncle, when thou expound'st a chapter to thy family.

Ald. You are always jerking at the Scriptures, and profaning the silent Ministers ; those are your commonplaces. They say, now, you take delight to be thought an Atheist and a Wit, forsooth.

Her. I confess I'd rather be thought an Atheist than not a Wit.

Ald. They go together, indeed ; impossible to part those two sins.

Her. They are as inseparable, I confess, as matrimony; an Atheist and a Wit are incorporated, and like man and wife become one flesh.

Ald. Or rather, grafted or inoculated into Belzebub, and so become one devil.

Her. The truth is, they are linked together like sausages.

Ald. Ay, and they will fry together like sausages one day.

Her. In hell, thou meanest ? They never value that, man, for they that believe nothing fear nothing.

Ald. Then you are counted the most notorious liar of all Norfolk, which is a shame and dishonour to the family of the Buffoons.

Her. Thou fool ! 'tis the only useful virtue belonging to a great family, and I am prouder of it, uncle, than thou art of thy great Bible with huge silver clasps.

Ald. A worthy virtue, indeed, when a liar's counted worse than a thief.

Her. Y' are a rascal, uncle ; lying is one of the

P

liberal sciences, and is the eminent'st profession
in the world but poetry.

Ald. A poet, indeed, is an excellent yoke-fellow
for a liar; the devil could not ha' matched them
better.

Her. A City Presbyter and a silenced Minister
are better matched by half.

Ald. Thou'rt a wicked fellow! Sure, there is
some secret delight in being a Wit, or else men
would never venture to be damned for't, as they
do.

Her. A man would venture anything to be a
Wit, uncle,—to have men honour and admire them,
and cry, There goes a Wit!—That gentleman's a
Wit! Oh, there's more glory in that than in being
a Monarch!

Ald. I believe I myself am a better Wit than
the best of them. I can repeat all Hopkins and
Sternal's psalms by rote; and that's more than any
Wit in England can brag of.

Her. Ha! ha! what a thing has this fool found
out for wit! Why, what the devil has wit to do
with religion?

Ald. Nay, sir, I have got a hundred thousand
pounds by my wit; that's the substantial part.
Your little flashy Wits! their pockets are always
as empty as their heads. Money is wit, purchasing
is wit, planting is wit; when they come to that,
I'll allow 'em to be Wits,—not before, I assure you.
But, where's your son? I mean to make a prentice
of him.

Her. I mean to make a Wit of him.

Ald. First make a prentice of him, and then he
is qualified for wit, or any honourable title in the
world. I would bind him prentice because I
would have him saved.

Her. Saved? I was a prentice myself, and I do not find I am like to be saved, for I learnt all my lying there. The first thing my master taught me was never to speak truth to a customer; and is that the way to be saved?

Ald. That is not lying, nephew, 'tis but the mystery of our professions; and for advantage of trade we all hold fraud to be a little lawful.

Enter ESQUIRE BUFFOON.

Her. Oh, here comes your heir and mine!—This is your uncle, sirrah.

Squ. Sirrah? Sir, if you were twenty fathers, I write myself Esquire.

Ald. Well said, boy! I commend thee.

Squ. Are you my reverend rich uncle, Alderman Buffoon?

Ald. Yes, sir.

Squ. I hope you'll excuse my father's rudeness for calling me sirrah; really, I am ashamed of him.—a poor country Knight, void of manners. I understand, uncle, you will make me your heir?

Ald. If you behave yourself like a Buffoon, I'll make you my heir.

Squ. Then pray you, uncle, pray to God to bless me. You are obliged indeed, sir, for I have not asked my father's blessing these seven years.

Ald. And if good times come, I'll make you a Lord.

Squ. Then I shall be the first Buffoon that ever was a Lord.

Her. Not by a hundred! There have been, there are, and will for ever be Lord Buffoons. We are an ancienter family than the La-Fools. We came in with William of Normandy, and the French Buffoons came out of the Irish Buffoons by a match with King Pippin; and there the Buffoons are fixed, and will be to the end of the world.

Ald. I honour thee, nephew, for thy learning, in deriving our pedigree in a diameter from the best blood of Europe.

Squ. But, uncle, setting the house of Pippin aside, I must needs go see the players.

Ald. Players! Thou foolish, profane boy,—players?

Squ. If you be not read in the history of players, both men and women, 'twill call your breeding in question. Besides, all the Princes in the world allow of players; and if the Buffoons should not, then where's your pedigree from the house of Pippin?

Ald. Nay, rather than call that in question, I'll allow of players freely.

Squ. We admire poets, too, in the country most mightily, uncle.

Ald. That's more than we do in London, I assure you, sir.

Squ. I pity all those that do not, uncle.—But, father, which do you hold to be the most honourable, your comic or heroic poet?

Her. Oh, your heroic, without doubt, because he comes nearer the romantic strain than the other.

Squ. Romantic! What signifies the word romantic?

Her. Why, it comes from the word romance, and romance is the Arabic word for a swinger, and swinger is the Hebrew word for a liar.

Squ. By this you prove the heroic poets to be liars?

Her. No, no, by no means; romantically inclined, only.

Ald. Nephew, I admire thy parts. I'll home and make thy entertainment to the dignity of the Buffoons, for I am more than proud that I spring from the loins of King Pippin.

[*Exit* ALDERMAN.

Squ. Uncle, we will most dutifully be with you forthwith.—I must see the players, father, for I have tokens to deliver to one of them from two country ladies.

Her. Prithee, Ned, which of the players is 't ?

Squ. 'Tis he that acts Drawcansir.* The ladies are damnably in love with him for killing whole armies, horse and foot. One of 'em said she would give a hundred pound to be with child by him of a young Drawcansir.

Her. Then he must get the other lady with child of a young army, for the young Drawcansir to conquer. But prithee, Ned, who are the ladies ? I'll warrant 'em both whipsters.

Squ. Like enough, for one is my sister, and the other my mother, i' faith.

Her. You damned rogue, to betray your mother and sister !

Squ. Betray ! if that be all, they have been betrayed long since. Come away, father !

Her. A plaguey witty dog this. [*Exeunt.*

---

* The extravagant language put by Dryden, in his Conquest of Grenada (1670), into the mouth of Almanzor, his hero, caused the Duke of Buckingham to ridicule that character, as Drawcansir, in his burlesque, the Rehearsal. Almanzor was originally played by Hart, one of the favoured lovers of the Countess of Castlemaine (Pepys, 7th April 1668) and other ladies of quality. It is understood that Nell Gwyn, for whom he entertained a passion, was elevated from the position of an orange-girl to that of an actress by him and Lacy.

ACT II.—SCENE I.

Enter GUARDIAN.—MARIANA *and* FIDELIA *meet him.*

Sel. Now, my Fidelia, how hast thou prospered? I know thou hast vigorously pressed her to obey, for thou art all duty.

Fid. Not I, indeed! this is your dutiful daughter, sir?

Sel. Is it possible? What charms, what fire didst thou use to thaw that frozen virtue in her, that common enemy to all honour and preferment?

Fid. I have made her more in love with greatness than e'er she was with virtue. Come, Lady Convert, down o' your knees and crave pardon for your stiffnecked rebellion, or out you turn to your old tattered granum, Goody Virtue.

Mar. Sir, I beg your pardon for all my disobedience, and tender my duty to whatever you command, and think it virtue in me to obey you.

Sel. I am overcharged, and want room to entertain the joy thy dear compliance brings. But now to our business. You two shall pass for my two nieces, and, in short, enjoy their fortunes.

Fid. Well, sir, if we must pass for these great fortunes, how will you dispose of the real ones?

Sel. They must be despatched! Let me see, we'll have 'em——

Fid. Murdered. Come, out with it, father!

Sel. That's too harsh a word for thy tender ear, is it not, my jewel?

Mar. Indeed it startles me; pray ye, give it a milder name; the word murder is enough to daunt a young beginner.

Fid. Fie, thou hast no mettle in thee. Think of honour; that will fright all bugbears that awe the simple conscience.

Sel. I'd give the world to have thee steeled and wrought to her hard temper.

Mar. I would not have 'em murdered, but they may be desired to take a journey into the other world.

Sel. There can be no offence in that; a tender zealot may allow of murder clad in such mild words.

Fid. A pretty equivocation the devil has helped us to to embolden us to murder.

Sel. Throw by your fears, or I'll throw by your lives. Bloody words suit best with bloody deeds, therefore I'll have no other phrase but murder; startle that dares!

Mar. Murder be it, then. Now I consider, sister, 'tis very foolish to scruple at the word when we so freely consent to the deed.

Fid. Father, I must laugh a little. To tell you true, this cunning baggage has but dissembled virtue all this while, on purpose to discover your inclinations.

Sel. Mine is to murder 'em, without the least fright or start of conscience; but if that were feigned virtue thou managed'st with such saint-like zeal, by heaven I shall honour thee as the metropolitan hypocrite of all thy sex.

Mar. And, sir, to show you how little I value virtue, their deaths already are contrived, and my faithful servant has undertaken it.

Sel. How, how, my dear child, how?

Mar. Thus, sir. My good, honest maid has a lover to whom she is contracted, and, being a seaman, has already hired a ship to spirit them away

into the north of Norway, where they shall never
more be seen or heard of.

Sel. The wisest of men could not ha' thought of
so secure a course. But when, oh when, shall this
be done?

Mar. Instantly! we have already prepared our
cousins for a journey, too. We told them you
would send them into France for better education,
before any suitors should be admitted.

Sel. And all this ready done? Let mankind
after this never deal in mischief. When there is a
work the devil cannot manage, a zealous woman
shall have the honour of it. I have prepared for
thee, my jewel, the brave Lord Arminger,—a man
that has no stain to blast his better parts, but has
a crystal fame that all the world may see through.

Fid. Then I find I must provide my own fool.

Sel. Thou art merry still. I have already rich
presents sent me by this Duke, that Marquis, the
other Earl. This Duchess for her kinsman writes,
that Countess for her brother,—will all send gifts.
I do not receive 'em, nor they carry 'em away, for
in that gentile manner great Ministers of State take
bribes.

Mar. Ay, sir, you have raised my spirits; the
thought of honour makes murder seem a little
crime.

Sel. Ay, there fix thy soul. Think on the blessings that attend on greatness; then who would
not wade to the chin in blood?

Fid. To the knees, father, is deep enough, in
conscience.

Sel. You are not known to the world, so that
you may pass for them securely; only the youngest,
that came from the north, the world has got some
hint of her country speech, which, if thou canst

imitate, we shall cozen the world, live in pleasure, and die in the bed of honour.

Fid. No, father; they that deal justly die in the bed of honour; we that cheat and cozen can die but in honour's truckle-bed.

Sel. Well said, good Madam Hudibras! Come, let us cheerfully despatch this murder, and that settles all our fortunes.

Mar. Our hands and hearts go all together.

Sel. This is the greatest satisfaction that ever yet my soul received. [*Exeunt.*

Scene II.

Enter Lord ARMINGER, BOWMAN, AIMWELL, *and* LATON.

Omnes. My Lord Arminger, your most humble servant!

Arm. I hope, gentlemen, you likewise think I am your's.

La. We come to invite your lordship to the sight of an extraordinary new sort of fool.

Arm. Not a finer than my Mr. Overwise, I hope?

La. Your lordship's is a more affected fool; he is for impossible projects, new words, and fine phrases.

Arm. Oh, he hates a common phrase as he does a common woman.

Bow. Then he is very impertinent. If he sees you kneeling, he will advise you how to pray; at dinner, how to eat; in bed, how to behave yourself.

Arm. Those things make him a fool; he would not be one else. He has one worse fault than all

those—he will whisper you eternally, always buzz-
ing in your ear like a Lincolnshire gnat.

Aim. But our fool makes lying one part of his
talent; 'tis Sir Hercules Buffoon.

Arm. Oh, I have heard of him; they say he has
a magazine of confidence.

Bow. Nay, faith, 'tis impudence, and the greatest
that e'er came out of Norfolk.

Aim. Sir, there are Buffoons in other countries
besides Norfolk.

Bow. I grant you more than that, sir; there are
as worthy gentry in Norfolk as are in the world,
and yet they may have a ridiculous Buffoon
amongst them.

Arm. Aimwell, methinks y'are very fine! this
dress is meant for love or war, a mistress or campaign. Oh, here comes my whispering fool, Overwise, i' faith.

Enter OVERWISE.

Over. My royal Earl! No, Earl is too common;
I will call thee my Royal Count. In thy haven I
ride safe at anchor from the surprising cogboats,
such as carry small burthens of sense; I mean
those whom men vulgarly call fops.

La. Prithee, Mr. Overwise, what is a fop?

Over. A fop! 'Tis strange thou shouldst not
know what a fop is, that art so great a one thyself.
I will tell thee. A fop is the fruit of a foplin, as a
Wit is the kernel of a witlin.

Bow. I have heard of a foplin but never of a
witlin before.

Arm. He has every day some ridiculous thing
would please the most morose creature in the
world.

Over. Aimwell, thou art as gay as a tulip, as

glorious as a milk-pail on a May day.—That is all new, my Count.

Arm. Thou art thyself every day new.

Over. I am upon a project, my Royal Count, of obtaining a charter for the sober society of the professors of coffee ; and I would honour the Peers and gentry so far as to make 'em free of the company.

Arm. It must needs be a great honour to be free of Coffee-House Hall.

Over. More honour than to be free of the Virtuosos'. But why, my Gallantissimos, do you not address to the rich heiresses ?

Arm. I declare the guardian has courted me ; but none must visit 'em till some time be expired. The reason I know not.

Over. My Count, why may not I address ? The ladies, perhaps, may love a wise man before a handsome man.

La. Where shall we find him ? Then let me put in ! perhaps they may love a peevish fellow that will beat 'em, before a civil man that will court 'em. I have a small miss that I use barbarously, and I dare swear that she loves me the better for it.

Aim. My French garniture, a pox on 'em, is not yet arrived from Paris.

Arm. The ladies will despise you if you have not all things French, for I suppose they are of the same air and humour that quality is subject to— that is, to admire a French fan before an English gown.

Bow. And a French dog before an English man.

La. The men do worse; for they admire a French feather above an English Lordship, and a French tailor above an English father and mother.

Arm. I must say this for the ladies,—where there is one female fool to admire 'em, there are forty male.

Over. Really, we are so fondly affected with the French that we shall in time send for Frenchmen to get our English children for us.

Bow. But they say, my Lord, the youngest heiress, that was bred in the north, is the prettiest kind of creature; everything she does or says becomes her.

Arm. Yes! and they say her northern speech is a great addition to her beauty, which is very strange; but, being a child, it may the better become her.

La. She has a Frenchwoman to wait on her, and she hates her mortally, and desires all people to help her to curse her home again.

Over. Really they say she puts up a paper every Sunday to the parson in the pulpit, to desire the curses of the congregation against all French tailors and tirewomen.

Bow. Then they say she plays at several sports, —as Rampscuttle, Clapperdepouch, and Come, mother, saw you my cock to-day? These sports declare her a sweet, innocent creature.

Arm. But you have forgot Sir Hercules Buffoon, gentlemen. Pray ye, let us go in search of him.

Am. My lord, we shall all wait upon your Lordship.

Over. I will go in search of that strange sport called, Come, mother, saw you my cock to-day? so I take leave.

Omnes. Ha, ha, ha, ha!   [*Exeunt.*

SCENE III.

Enter SELDIN, SEAMAN, *and* MAID.

Sel. I understand, sir, that you have undertaken the disposing of my two nieces ?

Sea. I'll set them ashore where no mankind inhabits, where they must be starved to death or torn to pieces by wild bears.

Sel. I honour thee because thou makest no scruple.

Sea. That's for children to boggle and be fearful. I'll give you an honest and a just account of their murder, sir ; and in so doing I hope I shall discharge my duty with a good conscience.

Sel. What a sweet minister of darkness has the devil sent me !

Lyd. He is my lover, sir, my honest lover. I have his heart as sure as my young ladies have mine. We two would commit more than murder to make them great.

Sel. Your worthy faith shall be rewarded.

Sea. 'Tis enough ! Come, call our foolish seamates, we must not lose our tide. Oh, here they come.

Enter MARIANA, FIDELIA, INNOCENTIA, *and* BELMARIA.

Sel. Alack, my sweet and lovely nieces, why do ye weep ? Such tears are too precious for so slight occasion ; all ladies rejoice at going into France.

Inn. I had rather gea to Yorkshire than to France. Now, good my honey nuncle, let us not gea to France, but send me back to my naunt at York again.

Sel. Alas, my sweet niece, 'tis for your breeding I send you. Why weep you, my lovely niece?

Bel. Something troubles me, I know not what, and prompts me to beseech you on my knees you'll give us leave to stay.

Sel. Alack, my dear jewels, it is by advice I send you into France. Your fortunes are great, and 'tis my duty to see your education answerable. I should be condemned by all the world else.

Bel. But, good uncle, why do you turn away our old servants, that have been with us from our cradles? They would be a comfort to us.

Sel. Because you shall have none but French about you; you'll never learn the language else.

Inn. Marra, the devilst learn French for me. By my saul, ean Yorkshire word, nuncle, 's worth ten thousand French cans.

Bel. Dear uncle, let us stay. We have both had horrid dreams last night, which waked us into such dreadful tremblings. No ague ever shook the body as those have done our fearful souls.

Sel. You are more a child than your sister; and what was your dream?

Bel. Why, sir, I dreamt I was set ashore by a seaman in a cold country, all frost and snow; and I called out, methought, to the wicked wretch that left me there, but he like a cruel man ran from me; and there I perished, without one bird or beast of the creation by to pity me.

Sel. I like not this.

Sea. [*Apart to Sel.*] Damn 'em, get 'em aboard! and then no matter what they dream. I hate peevish people that will not be murdered quietly when 'tis their turn. Come, despatch 'em, sir!

Sel. And what was your dream, you little fearful fool?

Inn. Marry, God help me, nuncle, I dreamed just sike ana grizely * man as that set me down in frost and snow, and ran away when he had done, and by and by there came three hujus bears, nuncle; then I cried and screamed out, and God wait not ean kerson saul came to help me; then I said, Good sweet honey bears, do not kill me, and yet the hard-hearted devils worried me all to bits, and left not ean morsel of me alive.

Sel. Is it possible instinct should give nature such hints of truths to come?—'Sdeath, what weep you for?

Mar. To practise hypocrisy; I may have occasion for 't. Besides, it is a kind of compliment to weep with them at parting.

Fid. Come, sir, away with 'em! I fear they will work upon your good nature too, and then all our hopes are cut off.

Sel. Thou wert always my comforter, but now my counsellor. I'll see 'em aboard presently. Come, my dear nieces, throw your idle dreams behind you. I send you to the splendid court of France, where all good manners and civil breeding grow.

Inn. We have better manners bith' half at York, that have we; and one Yorkshire jig's worth a thousand French dances, that it is.

Bel. Dear uncle, let our sweet cousins go with us, that they may have the same education that is allotted for us.

Sel. Not for the world: the town would report I bred my children at your charge, and so conclude I mean them part of your fortune.

Sea. They consider nothing.—Come, sir, the tide serves, and go we must.

* Frightful, ugly. – *Yorksh.*

Inn. Now, by my saul, that ill-looked beast
frights me. Ah, thou's an ill-favoured grizely-like
fellow, that is sa.

Sel. Not one word more, I charge you, of all
hands. I'll see you safe ashipboard, pray for you,
and farewell!

Inn. E'en God's benison and mine be with you,
cousins. My heart gives me I'st be dead, cousin;
and if I die, wae's me, we'st ne'er play at Clapperdepouch again.

Fid. Yes, yes, dear cousin, fear nothing!

[*Exeunt.*

SCENE IV.

Enter Lord ARMINGER, BOWMAN, LATON, AIM-
WELL, *and* Sir HERCULES.

La. Sir Hercules Buffoon, no man more glad to
see you! Here is a most worthy and honourable
Peer of the realm desires to know you.

Her. Not as a Lord, but as a man of parts, I
salute you.

La. My Lord has great parts and virtues, besides
a man of great wit.

Her. Wit? Prithee, my Lord, let's hear a little
of it.

Arm. When you give me occasion for't, you
shall; i' th' interim, assure yourself I have wit
enough to honour and admire you.

Her. Prithee, my Lord, let's honour and admire
one another till we find a reason for't.

Arm. If we stay till then, we shall admire one
another long enough.

La. Here's another worthy person; his name is
Bowman, sir.

Her. Bowman, Bowman ? by my life I honour
and admire you to the superlative degree. You
must needs be a swingeing liar.

Bow. Why so, sir ?

Her. Sir, I have a hound of your name, as
arrant a cur as e'er came in field. When my dogs
are hunting and at a fail, he is the first that opens ;
but the devil a hound i' th' pack will believe him,
for he ne'er spoke truth in 's life. So, sir, if you
be a true Bowman——

Bow. I'm as arrant a cur as your dog Bowman ?

Her. Despise not my dog ; for aught you know,
you may be both of a family.

Arm. This is an insufferable fool indeed !

Her. You'll not be angry, I hope ; a hound is a
gentleman's fellow in any ground in England.

Arm. In any hunting ground in England, I
grant you ; but we are men of no exceptions, nor
you, I hope.

Bow. Therefore, good Sir Hercules, let's have a
swingeing lie, now !

Her. You are a very idle fool, sir !

Bow. What mean you by that? I am no fool, sir !

Her. Then there's a lie for you, and that's what
you required.

Arm. 'Tis a kind of a witty lie, too.

Her. 'Tis so, my lord ; I have not spoke a word
of truth to-day. I said I honoured and admired
thee ; that's another lie, for the devil take me if I
either honour or admire thee — indeed I see nothing in thee to admire.

Arm. Oh, sir, Mr. Bowman is a man of most
accomplished parts.

Her. He's an ill-natured fellow, then, for he
keeps 'em to himself. I believe his good parts and
terra incognita will be found together.

Q

Arm. This is great wit, Knight, but very severe.

La. Come, Sir Hercules, be good-natured! and let's have a——

Her. Lie; I know your meaning, to tell you truth, sir. This is none of my lying days.

Aim. No! Hast thou in the whole course of thy life any intervals of truth?

Her. Oh, sir, I'm an old man, and must think o' th' other world; and therefore I'm allowed but three days a week to lie.

Bow. Prithee, Knight, who allows thee?

Her. Our parson. I was forced to give him a bull calf to allow me them; I'd been excommunicated else.

La. But prithee, Knight, what dost thou do the other four days?

Bow. He looks like an ass, I believe, when he speaks truth.

Her. I' faith, so I do; it is very childish, and therefore I hate it. However, of those days I'm very godly, and go to church.

Arm. How! to church, man? Dost thou think there's another world for thee?

Her. Yes, faith, do I—such a one as it is; but those days I go to church I would not speak a lie for the world's wealth.

Aim. That day thou goest to church. I dare swear, thou speakest truth.

Enter ESQUIRE BUFFOON.

Squ. You say right, gentlemen. I have been his son these eighteen years, and he has ne'er been at church since I was born.

Her. You impudent son of a whore you!

Arm. Oh, fie, Sir Hercules, who is this you call son of a whore?

Her. My own son of a whore; whose should he be ?

Arm. Nay, if he be the son of a whore, he ought to be thine.

Squ. Gentlemen, I'm not ashamed to own it ; I am my father's own son of a whore, upon my credit !

Arm. Bowman, the son is a finer fool than the father.

Squ. Yet my mother's virtuous enough, if it were not for——

Aim. What, what ? Prithee out with it !

Squ. Oh, sir, she will lie most shamefully ; that is, she would lie as a man would have her.

Her. By my life, the boy's i' th' right ; my wife will lie with any man in England.

Bow. Do you own her to be so common, sir ?

Her. No ; I mean she will tell a lie with any man in England. Why, the devil would not lie with her carnally, for she's as ugly as she's old. A man with all his neighing youth about him would not touch her with a pair of tongs.

Squ. She has not had a tooth in her head these thirty years, nor capable of man these forty.

Her. The boy's i' th' right ; the jade's as lean as a luke olive, and as dry as a mummy,—a skeleton fit only to read lectures on.

Bow. But, Squire, if your mother has not been capable of man these forty years, how came you to be but eighteen ?

Squ. I am none of her son, man. I'm but a by-blow my father got of a cinder woman one night a-serenading ; so that you cannot properly call me the son of a whore, but the son of a serenade.

Aim. Hark you, sir ! are not you a damned eternal lying rascal ?

Her. Ay, by my life, is he ; but I cannot be angry, he lies so impudently.

Squ. Oh, dear sir, now you compliment. I assure you, gentlemen, my father is the cock liar of all Norfolk.

Her. My son, i' faith! Besides, he is full of invention, and for that cause I mean to bind him prentice to a poet.

Omnes. Prentice to a poet? This is more than ridiculous.

Her. Yes; and my reason is, if he should prove dull, as 'tis many a poet's case, yet they cannot deny him to be a poet, because he has served his time for 't. Besides, as he is a poet, he sees plays for nothing, and that's considerable.

Bow. And must he needs be a poet when he has served his time? Faith, bind him prentice to a lord; by the same rule he'll be a lord when he's out of his time.

Her. Now you joke. Yes indeed must he; but, really, do you know ever a poet that wants a prentice?

Arm. Pray you, gentlemen, manage these fools; 'twill be worth while.

Aim. Sir, I know a rare poet, but he'll have two hundred pounds with a prentice.

Her. I stand not upon that; but I'm for one of the primest of 'em, one of those that swinges the Gods about.

Squ. No, father, I had rather be prentice to a comic poet; that's witty company. Some of your heroic poets, they say, write rarely well, yet are the heaviest, dull, insipid animals over a glass of wine in nature.

Her. Ay, and some of 'em will filch and steal out o' th' old plays, and cry down the authors when they've done.

Squ. They have no more invention than there is

in the head of a soused mackerel. Now they've turned cobblers; they vamp and mend old plays.

Her. Or rather turned tinkers, who stop one hole and make ten; so they mend one fault and make twenty.

Squ. But, gentlemen, am I to serve a seven years' prenticeship?

Aim. No, sir, but five. 'Tis with a poet as with a red or fallow deer; the fifth year he is a stag or buck o' th' first head; so he that writes.

Squ. A pretty kind of similitude! And pray you, sir, do the poets shed their heads yearly as the deer do?

Arm. No, sir, in that they differ, else they come nearest of all creatures. For every year they commence and have new titles; as, for example, a stag, —the first year he's a calf, the second a brocket, the third a brock, the fourth a staggard, and the fifth year a stag o' th' first head.

Bow. So he that means to be a poet, the first year he's an ass, the second a fop, the third a witlin, the fourth a wit, and the fifth year a poet o' th' first head.

Her. Aha, sirrah, here's learning in this! 'Tis ingenious and admirable.

Squ. But, sir, have not your wits their degrees too?

Bow. Oh yes; there are your first, second, third, fourth, and fifth-rate wits too.

Arm. Ay, and your first, second, third, fourth, and fifth-rate fools too.

Squ. That we have i' th' country. But why should a poet be an ass the first year?

Arm. A poet is not an ass; he is five years advanced above it. Yet let any man that has writ five years look back into what he writ the first year, and he will find himself an ass, I warrant you.

Squ. I believe I should make a good fop, but I am positive I shall never make an ass as long as I live.

Bow. Never despair! I'll help you to an hundred gentlemen shall make an ass of you presently.

Squ. I shall be extremely beholding to you, for the devil take me if I know which way to go about it myself.

Aim. Sir, your father must requite this courtesy.

Squ. Command him anything but his new play; he is mighty choice of that.

Her. I confess I am a little fond of my play.

Arm. That's more than any man else can be, I doubt.

Aim. Why is't not played? 'Twas made in Norfolk, I doubt.

Her. So all you fops cry, indeed; but your cock wits and your cock poets cry it up to the skies. It is so lashing a satire against the whole nation, I should ha' been hanged had it been played.

Bow. 'Tis a thousand pities 'twas not played, then. But I am told 'tis a damned play, worse than ever Mr. Bayes * writ in all his whole cartload.

Her. Sir, I had as lief you would stab me to the heart as speak ill of my play.

Aim. But, Knight, I hope you remember your promise to me?

Her. Upon my life, thou shalt have one of the rich heiresses; the guardian and I are the intimatest friends i' th' world. And so, gentlemen, let's go bind my son prentice to this famous poet.

Bow. Agreed, agreed! and there shall he be sufficiently abused.   [*Exeunt.*

* Dryden.

SCENE V.

Enter SIR MARMADUKE *and* MARIANA.

Sel. We are happy, Mariana. I saw my nieces
under sail below the Hope, with a fair wind to
blow 'em to destruction. We are happy in thy
sister too, for never was so ingenious a mimic.
She imitates her northern cousin ; no player ever
acted like her. And the necessity of it is great,
for there is such notice taken of her Yorkshire
speech, that, should her tongue be missing, we
were all in question.

Mar. She does it so well that she puts me but
too much in mind of my poor little cousin.

Sel. Death ! do you repent ? Value thyself upon
thy fortune ! Be proud ! mankind shall pay thee
homage as if it were thy due and their duty. My
heart is set upon the highest pinnacle of pride —
not for myself ; I am proud for thee, my jewel,
and had I power I would make the whole body of
the earth bow to thee, though it dropped out
o' th' frame, and dashed itself into eternal atoms.
Yet am I pleased to match thee to the great, the
virtuous, and the valiant Lord Arminger.

Mar. The noble character that you so oft have
given him has made an impression here so deep,
that before I see I love. Report has conquered
ere the siege is laid.

Sel. Those blessed words create me a new man,
young and vigorous. The course of nature, joined
with envious age, cannot prevent the sprightly
youth I now feel growing in me.

Enter SERVANT.

Ser. Sir, Alderman Buffoon is come to see you.

Sel. Alderman Buffoon, dost thou call him? Prithee, good foolane, tell Alderman Buffoon that he may come in. 'Tis Alderman Buffoon! I know him,—a vast rich citizen. Go you in, Mariana, no more my daughter, but my niece.

Mar. I understand you, sir. [*Exit* MARIANA.

Enter ALDERMAN.

Ald. Sir Marmaduke! I come to congratulate your good fortune.

Sel. Good fortune in what, sir?

Ald. In being sole guardian to your brother's daughters.

Sel. Where lies the good fortune of that?

Ald. Oh, sir, it gains you esteem in the world: besides, good advantage may be made on't.

Sel. Advantage? What! do you take me for a knave?

Ald. Fie, no! and yet I think you are no fool.

Sel. All the town knows their fortune; what advantage, then, can I make, unless I wickedly betray my trust?

Ald. Said like a worthy gentleman! I know your principles are honourable, your spirit high, but your fortune is low; consider that!

Sel. Pray you, come to your meaning, sir.

Ald. An honest advantage may be made, and I come to offer it.

Sel. I would have you know, were there no other but the common thing called honesty, that would guard me from corruption. But here's a stronger tie, a tender conscience. Alas! doomsday is ever in my thoughts, and I dare not hear you.

Ald. I wonder your high spirit and a tender conscience should agree so well ? 'Tis strange, too, that having been so lavish as to spend your great estate, you should now be so good a husband as to lay up for doomsday, a thing so far off.

Sel. Death, sir, do you come to affront me ?

Ald. No ; I say again, an honest advantage may be made, if there were twenty doomsdays. Will ten thousand pounds damn you ? Ask any man's opinion. But, case it would, I know twenty citizens with tender consciences, that make long prayers too, and yet would run the risk of doomsday for ten thousand pound.

Sel. Oh, most fearful! I hope you've better thoughts of me. Alas, I have a grave to think on. and in my chamber stands my coffin with my father's skull upon 't, and when I awake they are the first objects that my eyes encounter ; and can you ever hope to corrupt me then ?

Ald. I never knew a tender conscience afraid of an honest motion before. Since you're turned a simple precisian, farewell, sir !

Sel. Nay, pray stay, an honest motion may be heard at last.

Ald. Well said! Then thus it is : I have a nephew that I'll make my heir, and if you'll match your northern niece to him, I'll settle five thousand pounds a year on him, and at my death the rest. And I'll give you ten thousand pounds for your consent. You know I can make this good.

Sel. Where's your nephew ? Fetch him presently ; but I will take no money.

Ald. Well, well, who is your goldsmith ?

Sel. I have no goldsmith, nor will I take money; 'tis vicious bribery. Yet, now you talk of a gold-

smith, Mr. Cash is as just a man as can be dealt
with.

Ald. 'Tis enough! I understand you.

Sel. You must not understand me so, indeed,
sir.

Ald. Away, away! you're too modest, too honest
to live among men. I'll do it, and bring my
nephew presently.   [*Exit* ALDERMAN.

Sel. Ha, ha! I laugh to think how this fellow
will report my tender conscience to the citizens.
Well, if this fool will fall into a trap that never
was laid for him, then 'tis not I but fate destroys
him.   [*Exit.*

ACT III.—SCENE I.

Enter LORD ARMINGER, BOWMAN, AIMWELL,
POET, SERVANTS *and bottles.*

Arm. Gentlemen, pray ye salute my friend
Overwise! he has undertaken to be the poet to
whom the Squire is bound prentice.

Omnes. Your humble servant, Mr. Overwise.

Over. Gentle worthies, I am your contracted and
betrothed friend.

Arm. Can there be a finer-phrased fool than
this?

Bow. No, certainly; he is our contracted and
betrothed fool.

Over. My lord! No, the word lord is too common; it tastes of vulgerality.

Aim. God's so, there's a fine word! Vulgerality
is your own coining, sir?

Over. Stamped in my own mint, sir. I hope so

to refine the English tongue that the Dukes and
Peers of France will come over hither to learn the
language.

Aim. That's a great project. Do you hope to
see it in your own lifetime?

Over. No question, sir. Do you hope to see
Paul's built?

Aim. Yes, without doubt.

Over. At the same time I expect the Peers of
France to learn the English tongue.

Arm. But, Mr. Overwise, prithee what are those
squirts and bottles for?

Over. They are proper instruments to initiate
an ass withal. You must second me, as I have
ordered the ceremony; he will really be very
much abused.

Bow. Abused? Hang him! to murder him
requires no more compassion than drowning of a
kitlin.

Enter SIR HERCULES *and* SQUIRE.

Her. Save you, my lord! Save ye, gentlemen!
You honour me to come to this ceremony. Which
is my son's master, sirs?

Bow. This is the worthy person your son is
bound prentice to.

Her. Are you a poet, worthy sir?

Arm. Yes, sir; he is one of those that swinges
the Gods about.

Over. I am by my profession a poor poet, sir.

Her. That's no wonder, for I never heard of a
rich one in my life.

Over. Oh, sir, poets, like philosophers, despise
wealth. The fame of worthy wit is all we aim at.

Her. You may aim, but ne'er hit the mark, I

doubt; however, 'tis an honourable ambition.
Well, what is he to be the first year?

Over. The first year he takes his degree of ass.

Her. Oh, 'tis true; you told me of a ceremony to
enter or initiate him into the order of asshood.

Arm. I have heard of manhood, but never of
asshood before.

Over. Sir, the ceremony is great. The rule was
among the ancient poets, when a man took his
degree, to bathe in the liquor of the Gods; but we
modern wits steep our brains altogether in Burgundy and Pontack, and we find it does the business every whit as well.

Her. But how do you know that?

Over. By comparing the ancient and modern
wits together. Come, sir, you must strip to your
shirt. Get the bottles and glasses!

Bow. The ceremony to a stranger will seem to
be a gross abuse; however, I assure you it is no
more than what all men undergo that are bound
prentice to poets.

Omnes. That we all upon our honours do assure
you.

Squ. Nay, then, I will undergo it, whatsoever it
be.

Her. We can suffer as much abuse as any family
in England upon the score of poetry.

Over. Come, kneel down, sir! Now fill every
gentleman a bumper of claret. You must know
for six months together he must swallow daily two
verses; and by old custom he must begin with
Chaucer, and so go through all the English poets
till he come to modern Mr. Bayes. The ceremony
is an ancient copy of verses taken out of the
records of Parnassus.

Her. Is it possible? Pray, sir, oblige me with

a copy of verses out of the records of Parnassus.
What work shall we make i' th' country with 'em,
boy!

Squ. Ay, father!

Over. Are you all ready? Kneel down, sir.

Her. He will hurt his knees; pray ye, let him
have a cushion.

Arm. By no means; 'tis absolutely against the
record of Parnassus.

Squ. Then hang knees, father.

Her. 'Sheart! What a deal ado is here about
making one an ass!

Over. Silence! Stand all ready charged!

> Thy dull and stupid blockhead must be
> washed,
> And in thy face bumpers of claret dashed.
> > [*Throw the wine in his face.*
> Pour on his head the best Canary sack,
> And down his throat Burgundy and Pontack.
> > [*Pour wine.*
> Wash all his body with the choicest wine,
> That grows upon the fruitful river Rhine.
> Leave not e'en one dry thread upon his shirt,
> And do't with each of ye a lusty squirt.
> > [*They squirt him all over.*

Her. Hold! 'Sheart, hold! I think you mean
to make an ass of my son indeed.

Aim. Who the devil doubts it?

Bow. Why, sir, you know he is to be made
poetically an ass.

Her. 'Tis true; but yet 'twould stir a man's
blood to see one's child used at this roguish rate.

Arm. Sir, by the rules of Parnassus he ought to
take his degrees upon the rack.

Her. 'Sheart, I'll have no child of mine put upon the rack, my lord!

Bow. 'Tis not intended; that act was abolished by reason of the torment.

Squ. Nay, I'll endure any torment rather than not be a complete ass.

Her. I could find in my heart, the devil take me, to step to Parnassus, and see whether it be so or no.

Arm. You will not lose your labour, for really I have been there and read the record.

Squ. Pox of your records! my knees ache damnably. Do they use to have agues in Parnassus? My teeth chatter in my head, I am so wet and so cold.

Over. Come, we will make an end. Silence!

Here I produce a rare and precious pill,
Made by the doctors of Parnassus' Hill;
The virtue is, it will thy brain inspire
With th' airy flames of brisk poetic fire,
Having in it the refined quintessence
Of wit, true wisdom, and well-worded sense.
It being wrapt up in two lines of Chaucer,
You must with reverence swallow it down
    your maw, sir.

Her. Silence! Come, let's make an end!

In's face let each man throw a full beer glass.
        [*Full glasses thrown in his face.*
That ceremony done, rise up and pass
For a well-grounded and sufficient ass!

Squ. Do you call throwing of beer glasses in a man's face a ceremony?

Over. In Parnassus we do. Now, sir, I'll justify to the world you're an ass.

Arm. A pretty thing to brag of! Two such fools nature ne'er produced.

Her. I declare I like the pill wonderfully; I must have one of 'em.

Squ. For all this, I cannot fancy myself to be an ass yet.

Arm. Oh, yes; the very first minute you parted with your money you were an ass, I assure you.

Squ. How? You mean I was an ass for parting with my money, my lord?

Arm. I mean fairly by the rules of poetry.

Her. Then you're an ass upon record, sirrah! Now you're a prentice, your hat must not be on before your master.

Arm. That's your mistake; an ass puts off his hat to no man, but is void of all manners. His talent is to be bold, rude, and saucy, without regard to quality or any distinction of persons.

Her. If those qualifications will do, I'll warrant him a sufficient ass.

Bon. And now you are so, Squire, you must always have a cane, but not in your hand; 'tis to be worn ever under your arm, that when you turn about you may take the next man a slap over the face.

Squ. Adad, that's pretty! Look to your chops, father! But, sir, are them asses that wear their canes so?

Arm. They are shrewdly to be suspected.

Squ. I am an apt scholar. I do but what you teach me; ha!

Her. I am thinking, my lord, what contemptible titles a man must pass over before he attains to the honourable name of poet,—as ass, fop, and witlin.

Bow. Poet is an honourable title ; it admits of
no addition.

Squ. Oh, father, the fame of poetry is above all
mortal honour. Wealth and greatness perish, the
man of dignity dies, but poets are eminently and
prodigiously immortal.

Her. By my life, the boy speaks rarely well
already ! If he talk thus wittily being an ass,
how will he talk when he's a poet ?

Aim. Little better, I assure thee.

Squ. Poets are esteemed above Princes. I have a
reverend author for it called Taylor, the water poet.

" When nature did intend some wondrous thing,
  She made a poet, or at least a King."

Ben Jonson would ha' given a hundred pounds—
if he had had it, that is—to ha' been author of
those two lines.

Her. Did ever boy speak so rarely, gentlemen ?
The devil take me, I could find in my heart to
commence ass myself.

Arm. Commence changeling, for thou wert born
an ass.

Squ. Hark you, sir ! now I'm entered, I may
censure plays, may I not ?

Arm. Yes, yes ! to censure plays and women is
natural to an ass.   [*Exit* SQUIRE.

Over. Well, my Earl, I value myself much upon
this frolic.

Arm. So thou mayest.

Aim. Sir Hercules, 'tis time to remember your
promise, and to present me to the guardian. If
thy interest get me one of the heiresses, here's my
hand I'll not murder thee.

Her. 'Tis enough ! I'm so intimate with the
guardian, I'm certain he'll deny me nothing.

Enter FOOTMAN.

Foot. My lord, here's a letter from Sir Marmaduke Seldin.

Arm. 'Ods so, the guardian to the heiresses! Gentlemen, I must take leave, and for a while grow serious.

Her. My lord, I thank you for this honour. Bowman, prithee go with me !   [*Exeunt.*

SCENE II.

Enter SIR MARMADUKE *and* MARIANA *at one door,* FRENCH WOMAN *at another.*

Wom. O sir, sir, sir !

Sel. What is the matter that you stare so ?

Wom. Sir, my country north lady will no learn French of me. Me must learn Yorkshire of her or she will beat my brain.

Sel. That is just her humorous little cousin. 'Tis happy that she mimics her so well; that preserves us from suspicion.

Enter TAILOR.

Tail. Oh, sir, what sall me do? Me have brought my Yorkshire madam two new gown home, and begar she have cut off all her long train to de very calf of her leg !

Enter FIDELIA.

Sel. Here she comes ! Fie, fie, niece ! I must chide you, niece. They say you've cut the train off your gowns, and quite spoiled 'em, niece.

Fid. Nay, honey nuncle, they're ne'er the war for me; why, lack-a-day, they come down to the varra heels of me yet, my bearn.

R

Mar. Nay, sister, you must be ruled, and wear your clothes fashionably, as I do.

Fid. Now, oot upon thee, sister! yee wad have me wear a lang tail behind me, as my naunt's brown cow does at hame.

Mar. They are not tails, but trains, sister. Great persons wear them as ornaments of State, as an honourable distinction from those of lower quality.

Fid. By my troth, but I'se teld that naughty sluts wear 'em as well as your great Countesses.

Sel. Ay, but, niece, persons of quality have Pages,—boys a purpose to hold up their trains.

Fid. Have they boys to hold up their tails behind? Do not the unlucky lads peep in 'em sometime?

Sel. Fie, niece, what have you said? Those are paw * words indeed.

Fid. Why, nuncle, did I say bawdiness now?

Sel. No, not downright, but very near it, I assure you.

Fid. Nay, by my saul, sister, gin my naunt at York should but knaw that I said bawdiness, marra, she'd shatter my brains oot; faith wad she!

Sel. Come, sweet niece, be ruled, and let the French people dress you and make a fine lady of you.

Fid. Wad my French tailor were hanged; he stinks of wine as sour as a swine-trough. Beside he is varra saucy with ma, nuncle.

Sel. Saucy! how? saucy was he?

Fid. Oh, my saul, nuncle, gin I'd let him alane, he had taken measure o' th' inside of me as well as o' th' out.

Sel. You damned villain! ha! I never heard of such a rogue.

[*Draws; the Man runs out.*

* Paw-paw: naughty.—*Ver. dial.*

Fid. Nuncle, I'd have my naunt's tailor, Billy
Barton of York, make my gowns for me.

Sel. Prithee, who is Billy Barton of York?

Fid. Marra, he's the delicatest tailor in all
England; he makes my Lord Mayor of York's
gowns, and Lady Mairise's tee.

Enter ALDERMAN *and* SQUIRE.

Ald. Come, sir, I mean to marry you to the
Northern heiress.—Sir, I have brought my nephew
and my heir.

Sel. He is welcome. Pray you, sir, salute my
nieces.—I should scorn to have this Buffoon come
into the presence of my children but for the con-
veniency of destroying him.

Ald. Here's a bill upon Alderman Marrow for
ten thousand pound.

Sel. I'll not take it indeed, sir.

Ald. Come, come; you must and shall have it.

Sel. I'll not touch it, truly; give it my eldest
niece, if you please, to buy her pins. A proud
man may let his daughter stoop to ten thousand
pound.   [*A kiss.*

Ald. Fair lady, here's a paper of pins will last
you and your heirs for ever. Sir, I have brought
the deeds of my estate to peruse and to keep till
our Counsel settle things of all hands.

Sel. 'Tis enough; let us in and view the writings.

Squ. Sir, I swear by Parnassus, you have got
the most superlative paragon of the North. I am
struck with an amour as suddenly as he that fell
in love while he pulled on his boots.

Ald. Sir, you have taken Sir Marmaduke over
the face with your cane.

Squ. The mode must crave your pardon, not I. The whole congregation of Gallants use it as a novel lately come from France.

Sel. A most superlative fool! This is one of nature's bold strokes, niece. You see a monster there almost in the shape of a man; use him accordingly.

[*Exeunt* Sir Marmaduke *and* Alderman.

Fid. I understand you, sir; let me alone to abuse him, sir.—Is thou to be my husband, sweet honey bearn?

Squ. Honey? What a loving fool it is; she calls me honey at first sight.

Fid. Now, I prithee, honey, help me to curse my Frenchwoman.

Squ. Ay, with all my heart, honey. A pox upon her, and confound her! Where is she?

Fid. Honey, thou mun let me bang thee some time, then thou't be my good lad.

Squ. Ay, with all my heart, bang all the honey out of the hive of Parnassus.

Fid. Stand fair, then, honey; there's for thee now.   [*Box o' th' ear.*

Squ. The devil! You strike too hard, honey.

Fid. Hang thee, thou mun not frown; thou mun smile sweetly on me when I box thee; now thou's my defty.* And wilt thou play finely with me, and not hurt me?   [*Box o' th' ear; he smiles.*

Squ. Play finely with me and not hurt me? 'Sheart, I have got a little whore, I think.

Fid. Now, my bearn, thou mun lake† at, *Come, mother, saw you my cock to-day?*

* Qy. dawty?—one to be caressed and fondled.
† Play.
     "William wel with Meliors his wille than dede,
      And layked there at lyking al the long daye."
                              William and the Werwolf, p. 38.

Squ. Come, mother, saw you my cock to day?
'Sheart, 'tis a whore of a certain.

Fid. Thou mun play at Rampscuttle and Clapperdepouch with me, my honey.

Squ. Clapperdepouch? Devil, what a strange
kind of a wife shall I have! Come, then, show
me your Rampscuttle.

Fid. Thou mun first put on a petticoat. My
Frenchwoman shall make a lad-lass of thee.

[*Puts on a petticoat.*

Squ. Anything to please you, madam.

Fid. Then thou's my pretty Frenchwoman, and
I'll give thee a honey sugar kiss.

Squ. I'll do her the honour to give her a honey
sugar kiss too.

Mar. A great honour, indeed. What an absolute
fool is this!

Fid. Come, honey, learn Rampscuttle; begin
thus.   [*Dance.*

Squ. With all my heart. 'Slife, what a mad
couple shall we make!

Fid. That's my fool; wilt thou be my fool,
honey?

[*She turns round and claps down; then he.*

Squ. I'll be thy fool; nay, I'll be thy cuckold,
honey.

Fid. Wilt thou? I' faith, and we have mad
lads; we make swingeing cuckolds in Yorkshire.

Squ. That's nothing to be a cuckold, madam.
My father and mother are cuckolds; we can prove
our genealogy to be cuckolds from the very loins
of King Pippin.

Fid. Whaw, whaw, marra, the devil take thee
and thy King Pippin to boot! Now play at Clapperdepouch, my honey bearn. Clapperdepouch, clapperdepouch, clapperde, clapperde, clapperdepouch!

Squ. This is the finest wife for my turn that
ever mortal light on! Oh, devil! you have beat
out my teeth, honey!

[*She turns, and hits him on the face with his cane.*

Fid. The fashion mun crave thy pardon, honey,
not I; besides, all the teeth of thy genealogy have
been beaten out up to King Pippin. What's thy
name, honey?

Squ. I am proud of my name; I was christened
Squire Buffoon.

Fid. By my saul, Buffoon is a worse name than
King Pippin.

Squ. Honey, we are the ancientest family of
the nation; our mansionhouse is called Buffoon,
and our coat is three buffoons.

Fid. Methinks you should give three pippins
too, and that would show your descent plainly
from King Pippin.

Squ. If the heralds are to be bribed, I'll have
'em. Come, honey, shall we go behind the door
and play finely together, and get one another with
child of two young Pippins?

Fid. Marra, out upon the grizely beast! Wie
wad ta make a slut of me, and have me play at
bawdiness with thee? Help, help, help!

Enter ALDERMAN *and* SIR MARMADUKE.

Ald. How now, what's the matter?

Fid. Marra, he's e'en a foul beast; that is a,
nuncle, he wad have me go into the dark, and do
naughtiness with him.

Squ. She asked me to play finely with her and
not hurt her; then what could·I say less?

Sel. This rogue was composed of a coarser stuff
than the common creation, of unrefined clay, such

as bearwards and tinkers were made up of. You are content, sir, to settle all entirely upon my niece and her heirs?

Ald. Most freely; upon this match I'll make my nephew a lord.

Sel. There are so many Buffoons stolen into titles, that men would judge they came not lawfully by them. Come, sir, let us go settle this estate.

Squ. Why, honey, shall we not have one trial of skill for a young Pippin? [*Exeunt.*

SCENE III.

Enter SIR HERCULES, LATON, BOWMAN, SQUIRE, *and* CLERK.

La. Sir, be sure you make my peace, or all the world shall not save your throat. I will be at the door and hear all you say, sir. [*Exit* LATON.

Bow. If thou get'st off o' this, Knight, I'll prefer thee to the first form of Wits, and that's very honourable, I assure you.

Her. I had rather be an honourable first-rate Wit than a first-rate Alderman.

Enter JUDGE.

Bow. Thou art bravely disguised; have a good heart! here's the Judge.

Jud. Save ye, gentlemen! Are you Sir Thomas Lovill, sir?

Her. I am, Knight and Baronet, if you please, my Lord.

Jud. Then, sir, if you please, your business?

Her. Second me, sirs.—I come to inform your Lordship of the most notorious villain that ever

wore the figure of a man,—one Sir Hercules Buffoon.   The law, no doubt, will give your Lordship
damage enough for the scandalous things he has
said of you.

Jud. Of me, sir? Scandalous things of me?
Pray you, the words?

Bow. What the devil! does your father mean
to be hanged?

Squ. For a good lie he'll venture that at any
time.

Her. He said your Lordship loved a bribe above
your allegiance, and that you have unjustly given
away an estate for a bribe of fifteen hundred
guineas.

Jud. That's action enough; down with those
guineas.   What a villain 'tis!

Squ. Ay, you'd say so if you knew the rogue as
well as we do, my Lord.

Her. You dog, I do not allow you to abuse me
thus.

Jud. But, gentlemen, have you witness of this?

Her. Enough, my Lord; myself and two gentlemen more,—not these; they can witness another
thing.   One Laton, hearing how Buffoon had
abused your Lordship, comes to him, and had
downright killed him but for these two gentlemen.

Squ. 'Tis very true, my Lord; I got a broken
head with parting 'em, and this gentleman was
run through the arm.

Bow. A pox on him, I must own it now.—He
tells you true, my Lord.

Jud. Pray you, what Laton is it that has fought
for me thus?

Her. One Robin Laton, my Lord.   Buffoon's a
valiant fellow, and yet this Laton has cudgelled
and beaten him to stockfish, my Lord.

Jud. That Robin Laton is my kinsman. I turned him out of doors; 'tis much, then, he should fight for me.

Her. Your kinsman, my Lord? he might be your son by his desperate fighting for you.

Jud. Say you so? If this be true, gentlemen. I'll make him happy.

Bow. We can all witness it, my Lord. To say truth, Sir Hercules is a most pernicious, mischievous rascal.

Squ. A notorious villain, my Lord. There has not been a rogue hanged these seven years that has deserved it so much as he has done.

Her. You dog, remember this; I'll maul you for 't.

Jud. Well, I'll trounce the rogue, I warrant you. Has he an estate to make good the damages the law will give me?

Squ. Enough, enough, my Lord. Hang him! a damned rich hell-hound!

Her. Zounds! was ever man thus abused, Bowman?—Nay, he said your Lordship was a most gigantic whoremaster, and that you have nine bawds lie leaguer in the country to send up fresh virgins to you.

Jud. Pox on him, would he could make his words good! I'll firk the knave. How shall we do to take him?

Her. If your Lordship will grant me your warrant, I'll bring him before your honour to-morrow morning.

Jud. Clerk, write a warrant presently. I'll not leave him worth a groat; he shall rot in jail.

Her. To see that rogue a beggar would make me pray for your Lordship all the days of my life. The knave called me cuckold, my Lord, too.

Squ. Faith, sir, no child can say absolutely who was his father; wives will have their fancies, and why not yours?

Her. You abominable rogue!—My Lord, have not you an office in your gift?

Jud. Yes, I have, sir.

Bow. I'll tell you, my Lord; this Buffoon, after Mr. Laton had beaten him, promised to get this office of your Lordship for Mr. Laton, pretending that he had you at such a hank you durst not deny him.

Jud. I never saw the villain in my life.

Bow. Nay, my Lord, the next day he told your nephew he had got the office for him, and made him go presently to give your Lordship thanks for it.

Her. And the base fellow, they say, was never with your Lordship.

Jud. No, indeed, sir; and that made me angry with my nephew to give me thanks for that I never gave him. The man meant mischief.

Her. Was ever such a shameless fellow, my Lord? By my troth, give your kinsman the office, and I'll give your Lordship two brace of fat deer every season, as long as you live, my Lord.

Jud. Give it me under hand and seal, that I may demand them as my due, and I'll do it.

Her. With all my heart, my Lord.

Jud. Out of what park? for the place must be expressed in the writing.

Her. Zounds! I've ne'er a park; what shall I do?—Out Whetstone's Park, in the county of Middlesex, my Lord.

Jud. Whetstone? There is a place called Whetstone by Barnet, but I never heard of a park there.

Her. That's not the place. Whetstone's Park is

as well known as London. I would it were an
hundred miles off on't. I am so plagued with
Citizens that I cannot have a deer that's man's meat
but they steal it out of my park, my Lord.

Clerk. Here is the warrant against Sir Hercules
Buffoon.

Jud. I'll sign it. Clerk, draw an indenture for
two brace of deer yearly out of Whetstone's Park,*
in the county of Middlesex, upon forfeiture of five
hundred pounds, from Sir Thomas Lovill.

Bow. Here I shall burst out a-laughing ; I cannot hold.

Enter LATON.

La. My Lord, here's one to summon all the
Judges to court.

Jud. 'Ods so, I must away, then. Sir, I forgive
you for defending my reputation so well ; I give
you the office, and all my estate after my death.
Nephew, see Sir Thomas Lovill sign the obligation
for two brace of deer yearly out of Whetstone's
Park, in Middlesex ; and, sir, I hope you will
apprehend that rascal Buffoon for me.

[*Exit* JUDGE.

Her. I'll have him as sure as the day comes, my
Lord.

La. Dear Knight, thou art come off with honour ;
thou art my golden calf, and I'll worship thee.

---

* Whetstone's Park is referred to in Crowne's Country Wit.
See *Crowne's Works in this series, Vol. III.* See also *author's
address to Lee's* ' *Princess of Cleves.*' It was situated on the
Holborn side of Lincoln's Inn Fields, and was much frequented by women of the town. Granger, in his account of
Mother Cresswell, observes : "The daughters of iniquity
were much more numerous than the mothers. They were
dispersed through every quarter of the town, but Moorfields,
Whetstone's Park, Lukener's Lane, and Dog and Bitch Yard,
were their capital seraglios."

Bow. Never had man so much ado to forbear laughing as I have had at this Whetstone's Park.

Squ. I was fain to turn about and laugh.

Clerk. I had certainly laughed in the Judge's face, but for consideration of you, sir.

La. Clerk, take heed you be very just.

Clerk. As your own heart, i' faith.

Bow. How thou wilt get clear of the Judge when he comes to have his deer out of Whetstone's Park, I know not.

Her. I have a harder task by half; I am to help Aimwell to one of the rich heiresses. I have told him a damned lie.

La. Like enough ; prithee, what is it ?

Her. I told him the guardian and I were intimate friends, old acquaintance and schoolfellows, and the devil take me if I ever saw him in my life ; yet I am resolved to face him down that we are dear friends and old acquaintants, and that's as hard a task as ever impudence undertook.

Bow. Faith, so 'tis, considering the great spirit of the guardian.

Her. I'll do it for all that.

Squ. Give me thy hand, father ; I commend thy impudence, old——

La. Bravely resolved ! Come, I will first treat thee, then go with thee, and back thee manfully.

[*Exeunt.*

ACT IV.—SCENE I.

Enter LORD ARMINGER, GUARDIAN, MARIANA, *and* WAITERS.

Arm. Wait in the next room.

Sel. I am prouder to have the great Lord

Arminger under this mean roof than haughty
Princes are of empire ; and I bow with such reverence to your person as holy men do to the holy
altar, and with the same humility offer my obla-
tion up. Receive her as from Heaven, for she is
fraught with virtue equal with the angels.

Arm. Sir, I admire you with more than common wonder. Guardians usually make price of
the innocent orphans in their charge, but you are
more than just, you are kind, and to that degree
which parents have for children.

Sel. I shall betray myself with violent fondness :
such torrents of love flow in me, that I think the
world too little for her dower.

Mar. Indeed, my Lord, his tender care seems
to have more of father than guardian in 't, in
which we hold ourselves most highly blessed.

Sel. My good Lord, I leave you to make your
court where doubtless you'll find your love most
worthily and readily received.   [*Exit* SELDIN.

Arm. Madam, your uncle spoke largely of your
virtues to me, but nothing of your person ; and
now I see the cause, for 'tis impossible the capacity
of man should reach the character of so much
beauty as I now behold, and all the rest must
needs submit to crown you Goddess of your
admired sex.

Mar. My Lord, you answer not your character.
You were rendered to me the only man of honour,
truth, and justice, and I hear nothing but airy
compliment, fine poetical flattery ; fit only to catch
girls.

Arm. Madam, by my honour, and that's my
dearest treasure, I flatter not, but speak truth just
as my heart conceives it ; therefore I again declare
you are the only beauty that ever yet my eye

encountered, and I find a dotage stealing on me
more than common love.

Mar. Hold, my Lord, I command you! for sure
she may command that is so much admired?
therefore, by that precious gem, your honour, are
those sweet words you've spoken truth?

Arm. Madam, by all the bliss I hope for, I have
no falsehood in me.

Mar. Then stop and go no further in your love,
I charge you, for I must never be your wife.

Arm. How, madam? I came prepared by your
uncle this day to marry you.

Mar. Oh, my Lord, that day is further off than
the unknown, uncertain hour of doom.

Arm. Madam, if there be cause for this your
cruelty, reveal it; and by the original of all honour
here I swear, this bosom is your grave to bury all
your secrets.

Mar. I believe you, my Lord, with the same
faith I do religion.

Arm. Madam, you have reprieved my life, by
thinking me worthy of your thoughts, though unworthy of your love.

Mar. Oh, my honoured Lord, it is my unworthi-
ness, not yours, that must for ever keep this cruel
distance.

Arm. Whate'er the reason is, that cannot be it.
Say you're contracted unknown to your uncle;
say any cruel thing but that.

Mar. Then I declare the noble character my
uncle gave me of your Lordship sprung in me a
true and perfect love, which made my desires so
violent to see you, that since my life till now was
more uneasy than a sick man's restless night, and
yet must never marry.

Arm. Never was man pleased and startled so at

once! Infinitely pleased to hear you say you love,
but strangely startled that you ne'er must marry.
The thought frights me. The ghosts of murdered
men shake not guilty slaves as that resolve shakes
me. I find man is not fortified to bear the frights
of love. I beseech you, madam, if you have cause
for this your resolution, give me some ease by
imparting it.

Mar. It is so dreadful for a good man to hear;
but, if your Lordship will ask my uncle's leave to
carry me and my sister abroad, you then shall
know why you and I must never marry.

Arm. Your resolution has dispersed my spirits
so, they are never more to be collected. All
within me lies confused; a madman's blood's in
better temper, and I am all on fire till I am satisfied.

Mar. My Lord, I am destroyed if you reveal me.

Arm. You are more cruel in distrusting that
than in refusing me.

Mar. Your pardon; and henceforth my trust
shall ever rest in you.   [*Exeunt.*

SCENE II.

Enter SIR HERCULES, BOWMAN, AIMWELL, LATON,
and OVERWISE.

Aim. You have put me off from time to time,
and I am resolved to be no longer fooled; therefore, try your interest you boast of with the
guardian, or——

Her. Well, fool, doubt not me in the least.
—This is the greatest strait I ever was yet put to,
Bowman. For me to salute and impudently em-
brace a man of his high spirit, and face him down

that we are dear and intimate friends, and yet
never saw him—the devil take me, 'tis a damned
audacious task !

Bow. However, go forward ! here's my hand
thou shalt not suffer.

Her. Then, dear impudence, stand my friend
this one push, and I'll own thee for my patron all
my life.

La. Here comes the guardian ; bear up, Knight !

Omnes. Your most humble servant, sir.

Enter SELDIN.

Sel. Gentlemen, I am to crave your pardon, my
nieces are not this day to be seen ; however, the
freedom of my house I tender you with all the
respect imaginable.

Her. Sure, Sir Marmaduke, you will let your
intimate friend see your nieces. Dear rogue, how
dost thou do?—Own me for your friend and
schoolfellow ; 'twill be thousands in your way.—
This worthy gentleman, dear friend, thou must
know.

Sel. It will concern me more to know you, sir,
for in my life I never met such confidence.

Her. Why, how now, Marmaduke, has your
guardianship made you proud ? Have you forgot
yourself ?

Sel. What the devil means this fellow ? Gentlemen, who knows this creature ? or who brought
him hither?

Aim. We all know him, and he brought us
hither, pretending more interest in you than all
mankind besides.

Sel. Upon my honour, gentlemen, I never saw
the man before.

Her. Thou shameless fellow, canst thou with so
bold a face say thou know'st me not?

Aim. You are found out, i' faith, Knight!

Her. Hang him, he knows me better than he knows his housekeeper!

Sel. I am at a stand, and know not how in this case to behave myself.

Her. I commend thee, Marmaduke, for driving a jest so far. The devil take me, gentlemen, if I thought it had been in him. I loved thee dearly before, but this jocose humour of thine makes me admire thee. Dear rogue, let me hug and kiss thee, sweet boy.

Sel. Stand off, or, as I'm a gentleman, I'll strike you; which nothing could make me do in my own house, but such an impudent provocation.

Her. Did you ever in your lives see a jest so well managed, gentlemen? He does it so rarely well that I dare swear you all think him in earnest.

La. Yes, in good faith do we.

Her. By my life, so should I, but that I have known him these fifty years.

Sel. Pray ye, gentlemen, open the scene, and discover what buffoon this is.

Her. Buffoon! mark ye that; as if he did not know me, and yet name me. He'll carry it thus till I am angry with him.

Bow. Overwise is whispering of him; he'll trouble him worse than Buffoon.

Over. Sir, I am one that honours you. My name is Overwise; by that you may judge I am no fool, sir.

Sel. 'Sdeath! this is a worse fop than the other.

La. But, Knight, if Sir Marmaduke jokes, he does it rarely well.

Her. He is the devil at joking. But that I would not say it to disgrace him, he has been an old player at the Blackfriars.

S

Sel. You eternal dog, I'll cut your throat!
Gentlemen, come ye to affront me?

Bow. Hold, good sir! we come upon no such
unworthy design, I assure you, sir!

Over. Sir, read Seneca, and he will teach you
patience.

Sel. Damn thee, fop! is patience to be exercised
in thy company?

Her. But you, friend Marmaduke, now 'tis time
to leave fooling, and to own me for your old
friend, as you have done these fifty years, or hang
me if I do not declare you a proud foolish fellow.

Sel. Gentlemen, I love wit and joking—no man
more ; therefore, if this be a Court fool, or a public
buffoon, declare it, and he's welcome.

Her. Incomparable well ! incomparable ! Does
he not carry it rarely well, gentlemen?

Aim. I know not what to think. Are they
acquainted or no, for a wager?

Over. No more than thou art with a reverend
Divine, or the Emperor of Japan.

Aim. Then is this rogue Buffoon the original
of impudence, and the rest of mankind mere
copies.   [*He whispers.*

Sel. 'Sdeath, your whispering torments me more
than his impudence. Gentlemen, pray ye let me
know the name and quality of this confident person.

Her. Away, away, fools! 'Sheart, he knows
name and quality better than he knows his children. I'll show you by an infallible token that I
know him, for he has a mole of his right buttock
as broad as both my hands.

Sel. By my life, a villain, and he lies, gentlemen !

Her. Why, show the contrary, and that's de-
monstration. Sure he will not let down his
breeches to disprove me.

Sel. I know not whether to laugh or to be angry. Pray ye, gentlemen, let me know his name.

Bow. Sir, his name is Hercules Buffoon.

Sel. Oh, I have heard of him. Sir Hercules, I must be better known to you.

Her. A good jest! as if you and I need to be better known.

Sel. Nay, sir, I'll own anything you say, to keep up your humour.

Over. But one ear more with you, sir. I'm one that loves curiosities. Have you really such a mole o' your buttock?

Sel. I can be angry no longer. Where the devil wert thou bred that thou delightest so in lying?

Her. Now, sirs, I'll tell you how we two arch rogues robbed my mother's orchard of all her wall fruit, her peaches, heart cherries, and her great Dutch strawberries.

La. Pray ye, sir, are strawberries a wall fruit?

Her. You must know those were Greenland strawberries, and there they grow up to be vast great trees, and are nailed against the walls as vines are.

La. By reason of the great heat of the climate, I suppose; because Greenland, you know, lies under the line.

Her. It does so. Thou hast travelled, or read maps, I find. But, sir, to clear ourselves of robbing the orchard, we drew forty huge overgrown carps out of a pond, each six foot long at least.

Bow. How! carps six foot long! That's two yards, man.

Sel. But then you must consider they were overgrown carps.

Her. Right! a monstrous overgrown carp may

be nine foot long. But, sir, we put 'em in the peach-trees, then fetched my mother to see 'em; and when we came back, the carps were skipping from tree to tree, eating the fruit as the devil drove 'em. So my mother wondered at it, and we were cleared of the robbery, old boy.

Aim. Now the devil thy tutor take thee; for every motion of thy tongue thou deservest a whipping.

Her. This fellow is an infatuated Jew; believes nothing—not so much as a Greenland strawberry-tree.

Aim. Did you never tell a lie with Sir John Mandevil for a wager?

Her. Yes, and made an ass of him too. I'll tell you a thing that I am sure this fellow will give no credit to.

Aim. Now thou speakest truth, I am sure of it.

Her. Sir, I have been in a strange country, where all creatures are prodigiously bigger than in other parts of the world, though of the same species. For example, I have seen a bee as big as an eagle.

Bow. Pray you, how big were the hives then?

Her. Full as big as Westminster Hall, only they're round.

Over. A good simile; for we have a fort of English vermin that bring all the honey of the nation to that hive indeed.

Her. I have seen a cabbage-tree higher than the monument upon Fish Street Hill.

Omnes. Thou boy, thou boy!

Her. You do not believe me, then? The devil take me if these homebred fellows can be saved! They neither know nor believe half the creation.

Aim. The country thou speakest of is thy own creation.

Her. Marmaduke, upon my credit, all their mainmasts for their capital ships are made of cabbage stalks, and the planks of the ships are all cabbage leaves,—and better timber by half than your English oak.

Bow. If the planks of their ships be cabbage leaves, prithee what are the sails made of ?

Her. Upon my life, all their sails are made of spiders' webs.

Omnes. Ha, ha, ha !

Her. You ignorant fops, what do you laugh at ? A spider's web there is ten times stronger than all the canvas sails in the world. And the spiders are bigger than the King's fine cranes in the park, but twenty times longer legged. The first time I saw them, they looked like Lincolnshire men walking i' th' fens upon stilts.

Omnes. Ha, ha, ha !

Aim. If every man here should cut an inch of his tongue out, he would have enough left, I warrant ye, to tell a lie.

Over. Really, if one inch were off, 'tis possible he might speak truth ; and if one inch will not do, my opinion is to cut it clear out.

Bow. Prithee, Knight, what's the name of the country where these wonders grow ?

Her. 'Tis called—'tis called Terra Incognita. All the seamen i' th' world know it. Ne'er a sculler o' th' Thames but knows Terra Incognita, fool !

Bow. 'Tis as well known as the north-east passage to the Indies. The seamen know it as well as they know the Garden of Eden.

Her. Why, there's no question i' th' world of it, man.

Aim. If thou shouldst be condemned to speak truth all thy life, what a case wert thou in !

Her. I'll hold thee five guineas the next thing I speak of shall be truth, and deposit in Sir Marmaduke's hand.

Aim. Done for five guineas ! There, sir.

Her. And there, sir. You know I told ye, gentlemen, that the guardian and I were old acquaintants and intimate friends ; and may I perish if ever I saw him in my life before this hour. Speak truth, now, guardian.

Sel. The man speaks truth now, upon my honour, gentlemen.

Her. Then I have won. Now, I'll hold thee five guineas more that I ne'er speak truth again as long as I live.

Omnes. Ha, ha, ha, ha !

Enter SERVANT.

Ser. My Lord Arminger is come, and desires to see you.

Sel. Gentlemen, I must crave your pardon. Great business calls me from ye ; but I desire ye to take the freedom of my house.   [*Exit* SELDIN.

Enter ALDERMAN *and* SQUIRE.

Her. Uncle, what makes you here ?

Ald. I have matched our squire to the Northern heiress, and settled all my estate upon the lady.

Bow. Sir, your nephew cannot marry till he is out of his time, for he is prentice to a poet.

Ald. How ! Prentice to a poet !

Squ. Yes, and a greater honour than to be a Lord. Uncle, you would say so if you knew the records of Parnassus. I have taken the degree of ass already.

Ald. Ass! Poets are the wittiest men of our nation; then what relation can an ass have to a poet, blockhead?

Squ. Oh, uncle, you would ha' blessed yourself to ha' seen me pass the grand ceremony of an ass. First, I kneeled in my shirt, then all these gentlemen, according to the rules of Parnassus, threw a hundred bumpers of claret in my face.

Ald. Bumper! Prithee, what's a bumper?

Squ. For shame, uncle! Not know what a bumper is? Bumper is the Parnassus' word for a beer glass top full.

Her. Oh, the learning of Parnassus exceeds all the Greek, Hebrew, Scotch, Welsh, and Irish in the world!

Ald. I find they make an ass of thee indeed.

La. But you must know 'twas done by the laws of Parnassus, where the records of poetry are most sacredly kept.

Ald. Records of Parnassus! Prithee what place is Parnassus?

Squ. 'Tis a place of rest for the souls of the poets; for you must know they never go to Heaven, but when they die their souls are condemned to Parnassus, there to sing madrigals, every one in praise of his own poetry, to all eternity.

Aim. And that doubtless pleases them better than going to Heaven.

Ald. But will abusing a man inspire him with wit?

Her. The ceremony without question will; for never was boy so improved.

Ald. But will his wit get him an estate, as mine has done?

Her. Nay, by my faith, I cannot say that.

Ald. Then a wit is a pitiful poor creature, and,

I'll warrant you, one that will borrow money of his very father. I have more wit than a hundred of 'em.

Squ. Ay, uncle, you got your wit out of eternal Hopkins.

Ald. Come, let me see your master.

Over. I am the person that honours your nephew so far as to make him my prentice.

Ald. Honour him! He honours thee, thou vainglorious poet! But I do not blame thee, for 'tis natural to you all. But come, Sir Poet, I'll try whether you're a poet or no. Break a jest quickly—quickly, without studying, sir!

Over. Hold, sir; a jest is not so quickly at a poet's command.

Ald. Then you're a dull, insipid poet, and will never go to Parnassus. To tell you true, I like not your profession, therefore I'll buy the boy's time out. I'll give you a hundred pound that you may take some lawful calling; for poets and players are never useful but of a Lord Mayor's day, when they're mounted on a pageant.

Bow. What think you of the authority of the nation that allows them?

Ald. For all that, we citizens are always of our own opinion. And I say again, poets and players are never useful but when a king is crowned, or a lord mayor is chosen; and 'tis the opinion of the court of aldermen, and I'll stand in it. [*Exeunt.*

SCENE III.

Enter LORD ARMINGER *and* MARIANA.

Mar. I am here by promise, to give your Lordship reasons why you and I must never marry.

And prepare yourself, for I've a story; blood and horror are the least things in't.

Arm. Bless me! it startles all my spirits to hear sweet innocence talk of blood. You must be virtuous; such sweetness cannot deceive.

Mar. My Lord, I am false,—a lewd impostor, and not the heiress whom you came to marry.

Arm. How? You have not left me sense enough to wonder! My blood wants motion, and life is stealing from me, and not sensible. Speak again, for 'tis impossible you should e'er be wicked.

Mar. I am not the heiress, but Sir Marmaduke Seldin's own daughter; and the true heiresses, my dear and lovely kinswomen, are ——

Arm. Are what? Where? Speak!

Mar. Murdered! What opinion have you of my virtue now, my Lord ?

Arm. I rather fear your senses than your virtue yet. Some wild extravagancy hath seized your parts, and made your tongue strike false. Such a Heavenly fabric cannot be tenanted with devils. Therefore deliver truth, in short, and let me be at ease.

Mar. Our cruel father forced our consents to that more cruel murder; and had we refused, we had infallibly met our own deaths.

Arm. Hold! My heart has met so violent a storm, 'twill overset. I bear a weight of grief heavier than Atlas' burden. Pray you, speak of something else; my ears are filled with so much wickedness, they have no room for more. Pray you, speak the rest as softly as you can.

Mar. Then thus, my Lord. Having met my father in all his bloody purposes ——

Arm. Bless me! how unconcerned she talks of

blood! Her tongue persuades one way and her Heavenly form another.

Mar. But the contrivance of their deaths so infinitely surprised and pleased my father, that he trusted our engines with the bloody deed.

Arm. Bless me! how my opinion comes and goes! You seem to rejoice, madam.

Mar. Then hear me, sir. My own servant, having a seaman to her lover, hired a ship to carry them to the north of Norway, and there to set the innocent ashore where none but the merciless inhabit; and, being shipped, my jealous father saw them under sail below the Hope, and then returned well satisfied. But our servants, by our order, the next tide brought 'em back; and here, I thank Heaven, they are safe, and have escaped the wicked purpose of my father.   -

Arm. I thank Heaven too, both for your virtuous act and their preservation. How glorious do you now appear! You shine so bright, your dazzling virtues hurt my tender sight. I dare not gaze too much.

Mar. My Lord, preserve your fine managed tongue for the lovely beauty that deserves it. You came to court the true heiress, and fate has purposely preserved her for you.

Enter LYDIA.

Lyd. Oh, my sweet, dear lady, your cousins will receive you with such joy, I fear an ecstasy will follow. I'll call them presently.

Mar. Now you shall behold a beauty worthy of the Lord Arminger, whose parts and fortune parallel yours. But had she no wealth, and were as low as poor Mariana, the power of her beauty would humble the proudest of Monarchs, and make him stoop to court her.   .

Arm. Had she all this beauty, and the world's treasure in her own exchequer, she could no more tempt me to love her than she could tempt the dead. A marble statue her beauty may give life and motion to, force it to weep and tell its amorous passion, make it die for love, and so turn statue again. All this, I think, is in the power of love, and yet it cannot work a change in me; my heart is linked so firmly to your virtues, magic cannot break the chain.

Enter BELMARIA, INNOCENTIA, FIDELIA, LYDIA,
and SEAMAN.

Mar. Oh, my dear and lovely Belmaria! My pretty Innocentia!

Fid. We have embraced and kissed already, sister; wept for joy, and given thanks. Not so much as my ungodly seaman, old Captain Hammock, but has rendered thanks to see us together again.

Bel. Oh, you dear preservers! How shall we reward your virtues? How shall we proclaim the honour due to your merits? 'Tis fit the world should know that Heaven reigns in women.

Fid. Ay, but the wicked world will hardly believe it.

Inn. Oh, let me kiss, and clip,* and hug thee! Oh, thou's my goodly cousin; thou wad not let us be murdered, honey; no more wad thou, thou pratty creature thou.

Fid. Sister, whilst we rejoice to see each other, we lose ourselves in neglecting of my Lord.

Mar. My Lord, most earnestly I crave your pardon.

Arm. This precious love you show each other

* Embrace.

requires my praise and wonder, not my pardon.
Your servant, madam ; yours, lovely Innocentia.

Inn. What pratty words he said to me, cousin !

Bel. We ought to rejoice at the sight of these
miracles, these cherubins ; for such virtue, my
Lord, deserves such heavenly attributes.

Arm. Madam, you cannot say enough ; they are
angels, only wrapped up in mortality, disguised in
lovely flesh and blood, to show the world what
blessed creatures the whole sex of womankind
were meant.

Inn. Now, wae's me, cousin, that my tongue
could but tattle as prattily as this deft * lord's does !

Bel. My Lord, we intend equally to divide our
fortunes with them ; to be less grateful would
render us unworthy of our lives, which they so
virtuously have preserved.

Inn. Marra, sister, my cousin shall have half of
everything I have ! Thou'st have half my portion ;
nay, by my conscience, thou'st have half my husband when I have him !

Fid. But, cousin, suppose this brave Lord were
your husband, would you let me have half of
him ?

Inn. Now, by my saul, I think I should not.
A wattanerin † he's too pratty a man to part with,
cousin.

Arm. Lovely, sweet Innocence ! I thank your
kind opinion, madam.

Mar. Good Belmaria, did you say half your
portions ? My Lord, have they not brave and
generous souls ? Does it not add to their beauties,
and make them look more lovely ? Speak, my Lord.

Arm. With great astonishment I admire their

---

* Neat, dexterous. Still in use in the north.
† Qy. I am of opinion.

offer. The worst of men must needs adore such gratitude.

Mar. And the best of men despise us, should we accept the offer.

Arm. It was my fear you would, when you so highly extolled their generosity.

Mar. My Lord, if we have done good, the deed rewards itself. Virtue's a free gift from above, and to be bought and sold no more than Heaven.

Fid. Virtue was never mercenary yet; and if it should, my Lord, we have not such a stock as to sell it out by retail.

Bel. This is obstinacy, not honour, to refuse a friendship justly due to you. You'd make us ungrateful to raise yourselves a fame.

Inn. Let this deft honey Lord be judge now. They saved us fra being devoured by wild bears, honey Lord; then should not we give them half we have, thou pratty man, thou?

Fid. Dispute this no more, but come to the point. I present your Lordship with the real heiress; my sister was but a false ninepin put upon you.

Mar. 'Tis true, my Lord, this is your true prize, and worthy of your greatness.

Bel. Hold, cousin! Shall I be offered up to one that may refuse me? That would be a stain to my honour never to be cleared.

Inn. Marra, wad, to the Lord of Heaven, they wad all say so! Then I hope at last he wad come to be my sweet honey husband.

Mar. We are now to think of safety, for home we must not go; therefore we beg your Lordship to take us into your protection.

Omnes. We all desire that favour, my Lord.

Inn. Favour! marra, it's e'en a blessing! And,

good honey sister, let's ne'er go fra this pratty Lord whilst we live.

Arm. I receive you, ladies, with such care as tender mothers take of infants ; and if my honour, life, and fortune can preserve you from your father's cruelty, you are safe.

Sea. Your safety lies in securing your father, madam. Bring him to public justice, and then you're safe.

Mar. Oh, say that no more ! My Lord and Belmaria, you have milder tempers. We have preserved your lives, and to publish my father's shame were to murder us.

Fid. The ill he meant you see is mercifully prevented ; how ungrateful, then, would you all appear to us ! But thy nature, like thy horrid aspect, is all rough and furred. Thy love to her is furred all over like a sick man's tongue, so that love in thee is a perfect fever ; and when thou'rt well, it is no longer love, but turns again to brutish seaman.

Arm. What way can you propose to secure yourselves, and conceal your father's shame, ladies ?

Mar. If we could find a way to bring him to repentance.

Bel. Ay, dear cousin, that were a blessed work indeed ; we could all wish that ; but how ?

Mar. Why, thus. Your Lordship, we desire to get my father hither, and tell him we are fallen desperately ill—indeed, distracted. Say something has appeared to us and frighted us ; and desire him to come with all speed, lest we die before he has a sight of us.

Fid. Very good ! My two cousins, Lydia, and her seaman, shall appear at that window like ghosts, call him bloody murderer, bid him repent, and so vanish.

Mar. That must shake his spirits, being guilty and, I hope, may work upon his hardened heart.

Arm. We all hope that. I much approve of this contrivance, and, if you please, I'll instantly about it.

Bel. My Lord, we shall for ever own the obligation.

Inn. Good honey Lord, take heed my naughty nuncle do not kill you now.

Arm. Sweet lovely Innocentia, I thank you. Your faithful servant, ladies.   [*Exit* ARMINGER.

Inn. Faithful to us all? Marra, I'se sure I'st have the least share of you, then.

Bel. Come, dear Mariana; this trial, I hope will bring your poor father to an humble penitence.

Mar. It is the only blessing upon earth my soul prays for.

Fid. I hope for something else upon earth before I die, sister.

Omnes. We shall all rejoice to see you both enjoy your wishes.   [*Exeunt.*

———————

ACT V.—SCENE I.

Enter BUFFOON, BOWMAN, *and* LATON.

La. Oh, Sir Hercules, there's rods in piss for you, i' faith. My uncle is so incensed against thee for putting that damned joke of Whetstone's Park upon him, that he resolves to have the whole nation searched, but he will have thee.

Her. I thought a deer out of Whetstone's Park had been welcomer to him than all the venison i' th' world. How came he to know it?

Bow. Why, it seems he inquired of some of his brother lawyers whereabout in Middlesex a place called Whetstone's Park stood, and withal told 'em he had bargained for two brace of deer yearly out on't during his life.

La. Upon that they all fell a-laughing at him ready to split, and told him it was a park of bawdy-houses; which made him fall into so great a rage, that he has sent his clerk, constables, and devil, and all to search for thee.

Her. Why, you know, 'twas Sir Thomas Lovill with the wooden leg that put Whetstone's Park upon him. I'll go to him, as I am Sir Hercules, and bid him produce his lame knave, Sir Thomas Lovill. Hast thou the deed of thy father's estate, man?

La. I have it, old boy. He was so pleased that I fought with thee in the defence of his reputation, that he gave me the deed presently; and the lawyers assure me that it is as firm a deed as ever yet was made.

Her. Then never fear me; I'll get off well enough, I'll warrant you.

La. I'll own the whole to him. Come, we'll contrive it as we go. [*Exeunt.*

SCENE II.

Enter LORD ARMINGER *and* GUARDIAN.

Arm. Sir Marmaduke, I have something to impart to you; but you being subject to violent passions, I am not willing to communicate such unwelcome news to you.

Sel. My Lord, to show the dear respect I bear you, passion shall be my slave for once. I'll stop his violent source, and yoke him to humility. Therefore, let me know the worst of ill my cruel fate has destined.

Arm. In short, your nieces are fallen desperately ill.

Sel. Is that all, my Lord? If they be sick, we will have a doctor.

Arm. Not sick, but worse. A ghastly fear and trembling has possessed them. Something appears to 'em and frights 'em; for they ran to me and cried, Save us, save us! and asked me if I saw nothing, and pointed with their fingers, crying aloud, There they are! there they are! Have they ever had such fits before?

Sel. Often, my Lord, often. Ever, when they dream of hobgoblins, the next day they run to me for shelter. Damn 'em, their base womanish fear will destroy their glorious preferment.

Arm. Their desperate fits would make me think 'em guilty of murder, but for my full persuasion of their sweet and blessed innocence; and what unspeakable comfort it is to be innocent! What say you, sir?

Sel. Yes, it is a fine childish comfort. For to be innocent is to be ignorant; to be ignorant is to know nothing; and they that know nothing are unworthy to be reckoned of the race of man. And that is my opinion of innocence, my Lord.

Arm. I am troubled to hear this; it is no religious answer.

Sel. It was no religious question. I would see my nieces; are they here, my Lord?

T

Arm. Yes, they are here, bloody villain! I'll fetch those blessed innocents, which by thy virtuous daughters were preserved.   [*Ghost above.*

Sel. Ha, ha! What! thou art a foolish scarecrow called a ghost, art thou not?

Arm. Who is't you speak to? What is't you see?

Sel. Nothing. I speak to nothing; I see nothing. Do you, my Lord?

Arm. No, sir; but such distracted starts as those your nieces had.

Sel. Then, good my Lord, withdraw. In short, the devil and I have conference once a week, and now's the time.

Arm. I'll fetch your nieces; their virtues may fright your devil away.   [*Exit* ARMINGER.

Sel. Now, thou venomous serpent clad in ghostly white, come down, that I may kill thee over again, and so have thee doubly damned.

Sea. Thou canst not, fool, hurt me; I am an airy spirit.

Sel. Come down, and I'll knead and mould thy airy spirit into substance, that I may tear it into air again. What art thou?

Sea. A damned soul of thy preferring. Despatch and die! The devils are stark mad in hell that thou art so long on earth; therefore make haste, they want thee.

Sel. If the devil wants me, let him if he dares come fetch me. I dare him and his whole host of furies. Bring Proserpine, his wife, and in spite of all his guards, I'll keep her here on earth, and make Prince Pluto my cuckold. And what a shame 'twould be to hell to have it said, Miss Proserpine is kept!

Sea. Cease thy madness, fool! I am that

seaman who undertook the bloody murder of thy
nieces, but was prevented by being all drowned at
sea.

Sel. Drowned! Art thou sure of it?

Sea. Too sure.

Sel. Then take notice, I am their heir-at-law!
Come down, sweet ghost, and let me kiss thee;
for never did spirit bring such blessed news!

Bel. [*Entering above*] O wicked uncle, repent.

Inn. Repent, for thou's my naughty nuncle.

Sel. What! a Yorkshire ghost with Innocentia?
What northern devil is thy guardian now?

Sea. Since thou canst not, wretched man, repent,
behold us all in flesh and blood, and clad in pure
innocence.

Sel. Alive, all alive? Oh, happy hour! Oh,
blessed minute! Come, come down, dear nieces,
and behold your poor uncle rejoicing in his tears
to find you all thus secretly preserved. What
saint was't that saved you?

Bel. Your virtuous children. So we come, good
uncle.

Inn. Take heed thou dissemble not, good nuncle.
[*Exeunt above.*

Sel. My own daughters betray me? I that
thought my subtlety above the reach of devils, by
children to be deluded! Oh, damn 'em! How like
innocent truth their words fell from 'em, and I an
infatuated fool believed.

Enter Lord Arminger, Fidelia, Belmaria,
  Innocentia, Lydia, *and* Seaman.

Arm. Sir Marmaduke, I take you in my arms,
and am o'erjoyed to see such penitential tears flow
from you.

Sel. Oh, my Lord, I find my children have made

known my wicked purpose; and my shame confounds me so, I dare not look upon your virtuous figure. Oh, let me see my Heavenly babes!

Mar. Here, dear father, let us for ever kneel, and for evermore thank Heaven for this your blessed conversion.

Fid. Oh, dear sir, what comfort 'tis to see you satisfied that these are safe!

Sel. A blessed comfort indeed! They are saints, my Lord, too good to dwell on earth, and therefore shall to Heaven—thus, ye devils!

[*Stabs* MARIANA; LORD ARMINGER *and* SEAMAN *disarm him.*

Arm. Hold, thou cursed wretch! Take his sword from's side, whilst I disarm him of his dagger.

Fid. Run, run for surgeons! let all the household run!

Arm. Household? Employ the whole world for surgeons, and let all the business of the earth stand still till Mariana be recovered!

Mar. Have mercy on my distressed father, my Lord.

Sel. A curse on thee for a religious jilt!

Arm. What can he now expect but public justice? for all the records of hell cannot produce such wickedness as is in thee. But, for Mariana's sake, yet repent, and all shall be forgot.

Sel. Repent! Seaman, that Lord's turned fool. Did quality ever trouble itself with repentance before? it lies not in the road of greatness. Fetch me the devil, and I'll thank you. I have revengeful work for him and his whole tribe. Give me my sword.

Sea. You are in no condition to be trusted with a sword, sir.

Sel. Lord, of all mankind trust not that treacherous slave. He once seemed to me the bravest
and the bloodiest villain that ever man or devil
employed ; and the false dog turned tail, proved
honest, and betrayed me. My children, too,
proved false. Who would stay in this wicked
world ? I and my damned issue will out on 't.
To see them fry in torments would please me
better than to be a Monarch.

Arm. Thou wretch, think of thy soul, and then
repent.

Sel. I cannot. Revenge allows no time to think
of souls. The heralds know everything takes
place of penitence ; that comes sneaking behind.
and is allowed no place of honour. But vengeance
rides i' th' front o' th' battle, and I his right hand
man. Therefore this tongue shall never utter any
words but vengeance, furies, and torments ; torments, furies, and vengeance. Revenge, devils,
revenge !   [*Exit* SELDIN.

Arm. What an example of desperation's here !
Pray you, sir, be careful of him till I send Ministers to comfort him. I wonder so wicked a man
should have such virtuous children.   [*Exeunt.*

SCENE III.

Enter JUDGE *and* CLERK *at one door ;* BOWMAN,
LATON, BUFFOON, *and* SQUIRE *at another.*

La. Clerk. take heed, be sure you be true to us.
Clerk. I'll stick as close to you as your shirt, sir.
Her. Save you, my Lord ! I understand one
Lovill, a rogue with one eye and a wooden leg,
has informed you that I have with most reproach-

ful and ignominious words bespattered your Judge-
ship.

Jud. Oho ! then it seems you are Sir Hercules
Buffoon, that have, as you call it, bespattered me.
Write a warrant, clerk. I'll clap you up, and clap
an action of ten thousand pounds upon you for
scandal, sir.

Squ. That will be a damned clap indeed. Clap
him up, and clap an action ? This Judge talks
of nothing but claps; I believe he knows Whetstone's Park better than I do.

Her. Clap me up ? I scorn your words, my
Lord. Bring that villain Lovill to my face to
justify his words, if he dare.

Jud. I am afraid, clerk, he dares not come,
because of the roguish bargain he put upon me, of
two brace of deer out of Whetstone's Park,—it
seems a park of bawdy-houses. Rogue ! rogue !

Squ. My Lord, I'll take that bargain off your
hands. I'll give you two brace of fallow deer for
your two brace of Whetstone.

Jud. Yours is such another park as Whetstone,
I suppose. But for Lovill, I'll clap him up in a
jail, where he shall never come out.

Squ. Another clap ? This old fellow has been a
swinger in's days.

Her. He's a shirking knave, and no Knight, my .
Lord !

Jud. How came he to be called so, then ?

Bow. In the time of the civil wars he found
friends, it seems, to get a blank warrant for a
Baronet, and not finding a good customer for it, he
saucily bestowed the honour upon himself.

Jud. He is the first subject that ever made himself a Knight.

Her. Not by some few, my Lord. But I am

told you threaten to undo me, for which I'll clap
an action of the case upon you, my Lord.

Squ. Then there will be clap for your clap, and
the stone in your foot still, my lord.

Jud. If I find this Lovill, I'll purge your ill
manners for you.

Her. The rogue's oath will not be taken ; he has
been Knight of the post these twenty years.
There came in his Knighthood ; 'tis his trade, he
has nothing else to live on.

Jud. Did you ever hear two men rail at one
another thus, sir ?

Bow. I think the like was never known, my
Lord.

Jud. Well, till Lovill be found, I'll secure you,
sir.

Her. I defy both law and lawyers, for I have a
protection.

Jud. A protection ? I believe the devil voids
protections faster than children void worms. Let
me see it, sir.

Her. I have it not yet ; but if you'll call for a
pen and ink, I'll write myself one presently.

Jud. This fellow seems to be some jester rather
than a Knight.

Bow. He may be a jester, and yet a Knight too.

Jud. But hold, clerk, was not this gentleman
here with Sir Thomas Lovill ?

Bow. My Lord, I was not here. I have a twin
brother, indeed, very like me ; I suppose it might
be him.

Jud. That may be ; but I am certain this young
Squire was here, and said he was Lovill's son.

Squ. My Lord, I was not here. I have a twin
brother, indeed, very like me ; I suppose it might
be him.

Jud. This fellow's a fool, and not a Squire, sure.

Squ. My Lord, a fool and a Squire are twins too ; you'll scarce know one from the other.

Jud. Clerk, sure this is Sir Thomas Lovill's son.

Squ. I had rather be thought the son of a whore. Lovill's a rogue that deals with pickpockets, and can help people to stolen goods again.

Bow. This is you all this while, Knight.

Jud. You all deny the truth. Sir Buffoon, you'll deny, too, that my nephew cudgelled you ?

Her. I scorn to be cudgelled. I confess he caned me, indeed, and he kicked me so that my haunches look as black as Westphalia ham, or the traitors' quarters upon the city gates.

La. Upon my word, my Lord, I never caned nor kicked him, nor did I ever in my life see the man before this day.

Jud. Did you not beat him, then, for abusing me so grossly?

La. No, my Lord.

Jud. Then give me my deed again, sirrah.

La. No, my Lord.

Jud. Why did you own, you base fellow, that you were caned and kicked ?

Her. Because, my Lord, I take delight in lying ; 'tis my darling virtue. I love it better than you love Whetstone venison, my Lord.

Jud. You rascal, I'll have you cudgelled because you scorn it.

Bow. Oh, my Lord, exercise your patience and take some other course.

Jud. Then I suppose that you, sirrah, hired that rogue Lovill to tell me stories of your valour, to wheedle me out of my estate.

La. I did so, my Lord.

Jud. You impudent fellow! hast thou the face to justify it?

La. Yes, my Lord.

Jud. And this ridiculous Squire is Lovill, that rascal's son?

Squ. Yes, my Lord; and I am this Knight's son too, my Lord.

Jud. You abominable fool, how can that be?

Bow. Because, my Lord, Sir Hercules disguised himself with a black patch and a wooden leg, a purpose to put this trick upon you.

Jud. Clerk, bear witness, here are two Knights found in one person, both confessing each other to be notorious rogues. Here's a pillory in the case, besides whipping in abundance.

Her. You have done well. Ouns! what have you brought me to?

Jud. The misfortune is that these two Knights have but one back to bear all the whipping due to 'em both.

Her. I defy your whipping! Pull off my coat. Look you here, sir; I am the court fool, and here's my fool's coat to protect me.

Jud. Death! Had ever lawyer so many tricks put upon him? Cheated of my office, my estate! and not content with that, but thus grossly to abuse me too?

La. Your conscience knows you cozened my father grossly, and I have got it again by a trick: so there's trick for your trick, and the stone in your foot still.

Jud. I think there's a flaw in the deed; if there be, villain, I'll make thee the wretchedest beggar in the nation.

Bow. We have been with counsel, and they say it is the firmest deed that ever yet was drawn; so

that you have the credit of being the best convey-
ancer of all the town.

Jud. Then am I the first man that ever was
undone by being too good a lawyer. But I'll find
some other way to destroy thee, thou accursed
villain !   [*Exeunt* JUDGE *and* CLERK.

Squ. As angry as you are, I expect my bargain
of Whetstone's Park, my Lord.

Her. Now, boys, let's to the tavern ! eat, drink,
and rejoice ; for Dagon the law is beaten down, and
shall be no longer worshipped.   [*Exeunt.*

SCENE IV.

Enter FIDELIA *and* INNOCENTIA.

Fid. How do you, my dear Innocentia? My
soul mourns to hear you say you're sick, child.

Inn. Prithee, cousin, do not call me child. By
my saul, I have woman's thoughts in me ; my head
aches so it plays riveskin with me. Wae's me, my
heart gripes me too !

Fid. You mistake, jewel; 'tis the belly that
gripes, not the heart.

Inn. Nay, God waite, it's e'en my heart that is
it. I can do nought but think of that pratty Lord,
cousin ; then my heart gripes me so that I'se e'en
ready to be dead. What means that? hast thou
any skill to tell me, cousin?

Fid. Alas ! my dear cousin, I doubt you are in
love.

Inn. Now, wae's me, I'se quite undone then.
Thou knows, cousin, that sweet honey Lord kissed
my hand e'en now, and he kissed it so prattily
that I have kissed it a thousand times since, be-

cause that pratty Lord kissed it; and is that love,
thinkest thou, cousin?

Fid. Ay, and desperate love too. Shall I tell
him how you love him, cousin?

Inn. Ay, and e'en God's benison and mine light
on thee for it; but I doubt, cousin, thou'll speak
ean word for me, and twea for thyself.

Fid. Oh fie, cousin! do not think I am so treacherous.

Inn. By my saul, I'se sure I should serve thee
sea.

Fid. Poor, sweet jewel, I pity thee exceedingly!

Enter LORD ARMINGER.

Arm. Oh, Fidelia, rejoice! your sister's wound
proves but a scratch. All danger's past; she's
dressed and coming forth.

Fid. I heartily rejoice. But, my Lord, this
sweet creature is so in love with your Lordship,
that if you be not civil to her, I really think 'twill
kill her.

Arm. Heaven forbid, pretty lady! Be assured
I pay you my respects with all the love my honour
can give way to.

Inn. Let me but once a day look at thy pratty
face, and then kiss my hand for me, thou deft
pratty man, and that's all the blessing I desire in
the warld.

Enter MARIANA.

Arm. Assure yourself of those and thousands
more. But behold your sweet sister. Oh, my dear
Mariana, Providence, I hope, has lent you life, to
make mine easy to me.

Mar. Stop there, my Lord. Made not you a

contract with my father to marry Belmaria, the eldest heiress?

Arm. I grant I did so, madam.

Mar. And was not I without a fortune falsely put upon you? Did you not court me as Belmaria, and truly love me as Belmaria?

Arm. Your father's dagger is in every word you've spoke, and has not scratched, but wounded.

Inn. Now, wae's me! my pratty Lord's in love with thy sister, cousin.

Arm. Mariana, you accuse me as if I had broke my faith! By Heaven, I never yet was false!

Mar. You will be, if you persist in a love sprung from a false foundation. You made love to an impostor, a false woman; and now you know the cheat, are you so weak to think your honour is engaged to make that courtship good to that impostor?

Arm. An impostor is the welcomest blessing upon earth to me, if it appear in your lovely figure.

Inn. Now, by my saul, he's more in love with her than I'se with him, waes me!

Mar. I believe, my Lord, you truly love me, and that's my only curse.

Inn. Ten thousand sike curses fall on me! they would be my best blessings, cousin.

Mar. When I consider how falsely—how by a trick you came to love me, I must in honour pronounce my own doom, and say I'll never marry.

Inn. God in Heaven keep her ever in that mind!

Mar. The wrong else to Belmaria would look as if we saved her from one murder to execute a worse upon her.

Enter BELMARIA.

Bel. Mariana, you nor your Lord have injured ; but had your father proved faithful, perhaps I had been your bride, my Lord.

Inn. Wae's me, what shall I do ? My sister's in love with him too ! Wad I had been devoured with wild bears.

Mar. Had my father been faithful, Belmaria says you had been hers ; mark that, my Lord. Can you after this ever make court to me ? My Lord, this heart and every drop of blood within it has more love for you than Dido quitted life for ; yet all this can I conquer to be just, therefore must not in point of honour marry.—What strong arguments I use to destroy myself !   [*Aside.*

Fid. I thank fate I am not in love's lime-twigs, for here's the devil and all to do. In point of honour, forsooth, one will not marry, and the other will not marry ; so that I find the punctilios of honour will destroy generation. And is't not pity such a Lord should die without leaving some of his brood behind him, cousin ?

Inn. Ay, God he knows is it !

Arm. I know she loves me ; I'll try her with a small design. Mariana, I find your resolution fixed, and no persuasion can make you mine ; therefore I will take your advice, and apply myself to fair Belmaria ; so your servant, madam. Sweet Belmaria, now I address to you.

Mar. Hold, hold ! I die, I die !
    [*They run to her.*

Arm. Say you'll be my wife, and then I'll quit Belmaria.

Mar. Anything rather than see that cruel sight again.

Fid. Marry her presently, my Lord, lest honour get the upper hand again.

Inn. Help, help! my heart is broken quite in two.   *[Falls down.*

Fid. Alas, my sweet cousin! Do you take her up, my Lord, and she'll do well again.

Arm. How do you do, dear Innocentia?

Inn. Is it the pratty Lord that comes to help me? Then I is varra well again.

Mar. Then we are happy, my Lord, and I am wholly yours. But how does my father all this while?

Arm. He desires to go into the country with two Ministers, who gave me great assurance of his conversion. We will marry, then, with all convenient speed.

Bel. I hope, my Lord, you'll be our guardian, and let us live together, and we are satisfied.

Inn. And, good honey Lord, let us never part whilst we have one hour to live.

Arm. By my life, we would not quit you for all the world's wealth; and I'll make it my whole business to match you to honourable fortunes.

Enter ALDERMAN, SQUIRE, BOWMAN, LATON, *and* AIMWELL.

Ald. With your leave, my Lord Arminger! We hear Sir Marmaduke Seldin is distracted and dying, and that your Lordship is made guardian to the two heiresses?

Arm. The ladies are pleased to think me worthy of that trust, and I have undertaken it.

Ald. The northern lady is to marry my nephew, my Lord. To that end Sir Marmaduke caused me to settle my estate entirely upon her; the match is gone so far, my Lord.

Squ. Nay, 'tis gone further with us young folks, for we have played at clapperdepouch together; therefore 'tis too late to break off the match.

Inn. By my saul I never played at clapperdepouch with thee. Did my nuncle mean to wad me to sike an a fool as thee?

Squ. Why, this is not my clapperdepouch, uncle.

Fid. Why, no! I is thy clapperdepouch, honey.

Squ. What the devil! are there two clapperdepouches? I am sure one must be false.

Inn. I'se sure I'se the right Northern Heiress.

Squ. Then thou art the false one, honey. I have heard of false dice and false ninepins; but to have a false clapperdepouch put upon a man is more than ever I heard of.

Ald. My Lord, I will not stand to this bargain, for my estate is settled upon the Northern Heiress.

Arm. No, sir; I have read the deed, and it is settled upon Fidelia Seldin.

Ald. Then I am cozened, my Lord, and abused.

Arm. Not so, sir; 'twas your own voluntary act. Besides, I have married her sister, and I hope you'll think it no disparagement for me to call you uncle, and you me nephew, and to have your kinsman call me brother.

Ald. My Lord, I shall take it for the greatest honour in the world.

Squ. A much greater honour than our alliance with King Pippin; and so I receive Fidelia Seldin for my wife.

Ald. And I receive you, my Lord, as my nephew, and your lady as my niece.

Enter SIR HERCULES BUFFOON *and* OVERWISE.

Her. And I receive you as my son and daughter. By this match you honour us, as you are a noble

Lord ; and we honour you by making you a kinsman to King Pippin.

Over. My Earl of honour, I have one project, the
which, if your Lordship will countenance ——

Arm. You know I was always your friend, and
ever will be.

Over. Then, my Earl, you must know my ancestor
was the first inventor of shorthand, and you see of
what use it is to the world ; but at first it was
extremely laughed at, as, no doubt, my project
will be.

Bow. There is no question of it in the least.

Arm. Pray you let me hear your project as
briefly as you can.

Over. Briefly ? I find I am troublesome. I
humbly refuse, then, my Lord.

Aim. I would not give a doit to hear it.

Over. My Lord, I humbly grieve that I have
rudely refused. My project is this ——

Arm. I will not hear it now, sir.

Over. Then I pity you, my Lord. Young man,
thou shalt hear it.

Squ. By my faith but I will not.

Over. Now, sir, it is my opinion that you sprung
not from the loins of King Pippin.

Her. Sir, do you affront the family of the
Buffoons ?

Squ. I'll affront your coxcomb with Mahomet's
own scimitar that cut off Orene's head.

Over. My Lord, upon my honour that very
scimitar hangs up now in Gresham College.

Arm. Now, sir, I'll hear your project, for your
scimitar's sake at Gresham College.

Over. My Lord, you all know the world now
writes shorthand ; and my project is that, which I
am, I confess, really fond of.

Bow. That's more than any one else will be, I doubt. Well, what is it?

Over. Sir, I communicate only to my Lord. Ladies, you may hear if you please. My project is, ladies ; well, I value myself extremely upon it.

Inn. Marra, the devil ha ma gin this be not a worse fool than thy clapperdepouch cousin.

Over. Well, in short, as all the world writes shorthand, so I would teach all the world to speak shorthand, and by an Act of Parliament have it called the shorthand tongue.

La. Speak shorthand, and have it called the shorthand tongue? Jack Adams* for that ! Ha, ha, ha !

Omnes. Ha, ha, ha, ha !

Over. Did not I beforehand tell your Lordship I should be laughed at ?

Arm. You did so indeed, most prophetically.

Over. Nevertheless, my Lord, I shall proceed ; for I have really computed that a long-winded Minister shall preach a sermon in the shorthand tongue in as little time as a horse shall run a four miles' course, and that is exactly seven minutes, madam.

Omnes. Ha, ha, ha, ha !

Bow. Why do you laugh, gentlemen? I think 'twould be great service to the nation to have a sermon preached in seven minutes.

Aim. Then sermons would not be tedious, nor people would not sleep at church.

Her. Nor would they have time to make love there, as I have done often.

Squ. Nor would Sunday pies be burnt in the oven, nor meat over-roasted ; nor would farmers have time to make bargains at church.

---

* Astrological Professor of Clerkenwell, of whom there is a portrait, now very rare.

U

Over.. Right, sir. I will undertake to make the merchants of the 'Change and lawyers at the bar plead all their business in the shorthand tongue ; nay, and the Judges shall give sentence in the shorthand tongue.

Squ. And men shall be hanged in shorthand ropes, and then they will feel no pain.

Over. Right. And what ease would it be to the world to have all the whole business of a day done in seven minutes !

Squ. Then should we have all the rest of the day to be drunk in.

La. I believe thou speak'st shorthand already, Squire ; for always when thou'rt drunk thou put'st twelve words into one.

Squ. That is not shorthand ; 'tis called clipping the King's English. I hope, sir, you'll teach women to scold in shorthand tongue, and that would be great service to the nation.

Bow. Good my Lord, let us laugh this insufferable shorthand fool quite out of the land.

Omnes. The shorthand tongue ! Ha, ha, ha ! away, fool, away !

Over. I'll make you all fools with one philosophical question. Tell me whether at the great or the small end of a spider's egg does nature make production ?

La. Thou art the product of an ass, I'm sure.

Squ. Pray you, sir, let me ask you one question. Is your name Overwise or Otherwise ?

Over. It is not proper for me to say I'll quarrel with you ; but, sir, I'll make a cessation of friendship with you, and so draw upon you.

Bow. Hold, hold ! put up, put up ! Away, shorthand ass !

Over. Well, I pity all fools ; from the gentleman to the lord and lady fools; and so I take my leave.   [*Exit* OVERWISE.

Squ. I hope you'll take your leave in the short-hand tongue.

Aim. My Lord, we hope you will befriend us so far as to admit us suitors to these heiresses.

Arm. Gentlemen, were I not concerned, I would serve you frankly; but being their guardian, were you my brothers I would not betray my trust, but will match them to men of such honour and wealth as shall deserve their fortunes; and this resolution you cannot take unkindly.

La. No, my good Lord, your answer has fully satisfied us.

Bel. What a noble Lord is this, cousin!

Mar. Come, pretty cousin, I'll give you half I have now; nay, I'll give you half my husband.

Inn. Thank you, honey cousin; but I'st be a little whore then, shall I not?

Mar. No, sweet cousin, I'll have a care of that.

Fid. My Lord, we must see honest Captain Hammock here and his Miss well rewarded, and all's done.

Arm. And it shall be done to their satisfaction.

EPILOGUE.

Wrote and spoke by J. H. Com.

METHINKS, right worthy friends, you seem to sit
As if you had all ta'en physic in the pit.
When the play's done, your jaded fancies pall;
After enjoyment, thus 'tis with us all.
You are
Mere epicures in thinking; and, in fine,
As difficult to please in plays as wine.
You've no true taste of either, judge at random,
And cry, *De gustibus non disputandum.*
One's for Vin d'Hermitage, love's lofty inditing;
Another Old Hock, he a style that's biting;
Both hate Champagne, and damn soft natural
   writing.
And some, forsooth,
Love Rhenish wine and sugar, plays in metre;
Like dead wine, swallowing nonsense rhymes make
   sweeter.
There's one's for a cup of Nantes, and he, 'tis odds,
Like old Buffoon, loves plays that swinge the Gods.
True English topers Racy Sack ne'er fail;
With such Ben Jonson's humming plays prevail;
Whilst some at tricks and grimace only fleer;
To such must noisy frothy farce appear;
These new Wits relish small smart bottle beer.
French goûts, that mingle water with their wine,
Cry, Ah de French song, gosoun, dat is ver' fine.
Who never drink without a relishing bit;
Scapin, methinks, such sickly tastes might hit.

Where w' entertain each squeamish nicer palate
With sauce of dances, and with songs for salad.
Since, then, 'tis so hard to please with choicest diet
Our guests, wh' in wit and sense do daily riot ;
Since wit is damned by those whom wits we call,
As love that stands by love, by love does fall ;
When fools, both good and bad, like whores,
    swallow all,—
" I wish for your sakes the sham Wits o' th' nation
" Would take to some honest, some thriving voca-
    tion.
" The Wit of our feet, you see every night,
" Says more to our purpose than all you can write.
" Since things are thus carried, a Wit's such a tool,
" He that makes the best plays does but best play
    the fool."
            A dreaded fool's your bully,
            A wealthy fool's your cit,
            A contented fool's your cully,
            But your fool of fools your wit.
        They all fool cit of 's wife,
            He fools them of their pelf ;
        But your Wit's so damned a fool,
            He only fools himself.
Oh, Wits, then face about to sense ! Alas !
I know it by myself, a Wit's an ass.
For, like you, in my time
I've been foolish in rhyme ;
But now so repent the nonsensical crime,
I speak it in tears, which from me may seem oddly,
Henceforth I'll grow wiser—damn wit, I'll be
    godly !
That when by new grace I have wiped off old
    stains,
In time I may pass, not for Count, but Sir Haynes.

SAUNY THE SCOT;

THE TAMING OF THE SHREW.

Sauny the Scot; or, The Taming of the Shrew: A Comedy. As it is now acted at the Theatre-Royal. Written by J. Lacy, Servant to His Majesty, and never before printed. London: Printed and sold by E. Whitlock, near Stationers' Hall. 1698. 4to.

Ib.—As it is now acted at the Theatre Royal in Drury Lane, by Her Majesty's Company of Comedians. Written by John Lacy, Esq.

> Then I'll cry out, swell'd with Poetick Rage,
> 'Tis I, John Lacy, have reformed your Stage.
> —*Prol. to Rehearsal.*

London: Printed for R. Bragge, in Paternoster Row. 1708. 4to.

THIS piece, altered from Shakespeare's *Taming of a Shrew*, has been attributed to Lacy, and with all show of probability, inasmuch as internal evidence is strong in his favour. The language of Sauny, for instance, is closely allied to, if not identical with, that of the Yorkshire heiress in the comedy of *Sir Hercules Buffoon*, just preceding. It is not Scotch in its idiom or apparent pronunciation, but savours strongly of the meridian of Doncaster, Lacy's birthplace. Having some resemblance, some very remote resemblance, to Scotch, the difference between it and the reality at the time when the piece was first produced would not be detected in London; and even at the present day a mongrel mixture of Scotch, Yorkshire, Somerset, and other provincial dialects, is, it is to be feared with consent of the Scotch residenters there, accepted on the London stage as the language spoken in one and all or any of these several places. As regards provincial *patois*, it is recorded by Aubrey that from Lacy "Ben Jonson tooke a note of his Yorkshire words and proverbs for his *Tale of a Tub.*" Aubrey, however, more probably meant Jonson's *Sad Shepherd*, as the phrases introduced in the *Tale of a Tub* are not northern but western, while in the *Sad Shepherd* the Yorkshire phraseology obtains.

Although Langbaine evinces a partiality for Lacy, and *Sauny the Scot* was produced at the Theatre Royal on 9th April 1667, he makes no mention of it whatever in his account of *English Dramatic Poetry*. Lacy himself acted "Sauny." The play was not printed until 1698, seventeen years after Lacy's death, but without the performers' names. It would seem to have been revived at that time to afford Bullock an opportunity of performing "Sauny." Geneste gives this further portion of the cast:— *Petruchio*, Powell; *Woodall*, Johnson; *Winlove*, Mills; *Tranio*, Harland; *Geraldo*, Thomas; *Snatchpenny*, Pinkethman; *Jamie*, Haines; *Margaret, the Shrew*, Mrs. Verbruggen; *Biancha*, Mrs. Cibber.

Pepys thus notices its first production:—"9th April 1667. To the King's house, and there saw *The Taming of a Shrew*, which hath some very good pieces in it, but generally is but a mean play; and the best part, 'Sauny,' done by Lacy;

and hath not half its life, by reason of the words, I suppose, not being understood, at least by me."

In this alteration of Shakespeare's play, the dialogue is shortened and converted into prose, the scene is changed from Padua to London, Grumio is turned into Sauny, and the fifth act is almost altogether new. It was acted with success. Shakespeare's play was partially taken from the older comedy *The Taming of a Shrew*, and partly from *The Supposes*, a comedy by George Gascoigne. The subject has been frequently dealt with in other plays, and among the offshoots of Shakespeare's piece may be instanced *The Cobbler of Preston*, by Charles Johnson, again altered by Christopher Bullock, son of the actor who played "Sauny" in Lacy's version, and *The Devil to Pay*, by Jevon.

In the old play *Taming of a Shrew*, on which Shakespeare founded his comedy, the character called by him Grumio was named Sander, and probably from this circumstance Lacy derived the idea of representing it under the garb of a Scotchman. The original play (1594) was reprinted for the Shakespeare Society in 1844, from the copy supposed to be unique in the library of the Duke of Devonshire. Stevens had previously reprinted the edition of 1607 of this play, in "six old plays, on which Shakespeare founded his *Measure for Measure, Comedy of Errors, Taming the Shrew, King John, King Henry IV. and King Henry V., King Lear.*" Lond. 1779. 8vo.

The dedication "to the Right Honourable the Earl of Bradford," which follows, is attached only to the edition of 1708, and apparently emanates from the publisher. Although not a great literary effort, it is worth while preserving.

Francis Newport, the first Earl of Bradford, who obtained that honour in 1694 from William and Mary, was the eldest son and heir of Richard Newport, who for his loyalty was created by Charles I., in 1642, Lord Newport of High-Ercall. After the King's death, he having suffered much during the Civil War, retired to France, where he died in 1650. Before the Restoration, Francis, the future earl, was appointed Comptroller and Treasurer of the Royal Household. He was created Viscount Newport of Bradford in 1675. He married Lady Diana Russell, daughter of Francis, Earl of Bedford, by whom he had five sons and four daughters, and died in 1708, when he was succeeded by his son Richard. All the honours became extinct upon the death of Thomas, the fifth and last earl, who died a lunatic on the 18th of April 1762.

THE EARL OF BRADFORD.

WHEN, by this way of address, I gain an admission
into your Lordship's honourable walls, the full
view of that venerable brow I meet there, and all
the radiant glories round it, demands the humblest
bending knee from so bold an intruder.

'Tis here I survey the bountiful smiles of the
great and gracious Dispenser of blessings, in de-
volving on so deserving a head so unbroken a
chain of continued prosperity, through your Lordship's long and still unfinished race of honour.

'Tis thus, through the various administrations of
so many successive sovereign heads, the throne has
ever found your Lordship a vigorous supporter;
your country a faithful and unshaken patriot ; your
altars a constant and zealous devotee ; your equals,
the more exalted veins, a leading worthy among
them ; whilst your Lordship has so signally distinguished your conspicuous merits, that the elder
heads of honour have all the reason in the world
to pride themselves in so eminent a pattern of
virtue, and the younger to copy from it.

'Tis thus, my Lord, you have enjoyed a long
blest life,—more a reward than gift, a donation
more from the divine gratitude than favour. For
true virtue is so much and so justly the darling

of Heaven, that the blessings that fall on such a favourite head are not the random showers of Providence.

Your Lordship's austere profession of piety has not the least tincture of bigotry ; for, as your Lordship has ever made it your care thoroughly to read the world, yet so equally have you divided the work of life, that in all the greatest load of private or public affairs your Lordship still never wanted leisure or application to the sublimer study of heaven. 'Tis from this you can equally taste the innocent blessings of this life, and yet at the same time make the wisest and securest provision for a richer feast in the next.

Amongst these innocent enjoyments, your Lordship has ever had a particular relish to the diversions of the theatre ; and 'tis this consideration only has animated my presumption in making your Lordship this public presentation. And, as the offering I humbly make your Lordship is a piece that took its original from the celebrated pen of the famous Shakespeare, and afterwards received its finishing stroke from that ingenious comedian Mr. Lacy, and thereby has acquired the merit of appearing so often on the stage, handed down through so long an age, and even to continue its reputation to the present generation a still darling entertainment,—'tis from hence alone it has arrogated a little more boldness in laying itself at your Lordship's feet, by the hand of,

My Lord,

Your Lordship's most dutiful

and most devoted Servant.

DRAMATIS PERSONÆ.

1708.

MEN.

LORD BEAUFOY, *Father to Margaret and Biancha,* . . . Mr. KEEN.

WOODALL, *a rich old Citizen, courts Biancha,* . . . Mr. JOHNSON.

PETRUCHIO, *the Tamer,* . . Mr. MILLS.

GERALDO, *another Pretender to Biancha,* . . . . Mr. HUSBANDS.

TRANIO, *young Winlove's Servant,* Mr. FAIRBANK.

SIR LYONEL WINLOVE, *a Country Gentleman,* . . Mr. CROSS.

WINLOVE, *his Son,* . . . Mr. BOOTH.

SNATCHPENNY, *a Town Sharper,* Mr. PACK.

JAMY, *Servant to Winlove,* . Mr. NORRIS.

SAUNY, *Petruchio's Scotch Footman,* Mr. BULLOCK.

CURTIS, NICK, PHILIP, *and other Servants to Petruchio.*

WOMEN.

MARGARET, *the Shrew,* . . Mrs. BRADSHAW.

BIANCHA, *her Sister,* . . Mrs. MILLS.

WIDOW.

SCENE : LONDON.

SAUNY THE SCOT;

OR,

THE TAMING OF THE SHREW.

———◆———

ACT I.

Enter WINLOVE *and his man* TRANIO.

Win. I am quite weary of the country life. There is that little thing the world calls *quiet,* but there is nothing else. Clowns live and die in't, whose souls lie hid here, and after death their names. My kinder stars, I thank 'em, have winged my spirit with an active fire, which makes me wish to know what men are born for. To diet a running horse, to give a hawk casting, to know dogs' names? These make not men; no, 'tis philosophy, 'tis learning, and exercise of reason to know what's good and virtuous, and to break our stubborn and untempered wills to choose it. This makes us imitate that great Divinity that framed us.

Tra. I thought you had learn'd Philosophy enough at Oxford. What betwixt Aristotle on one side, and bottle-ale on the other, I am confident you have arrived at a pitch of learning and virtue sufficient for any gentleman to set up with in the country—that is, to be the prop of the family.

Win. My father's fondness has kept me so long in the country, I've forgot all I'd learned at the university. Besides, take that at best, it but rough-casts us. No; London is the choicest academy; 'tis that must polish us and put a gloss upon our country studies. Hither I'm come at last, and do resolve to glean many vices. Thou, Tranio, hast been my companion; still one bed has held us, one table fed us; and though our bloods give me precedency,—that I count chance,—my love has made us equal, and I have found a frank return in thee.

Tra. Such a discourse commands a serious answer. Know, then, your kindness tells me I must love you; the good you have taught me commands me to honour you; I have learned with you to hate ingratitude. But, setting those aside, for thus I may seem to do it for my own sake, be assured I must love you though you hate me; I neither look at vice nor virtue in you, but as you are the person I dote on.

Win. No more; I do believe and know thou lov'st me. I wonder Jamy stays so long behind. You must look out to get me handsome lodgings, fit to receive such friends the town shall bring me. You must take care of all, for I'm resolved to make my study my sole business. I'll live handsomely—not over high, nor yet beneath my quality.

Enter BEAUFOY, MARGARET, BIANCHA, WOODALL, *and* GERALDO.

But stay a little! what company's this?

Beau. Gentlemen, importune no farther; you know my firm resolve not to bestow my youngest daughter before I have a husband for the elder. If either of you both love Peg, because I know you well and love you well, you shall have freedom to court her at your pleasure.

Wood. That is to say, we shall have leave to have our heads broken; a prime kindness, by'r lady! She's too rough for me. There, Geraldo, take her for me, if you have any mind to a wife; you are young, and may clap trammels on her, and strike her to a pace in time. I dare not deal with her; I shall never get her out of her high trot.

Mar. 'Tis strange, sir, you should make a stale of me among these mates thus.

Ger. Mates, madam? Faith, no mates for you, unless you were a little tamer! · Woe worth him that has the breaking of you!

Mar. Take heed I don't bestow the breaking of your calf's head for you. You mate? marry come up! Go, get you a seamstress, and run in score with her for muckinders to dry your nose with, and marry her at last to pay the debt. And you there, goodman turnip-eater, with your neats-leather phisnomy, I'll send your kitchen-wench to liquor it this wet weather. Whose old boots was it cut out of?

Ger. From all such petticoat devils deliver us, I pray!

Tra. Did you ever see the like, sir? That wench is either stark mad or wonderful froward.

Wood. I can't tell, but I had as live take her dowry with this condition, to be whipped at Charing Cross every morning.

Ger. Faith, as you say, there's small choice in rotten apples; but since 'tis as 'tis, let us be friendly rivals, and endeavour for a husband for Margaret that Biancha may be free to have one, and then he that can win her wear her.

Wood. I would give the best horse in Smithfield to him that would throughly woo her, wed her,

X

and bed her, and rid the house of her, to carry
her far enough off.   Well, come, agreed !   [*Exit.*

Tra. But pray, sir, is 't possible that love should
of a sudden take such hold of you ?

Win. Oh, Tranio, till I found it to be true I
never found it possible ; but she has such attractive
charms, he were a stone that did not love her.   I
am all fire ; burn, pine, perish, Tranio, unless I
win her.   Counsel me and assist me, dear Tranio.

Tra. Are all your resolutions for study come to
this ?   You have got a book will hold you tack ;
you are like to be a fine virtuoso.   Now must we to
a chemist, to set his still a going for philters, love
powders, and extracts of sighs and heighos.

Win. Nay, Tranio, do not make sport with my
passion ; it is a thing so deeply rooted here, it cannot die but it must take me with it.   Help me, or
hope not long to see thy master.

Tra. Nay, sir, if you are so far gone there's no
remedy, we must contrive some way, but 'twill
be difficult ; for you know her father has mewed
her up, and till he has rid his hands of her sister
there's no coming near her.

Win. Ah, Tranio, what a cruel father's he.   But
don't you remember what care he took to provide
masters for her ?

Tra. Ay, sir, and what of all that ?

Win. Y' are a fool !   Can't I be preferred to her
to teach her French ?   I have a good command of
the language, and it may be easily done.

Tra. I don't apprehend the easiness of it ; for
who shall be Sir Lyonel's son here in town,—to
ply his studies, and welcome his friends, visit his
kindred, and entertain 'em ?

Win. Be content ! I have a salve for that too.
We have not yet been seen in any house, nor can

be distinguished by our faces for man or master.
Then it follows thus : You, Tranio, must be young
Winlove in my stead, and bear yourself according
to my rank. I'll be an ordinary French master
about the town ; the time I stayed in France in
that will help me ; it must be so. Come, come,
uncase ! and take my clothes, and when we're at
our lodgings we'll make a full change. When
Jamy comes he waits on thee; but first I'll charm
his tongue.

Tra. 'Twill be needful. Since this is your pleasure I'm tied to be obedient, for so your father
charged me at your parting, although, I think,
'twas in another sense ; in short, I'm ready to
serve you and assist you in your enterprise.

Enter JAMY.

Win. Here comes the rogue. Sirrah, where
have you been ?

Jamy. Where have I been ? Pray, how now,
master, where are you, master ? Has Tranio
stolen your clothes, or you his, or both ?

Win. Sirrah, come hither ! this is not the time
to jest. Some weighty reasons make me take this
habit. Enquire not ; you shall know 'em time
enough. Meanwhile, wait you on Tranio in my
stead, I charge you, as becomes you. You understand me ?

Jamy. I, sir ? ne'er a whit.

Win. And not of Tranio one word in your
mouth ; he's turned to Winlove.

Jamy. The better for him ; would I were so too !

Tra. When I am alone with you, why, then, I
am Tranio still ; in all places else, your master,
Winlove.

Win. Tranio, let's go. One thing yet remains,

which you must by no means neglect, that is, to
make one amongst these wooers. Ask me not
why, but be satisfied my reasons are both good
and weighty.

Tra. I obey, sir !   [*Exeunt.*

ACT II.

Enter PETRUCHIO *and his Man,* SAUNY.

Pet. Sirrah, leave off your Scotch, and speak me
English, or something like it.

Sau. Gud will I, sir.

Pet. I think we have ridden twenty miles in
three hours, Sauny. Are the horses well rubbed
down and littered ?

Sau. Deil o' my saul, sir, I ne'er scrubbed mysel'
better than I scrubbed your nags.

Pet. And thou need'st scrubbing, I'll say that
for thee, thou beastly knave ! Why do ye not get
yourself cured of the mange ?

Sau. 'Sbreed, sir, I wud nea be cured for a
thousand pund; there's nea a lad in a' Scotland
but loves it. Gud, Sauny might hang himsel' an
it were not for scratten and scrubben.

Pet. Why so, prithee ?

Sau. When ye gea 'tull a lady's house ye are
blithe and bonny, sir, and gat gud meat, but the
deil a bit gats Saundy, meer than hunger and
cawd, sir. Ba then, sir, when a' the footmen
stan' still, sir, and ha nothing to dea, then gaes
Saundy tull his pastime, scratten and scrubben.

Pet. Dost call it pastime ?

Sau. A my saul dea I, sir. I take as muckle
pleasure, sir, in scratten and scrubben as ye dea in
tippling and mowing.

Pet. Nay, if it be so, keep it, and much good may it d' ye. This is my old friend Geraldo's lodgings, for whose sake now I am come to town. I hope he's at home ; there, Sauny, knock.

Sau. Wuns, sir, I see nean to knock boe' yer eansel', sir.

Pet. Sirrah, I say knock me soundly at this gate.

Sau. Out, out, in the muckle deil's name t' ye ! You'll gar me strike ye, and then ye'll put me awa, sir. With yer favour I'se ne'er do 't, sir. Gud, an ye nea ken when ye an a gued man, 'sbreed, I wot when I've a gued master. Ye's bang yersel' for Saundy.

Pet. Rogue ! I'll make you understand me.

[*Beats him.*

Sau. Gud, an ye'd give Saundy ea bang ai twa meer i' that place, for I can ne'er come at it to scrat it mysel', sir.

Pet. Yes, thus, sir ! [*Beats him again.*

Sau. The deil fa' yer fingers ! I may not beat yea o' ye'er ean dunghill, sir ; bot gin I had yea in Scotland, I'se nea give yea a bawbee for your lugs.

Enter GERALDO.

Ger. How now, Sauny ? What ! crying out ? Dear Petruchio, most welcome ! When came you to town ? What quarrel is this 'twixt you and Sauny ? I pray, let me compose the difference ; and tell me, now, what happy gale drove you to town, and why in this habit ?—why in mourning ?

Pet. A common calamity to us young men ; my father has been dead this four months.

Ger. Trust me, I am sorry. A good old gentleman.

Sau. Gee yer gate, sir, gee yer gate! On ye be fow a grief ye're nea friend, sir. We are blithe and bonny, sir; we ne'er woe for't.

Pet. Sirrah, you long to be basted.

Sau. Gud, do I not, sir.

Pet. Hither I come to try my fortunes, to see if good luck and my friends will help me to a wife. Will you wish me to one?

Ger. What qualifications do you look for?

Pet. Why, money—a good portion.

Ger. Is that all?

Pet. All, man? All other things are in my making.

Ger. I shall come roundly to you, and wish you to a rich wife; but her face——

Pet. That shall break no squares—a mask will mend it; wealth is the burthen of my wooing song. If she be rich, I care not if she want a nose or an eye; anything with money.

Sau. De ye nea gie him creedit, sir. I wud a halpt him tull a Heeland lady with twanty thousand pund. Gud, he wud nea have her, sir!

Pet. Sirrah, your twenty thousand pounds Scotch will make but a pitiful English portion.

Sau. Gud, sir, bo a muckle deal of Scotch punds is as gued as a little deal of English punds.

Ger. She has nothing like this, but a thing worse; she has a tongue that keeps more noise than all that ever moved at Billingsgate.

Pet. Pish, a trifle! Where lives she? I long to be wooing her. Let me alone with her tongue; I'm in love with the news of it. Who is't? who is't? I'm resolved for her or nobody.

Ger. But look before you leap, sir, and say you were warned.

Sau. Out, out, he can nea break his cragg upon
her. Gud, an ye'd venter your bonny lass, I'se
venter my bonny lad at her, sir.

Ger. Her father is the brave, noble Beaufoy;
her name Margaret, famed about town for a vixen.

Pet. The town's an ass! Come, prithee, show
me the house; I will not sleep till I see her. I
know her father. Nay, I am resolved, man;
come, prithee, come!

Sau. Wuns, man, an she be a scawd, awa' with
her, awa' with her, and Johnee Johnston's curse *
gang with her!

Ger. Prithee, what's that?

Sau. That is, the deil creep into her weem t'ith'
very bottom on't, that's to the croon, gued faith, of
her head.

Ger. Well, sir, if you are resolved, I'll wait on
you. To say the truth, 'twill be my great advantage; for if you win her, I shall have liberty to
see her younger sister, sweet Biancha, to whose
fair eyes I am a votary. And you, in order to my
love, Petruchio, must help me. I'll tell you why,
and how you must prefer me as a Music-master to
old Beaufoy.

Pet. I understand you not.

Sau. He'd ha' ye make him her piper, sir. Gud,
at ye'd make Saundy her piper, wuns, I'd sea
blea her pipe.

Pet. Sirrah, be quiet. What I can I'll serve you
in. But who comes here, Geraldo?

Enter WOODALL *and* WINLOVE *disguised.*

Ger. 'Tis Mr. Woodall, a rich old citizen, and
my rival. Hark!

Sau. Out, out! What sud an auld carle do with

---

* Qy. Johnstone, the Laird of Warriston's, curse?

a young bonny lass? Are ye not an aud thief, sir?

Wood. How?

Sau. Are ye not an aud man, sir?

Wood. Yes, marry am I, sir.

Sau. And are not ye to marry a young maiden?

Wood. Yes; what then?

Sau. And are not ye troubled with a sear grief, sir?

Wood. A sear grief?—what sear grief?

Sau. You're troubled with a great weakness i' th' bottom of your bally. What sid ye dea with a young maiden? Out, out, out!

Wood. You understand me? Your French books treat most of love; those use her to, and now and then you may urge something of my love and merit. Besides her father's bounty, you shall find me liberal.

Win. Mounsier, me will tell her the very fine ting of you; me vill make her love you whether she can or no.

Wood. Enough! peace! here's Geraldo. Your servant, sir. I am just going to Sir Nicholas * Beaufoy, to carry him this gentleman, a French-man, most eminent for teaching his country language.

Ger. I have a master for Biancha too; but, waiving that, I have some news to tell you. I have found out a friend that will woo Margaret. What will you contribute? for he must be hired to 't.

Wood. Why, I will give him forty pieces † in hand, and when he has done 't, I'll double the sum.

Ger. Done, sir! I'll undertake it.

* My Lord.—*Ed.* 1708. † Fifty guineas.—*Ib.*

Sau. 'Shreed, sir, I'se gat it done muckle cheaper; for twanty punds I'se dea it mysel'.

Ger. Come! down with your money! and the bargain's made.

Wood. But if he should not do it? I don't care for throwing away so much money.

Ger. If he don't, I'll undertake he shall refund.

Wood. Why, then, here's ten pieces,* and that ring I'll pawn to you for t'other forty—'tis worth a hundred. But does the gentleman know her qualities?

Pet. Ay, sir, and they are such as I am fond on. I would not be hired for anything to woo a person of another humour.

Enter TRANIO *brave, and* JAMY.

Tra. Save you, gentlemen! Pray, which is the way to Sir Nicholas Beaufoy's † house?

Wood. Why, sir, what's your business there? You pretend not to be a servant to either of his daughters, d'ye?

Tra. You are something blunt in your questions. Perhaps I do.

Pet. Not her that chides, on any hand, I pray?

Tra. I love no chiders. Come, Jamy!

Ger. Pray stay, sir! is it the other?

Tra. Maybe it is; is it any offence?

Wood. Yes, 'tis, sir! she is my mistress.

Ger. I must tell you, sir, she is my mistress too.

Tra. And I must tell you both she is my mistress. Will that content you? Nay, never frown for the matter.

Sau. And I mun tell ye all, there's little hopes for Saundy then.

Win. The rogue does it rarely.

* Guineas.—*Ed.* 1708.   † My Lord.—*Ib.*

Pet. Nay, nay, gentlemen, no quarrelling, unless it were to the purpose. Have you seen this young lady, sir?

Tra. No, sir; but I'm in love with her character. They say she has a sister moves like a whirlwind.

Pet. Pray spare your description, sir. That furious lady is my mistress, and, till I have married her, Biancha is invisible. Her father has sworn it, and, till then, you must all move forty foot off.

Tra. I thank you for your admonition; I should have lost my labour else. And, since you are to do all of us the favour, I shall be glad to be numbered among your servants, sir.

Pet. You will honour me to accept of me for yours. But pray, sir, let me know who obliges me with this civility.

Tra. My name is Winlove, sir, a Worcestershire gentleman, where I have something an old man's death will entitle me to, not inconsiderable. Come, gentlemen, let's not fall out, at least till the fair Biancha's at liberty. Shall we go sit out half-an-hour at the tavern, and drink her health?

Sau. Do, my bearns; and I'se drink with ye to countenance ye.

Pet. Ay, ay, agreed. Come! and then I'll to my mistress.

Sau. Gud, these lads are o' Saundy's mind; they'll rather take a drink nor fight.   [*Exeunt.*

Enter MARGARET *and* BIANCHA.

Mar. Marry come up, proud slut! must you be making yourself fine before your elder sister? You are the favourite, are you? but I shall make you know your distance. Give me that necklace and those pendants. I'll have that whisk too.

There's an old handkerchief, good enough for you!

Bian. Here, take 'em, sister! I resign 'em freely. I would give you all I have to purchase your kindness.

Mar. You flattering gipsy! I could find in my heart to slit your dissembling tongue. Come, tell me, and without lying, which of your suitors you love best. Tell me, or I'll beat you to clouts, and pinch thee like a fairy.

Bian. Believe me, sister, of all men alive, I never saw that particular face which I could fancy more than another.

Mar. Huswife, you lie; and I could find in my heart to dash thy teeth down thy throat. I know thou lov'st Geraldo.

Bian. If you affect him, sister, I vow to plead for you myself, but you shall have him.

Mar. Oh, then, belike you fancy riches more; you love old Woodall?

Bian. That old fool? Nay, now I see you but jested with me all this while. I know you are not angry with me.

Mar. If this be jest, then all the rest is so. I'll make ye tell me ere I have done with you, gossip.

[*Flies at her.*

Enter BEAUFOY.

Beau. Why, how now, Dame! whence grows this insolence? Biancha, get thee in, my poor girl!—[*She weeps.*]—Fie, Peg! put off this devilish humour. Why dost thou cross thy tender, innocent sister? When did she cross thee with a bitter word?

Mar. Her silence flouts me, and I'll be revenged!

[*Flies at* BIANCHA.

Beau. What! in my sight too? You scurvy,

ill-natured thing! Go, poor Biancha, get thee out
of her way.   [*Exit.*

Mar. What! will you not suffer me? Nay,
now I see she is your treasure. She must have a
husband, and I dance barefoot on her wedding day,
and, for your love to her, lead apes in hell. I see
your care of me; I'll go and cry till I can find a
way to be quit with her.   [*Exit.*

Beau. Was ever poor man thus plagued?

Enter WOODALL, *with* WINLOVE *disguised, with*
JAMY *carrying a lute and books, and* TRANIO.

How now? Who's here?

Wood. Sir, your servant. I am bold to wait on
you, to present you this gentleman, an acute
teacher of the French tongue; his name's Mounsieur Maugier. Pray accept his service.

Beau. I am your debtor, sir. Mounsieur, you're
welcome.

Win. Me give you humble thanks, sir.

Beau. But what gentleman is that?

Wood. I don't love him so well to tell you his
errand, but he would come along with me. You
had best ask him.

Tra. I beg your pardon for my intrusion. We
heard your fair and virtuous daughter Biancha
praised to such a height of wonder, fame has
already made me her servant. I've heard your
resolution not to match her till her eldest sister
be bestowed; meanwhile, I beg admittance, like
the rest, to keep my hopes alive. This lute, sir,
and these few French romances, I would dedicate
to her service.

Beau. Sir, you oblige me; pray, your name?

Tra. 'Tis Winlove, son and heir to Sir Lyonel
Winlove.

Beau. My noble friend, he has been my school-fellow. For his sake you are most kindly welcome; you shall have all the freedom I can give you.

Enter SAUNY, *and* GERALDO *disguised.*

Sau. Hand in hand, sir, I'se go tell him mysel'. Whare is this laird?

Beau. Here, sir; what would you have? What are you?

Sau. Marry, I'se ean a bonny Scot, sir.

Beau. A Scotchman! Is that all?

Sau. Wuns! wud ye have me a cherub? I ha' brought ye a small teaken, sir.

Beau. But d'ye hear, you Scot, don't you use to put off your cap to your betters?

Sau. Marry, we say in Scotland gead morn till ye for a' the day, and sea put on our bonnets again, sir. Bud, sir, I ha' brought ye a teaken.

Beau. To me? Where is't? From whence is your teaken?

Sau. Marry, from my good master, Petruchio, sir. He has sen' ye a piper to teach your bonny lasses to pipe; but gin ye'd lit Sauny teach 'em, I'se pipe 'em sea—whim, whum—their a . . s shall ne'er leave giging and joging while there's a tooth in their head.

Beau. Petruchio? I remember him now. How does thy master?

Sau. Marry, sir, he means to make one of your lasses his wanch—that is, his love and his ligby.

Beau. You are a saucy rogue.

Sau. Gud wull a, sir. He'll tak your lass with a long tang that the deil and Saundy wunna venter on; but he's here his aunsel, sir.

Enter PETRUCHIO.

Pet. Your most humble servant !

Beau. Noble Petruchio, welcome ! I thank you for your kindness to my daughters. Within there !

Enter SERVANT.

Conduct these gentlemen to my daughters. Tell 'em these are both to be their masters; bid 'em use 'em civilly. Take in that lute and those books there ! Petruchio, I hear you have lost your father lately.

Pet. 'Tis true, but I hope to find another in you. In short, I hear you have a fair daughter called Margaret. The world says she is a Shrew, but I think otherwise. You know my fortune; if you like my person, with your consent I'll be your son-in-law.

Beau. I have such a daughter, but I so much love you I would not put her into your hands; she'll make you mad.

Sau. Gud, he's as mad as heart can wish, sir; he need nea halp, sir.

Pet. I'll venture it, father—so I'll presume to call ye. I'm as peremptory as she's proud-minded; and where two raging fires meet together, they do consume the thing that feeds their fury. My father's estate I have bettered, not embezzled; then tell me, if I can get your daughter's love, what portion you will give ?

Beau. After my death the moiety of my estate; on the wedding day three thousand pounds.

Pet. And I'll assure her jointure answerable. Get writings drawn; I'll warrant you I'll carry the wench.

Beau. Fair luck betide you !

Enter GERALDO, *bleeding.*

How now, man, what's the matter? Will my daughter be a good lutanist?

Ger. She'll prove a better cudgel-player; lutes will not hold her.

Beau. Why, then, thou canst not break her to thy lute?

Ger. No, but she has broke the lute to me. I did but tell her she mistook her frets, and bowed her head to teach her fingerings. "Frets call you these?" quoth she, "and I'll fret with you;" so fairly took me o'er the pate with the lute, and set me in the pillory; and followed it with loud volleys of rogue, rascal, fiddler, Jack, puppy, and such like!

Pet. Now, by the world, I love her ten times more than e'er I did!

Sau. Gud! bo' the deil a bit ye's wad her, sir. Wuns! I'se nea gi' twa pence for my lugs gin you make her yer bride.

Pet. I'll warrant you, Sauny, we'll deal with her well enough.

Beau. Well, sir, I'll make you reparation. Proceed still with my youngest daughter; she's apt to learn. Petruchio, will you go with us, or shall I send my daughter to you?

Pet. Pray do, sir, and I'll attend her here.

[*Exeunt. Manent* PETRUCHIO *and* SAUNY.

Sau. Gud! at yed gi' Saundy a little siller to gea to Scotland agen?

Pet. Why, Sauny, I have not used thee so unkindly.

Sau. Gud! I'se nea tarry with a scauding quean, sir; yet the deil fa' my lugs if I'se ken which is worse, to tarry and venture my crag, or gea heam to Scotland agen.

Enter MARGARET.

Pet. Peace, sirrah, here she comes! Now for a rubber at cuffs. Oh, honey, pretty Peg, how dost thou do, wench?

Mar. Marry come up, Ragmanners! Plain Peg? Where were you bred? I am called Mrs. Margaret.

Pet. No, no, thou liest, Peg. Thou'rt called plain Peg, and bonny Peg, and sometimes Peg the cursed; take this from me. Hearing thy wildness praised in every town, thy virtues sounded, and thy beauty spoke of, myself am moved to take thee for my wife.

Mar. I knew at first you were a moveable.

Pet. Why, what's a moveable?

Mar. A joint-stool.

Pet. Thou hast hit it, Peg. Come, sit upon me.

Mar. Asses were made to bear, and so were you.

Pet. Why, now I see the world has much abused thee. 'Twas told me thou wert rough, and coy, and sullen; but I do find thee pleasant, mild, and courteous. Thou canst not frown, nor pout, nor bite the lip, as angry wenches do. Thou art all sweetness!

Mar. Do not provoke me; I won't stand still and hear myself abused.

Pet. What a rogue was that told me thou wert lame! Thou art as straight as an osier, and as pliable! Oh, what a rare walk's there! Why, there's a gait puts down the King of France's best great horse!

Sau. And the King of Scotland's tea.

Pet. Where didst thou learn the grand pas, Peg? It becomes thee rarely.

Mar. Does it so, saucebox? How will a halter become you, with a running knot under one ear?

Pet. Nay, no knot, Peg, but the knot of matrimony 'twixt thee and me. We shall be an excellent "mad couple well matched."*

Mar. I matched to thee? What? to such a fellow with such a gridiron face? with a nose set on like a candle's end stuck against a mud wall, and a mouth to eat milk porridge with ladles? Foh! it almost turns my stomach to look on't.

Sau. Gud, an your stomach wamble to see his face, what will ye dea when ye see his a . . e, madam?

Mar. Marry come up, Aberdeen! Take that— [*hits him a box on the ear*]—and speak next when it comes to your turn.

Sau. 'Sbreed! the deil tak' a gripe o' yer faw fingers, and driss your doublat for ye!

Pet. Take heed, Peg, Sauny's a desperate fellow.

Mar. You're a couple of loggerheads, Master and Man, that I can tell you! [*Going.*

Pet. Nay, nay, stay, Peg! For all this I do like thee, and I mean to have thee; in truth, I am thy servant.

Mar. Are you? Why, then, I'll give you a favour, and thus I'll tie it on; there's for you! [*Beats him.*

Sau. Out, out! I'se gea for Scotland. Gud, an she beat ye, Saundy's a dead man.

Pet. I'll swear I'll cuff you, if you strike again.

Mar. That's the way to lose your arm. If you strike a woman you are no gentleman.

Pet. A herald, Peg! Prithee, blazon my coat.

Mar. I know not your coat, but your crest is a coxcomb. [*Offers to go away.*

* A successful comedy by Richard Brome. 8vo. 1653.

Y

Pet. Stop her, sirrah ; stop her !

Sau. Let her gea her gate, sir, an e'en twa deils an' a Scotch wutch blaw her weem full of wind.

Pet. Stay her, sirrah ; stay her, I say !

Sau. 'Sbreed, sir, stay her yersen ! But hear ye, sir, an her tail gea as fast as her tang, Gud ! ye ha' meet with a whupster, sir!

Pet. Prithee, Peg, stay, and I'll talk to thee in earnest.

Mar. You may pump long enough ere you get out a wise word. Get a nightcap to keep your brains warm.

Pet. I mean thou shalt keep me warm in thy bed, Peg. What thinkst thou of that, Peg ? In plain terms, without more ado, I have your father's consent, your portion's agreed upon, your jointure settled, and, for your own part, be willing or un-willing all's one, you I will marry ; I am resolved on't.

Mar. Marry come up, Jack-a-Lent ! Without my leave ?

Pet. A rush for your leave ! here's a clutter with a troublesome woman. Rest you contented, I'll have it so.

Mar. You shall be baked first, you shall. Within there ! Ha !

Pet. Hold ! get me a stick there, Sauny. By this hand, deny to promise before your father, I'll not leave you a whole rib ; I'll make you do't and be glad on't.

Mar. Why, you will not murder me, sirrah ? You are a couple of rascals. I don't think but you have picked my pockets.

Sau. I'se sooner pick your tang out o' your head nor pick your pocket.

Pet. Come, leave your idle prating. Have you

I will, or no man ever shall. Whoever else attempts it, his throat will I cut before he lies one night with thee ; it may be, thine too for company. I am the man am born to tame thee, Peg.

Enter BEAUFOY, WOODALL, *and* TRANIO.

Here comes your father. Never make denial ; if you do, you know what follows.

Mar. The devil's in this fellow, he has beat me at my own weapon. I have a good mind to marry him, to try if he can *tame* me.

Beau. Now, Petruchio, how speed you with my daughter ?

Pet. How, but well ? It were impossible I should speed amiss ; 'tis the best - natured'st lady——

Beau. Why, how now, daughter ! in your dumps ?

Mar. You show a father's care, indeed, to match me with this mad, hectoring fellow.

Pet. She has been abused, father, most unworthily. She is not cursed unless for policy ; for patience, a second Grizel. Betwixt us we have so agreed, the wedding is to be on Thursday next.

Sau. Gud ! Saundy's gea for Scotland a Tuesday, then.

Wood. Hark, Petruchio ! she says she'll see you hanged first. Is this your speeding ? I shall make you refund.

Pet. Pish ! that's but a way she has gotten. I have wooed her, won her, and she's my own. We have made a bargain that before company she shall maintain a little of her extravagant humour, for she must not seem to fall off from 't too soon. When we are alone, we are the kindest, lovingest, tenderest chickens to one another ! Pray, father,

provide the feast and bid the guests; I must home
to settle some things, and fetch some writings in
order to her jointure.   Farewell, Gallants!   Give
me thy hand, Peg.

Beau. I know not what to say; but give me
your hands.   Send you joy!   Petruchio, 'tis a
match.

Wood. Tra. Amen say we; we all are witnesses.

Mar. Why, sir, d'ye mean to match me in spite
of my teeth?

Pet. Nay, peace, Peg, peace! thou need'st not
be peevish before these; 'tis only before strangers,
according to our bargain.   Come, Peg, thou shalt
go see me take horse.   Farewell, father!

Mar. As I live I will not.

Pet. By this light but you shall.   Nay, no testy
tricks; away!   [*Exeunt.*

Sau. Gud! I'se be your lieutenant, and bring up
your rear, madam.   [*Exit.*

Wood. Was ever match clapped up so suddenly?

Beau. Faith, gentlemen, I have ventured madly
on a desperate mart.

Wood. But now, sir, as to your younger daughter; you may remember my long love and service.

Tra. I hope I may, without arrogance, sir, beg
you to look on me as a person of more merit.

Beau. Content ye, gentlemen, I'll compound
this strife; 'tis deeds not words must win the
prize.   I love you both, but he that can assure my
daughter the noblest jointure has her.   What say
you, sir?

Wood. I'll make it out my estate is worth, *de
clara*, full twenty thousand pounds, besides some
ventures at sea; and all I have at my decease I
give her.

Tra. Is that all, sir?   Alas! 'tis too light, sir.

I am my father's heir and only son, and his estate
is worth three thousand pound per annum; that
will afford a jointure answerable to her portion.
No debts nor incumbrances, no portions to be
paid.—Have I nipt you, sir?

Beau. I must confess your offer is the best; and
let your father make her this assurance, she is
your own, else you must pardon me, if you should
die before him, where's her power?

Tra. That's but a cavil; he's old, I young!

Wood. And may not young men die as well as
old? Have I nipt you there again?

Beau. Well, gentlemen, I am thus resolved. On
Thursday my daughter Peg is to be married. The
Thursday following Biancha's yours if you make
this assurance; if not, Mr. Woodall has her. And
so I take my leave, and thank you both. [*Exit.*

Wood. Sir, your servant; now I fear you not.
Alas! young man, your father is not such a fool to
give you all, and in his waning age set his foot
under your table. You may go whistle for your
mistress. Ha, ha, ha! [*Exit.*

Tra. A vengeance on your crafty, withered hide.
Yet 'tis in my head to do my master good. I see
no reason why this supposed young Winlove
should not get a supposed father called Sir Lyonel
Winlove. And that's a wonder; fathers commonly
get their children, but here the case must be
altered.

Love brings such prodigies as these to town,
For that at best turns all things upside down.
[*Exit.*

ACT III.

Enter WINLOVE, GERALDO, *and* BIANCHA. *Table covered with velvet. Two chairs and a guitar. A paper pricked with songs.*

Ger. Pray, madam, will you take out this lesson on the guitar?

Win. Here be de ver fine story in de varle of Monsieur Apollo and Mademoiselle Daphne; me vill read you dat, madam.

Ger. Good madam, mind not that Monsieur Shorthose, but learn this lesson first.

Win. Begar, Monsieur Fiddeller, you be de vera fine troublesome fellow; me vill make de great hole in your head wid de gittar, as Mrs. Margaret did.

Ger. This is no place to quarrel in. But remember——

Bian. Why, gentlemen, you do me double wrong, to strive for that which resteth in my bare choice. To end the quarrel, sit down and tune your instrument, and by that time his lecture will be done.

Ger. You'll leave his lecture, when I am in tune?

Bian. Yes, yes; pray be satisfied. Come, Monsieur! let's see your ode.

Win. I do suspect that fellow. Sure he's no lute-master.

Bian. Here's the place! come, read.

[*Reads.*]—"Do not believe I am a Frenchman. My name is Winlove; he that bears my name about the town is my man Tranio. I am your passionate servant, and must live by your smiles. Therefore be so good to give life to my hopes."

Ger. Madam, your guitar is in tune!

Bian. Let's hear.   Fie ! there's a string split.

Win. Make a de spit turn in the hole, man, and tune it again.

Bian. Now let me see.—[*Seems to read.*]—" I know not how to believe you, but, if it be true, noble Mr. Winlove deserves to be beloved ; and, in the meantime, keep your own counsel, and it is not impossible but your hopes may be converted into certainties."

Ger. Madam, now 'tis perfectly in tune.

Win. Fie, fie ! begar, no tune at all !

Bian. Now, sir, I am for you.

Ger. Monsieur, pray walk now ! and give me leave a-while ; my lesson will make no music in three parts.

Win. Me vill no trouble you, Monsieur Fiddeller ; I am confident it is so.   This must be some person that has taken a disguise, like me, to court Biancha.   I'll watch him.   [*Aside.*

Ger. First, madam, be pleased to sing the last song that I taught you, and then we'll proceed.

Bian. I'll try, but I am afraid I shall be out.

SONG.

Ger. Madam, before you proceed any farther, there be some few rules set down in this paper, in order to your fingering, will be worth your perusal.

Bian. Let's see.—[*Reads*]—" Though I appear a lute-master, yet know, my fair Biancha, I have but taken this disguise to get access to you, and tell you I am your humble servant and passionate admirer, Geraldo."   Pish ! take your rules again, I like 'em not ; the old way pleases me best.   I do not care for changing old rules for these foolish new inventions.

Enter SERVANT.

Serv. Madam, my Lord calls for you to help
dress the Bride.

Bian. Farewell, then, Master! I must be gone.
[*Exeunt.*

Ger. I know not what to think of her. This
fellow looks as if he were in love, and she caresses
him. These damned Frenchmen have got all the
trade in town. If they get up all the handsome
women, the English must e'en march into Wales
for mistresses. Well, if thy thoughts, Biancha,
are grown so low, to cast thy wandering eyes on
such a kickshaw, I'm resolved to ply my Widow.
[*Exit.*

Win. I'm glad I'm rid of him, that I may speak
my mother tongue again. Biancha has given me
hopes ; I dare half believe she loves me.

Enter BEAUFOY, WOODALL, TRANIO, MARGARET,
BIANCHA, *and* ATTENDANTS.

But, here's her father !

Beau. Believe me, gentlemen, 'tis very strange !
This day Petruchio appointed, yet he comes not.
Methinks he should be more a gentleman than to
put such a slur upon my family.

Mar. Nay, you have used me finely, and like a
father. I must be forced to give my hand against
my will to a rude, mad-brained fellow here, who
wooed in haste and means to wed at leisure. This
comes of obeying you. If I do't again, were you
ten thousand fathers, hang me !

Tra. Be patient, madam ; on my life he'll come.
Though he be blunt and merry, I'm sure he's noble.
Good madam, go put on your wedding clothes ;
I know he'll be with you ere you be dressed.

Mar. Wedding clothes? I'll see him hanged
before I'll have him, unless it be to scratch his
eyes out. [*Exit weeping.*

Beau. Poor girl! I cannot blame thee now to
weep, for such an injury would vex a saint.
Though I am old, I shall find somebody will call
him to a strict account for this.

Enter JAMY.

Jamy. Oh, master! news, news! and such news
as you never heard of!

Beau. Why, what news have you, sir?

Jamy. Is't not news to hear of Petruchio's
coming?

Beau. Why, is he come?

Jamy. Why, no, my Lord.

Beau. What then, sirrah?

Jamy. He's coming, sir.

Beau. When will he be here?

Jamy. When he stands where I am and sees you
there.

Beau. Well, sirrah, is this all the news?

Jamy. Why, Petruchio is coming in a new hat
and an old jerkin, a pair of breeches thrice turned,
a pair of boots that have been candle-cases; an old
rusty sword with a broken hilt and never a chape;
upon an old, lean, lame, spavined, glandered,
broken-winded jade, with a woman's crupper of
velvet, here and there pieced with packthread.

Tra. Who comes with him?

Jamy. Oh, sir, his man Sauny, and in an equipage
very suitable to his master; he looks no more like
a Christian footman than I look like a windmill.

Wood. This is a most strange, extravagant
humour.

Beau. I'm glad he comes, however he be.

Enter PETRUCHIO *and* SAUNY, *strangely habited.*

Pet. Come, where be these Gallants? Who's at home?

Beau. You're welcome, sir! I'm glad you're come at last.

Tra. I think I have seen you in better clothes.

Pet. Never, never, sir; this is my wedding suit. Why, how now, how now, gentlemen? What d'ye stare at? D'ye take me for a monster?

Wood. Faith, in that habit you might pass for one in the fair.

Pet. Oh, you talk merrily; my tailor tells me it is the newest fashion. But where's my Peg? I stay too long from her; the morning wears, 'tis time we were at church.

Tra. Why, you won't visit her thus?

Pet. Marry, but I will.

Sau. And sea will Saundy tea, sir.

Beau. But you will not marry her so, will you?

Sau. A my saul sall he, sir.

Pet. To me she's married, not to my clothes. Will you along, father and gentlemen? I'll to church immediately, not tarry a minute.

Sau. Hear ye, sir; ye sall marry her after the Scotch Directory; then, gin ye like her not, ye maw put her awa. How say ye, now?

[*Exeunt* PETRUCHIO *and* SAUNY.

Tra. He has some meaning in this mad attire; but you must persuade him to put on a better ere he goes to church.

Beau. Let's after, and see what will become of it.   [*Exit.*

Tra. Well, sir, you find there's no other way; 'tis too short warning to get your father up. Should you steal the match, who knows but both the old fools would so deeply resent it to your prejudice.

Win. Why, prithee, this way it will be stolen; for 'tis but a cheat, which will, in a little time, be discovered.

Tru. That's all one ; it carries a better face, and we shall have the more sport. Besides, ere it comes out, your father may be wrought to like it, and confirm my promises. She is suitable to you every way, and she is rich enough to do it, and loves you well enough besides.

Win. Well, if it must be so, let's contrive it handsomely.

Tru. Let me alone ; Jamy shall do the business. He shall find out some knight of the post that shall be old Sir Lyonel Winlove here, and make assurance of a greater jointure than I proposed. Ne'er fear it, sir; I'll so instruct him it shall be carried without the least suspicion.

Win. Ay ; but, you know, old Beaufoy knows my father.

Tru. That's nothing ; 'tis so many years since he saw him, he will never distinguish him by his face.

Win. This may be done. But, notwithstanding all, did not my fellow-teacher, that damned lute-master, so nearly watch us, 'twould not be amiss to steal a marriage ; and, that once performed, let all the world say no, I'll keep my own !

Tra. That we may think on too. This same lute-master I more than half suspect.

Win. And so do I.

Tra. I have missed a gentleman out of the gang a good while. But let that pass ; I have already sent Jamy to find a man.

Enter WOODALL.

To our postures ; here's Mr. Woodall ! He must be
choused too among the rest. — Save you, sir !
Came you from the church ?

Wood. As willingly as e'er I came from school.

Tra. And is the bride and bridegroom coming
home ?

Wood. A bridegroom ? Why, he's a bridegroom
for the devil ! A devil ? A very fiend !

Tra. Why, she's a devil, an arrant devil ! nay,
the devil's dam !

Wood. But she's a lamb, a dove, a child to him !
When the priest asked if he would take Margaret
for his wife, " Ay, by Gog's wounds," quoth he, and
swore so loud that, all amazed, the priest lets fall
the book ; and as the sexton stooped to take it up,
this mad-brained bridegroom took him such a cuff
that down fell sexton, book and all, again. " Now
take it up," quoth he, " if any list."

Tra. What said the poor bride to this ?

Wood. Trembled and shook like an aspen-leaf.
After this, just as the parson joined their hands,
he called to his roguey Scotchman for a glass of
muscadine, drank his wife's health, and threw the
toast in the clerk's face because his beard grew
thin and hungry ; then took the bride about the
neck, and gave her such a smack the church echoed
again. The sight of this made me run away for
shame ; I know they are following by this time.
But hark ! I hear the minstrels.   [*Music.*

Enter BEAUFOY, PETRUCHIO, MARGARET,
BIANCHA, GERALDO, SAUNY, *etc.*

Pet. Gentlemen and friends, I thank you for
your pains. I know you think to dine with me

to-day, and have prepared great store of wedding cheer; but, so it is, grand business calls me hence, and I take my leave.

Beau. Is't possible you will away to-night?

Pet. I must immediately; if you knew my business you would not wonder.—Well, honest gentlemen, I thank you all, that have beheld me give away myself to this most patient, sweet, and virtuous wife. Dine with my father, here, and drink my health, for I must hence; so farewell to you all!

Sau. Wuns! will ye nea eat your wadden dunner, sir?

Tra. Let us entreat you to stay till after dinner!

Pet. It must not be.

Mar. Let me entreat you!

Pet. That will do much; I am content.

Mar. Are you content to stay?

Pet. I am content you should entreat me; but yet I will not stay, entreat me how you can.

Mar. Now, if you love me, stay!

Pet. I cannot.—Sauny! the horses.

Sau. They have nea eat their wadden dunner yet.

Pet. Sirrah, get the horses!

Mar. Nay, then, do what thou canst, I won't go to-day, nor to-morrow, nor till I please myself. The door is open, sir, there lies your way; you may be jogging while your boots be green.

Pet. Oh, Peg, content thee; prithee be not angry!

Mar. I will be angry! What hast thou to do?—Father, be quiet; he shall stay my leisure!

Wood. Ay, marry, sir, now it begins to work.

Mar. Gentlemen, forward to the bridal dinner. I see a woman may be made a fool of if she want spirit to resist.

Pet. They shall go forward, Peg, at thy command. Obey the bride, you that attend on her. Go to the feast, revel, carouse, and dance, be mad or merry, or go hang yourselves; but for my bonny Peg, she must with me. Nay, look not big upon't, nor stamp, nor stare, nor fret. Come, come— gently—so, so; so—that's my good Peg. I will be master of my own. She is my proper goods and chattels; my house, my ox, my ass, my anything. Look, here she stands; touch her who dare! I'll make him smoke that offers to stop me in my way. Sauny, unsheath thy dudgeon* dagger; we are beset with thieves! Rescue thy mistress if thou beest a man.—Fear not, sweet wench, I'll buckler thee against a million. Nay, come!

Mar. Will none of you help me?

Sau. The deil a bit of dunner ye gat! Gud, at ye would speak to your cuke to gie Saundy a little mutton and porridge to put in his wallet.

[*Exeunt* PETRUCHIO, MARGARET, *and* SAUNY.

Beau. Nay, let 'em go—a couple of quiet ones.

Tra. Never was so mad a match.

Beau. Well, gentlemen, let's in; we have a dinner, although we want a bride and bridegroom to it. Biancha, you shall take your sister's room, and, Mr. Winlove, you may practise for a bridegroom. [*Exeunt.*

Wood. Monsieur, how do you find my mistress inclined?

Win. Me can no tell dat yet, but in time, Monsieur, me sall inform you.

---

* With the haft made of box-wood. "Dudgeon" is frequently used to express the dagger itself:—

  "It was a serviceable dudgeon,
  Either for fighting or for drudging."
  —*Hudibras.*

Wood. Pray, ply her close ; here's something for you.   [*Exit* WOODALL.

Win. Me tank you, sir.—Ha, ha, ha! I must go tell this to my Biancha.   [*Exit* WINLOVE.

Tra. Hark ye, sir, you may inform me ; pray, what think you, does Madam Biancha fancy any other but myself? She bears me' fair in hand. Pray discover, sir ; I shall not be ungrateful.

Ger. Troth, sir, I think she's as all other women are.

Tra. How is that, pray?

Ger. Why, fickle and foolish.

Tra. Why d'ye think so of her?—she was always held discreet.

Ger. No sober man will think so. I tell you, sir, she cares neither for you nor any man that's worth caring for. She's fallen in love with a Monsieur Jackdaw, a fellow that teaches bad French in worse English!   .

Tra. That fellow?—why, 'tis impossible !

Ger. 'Tis true, though.

Tra. Why, I am confident he was employed by old Woodall as his instrument to court her for him.

Ger. If he were, he has spoken one word for him and two for himself.

Enter WINLOVE *leading* BIANCHA.

See, here they come hand in hand. Stand close ! perhaps your eyes may convince you.

Win. Madam, you need not doubt my passion. By those fair eyes I swear, an oath inviolable, you have made a conquest over me so absolute that I must die your captive.

Tra. What does he say? what does he say?

Ger. I cannot hear ; listen !

Bian. I must believe you, sir, there's some

strange power attends your words, your attractive
actions, and your person, which is too strong for
my weak resistance. You have won, but do not
boast your victory.

Tra. Nay, then, I see 'tis so; I cannot hold!—
Madam, you must forgive my interruption : you
have used me kindly, fooled me with fine hopes ;
your Monsieur, there, has read excellent lessons
to you.

Bian. Sir, I understand you not.

Ger. That is, you won't.

Win. What be de matter, Monsieur Fiddeller?

Ger. No fiddler, nor no lutanist, Monsieur No-
point, but one that scorns to live in a disguise for
such a one as leaves a gentleman to doat upon a
pardon-a-moi Jack-pudding. Know I am a gentleman, my name Geraldo!

Bian. Alas, sir! And have you been my master
all this while, and I never knew it?

Ger. Yes, sweet lady, you did know it. I see
you have a little spice of Peg in you ; but I have
done with you. Mr. Winlove, pray tell me, don't
you hate this gentlewoman now?

Tra. I cannot say I hate her, but I'm sure I
don't love her for this day's work. Would she
court me, I swear I would not have her!

Ger. Nor I, by heavens! I have sworn, and
will keep my oath.

Bian. Why, gentlemen, I hope you will not
both give the willow garland.

Ger. Go, go ; you are a scurvy woman! I have
a widow that has loved me as long as I have loved
you. Sweet lady, I am not bankrupt for a mistress. 'Tis true she's something of your sister's
humour, a little wayward, but one three days'
time at the taming school will make her vie with

any wife in England ; and then I can pass by you unconcerned.

Bian. The taming school! For heaven's sake where is that, sir ?

Ger. Why, your brother Petruchio's house. I doubt you must there too ere you'll be good for anything. I'll to him immediately. Farewell, thou vile woman ! [*Exit.*

Bian. Ha, ha, ha ! this is excellent !

Tra. Madam, I beg your pardon ; but I hope my boldness with you has done my master some service.

Win. Believe me has it, Tranio, and I must thank thee.

Enter JAMY.

Now, sirrah, whither away in such haste ?

Jamy. Oh, master, I have found him !

Win. What ?—Who hast thou found ?

Jamy. A rare old sinner in the Temple Cloisters —will do the feat to a hair.

Bian. What feat ?—What's to be done ?

Win. That which I told you of, my fairest.— Where is he?

Jamy. Here, here ! he walks in the court. [*Exit.*

Bian. Well, I must in or I shall be missed. Carry the matter handsomely, and let me not suffer. [*Exit.*

Win. Fear not, madam !—Call him in, Tranio ! You must instruct him ; I'll not be seen in 't. [*Exit.*

Enter JAMY and SNATCHPENNY.

Tra. Now, friend, what are you ?

Snatch. Anything that you please, sir.

Tra. Anything ! Why, what can you do ?

Snatch. Anything, for so much as concerns swear-

z

ing and lying to your worship's service and to get
an honest livelihood ; so please you to employ me.

Tra. Why, thou may'st serve turn, I think.
But I'll put thee to no swearing ; bare lying and
impudence will serve for my occasion. You must
bate of the price for that.

Snatch. Faith, sir, they're both of a price, take
'em or leave 'em.

Tra. But canst thou manage and carry off a
good, well-contrived lie to the best advantage ?

Snatch. I should be very sorry else ; it has been
my trade these seven-and-thirty years. Never
fear it, sir.

Jamy. Nay, I picked him out amongst half-a-
score. I fancied he had the best lying face
amongst 'em.

Tra. Well, come along with me, and I'll instruct
you ; but if you fail, look to your ears, if you have
any !

Snatch. I'll venture neck and all to do it, sir. [*Exit.*

PETRUCHIO'S *House.* *Enter* SAUNY *and* CURTIS
severally.

Curt. Honest Sauny ! welcome, welcome !

Sau. Saundy's hungry ; can't you get a little
meat, sir ?

Curt. Yes, yes, Sanny.

Sau. Ye mun gat a gued fire, sir. Mrs. Bride
has gat a fa' intull a dyke ; she's a' wet, sir—Gud,
she has not a dry thread to her a . . e !

Curt. Is master and mistress coming, Sauny ?

Sau. Gud are they, gin they be nea frozen to
the grund. Bo where's your fire, man ?

Curt. 'Tis making, 'tis making ; all things are
ready. Prithee, what news, good Sauny ? What
kind of woman is our mistress ?

Sau. Ken ye twa-and-twanty deils, sir?

Curt. Marry, Heaven defend us!

Sau. Gud, she has e'en twa-and-twanty deils; I'se nea bate ye ean of 'em.

Curt. They say she's a cruel shrew.

Sau. O' my saul, sir, I'se haud a thousand pund, she's set up her tang and scaud fra Edinbrough to London and ne'er draw bit for 't!

Curt. What shall we do, then? there will be no living for us.

Sau. Gud will there not. Wuns, I think the deil has flead off her skin and put his dam intul 't! Bo where's Philip, and George, and Gregory?

Curt. They're all ready. What, ho! come forth here! Philip, George, Joseph, Nick! where are you?

Enter four or five SERVING-MEN.

Phil. Honest Sauny, welcome home!

Sau. Gat me some meat, and I'll believe ye, sir.

Geo. I am glad to see thee, Sauny.

Sau. Gat me a drink and I'se believe ye tea.

Jos. What? Sauny come to town again? Welcome!

Sau. Wuns, walcome, walcome! Gat me gued meat and drink; that is walcome, sir.

Nick. Old lusty fellow, Sauny, welcome!

Sau. How d'ye, Wully?

Nick. D'ye hear the news, Sauny? Wully Watts is dead.

Sau. 'Sbreed! nea man that geas on twa legs could slay Wully Watts, sir.

Nick. True, for he was fairly hanged.

Sau. I was sure nea man that went on twa legs could slay him.

Nick. You are in the right, Sauny, for 'twas one

with three legs—'twas Mr. Tyburn; for he was
fairly hanged.

Sau. 'Sbreed, ye lie, sir! The gallows might kill
him, and break his stout heart, but it could nea
hang him. 'Tis hang an Englishman!

Nick. Well, but what kind of woman is our
mistress, Sauny?

Sau. Ye'll ken soon enough tea your sorrow and
wea, sir. Ye've a' twa lugs apiece o' your head:
a my saul, I'se nea gea ye twa pennies for them
by th' morn. How say ye now?

Enter PETRUCHIO *and* MARGARET.

Pet. Where be these idle rogues? What! no
more at door to hold my stirrup or take my horses?
Where's Curtis, Philip, Nick, and Gregory?

All. Here! here! here! sir!

Pet. Here, here, here, you loggerheaded curs?
What! no attendance?—no regard?—no duty?
Where's that foolish knave I sent before?

Sau. Wuns, sir, I'se be sea hungry and sea
empty, ye may travel quite through me and ne'er
faw your fingers, sir.

Pet. You mangy rogue! did not I bid you
meet me in the park and bring these rascals with
you?

Sau. Gud did ye, sir; bo I'se sea hungry I'se
ha' nea memory. Deliver your message yoursel',
sir.

Pet. Begone, you slaves, and fetch my supper in!
Rogues! do I speak, and don't you fly to make
haste?—[*Exeunt two or three* SERVANTS.]—Sit
down, Peg, and welcome. Why, when, I pray?
nay, good sweet Peg, be merry; these are country
clownish fellows—prithee be merry.—Off with my
boots, sirrah! you rogues! ye villains!—When

Sings.

It was the orders of the friar grey,
As forth he walked on his way.

Mar. Sure, he will run himself out of breath,
and then it will be my turn.

Pet. Out, you rogue! you pluck my boot awry!
Take that, and mend it in pulling off the other.—
Be merry, Peg.—Some water here, ho!—Where's
my spaniel, sirrah?—Make haste, and desire my
cousin Ferdinand to come hither—one, Peg, you
must kiss and be acquainted with.—Where are
my slippers?—Shall I have some water?—Come,
Peg, wash and welcome, heartily!

Sau. Wuns, bo whare is the meat to mak her
welcome?

Mar. We shall fall out if we wash together.*

Pet. You whorson villain! will you let it fall?

Mar. Pray, sir, be patient! 'twas an unwilling
fault.

Table covered.   Enter SERVANTS *with meat.*

Pet. An idle, careless, beetle-headed slave! Come,
Peg, sit down; I know you have a stomach.   Will
you give thanks, sweet Peg, or shall I, or each for
ourselves?   Come, fall to!—What's this?—mutton?

Sau. Gud, it is, sir.

Pet. Who bought it?

Curt. I did, sir.

Pet. You rascal you, 'tis not mutton! 'tis the
breast of a dog!   What curs are these!   'Tis dried
and burnt to a coal, too!   Where is this rascal
cook?   How dare you bring such rotten meat to

---

* There still exists the vulgar belief, that if two persons
wash their hands in the same vessel, they are certain to
quarrel shortly.

my table? Why, d'ye mean to poison me, ye
heedless joltheads, ye ill-mannered whelps? What!
d'ye grumble?—I'll be with you straight.

Mar. Pray, husband, be content. The meat is
good meat, and I am very hungry; I must and
will eat some of it.

Pet. Not for the world, Peg; I love thee better
than so. 'Tis burnt, and will engender choler, a
disease we are both too subject to. I love thee too
well to give thee anything to hurt thee. We'll fast
to-night; to-morrow we'll make it up.

Mar. Say what you will, sir, I'll eat some of it!
Did you bring me hither to starve me?

Pet. Why, ye rascals, will ye stand still and see
your mistress poison herself? Take it away out
of her sight quickly!

[*Throws the meat at them;* SAUNY *gets it.*

San. Gud, Saundy will venture, poison an
't will!

Pet. Well, Peg, this night we'll fast for company. Come, I'll bring thee to the bridal chamber.

Mar. I must eat something, I shall be sick else;
—but an egg.

Pet. No, no; prithee don't talk on't! To bed
upon a full stomach?

Mar. But a crust of bread.

Pet. To-morrow, to-morrow. Come, prithee,
away.   [*Exeunt.*

Geo. Didst ever see the like?

Curt. He kills her in her own humour.

Phil. Have you said grace, Sauny?

Sau. Gud, I was sea hungry I forgot grace.—O
thou that hast filled our boyes and our blathers,
keep us a' from whoredom and secrecy.

Nick. Secrecy? Why, Sauny?

Sau. Wuns, man, it is wutchcraft! Peace! you

· put me out, with the deil's name to ye !—Keep us
a' from whoredom and secrecy. Fro' the dinger o'
the swatch to the gallow-tree, keep us a', we beseech thee.—Tak' a drink, man.

Phil. Are ye full now, Sauny?

Sau. As fow as a piper. Ye may put ean finger
in at my mouth, and another in mine a . . e, and feel
beath ends o' my dinner. [*Exeunt.*

Enter, as in a Bed-chamber PETRUCHIO, PEG,
SERVANTS, *and* SAUNY.

Pet. Where are you, you rogues? Some lights
there!—Come, Peg, undress; to bed, to bed!

Mar. Pray send your men away, and call for
some of your maids.

Pet. Maids? hang maids! I have no such vermin about my house; any of these will do as well.
Here, Sauny! Come hither, sirrah, and undress
your mistress.

Sau. O' my saul, sir, I'se put on my headpiece.
Now, an ye'll bind her hands behind her, I'se
undress her. [*Goes to take up her coats.*

Pet. What dost thou do?

Sau. In Scotland we a'ways begin at the nether
end of a bonny lass.

Pet. Who made this bed? What, rascals, are
these? Foh, these sheets are musty as the devil!
and what rags are here upon my bed! Is this a
counterpane?—'tis a dishclout!

Mar. Why, the counterpane is well enough and
rich enough, and the sheets are as clean and as
sweet as may be.

Pet. Fie, fie, Peg! thou hast got a cold, and lost
thy smelling. I tell thee they are all damp and
musty; I would not have thee to venture to lie in
'em for the world, it would be thy death.—Here,

take 'em away !—We must e'en sit up ; there's no remedy.

Mar. Pray, sir, talk not of sitting up ; I am so sleepy I can't hold my eyes open. I must to bed.

Pet. I'll keep thee waking, I warrant thee.—Ho, Curtis ! bring us a flagon of March beer, and some tobacco and clean pipes ; we'll be merry.

[*Exit* CURTIS.

Mar. Why, what d'ye mean ?   Are you mad ?

Pet. Mad ?—ay, what should we do—I mean thou and I ? hand to fist we'll drink a health to my father, and my sister, and all our good friends at London.

Enter SERVANT *with beer and tobacco.*

Mar. Why, you don't take me to be one of your fellow tosspots ?

Pet. I mean to teach thee to drink : thou must learn that, or thou'rt no wife for me.   Here, Peg ! to thee with all my heart, a whole one, and thou art welcome.   My father's good health ; Peg, you shall pledge it.

Mar. I can't drink without eating ; 'twill make me sick.

Pet. Pish, pish ! that's but a fancy.   Come ! off with it, or thou shalt neither eat nor drink this month.

Mar. Shall I go to bed when I have drank it?

Sau. Gud, at ye gi' Saundy a little drink, madam ?

Pet. Talk of that anon.—[*She drinks.*]—So— here, Peg, here's a pipe I've filled for thee myself ; sit down and light it !

Mar. D'ye mean to make a mere hackney horse of me ? What d'ye offer me your nasty tobacco for?

Pet. Nay, ne'er make so shy ; I know thou

lov'st it. Come; young ladies are often troubled
with the toothache, and take it in their chambers,
though they won't appear good fellows amongst
us. Take it, or no sleep nor meat, Peg. D'ye
hear?

Mar. Yes, to my grief. I won't be abused thus!
[*Weeps.*

Pet. Nay, nay, go where thou wilt, I'll make
thee smoke before I sleep. [*Exeunt.*

ACT IV.

Enter PETRUCHIO *and* SAUNY.

Pet. Sirrah, wait on your mistress! Say what
you will to her, and vex her, but do not touch her;
and let her have no meat, I charge ye!

Sau. 'Sbreed, sir, send her into the Highlands
in Scotland; there's hunger and caud enough;
there she may starve her bally fu'.

Pet. Well, sirrah, do as I direct you. [*Exit.*

Sau. O' my saul wull I, sir. Ye'll let me take
my headpiece to defend me, sir?

Enter MARGARET.

Mar. What! Gregory! Philip!—Nobody near
me? Sauny, where are you?

Sau. I'se e'en hard at your a . . e, madam.

Mar. Where's your master?

Sau. He's gone to the market himself, and he'll
bring ye heam a braw bull's puzzle to swaddle your
weam with.

Mar. And in the meantime I am famished.—
Was ever woman used so damnably? I am

starved for meat, giddy for want of sleep; and that which spites me more than all the rest is, he pretends 'tis out of care and love to me.—Prithee, good Sauny, give me some meat!

Sau. O' my saul, Saundy would be hanged gin I sud bestow an auld liquored bute; Sauny will cut it into tripes to stuff your weam with.

Mar. Good Sauny, here's money for thee. But one little bit of anything to stay my fainting spirits.

Sau. What will ye eat?—a bit of beef?

Mar. Ay, good Sauny.

Sau. Will ye eat some mustard to't?

Mar. Ay, good Sauny, quickly.

Sau. Mustard is nea gued for your tang; 'twill make it tea keen, and ye can scaud fast enough without.

Mar. Why, then, the beef without mustard.

Sau. Gud, beef is nea gued without mustard. Sauny will fetch ye some meal and water; ye'st make ye a Scotch pudding; ye'st eat of that tull your weam crack.

Mar. You abusive rogue, take that!—[*Beats him.*] —Must I be braved thus by my own servant?

Sau. The deil wash your face with a fou' clout.

Enter GERALDO.

Ger. Why, how now, sirrah! will you strike your mistress? You cowardly rogue—strike a woman?

Sau. 'Sbreed, sir, d'ye ca' a Scotchman a coward? Gin I'se had ye in Scotland, I'se put my whinyard in your weam gin ye were as stout as Gilderoy.

Ger. Why, Gilderoy was as arrant a coward as thou art.

Sau. Wuns, ye'd be lath to keep the grund

that Gilderoy quits; yet I must confess he was a little shamefaced before the enemy.

Mar. Oh, Mr. Geraldo, never was poor woman so used! For charity sake, convey me home to my father!

Enter PETRUCHIO *with a dish of meat.*

Pet. Here, Peg, here's meat for thee. I have dressed it myself, my dear.—Geraldo, welcome! This was kindly done, to visit Peg and me.—Come, Peg, fall to; here's an excellent piece of veal.

Mar. Why, 'tis a pullet.

Pet. Why, 'tis veal. Art thou mad?

Mar. You won't persuade me out of my senses. 'Tis a pullet.

Sau. A gud is it, sir.

Pet. What an unhappy man am I! my poor dear Peg's distracted! I always feared 'twould come to this.—Take the meat away, Curtis. Is the room ready as I ordered? are the lights dammed up?

Curt. Yes, sir.

Mar. Why, what d'ye mean to do with me?

Pet. Poor Peg, I pity thee; but thou shalt want no help for thy cure. You must be kept from the light; it troubles the brain.

Ger. I see I shall learn; he's an excellent teacher.

Mar. Why, sir, pray tell me, have you a mind to make me mad? This is the way indeed. How have I injured you that you use me thus inhumanly? Did you marry me to starve me?

Sau. He means to bring down your weam for a race; for we a'ways cry, A nag with a weam, but a mare with nean.

Pet. No, no, good Peg; thou know'st I have a

care of thee. Here's a gown just brought home
for thee, Peg. Now thou art empty, it will sit
handsomely.—Where is this tailor? Call him in,
Sauny!—If it fits you, you shall put it on and we'll
gallop o'er to London, and see your father. Your
sister's wedding is at hand; you must help her.

Enter TAILOR *with a gown.*

Mar. If she be matched as I am, heaven help
her! But there's some comfort in going home;
there's meat and sleeping room.

Pet. Come, tailor, let's see the gown. How
now, what's here? Bless me, what masquing
suit is this? What's this?—a sleeve? Why, 'tis
like a demi-cannon. Why, what a devil, tailor,
dost thou mean?—is this a gown?

Tail. A gown, sir? Yes, sir; and a handsome
gown as any man in London can make; 'tis the
newest fashion lately come out of France.

Pet. What a lying knave art thou! My great-
grandmother's picture in the matted gallery is just
such another.

Sau. It is like the picture of Queen Margaret in
Edinbrough Castle, sir.

Mar. I never saw a better fashioned gown in
my life, more quaint,* nor better shaped. I like
the gown, and I'll have this gown or I'll have
none. Say what you will, I like it; 'tis a handsome gown!

Pet. Why, thou say'st true, Peg; 'tis an ugly,
paltry gown. I am glad to hear thee of my mind;
'tis a beastly gown.

Mar. Why, I say 'tis a good gown, a handsome,
fashionable gown. What! d'ye mean to make a
puppet of me?

* Modish. *Ed.* 1708.

Pet. Ay, this fellow would make a puppet of thee.

Tail. She says your worship means to make a puppet of her.

Pet. Thou impudent, lying, thread, bodkin and thimble flea! thou nit! brave me in my own house? Go; take it! I'll ha' none on't.

Tail. Sir, I made it according to your directions, and I cannot take it again.

Sau. Tak' it awa', or the deil o' my lugs but ye'st tak' my whinyard!

Mar. He shall not take it again. What need you trouble yourself about it as long as it pleases me?—Lay it down there.

Pet. Sirrah, take it away, I say; we shall find more tailors. I won't have my wife so anticly dressed that the boys should hoot at her.

Mar. Come, come, all this is but fooling; you don't understand what belongs to a gown. Say what you will, I'm resolved to have it; if it were an ugly one I would wear it, an it were but to cross you!

Sau. Now the deil's a cruppen untill her mouth, sir; you may see a little of his tail hang out—it looks for a' the world an it were a sting, sir.

Pet. Why, that's my good Peg; I know thou dost not care for it. Say no more, prithee; thou shalt have another.

Mar. I know not what you mean to do with me, but methinks I might have leave to speak, and speak I will! I am no child, no baby! Your betters have endured me to speak my mind, and if you cannot you had best stop your ears; 'tis better set my tongue at liberty than let my heart break.

Pet. Speak, Peg, by all means; say what thou

wilt.—Sirrah, carry that tawdry thing away.—
Geraldo, tell him you'll see him paid—[*aside*]—
and bid him leave it.—Come, what say'st thou,
Peg?

Ger. Leave the gown in the next room, tailor,
and take no notice of what he says; I'll see you
paid for't.   [*Aside. Exit Tailor.*

Mar. Why, I say I will have that gown, and
everything I have a mind for! I did not bring
you such a portion to be made a fool of!

Pet. Very true! thou'rt in the right, Peg. Come,
let's to horse; these clothes will serve turn at present till we can get better.—Go, sirrah, lead the
horses to the land's end; thither we'll walk afoot.
—Let's see, I think 'tis about seven o'clock: we
shall reach to my father-in-law's by dinner-time
with ease.

Mar. 'Tis almost two; you cannot get thither
by supper-time.

Pet. It shall be seven ere I go! Why, what a
mischief's this?—what I say or do you are still
crossing it.—Let the horses alone! I will not go
to-day, and ere I do it shall be what o'clock I
please.

Mar. Nay, sir, that shan't stop our journey; 'tis
seven, or two, or nine, or what o'clock you please.
Pray let's go.

Sau. Ye's have it what hour you wull, sir.

Pet. Very well, it is so; get ready quickly.—
Come, Geraldo, let's all go; we shall help mend
the mirth at my sister's wedding.

Ger. I'll wait on you.

Pet. Come, Peg, get on your things!

Mar. Let me but once see Lincoln's Inn Fields
again, and yet thou shalt not tame me! [*Exeunt.*

Enter TRANIO *and* SNATCHPENNY.

Tra. Now, sirrah, be but impudent enough, and keep state like the old knight, and thou art made for ever.

Snatch. I warrant ye, sir, I know it to a hair. My Lord Beaufoy and I were schoolfellows together at Worcester; my estate lies in the vale of Evesham — three thousand pound a year, and fifteen hundred a year I settle upon you upon the marriage. Let me alone! I am Sir Lyonel himself.

Tra. Right, right! Excellent brave!—How now?

Enter JAMY.

Jamy. To your postures, old sinner! Be an exquisite rascal, and then thou shalt be a rogue paramount. Thou shalt lay the dragon asleep while my master steals the pippins.

Tra. Well, Jamy, what hast thou done?

Jamy. I have been with my Lord Beaufoy, presented your father's and your service to him, and told him the old knight was happily come to town, and, hearing of your love to Biancha, was so overjoyed he would settle all upon you.

Tra. Well, and what said he?

Jamy. He gave me a piece* for my news. I told him Sir Lyonel desired his company just now to treat upon the match. He's coming in all haste; he longs to be cozened, and, Snatchpenny, if thou dost not do it—

Snatch. Then hang me.

Jamy. Mum, look to't; he's here!

Enter BEAUFOY *and* WINLOVE.

Beau. Mr. Winlove, your man tells me your

* Guinea. *Ed.* 1708.

father is just happily come to town. Where is
he?

Tra. Here, sir; this is my father. Time has
been too bold to wear ye out of each other's
memory.

Snatch. Is this my Lord Beaufoy, sir?

Tra. Yes, sir.

Snatch. My Lord, your humble servant! I'm
happy at last to meet a person I have formerly
so much loved.

Beau. Noble Sir Lyonel, I joy to see you.

Snatch. Oh! the merry days that you and I have
seen, my Lord! Well fare the good old times, I say!

Beau. Ay, Sir Lyonel, when you and I were
acquainted first.

Snatch. Ay, marry, these were golden days indeed—no cozening, no cheating. The world is
altered.

Beau. But we will remember these times, and
be honest still.

Snatch. That's e'en the best way. There's
hopes we may have honest grandchildren too, if
all be true as I hear. My son tells me your
daughter has made a captive of him.

Beau. I would she were better for his sake.
She's a good girl, and a handsome one, though I
say it; if she were not, I would give her somewhat should make her so.

Tra. It takes rarely.   [*Aside.*

Snatch. I'm even overjoyed that you think my
son worthy your alliance. I'll give something
they shall make a shift to live on. In plain, and in
brief, if you'll approve of it, I'll settle fifteen hundred pounds a year upon him at present, which
shall be her jointure; after my death, all I have
with a good will. What say you, my Lord?

Beau. Sir Lyonel, your freedom pleases me;
I see you are an honest-meaning gentleman. The
young folks, if I am not mistaken, like one another.
Well, I say no more; it is a match.

Tra. You bind me to you ever; now I may
boldly say I am truly happy. Where will you
please to have the business made up?

Beau. Not in my house, son; I would have it
private. Pitchers have ears, and I have many
servants; besides, old Woodall will be hindering
of us. He's hearkening still, and will be interrupt-
ing.

Tra. Then at my lodging; there my father lies,
and there the business may be all dispatched.
Send for your daughter by this gentleman; my
boy shall fetch a scrivener presently. The worst
on 't is, 'tis too small a warning; you are like to
have but slender entertainment.

Beau. No matter, no matter; I shall like it.

Snatch. I would fain see your daughter, my
Lord; I have heard great commendations of her.

Beau. That you shall presently.—Monsieur,
pray go to Biancha, and tell her from me she
must come hither with you immediately. You
may tell her too, if you will, what has happened,
and that she must prepare to be Mr. Winlove's
bride.

Win. My Lord, me vill fetch her presant.

Tra. My Lord, will your Lordship please to walk
in with my father? This is my lodging.

Beau. Ay, sir.—Come, Sir Lyonel, I'll follow
you.

Snatch. Good my Lord, I will wait upon you.

[*Exeunt* BEAUFOY, SNATCHPENNY, *and* TRANIO.

Win. Thus far 'tis well carried on, Jamy; but
how shall we prosecute it?

2 A

Jamy. Why, there is but one way in the world, sir.

Win. And what's that?

Jamy. Why, thus: I have got a parson ready for the purpose; when you have got Biancha abroad, whip her into Covent Garden Church, and there marry her, and your work's done.

Win. Troth, thou say'st true. But is the parson orthodox and canonical? I would not have an Obadiah to make us enter into covenant of matrimony.

Jamy. Trust me, sir, he's as true as steel. He says all matrimony without book—he can christen, wed, and bury blindfold.

Win. Well, I'll take thy counsel, if I can persuade her to 't, as I hope I shall, for I know she loves me. Fair luck betides me.—But who comes here?

Enter WOODALL.

Jamy. 'Tis the old grub, Woodall. What shall we do with him?

Win. We must contrive some way to get him off.

Wood. I don't like those shuffling matters; I doubt there's some false play towards me in hand. Here's my Monsieur! he may inform me.—Monsieur!

Win. Che dict a vouz, Monsieur? Monsieur, your servant!

Wood. Monsieur, prithee tell me, if thou canst, how affairs go? Things are carried very closely. How stands my mistress affected?

Win. Moi foi, Monsieur, me tell you de bad news in the varle. Mademoiselle Biancha no stand affected to you at all. My Lord has sent

me to fetch her just now to be marry to Monsieur
—vat you call—Monsieur Le——

Wood. What! not to Winlove?

Win. Yes, to Monsieur Winlove. Begar, me be
very sorry, but me canno help dat.

Wood. Is old Beaufoy mad, to match her to him
without his father's privity?

Win. Here be de ver fine old man new come to
town; me Lord be wid him now.

Wood. Upon my life! old Sir Lyonel? Nay,
then, she's lost quite. Hark you, Monsieur; yet
'tis in your power to make me a happy man.

Win. Oh, Monsieur, me be your humble servant.

Wood. Why, look you, you are to fetch her—
here's forty pound in gold* to buy you a pair of
gloves — let me take her from you as you are
carrying her thither. I will have two or three
with me, and you may safely say she was forced
from you.

Win. Monsieur, begar, me do you all de service
in the varle; but me sall be the grand sheat knave
then.

Wood. That's nothing. Here's more money; I'll
save you harmless. Come, you shall do it.

Win. Monsieur, me have no mind to be van
knave; but to do you service, if you will meet me
upon de street—

Wood. Fear not, I'll secure you. Honest Monsieur, farewell; I will be your friend for ever.

[*Exit.*

Win. Ha, ha, ha! this is rare. What an ass
this fellow will make himself, do what we can!
Here, Jamy, thou shalt share with me.

Jamy. Thank you, sir; would we had such a
windfall every day. But come, sir, you must

* Guineas. *Ed.* 1708.

make haste. This is the critical minute; if you miss it, you lose Biancha.

Win. Thy counsel's good; away! I'll buy a ring and pay the priest with some of Woodall's money. Ha, ha, ha!   [*Exeunt.*

Enter PETRUCHIO, MARGARET, GERALDO, *and* SAUNY.

Pet. Walk your horses down the hill before; we shall reach London time enough. 'Tis a fair night; how bright and goodly the moon shines!

Mar. The moon !—the sun; 'tis not the moonlight now.

Pet. I say 'tis the moon that shines so bright.

Mar. I say 'tis the sun that shines so bright.

Pet. Now, by my mother's son, and that's myself, it shall be the moonlight, or what I please, before you set sight of your father's house.—Sirrah, go fetch the horses back!—Evermore crossed, and crossed, and nothing but crossed.

Ger. Say as he says, or we shall never go.

Mar. Forward, I pray sir, since we are come so far, and be it sun, or moon, or what you please. Nay, if you call it a rush-candle, henceforth it shall be so for me.

Pet. I say 'tis the moon.

Sau. 'Sbreed! but I say nay, sir. Out, out! a' lies.

Mar. I know 'tis the moon.

Pet. Nay, then, you lie; 'tis the blessed sun.

Mar. Why, Heaven be blessed for't, 'tis even what you have a mind to. Pray, let us forward.

Ger. Petruchio, go thy ways, the field is won.

Pet. Well, forward, forward! Now the bowl runs with a right bias;—but soft, here's company!

Enter SIR LYONEL WINLOVE.

Lyon. Boy, bid the coachman drive gently down the hill. I wonder I meet nor overtake no passengers to-day. Stay! I think here be some.

Pet. I will have one bout more with thee, Peg.—Good-morrow, gentle lady ; which way travel you?—Come hither, Peg. Didst thou ever behold so exquisite a beauty as this fair virgin bears about? Go to her, Peg, and salute her.

Mar. Are you mad? 'tis an old man.

Pet. Beat back again, then ;—still cross? Will you do it?

Sau. Why, i' th' deil's name, what mean ye? Its nea bonny lass, sir. 'Sbreed, its an a' fa' thief!

Ger. He'll make this old man mad.

Mar. You budding virgin, so fair, so sweet, so fresh, which way travel you? How happy should we be in the enjoyment of so fair a fellow traveller!

Sau. The deil has built a bird's nest in your head. Gud, ye're as mad as he ; and he as mad as gin he were the son of a March hare, sir.

Lyon. Why, what do ye mean, gentlewoman?

Pet. Why, now, now, Peg, I hope thou art not mad! A virgin, quotha? 'tis an old, wrinkled, withered man.

Mar. Reverend sir, pardon my mistaking eyes, that have been so dazzled with the moon—sun, I mean—I could not distinguish you. I now perceive you are a grave old man ; pray, excuse me.

Lyon. Indeed you are a merry lady. Your encounter has amazed me ; but I like such cheerful company. I am for London, to see a son of mine that went lately from me thither.

Pet. We shall be glad of your company. You must pardon my wife's error; she has not slept well to-night, and I could not persuade her but she would come out fasting, which makes her fancy a little extravagant.

Sau. The deil o' my saul, but you are a false trundle-tail tyke. The deil a bit he'd lat her eat these three days, sir.

Mar. Curse upon your excuse and the cause of it! I could have eaten my shoe soles if I might have had 'em fried.

Pet. Your name, I beseech you, sir?

Lyon. I am called Sir Lyonel Winlove in the country.

Pet. Father to young Mr. Winlove?

Lyon. The same, sir.

Pet. Then I am happy indeed to have met you. I can tell you some news perhaps may not be unwelcome to you. Your son is in a fair probability of calling me brother within these two days.

Lyon. How so, I pray, sir?

Pet. Why, he's upon marrying my wife's sister, my Lord Beaufoy's youngest daughter—a brave match, I can assure you, and a sweet bedfellow!

Sau. Gud, she's tea gued for any man but Saundy. Gud, gin poor Saundy had her in Scotland, wuns! I'd sea swing her about!

Lyon. You amaze me! Is this true? or have you a mind, like a pleasant traveller, to break a jest on the company you overtake?

Ger. Upon my word, sir, 'tis very true. 'Twas so designed, but I don't think he'll marry her; he's forsworn if he do.

Lyon. You make me wonder more and more.

Pet. Mind him not! he's a party concerned; 'tis true.

Lyon. Pray, gentlemen, let's make haste; I must look after this business. It sounds strangely; he would not do't without my consent. He's my only son, my heir, the prop of my family. I must be careful.

Pet. I see you are jealous, sir, but you need not; he cannot have a better match.

Lyon. I doubt it not, if all be fair. I should be glad of my Lord Beaufoy's alliance. He was my schoolfellow, but time, I doubt, has worn out our old acquaintance. Gentlemen, I must hasten to prevent the worst.

Sau. What mean ye, sir? Ye will nea bawk the bonna lad, and tak' fro' his mattle, sir?

Ger. Well, Petruchio, thou hast put me in a heat. Have at my widow now!　　　　　[*Exeunt.*

Enter WINLOVE, BIANCHA, *and* JAMY.

Win. How good you are, my fair one!—Jamy, art sure the priest is ready for us?

Jamy. I warrant you, sir. Pray make haste; some devil or other may come else and cross it. Don't stay thrumming of caps. Here! body o' me, away! Here's Woodall! shift for yourselves—all will be spoiled else.

　　　　　[*Exeunt* WINLOVE *and* BIANCHA.

Enter WOODALL *with three or four* FELLOWS.

Wood. Be sure you seize on her, and clap her into a chair, and one stop her mouth. Fear not! I'll save you harmless.

1 Fel. I warrant you, sir.

Wood. What a devil makes this rogue poaching here?

Jamy. Tum, te dum, te dum! Sing *old Coale of London.*　　　　　[*Sings.*

Wood. Now, Jamy, what walk you here for?

Jamy. Why, to look about me.—Te dum, te dum, *etc.*

Wood. They say your master is to be married to Madam Biancha to-day.

Jamy. Why, then, we'll be merry at night.—Te dum, te dum, *etc.*

Wood. The rogue won't be gone.—What! hast no business? Thou look'st as if thou hadst not drank to-day. There's something for thee; go, get thy morning's draught.

Jamy. I thank your worship. Will you take part of a pot of ale and a toast!

Wood. No, sirrah! I drank coffee this morning.

[*Exit* JAMY.

So, he's gone! I wonder Monsieur appears not with Biancha.

Enter PETRUCHIO, MARGARET, SIR LYONEL, GERALDO, *and* SAUNY, *with* ATTENDANTS.

Wood. Ha! Who comes there?

Ger. Now you are there, I'll take my leave. Your servant.   [*Exit.*

Pet. Sir Lyonel, you are welcome to town. There's your son's lodgings! my father lives on the other side. Thither we must, and therefore here I take my leave.

Lyon. Pray, stay a little! maybe he's not within. If so, I'll wait upon you to the Lord Beaufoy.

San. O' my saul, nea ean could have begged [*Knocks*] dunner better than this au'd thief has done.

Wood. They are all busy within, sir; you must knock louder if you mean to be heard.

[SNATCHPENNY *above.*

Snatch. Who is that knocks as if he would beat down the gate?

Lyon. Is Mr. Winlove within?

Snatch. He is within, but not to be spoken with.

Lyon. What if a man bring him a hundred pounds or two to make merry withal?

Snatch. Keep your hundred pounds for yourself; he shall need none as long as I live.

Pet. Nay, I told you, sir, your son was well beloved in London.—D'ye hear, sir? Leaving your frivolous circumstances, pray tell him his father's just now come out of the country to see him, and is here at the door to speak with him.

Snatch. That is a lie, sir. His father came to town yesterday, and is now here looking out at window.

Lyon. The devil he is! Are you his father?

Snatch. Ay, sir; so his mother says, if I may believe her.

Sau. Can they hang him for having twa fathers, sir? Gud, and 'twas sea, poor Saundy would be hanged, sure enough!

Pet. Why, hast thou two fathers?

Sau. Gud have I, and twa and twa to that, sir.

Pet. Why, how now, gentlemen? this is flat knavery, to take another man's name upon you.

Snatch. Lay hands upon this villain! I believe he means to cheat somebody here under my counter-name.

Enter JAMY.

Jamy. I have seen the Church on their back; send them good speeding.—Ha! how now?—my old master, Sir Lyonel!—'Sfoot, we are all lost, undone! I must brazen it out.

Lyon. Come hither, Crack-hemp.

Jamy. You may save me that labour, and come to me, if you have anything to say to me.

Lyon. Come hither, you rogue! What! have you forgot me?

Jamy. Forgot you, sir? I could not forget you, for I never saw you in all my life before.

Lyon. You notorious villain! didst thou never see thy master's father, Sir Lyonel Winlove?

Jamy. What! my worshipful old master? Yes, marry, sir. See where his worship looks out of the window.

Lyon. Does he so, sir? I'll make you find him below stairs.   [*Beats him.*

Jamy. Help, help! here's a madman will murder me!

Sau. Dea ca' yoursel' Jamy, and wull ye be beten by an a' fa' thief? An ye ca' yoursel' Jamy eance meare, I'se bang ye tea cloots; breed a gud will I, sir!

Snatch. Help, son! help, brother Beaufoy!— Jamy will be killed.

Pet. Prithee, Peg, stand by to see this controversy.

Enter SNATCHPENNY *with* SERVANTS, BEAUFOY, *and* TRANIO.

Tra. 'Sheart, 'tis Sir Lyonel! but we must bear it a little.—Sir, what are you that offer to beat my servant?

Lyon. What am I, sir? Nay, what are you, sir? —O Heaven, what do I see? Oh, fine villains, I'm undone! While I play the good husband at home in the country, my son and my servants spend my estate lavishly at London.

Sau. Your son sall allow you siller to keep an au'd wutch to rub your shins; and what to anger would ye ha' meer, sir?

Tra. How now, what's the matter?

Beau. Is the man frantic?

Tra. Sir, you seem a sober, ancient gentleman by your habit, but your words show you a madman. Why, sir, what concerns it you what rich clothes I wear? I thank my good father I am able to maintain it.

Lyon. Thy father? Oh, villain! he's a hemp-dresser in Partha.

Sau. Marra, the deil stuff his weam fu' o' hemp, and his dam spin it out at his a . . e.

Beau. You mistake, you mistake. What d'ye think his name is?

Lyon. His name?—as if I knew not his name. I have bred him up e'er since he was three years old, and his name is Tranio.

Snatch. Away, away, mad ass! His name is Winlove, my only son, and heir to all my estate in the vale of Evesham.

Lyon. Heavens! he has murdered his master. Lay hold on him, I charge you, in the King's name! Oh, my son!—Tell me, thou villain! where is my son, Winlove?

Tra. Run for an officer to carry this mad knave to the jail! Lay hold on him, I charge ye, and see him forthcoming.

Sau. Awa', awa' with the hampdresser, sir.

Lyon. Carry me to the jail, ye villains?

Pet. Hold, gentlemen.—Your blessing, father?

Beau. Son Petruchio, welcome. You have it, and you, Peg. How d'ye? Know ye anything of this matter?

Pet. My Lord, take heed what you do. So much I know, I dare swear this is Sir Lyonel Winlove, and that a counterfeit.

Sau. Wuns, I think sea tea. Gud, an' ye please, I'se take the covenant on't.

Wood. So durst I swear too, almost.

Snatch. Swear if thou durst!

Wood. Sir, I dare not swear point-blank.

Tra. You had best swear I am not Winlove neither.

Wood. Yes, I know you to be Mr. Winlove.

Beau. Away with the dotard! to the jail with him!

Lyon. Are you all settled to do mischief to me? Why, my Lord Beaufoy, methinks you might know me.

Tra. Away with him to my lodgings for the present, till we can get a constable to charge him upon. We shall have a hubbub in the streets. Drag him, I say.

Lyon. Rogues, villains, murderers! I shall have justice.   [*Exeunt with* SIR LYONEL.

Wood (*Manet.*) These are strange passages! I know not what to think of 'em. But I am glad Biancha came not when they were here. Sure my Monsieur will not fail me.

Enter WINLOVE *and* BIANCHA.

Win. Now, my Biancha, I am truly happy; our loves shall, like the spring, be ever growing.

Bian. But how shall we escape my father's anger?

Win. Fear not; I'll warrant thee.

Wood. Oh, here's Biancha!—How now, Monsieur brave, what fancy's this?

Win. Oh, Monsieur, te vous la menes. How d'ye do, good Mr. Woodall? How d'ye like my new bride?

Wood. How, how, how, sir?—your bride? Seize on her quickly.

Win. Hands off! She's my wife; touch her

who dares! Will you have your teeth picked?
What d'ye think of giving twenty pieces* to teach
your mistress French?

Wood. Oh, rogue, I'll have thee hanged!

Win. Or forty pieces* to buy a pair of gloves
to let you steal Madam Biancha? This ring was
bought with some of it—ha, ha, ha!

Wood. Down with him!—down with him!—a
damned rascal!

Win. Ay, do. Which of you has a mind to
breathe a vein?

2 Fel. Nay, if she be his wife, we dare not
touch her.

Wood. I'll fetch somebody that shall. Oh,
devil! [*Exit.*

Win. Ay, do. I am your poor Monsieur; ha,
ha, ha!—Fear not, Biancha; he'll fetch 'em all, I
know. I warrant thee we shall appease thy
father easily.

Bian. Trust me, sir, I fear the storm.

Enter BEAUFOY, TRANIO, PETRUCHIO, MARGARET,
SAUNY, SNATCHPENNY, JAMY, SIR LYONEL,
WOODALL, *and* ATTENDANTS.

Wood. That rogue, that damned counterfeit
Frenchman, has stolen your daughter and married
her! Here they are.

Win. Bless me! What do I see yonder? my
father in earnest? Dear sir, your blessing and
your pardon.

Lyon. My dear son, art thou alive? then take it.

Bian. I must beg your pardon too, sir.

Win. And I, most honoured father.

Beau. Why, what's the matter?—what hast

* Guineas. *Ed.* 1708.

thou done? Woodall tells me thou hast married the Frenchman.

Win. Me she has married, but no Frenchman. The right Winlove, son to the right Winlove, is her husband and your son-in-law.

Sau. 'Sbreed, sir, ye act twa parts; ye were but a hampdresser in the last act, sir.

Snatch. 'Tis time for us to be going; I feel one ear going off already.   [*Exit.*

Beau. You amaze me! Are not you the Frenchman Mr. Woodall preferred to teach my daughter?

Bian. No, my Lord; he put on that disguise to court me; he is the true Winlove.

Lyon. Marry is he my son, sir.

Win. Those were but counterfeits of my making.

Wood. Here's patching with a mistress. I'm sure I am gulled.

Beau. But d'ye hear, sir? Have you married my daughter without my consent?

Lyon. Come, my lord, now you must know me. I will beg both their pardons, and secure her a jointure worthy her birth and fortune.

Win. You are a father now indeed.

Beau. Sir Lyonel, excuse my rashness; I accept your noble proffer.—You are forgiven!

Sau. 'Sbreed, sir, we sall ne'er go to dunner, sir. The deil forgat and forgive you a', sir.

Lyon. But where is that rogue that would have sent me to jail? I'll slit his nose for him.

Win. I must beg his pardon, for he did all for my sake.

Lyon. Well, sir, for your sake I pardon him.

Beau. Come, gentlemen all, to my house; we shall there end all our doubts and drown our fears.

Wood. Sir, I shall expect my money back again ;
'tis enough to lose my mistress.

Win. No, faith, 'tis in better hands already.
You'll but fool it away ; you'll be hiring Frenchmen again.

Wood. Well, mock on ! I'll in, and eat out part
of it.

Beau. Come, gentlemen !

Mar. Husband, will you not go with my father ?

Pet. First kiss me, Peg, and I will.

Mar. What ! in the middle of the street ?

Pet. What ! art thou ashamed of me ?

Mar. Not so, sir, but ashamed to kiss so openly.

Pet. Why, then, let's home again.—Sauny, lead
the way.

Sau. Gud, the deil a bit will Saundy budge
before dunner, sir.

Mar. Nay, I will give thee a kiss ; nay, pray
now, stay.

Pet. So—is not this well ? Come, my sweet
Peg.

Bian. Sister, I hope we shall be friends now.

Mar. I was never foes with you.

Win. Come, fairest ! all the storms are over-
blown.

Love hath both wit and fortune of her own.

[*Exeunt.*

ACT V.

Enter MARGARET *and* BIANCHA.

Bian. But is't possible, sister, he should have
used you thus ?

Mar. Had I served him as bad as Eve did
Adam, he could not have used me worse ; but I

am resolved, now I'm got home again, I'll be revenged. I'll muster up the spite of all the curs'd
women since Noah's flood to do him mischief and
add new vigour to my tongue. I have not pared
my nails this fortnight; they are long enough to
do him some execution, that's my comfort.

Bian. Bless me, sister, how you talk!

Mar. Thou art a fool, Biancha! come, learn of
me : thou art married to a man too; thou dost
not know but thou mayest need my counsel, and
make good use on't. Thy husband bears thee
fair yet; but take heed of going home with him,
for, when once he has thee within his verge, 'tis
odds he'll have his freaks too—there's no trusting
these men. Thy temper is soft and easy; thou
must learn to break him, or he'll break thy heart.

Bian. I must confess I should be loth to be so
used; but sure Mr. Winlove is of a better disposition.

Mar. Trust him and hang him; they're all alike.
Come, thou shalt be my scholar; learn to frown
and cry out for unkindness, but brave anger;
thou hast a tongue, make use on't—scold, fight,
scratch, bite—anything. Still take exceptions at
all he does, if there be cause or not; if there be
reason for 't, he'll laugh at thee. I'll make
Petruchio glad to wipe my shoes or walk my
horse ere I have done with him.

Enter PETRUCHIO, WINLOVE, *and* SAUNY.

Bian. Peace, sister! our husbands are both here.

Mar. Thou child; I am glad on 't, I'll speak
louder.

Pet. Well, brother Winlove, now we are truly
happy. Never were men so blessed with two such
wives.

Win. I am glad to hear you say so, sir. My own I'm sure I'm blest in.

Pet. Yours?—why, Biancha's a lion, and Margaret a mere lamb to her. I tell thee, Winlove, there's no man living, though I say 't,—but 'tis no matter, since she does not hear me,—that has a wife so gentle and so active and affable. Poor thing, I durst be sworn she would walk barefoot a hundred miles to do me good.

Mar. No, but she would not; nor one mile neither.

Sau. Now have at your lugs, sir!

Pet. Oh, Peg, art thou there? How dost thou do, my dear?

Mar. You may go look; what's that to you?

Sau. Stand o' yer guard, sir. Gud, Saundy will put on his headpiece.

Pet. I am glad to hear thee say thou'rt well, in troth.

Mar. Never the better for you, which you shall find.

Pet. Nay, I know thou lov'st me. Prithee, take up my glove, Peg.

Mar. I take up your glove? Marry come up! command your servants. Look you, there it lies.

Pet. I am glad to see thee merry, poor wanton rogue.

Mar. 'Tis very well; you think you are in the country, but you are mistaken. The case is altered; I am at home now, and my own disposer. Go, swagger at your greasy lubber there, your patient wife will make you no more sport; she has a father will allow her meat and lodging, and another gaits* chambermaid than a Highlander.

Sau. Gud, an ye were a-top o' Grantham Steeple,

* Manner, kind of.

2 B

that a' the toon may hear what a scauden quean
ye are! Out, out!

Pet. Why, what's the matter, Peg? I never
saw thee in so jolly a humour. Sure thou hast
been drinking?

Sau. Gud has she.—Haud ye tang, ye fa'
dranken swine! Out, out, out! was ye tak' a
drink and ne'er tak' Saundy to ye? Out, out,
out!

Mar. 'Tis like I have. I am the fitter to talk
to you, for no sober woman is a companion for
you.

Pet. Troth, thou say'st right! we are excellently
matched.

Mar. Well, mark the end on't. Petruchio,
prithee come hither, I have something to say to
you.

Sau. De ye nea budge a foot, sir. Deil o' my
saul, bo she'll scratch your eyn out.

Pet. Well, your pleasure, madam?

Mar. First, thou art a pitiful fellow, a thing
beneath me, which I scorn and laugh at—ha, ha,
ha!

Win. She holds her own yet, I see.

Mar. I know not what to call thee. Thou art
no man; thou couldst not have a woman to thy
mother. Thou paltry, scurvy, ill-conditioned
fellow! dost thou not tremble to think how thou
hast used me? What! are you silent, sir?—Biancha,
see! looks he not like a disbanded officer with that
hanging-dog look there?—I must eat nothing
because your cook has roasted the mutton dry, as
you used to have it when your worship was a
bachelor. I must not go to bed, neither, because
the sheets are damp.

Pet. Mark you, Peg, what a strange woman are

you to discourse openly the fault of your servants in your own family.

Mar. No, no, sir, this won't serve your turn; your old stock of impudence won't carry you off so. I'll speak your fame, and tell what a fine gentleman you are—how valiantly you and half-a-dozen of your men got the better of a single woman, and made her lose her supper.

Sau. Gud, she lies, sir. I would ha' gin her an aud boot tull a made tripes on, and it wud a bin braw meat with mustard, and she would nea have it.

Mar. My faults? No, good squire of the country, you thought to have tamed me, I warrant, in good time. Why, you see I am even with you—your quiet, patient wife that will go no more in the country with you, but will stay in town, to laugh at your wise worship and wish you more wit.

Pet. I should laugh at that; why, we are just now a-going. — Sauny, go get the horses ready quickly.

Sau. Gud will I, sir. I'se saddle a Highland wutch to carry your bride.—Gud, she'll mount your a . . e for you, madam!

Mar. Sirrah, touch a horse and I'll curry your coxcomb for you!—No, sir, I won't say, Pray let me not go, but boldly, I won't go; you force me if you can or dare. You see I am not tongue-tied, as silent as you thought you made me.

Pet. Prithee, Peg, peace a little! I know thou canst speak. Leave now, or thou'lt have nothing to say to-morrow.

Mar. Yes, I'll say this over again, and something more if I can think on 't, to a poor despised man of clouts.—Sister, how he smokes now he's off his own dunghill.

Pet. Prithee, Peg, leave making a noise! i' faith, thou'lt make my head ache.

Mar. Noise?—why, this is silence to what I intend. I'll talk louder than this every night in my sleep.

Sau. The deil shall be your bed-fellow for Saundy, then.

Mar. I will learn to rail at thee in all languages. Thunder shall be soft music to my tongue.

Sau. The deil a bit Scots ye gat to brangle in! Marry, the deil gie ye a clap wi' a French thunderbolt.

Pet. Very pretty! Prithee go on.

Mar. I'll have a collection of all the ill names that ever was invented, and call you over by 'em twice a day.

Pet. And have the catalogue published for the education of young scolds. Proceed, Peg!

Mar. I'll have you chained to a stake at Billingsgate, and baited by the fishwives, while I stand to hiss 'em on.

Pet. Ha, ha, ha! Witty Peg! forward.

Mar. You shan't dare to blow your nose but when I bid you; you shall know me to be the master.

Sau. Wuns, gat her to the stool of repantance, sir.

Pet. Nay, I believe thou wilt go in breeches shortly. On, on! What! have you no more on't? Ha, ha, ha!

Mar. D'ye laugh, and be hanged! I'll spoil your sport.   [*Flies at him.*

Pet. Nay, Peg, hands off! I thought you would not have disgraced your good parts to come to blows so soon. Prithee, chide on; thou canst not believe what delight I take to hear thee, it does

become thee so well. What! pumped dry already?
Prithee, talk more, and longer, and faster, and
sharper; this is nothing.

Mar. I'll see you in the Indies before I'll do
anything to please you. D'ye like it?

Pet. Extremely! On, Peg; you'll cool too fast.

Mar. Why, then, mark me; if it were to save
thee from drowning or breaking thy neck, I won't
speak one word more to thee these two months.

[*Sits sullenly.*

Sau. Ah, gud, an ye do nea lie, madam.

Pet. Nay, good Peg, be not so hard-hearted.
What! melancholy all o' th' sudden? Come, get
up; we'll send for the fiddlers and have a dance.
Thou'lt break thy elbow with leaning on that hard
table.—Sauny, go get your mistress a cushion.—
Alas! I doubt she's not well; look to her, sister.

Bian. Are you not well, sister? What ails you?
Pray speak, sister.—Indeed, brother, you have so
vexed her she'll be sick.

Pet. Alas, alas! I know what's the matter with
her; she has the toothache—see how she holds her
cheek. The wind has gotten into her teeth, by
keeping her mouth open this cold weather.

Bian. Indeed it may be so, brother; she uses
to be troubled with that pain sometimes.

Pet. Without all question. Poor Peg, I pity
thee. Which tooth is it? Wilt thou have it
drawn, Peg? The toothache makes fools of all
the physicians; there is no cure but drawing.
What say'st thou?—wilt thou have it pulled out?
Well, thou shalt.—Sauny! run, sirrah, hard by,
you know, where my barber lives that drew me a
tooth last week; fetch him quickly! What d'ye
stand staring at? Run and fetch him immediately,
or I'll cut your legs off.

Sau. Gud, I'se fetch ean to pull her head off, an'
ye wull.   [*Exit.*

Win. This will make her find her tongue again,
or else for certain she has lost it.

Pet. Her tongue, brother? Alas! you see her
face is so swelled she cannot speak.

Bian. You jest, brother; her face is not swelled.
Pray let me see, sister; I can't perceive it.

Pet. Not swelled? Why, you are blind, then.
Prithee let her alone; you trouble her.

Enter SAUNY *and* BARBER.

Here, honest barber, have you brought your instruments?

Bar. Yes, sir. What must I do?

Pet. You must draw that gentlewoman a tooth
there. Prithee do it neatly, and as gently as thou
canst; and, d'ye hear me, take care you don't
tear her gums.

Bar. I warrant you, sir.

Sau. Hear ye, sir; could not ye mistake, and pull
her tang out instead of her teeth?

Bian. I'll be gone; I can't endure to see her
put to so much pain.   [*Exit.*

Bar. Pray, madam, open your mouth, that I
may see which tooth it is.—[*She strikes him.*]—
Why, sir, did you send for me to abuse me?

Sau. Gud, be nea angry; ye ha' nea a' yer pay
yet, sir! Cud ye not mistake and draw her tang
instead of her teeth, sir?

Pet. No, no; but it seems now she won't have
it drawn. Go; there's something for your pains,
however.   [*Exit* BARBER.

Sau. Ye sid ha' taken my counsel, sir.

Win. This will not do, sir; you cannot raise
the spirit you have laid, with all your arts.

Pet. I'll try ! have at her once more. Winlove,
you must assist me ; I'll make her stir if I can't
make her speak.—Look, look ! alas ! how pale she
is ! She's gone o' th' sudden ! Body o' me, she's
stiff, too ! Undone, undone ! what an unfor-
tunate man am I. She's gone ! she's gone !
Never had man so great a loss as I. Oh, Winlove, pity me ; my poor Peg is dead. Dear Winlove, call in my father and the company, that they
may share in this sad spectacle, and help my
sorrows with their joining griefs.—[*Exit* WINLOVE.]
—Speak, or by this hand I'll bury thee alive.—
Sauny, thou seest in how sad a condition thy poor
master is ; thy good mistress is dead. Haste to the
next church, and get the bier and the bearers hither !
I'll have her buried out of hand. Run, Sauny.

Sau. An' you'll mak' her dead, we'll bury her
deep enough ; we'll put her doon intill a Scotch
coalpit, and she shall rise at the Deil's a . . e o'
peak.* [*Exit.*

Pet. I will see that last pious act performed,
and then betake myself to a willing exile ; my own
country's hell, now my dear Peg has left it.—Not
yet ? Upon my life, I think thou hast a mind to
be buried quick. I hope thou hast.

Enter WINLOVE, BEAUFOY, SIR LYONEL, WOOD-
ALL, BIANCHA, TRANIO, JAMY, *etc.*

Beau. Bless me, son Petruchio, is my dear
daughter dead ?
Pet. Alas, alas ! 'tis but too true. Would I had
ta'en her room !
Beau. Why, methinks she looks brisk, fresh,
and lively.

* A natural cavern at Castleton, Derbyshire, called one of
the wonders of the Peak.

Pet. So much beauty as she had must needs leave some wandering remains to hover still about her face.

Beau. What could her disease be ?

Pet. Indeed I grieve to tell it, but truth must out—she died for spite; she was strangely infected.

Biun. Fie, sister ! for shame, speak ! Will you let him abuse you thus ?

Pet. Gentlemen, you are my loving friends, and knew the virtues of my matchless wife ; I hope you will accompany her body to its long home.

All. We'll all wait on you.

Beau. Thou wilt break her heart indeed.

Pet. I warrant you, sir, 'tis tougher than so.

Enter SAUNY *and* BEARERS *with a bier.*

Sau. I bring you here vera gued men. An' she be nea dead, sir, for a croon more they'll bury her quick.

Pet. Oh, honest friends, you're welcome ; you must take up that corpse. How ! hard-hearted ?—why do ye not weep the loss of so much beauty and goodness ? Take her up, and lay her upon the bier.

1 *Bear.* Why, what d'ye mean, sir ? She is not dead.

Pet. Rogues ! tell me such a lie to my face ? Take her up or I'll swinge ye.

Sau. Tak' her up, tak' her up ; we'll mak' her dead, Billy—ye'st ha' twa croons mear. Tak' her her up, man.

1 *Bear.* Dead or alive, all's one to us, let us but have our fees.

Pet. There. Nay, she is stiff ; however, on with her.—Will you not speak yet ?—So, here, take these strings and bind her on the bier; she had an active, stirring body when she lived, she may chance fall off the hearse now she's dead. So, now, take her up and away! Come, gentlemen, you'll follow? I mean to carry her through the Strand as far as St. James'; people shall see what respect I bore her, she shall have so much ceremony to attend her now she's dead. There my coach shall meet her and carry her into the country. I'll have her laid in the vault belonging to my family. She shall have a monument. Some of you inquire me out a good poet to write her epitaph suitable to her birth, quality, and conditions—pity the remembrance of so many virtues should be lost. March on! I would say more, but grief checks my tongue.

Mar. Father, sister, husband! are you all mad? Will you expose me to open shame? Rogues! set me down, you had best.

Pet. A miracle! a miracle! She lives! Heaven make me thankful for 't. Set her down!—Liv'st thou, my poor Peg?

Mar. Yes, that I do, and will, to be your tormentor.

Sau. Out, out, gea her nea credit; gud, she's as dead as mine grannam. Tak' her, away with her, sir!

Pet. Bless me, my hopes are all vanished again; 'tis a demon speaks within her body! Take her up again; we'll bury 'em together.

Mar. Hold, hold, my dear Petruchio; you have overcome me, and I beg your pardon. Henceforth I will not dare to think a thought shall cross your pleasure. Set me at liberty, and on my knees I'll make my recantation.

All. Victoria, victoria! the field is won!

Pet. Art thou in earnest, Peg?—may I believe thee?

Sau. You ken very well she was a'ways a lying quean when she was living, and wull ye believe her now she's dead?

Mar. By all that's good, not truth itself truer.

Pet. Then thus I free thee, and make thee mistress both of myself and all I have.

Sau. 'Sbreed, bo ye'll nea gi Saundy tull her, sir?

Wood. Take heed of giving away your power, sir.

Pet. I'll venture it, nor do I fear I shall repent my bargain.

Mar. I'm sure I will not give you cause. You've taught me now what 'tis to be a wife, and I'll still show myself your humble handmaid.

Pet. My best Peg, we will change kindness, and be each other's servant. Gentlemen, why do you not rejoice with me?

Beau. I am so full of joy I cannot speak. May you be happy. This is your wedding day.

Sau. Shall Saundy get her a bridecake and brake o'er her head, sir?—and we's gat us a good wadding dunner?

Enter GERALDO.

Ger. Save ye all, gentlemen! Have ye any room for more guests? I am come to make up the chorus.

Pet. My noble friend, welcome! Where have you been so long?

Ger. I have been about a little trivial business; I am just now come from a wedding.

Pet. What wedding, I pray, sir?

Ger. Troth, e'en my own; I have ventured upon 't at last.—Madam, I hope you'll pardon me?

Bian. Yes, sir; and so will this gentleman.

Sau. Are not you a gentleman hampdresser?

Pet. 'Tis e'en so; this proves to be Winlove in earnest.

Ger. Good gentlemen, undo this riddle; I'm all in the dark.

Pet. You shall know anon, in the meantime believe it, gentlemen. We want another woman, or we might have a dance.

Ger. My Widow is within; she'll supply you.

Beau. Good Peg, go and wait on her! and you, Biancha, too. [*Exeunt* MARGARET *and* BIANCHA.

Pet. I tell thee, Geraldo, never had man so obedient and loving a wife as I have now. I defy the world to equal her.

Win. Nay, brother, you must except her sister.

Ger. You must except mine too, or I shall have a hard bargain of it; my Widow is all obedience.

Pet. I'll tell you what I'll do with you. I'll hold you ten pieces,* to be spent in a collation on them, that mine has more obedience than both them; to try which, each send for his wife, and if mine come not first I'll lose my bet.

Sau. Gud, ye'll lose your siller sure enough, sir.

Both. A match!

Wood. I'll be your halves, Geraldo, and yours, Mr. Winlove, too.

Win. Jamy, go tell your mistress I desire her to come hither to me presently. [*Exit* JAMY.

Pet. A piece more she does not come.

Beau. You'll lose, son, you'll lose! I know she'll come.

---

* Pounds. *Ed.* 1708.

Pet. I know she won't. I find by instinct I shall win my wager.

Enter JAMY.

Jamy. Sir, she says she's busy, and she can't leave Mr. Geraldo's lady.

Pet. Look ye there, now! Come, your money!

Ger. Prithee go again and tell my wife I must needs speak with her immediately. [*Exit* JAMY.

Pet. I shall win yours too, as sure as in my pocket.

Ger. I warrant you no such matter. What will you give to be off your bet?

Pet. I won't take forty shillings.—

Enter JAMY.

How now?

Jamy. Sir, she says you have no business with her; if you have, you may come to her.

Pet. Come, produce! I knew 'twould be so.— Sauny, go and tell Peg from me I command her to come to me instantly.

Sau. I'se gar her gea wuth me, sir, or I'se put my durk to the hilt in her weam.

Wood. Yet you won't win; I'll hang for't if she'll come.

Pet. Yes, but she will, as sure as you gave forty pieces to court Biancha. I'll venture them to twenty more upon't with you.

Wood. Nay, I have lost enough already.

Enter MARGARET *and* SAUNY.

Pet. Look ye here, gentlemen!

Sau. O' my saul, she's can a daft gued lass.

* Guineas. *Ed.* 1708.

She's at your beck; streake her and kiss her, man.

Mar. I come to receive your commands, sir.

Pet. All I have to say to thee, Peg, is to bid thee demand ten pounds of these two gentlemen; thou hast won it.

Mar. I, sir?—for what?

Pet. Only for being so good-natured to come when I send for you.

Mar. It was my duty, sir.

Pet. Come, pay, pay; give it her! I'll not bate ye twopence.

Ger. There's mine.

Win. And mine, sister; much good may it do ye.

Beau. Well, Peg, I'll find thee one thousand pound the more for this.

Sau. Bo what wull ye gie Saundy, that halpt to mak' her gued and tame? Wuns, she was as wild as a Galloway colt!

Enter BIANCHA *and* WIDOW.

Win. Look! here they come at last.

Bian. What did you send for me for?

Win. Why, to win me five pounds, if you had been as obedient as you should ha' been.

Bian. You have not known me long enough to venture so much upon my duty. I have been my sister's scholar a little.

Sau. Bo put her to Saundy to teach; gud, I'se mak' her sea gentle ye may streake her and handle her all o'er, sir.

Ger. You might have got me five pounds if you had done as you should do.

Wid. Were it to do again, you should be sure to lose.

Mar. Fie! ladies, for shame! How dare you infringe that duty which you justly owe your husbands? They are our Lords, and we must pay 'em service.

Beau. Well said, Peg! you must be their tutor. Come, son, if you'll have a dance, dispatch it quickly; the music's ready, and the meat will be spoiled.

Pet. Come, then, play, play!

DANCE.

Now let us in and eat, the work is done,
Which neither time nor age can wear from
  memory;
I've tamed the shrew, but will not be ashamed
If next you see the very tamer tamed.

FINIS.